A Sicilian Affair

Susan Lewis is the internationally bestselling author of over fifty sensational novels across the genres of family drama, thriller, suspense, crime and romance – including the Richard and Judy picks *One Minute Later* and *I Have Something to Tell You*. She is also the author of *Just One More Day* and *One Day at a Time*, the moving memoirs of her childhood in Bristol during the 1960s. Following periods of living in Los Angeles and the South of France, she currently lives in Gloucestershire with her husband, James, and their beloved, naughty little dog, Mimi.

To find out more about Susan Lewis:

www.susanlewis.com

/SusanLewisBooks

@susanlewisbooks

@susanlewisbooks

@susanlewisbooks

Also by Susan Lewis

Fiction
A Class Apart
Dance While You Can
Stolen Beginnings
Darkest Longings
Obsession
Vengeance
Summer Madness
Last Resort
Wildfire
Cruel Venus
Strange Allure
The Mill House
A French Affair
Missing
Out of the Shadows
Lost Innocence
The Choice
Forgotten
Stolen
No Turning Back
Losing You
The Truth About You
Never Say Goodbye
Too Close to Home
No Place to Hide
The Secret Keeper
One Minute Later
I Have Something to Tell You
I Know It's You

Books that run in sequence
Chasing Dreams
Taking Chances

No Child of Mine
Don't Let Me Go
You Said Forever

Featuring Detective Andee Lawrence
Behind Closed Doors
The Girl Who Came Back
The Moment She Left
Hiding in Plain Sight
Believe in Me
Home Truths
My Lies, Your Lies
Forgive Me
The Lost Hours
Who's Lying Now?
No One Saw It Coming

Featuring Laurie Forbes and Elliott Russell
Silent Truths
Wicked Beauty
Intimate Strangers
The Hornbeam Tree

Memoirs
Just One More Day
One Day at a Time

SUSAN LEWIS

A Sicilian Affair

HarperCollins*Publishers*

HarperCollins*Publishers* Ltd
1 London Bridge Street,
London SE1 9GF

www.harpercollins.co.uk

HarperCollins*Publishers*
Macken House, 39/40 Mayor Street Upper
Dublin 1, D01 C9W8

This paperback edition published 2024

2

First published by HarperCollins*Publishers* Ltd 2024

ISBN: 978-0-00-847200-9

Typeset in Sabon LT Std by Palimpsest Book Production Ltd,
Falkirk, Stirlingshire

Printed and bound in the UK using
100% renewable electricity by CPI Group (UK) Ltd

MIX
Paper | Supporting
responsible forestry
FSC™ C007454

This book contains FSC™ certified paper and other controlled sources
to ensure responsible forest management.

For more information visit: www.harpercollins.co.uk/green

*To everyone, everywhere who
loves a love story*

CHAPTER ONE

This is, without a doubt, a crazy thing to do. She knows it, but she's going to do it anyway. She has to. A growing sense of urgency is driving her, pushing her on, telling her it's necessary, vital even. Maybe people who commit murder feel the same way; or a drug addict in need of a fix; or a prisoner with a panicked urge to escape. It overrides everything, and until the compulsion is met it won't go away, will only get stronger, and she can't wait any more. She knows she could pay a high price for her decision, but, God help her, she's willing to take the risk.

Catie MacAllister finishes reading the note that says all she wants to for now, folds it and slots it into an envelope. It feels like folding up a part of herself, tucking it into a safe space for the time being, while the rest of her is preparing to vanish from life as she knows it.

She props her goodbye against the empty wooden fruit bowl at the centre of the kitchen table – a bowl that has been there for so many years she can't even remember a time before its existence. Maybe it came with the house. That's likely, a lot had.

Checking her mobile, she sees that the Uber is ten minutes away and goes out to the hall. Plenty of time to drag her suitcases to the porch and check that all doors and windows are locked before she leaves.

After parking her luggage, she moves quietly, unhurriedly, through the downstairs rooms, each of them as silent as the familiar furniture within. Worn sofas and deep, sagging armchairs, flattened rugs, an empty fireplace; an abandoned play area at one end, no toys now, but shelves cluttered with books and memorabilia and doors that open onto a mossy patio. She returns to the kitchen. It seems uneasy, as though it's holding its breath, waiting to see if she'll really leave. A solitary drop of water clings to the tap; the windows give the impression of watching her instead of inviting a glorious view of the garden beyond. How much life has been lived in that garden: all the football and cricket practice, play wrestling, racing of guinea pigs, snails and worms, and pitching of tents. At the far end of the lawn, beside the raised beds, is a quaint thatched cottage with its own short driveway and fruit trees. No one has been inside for a while, and she won't go there now.

Her next stop is across the hall, the other side of the staircase, where the dining-room door is ajar, scene of many Christmases and birthdays. Next to it is the music room. With its neglected but treasured piano, an electronic keyboard, a collection of prized acoustic guitars, and several gig bags slumped against amplifiers. This room is the holder of so many memories that she hardly knows where to begin. She doesn't try, simply lets her eyes rest for a moment on the old-fashioned globe at the side of her desk, a guiding light in a darkening world. Close to it is the most precious of her instruments, a trumpet that's no longer played, or even handled. It simply sits quietly inside a large glass box, like a museum exhibit attached to the wall. It's as if all its power and beauty, all its memories and many voices are locked up in the case with it. If she were to open it, they might all come tumbling out and she'd feel crushed under the weight.

Her gaze moves on to the turntables – one digital, the other from the Sixties – side by side atop a decades-old stereogram that no longer works. They might be from different eras, but they are, and always will be, inextricably linked by the vinyl albums that fill most of one wall. Blues, soul, swing, jazz . . . A few have her face on the cover; others belong to Billie, Ella, Sarah, Etta – and, of course, Aretha, Roberta and Nina.

And then there are the men, so many more of them, starting all the way back with Scott Joplin, King Oliver, Jelly Roll Morton, Count Basie and Louis, always Louis . . . The greatest trumpeter of all. Even to think of him can evoke the opening of 'Summertime'.

She returns to the entrance hall. As she climbs the stairs, she's passing dozens of framed photographs of babies, small boys, happy parents, teenagers, holidays, achievements, and medals, lots of medals.

She checks the bedrooms. The beds, drapes and furniture have changed over time, as have the posters that used to cover the walls: superheroes, sporting legends, J. Lo, Britney, Oasis, Springsteen, Amy Winehouse . . .

She can't, won't, allow the past to derail or swamp her now.

Soon she is back in the hallway, where a lazy shaft of sunlight is spilling through the open front door onto the black-and-white chequered tiles.

The Uber is less than five minutes away. There's still time to stop it, but she won't.

She glances up at the mirror that probably also came with the house, she can't quite recall. The comings and goings it has seen, the secrets it will never share. Her reflection shows a woman who doesn't make much sense to her. She should look older than the person staring back at her, have more lines around her eyes, an abundance of grey hair, maybe even sagging jowls, and yet this familiar stranger is not like that at all. Her hair is dark and curly, tumbling to her shoulders, and has retained all its colours – ebony, chocolate, copper, golden-brown and, yes, maybe there is a little silver here and there, now she looks closer. She clips it into a low ponytail and watches the natural curls spring free around her face. Some say a woman of her age shouldn't have long hair, but she'd hated having it short while in prison and can't see a time now when she'd consider cutting it again.

Her eyes, almond-shaped and sky blue, show nothing of her experiences, and yet they feel heavy and dark. The lashes are still luxuriant, even without mascara; she wears none today. The pupils are watchful, wary in a way that almost makes her smile. She thinks about how they have no feelings of their own, can only reflect what is happening in the heart. The same goes for her mouth, with prominent twin peaks on her upper lip and upwardly tilted corners. Mouths have no feelings of their own, they merely change shape according to what is driving the emotions, or what is needing to be said.

She tilts her head to one side and, for fleeting moments, she sees herself in the posters that used to hang in the music room, showing her laughing and sultry, carefree, windswept, singing from the heart and dancing in moonlight. She'd torn them all down several weeks ago and put them out for recycling. It hadn't been possible to do the same with the hundreds of photographs that spanned so many years, all tucked into albums now and stored in boxes under the beds. The newer ones are on her old phone, locked in a drawer of her desk.

She has a new phone now, with a different number that only one person has.

Time is ticking on. The Uber is one minute away.

An expected sense of dread flutters inside her, but there is a promising drift of anticipation too. Yes, it's a risk, and not one she'd ever advise anyone else to take, but she's as determined as ever to go through with it.

Before going to the door, she looks down at her shoes, flat, black and easy for walking. She could be doing a lot of that today; most airports demand it. She's wearing narrow black trousers, a light blue sweater with a plain round neck and a cobalt blue silk scarf knotted at her neck. Smart, but not outstandingly so.

Hearing a car pull into the drive, she reaches for her sand-coloured pea coat. Though slouchy, it's also stylish. According to a good friend, she has a way of making most things look better than they are. Even during the period of waiting for her hair to grow, she'd managed to look, in her friend's words, gamine and vulnerable and weirdly classy.

'Can I take this for you?'

She looks up to find the driver at the door, reaching for her bags.

'Thank you,' she says, and adds as a caution, 'they're heavy.'

His smile reveals deep dimples in round, fleshy cheeks. He shows no sign of exertion as he heaves the larger silver case into the boot of his Passat.

Shouldering the leather tote-bag that contains her passport, laptop and Kindle, she steps outside, quickly pulls the front door closed behind her and doesn't look back as she goes to the car. Her own car is parked at the side of the house, not far from the centuries-old oak with its widely spread branches and a swing that's been there for ever.

As they drive along the street of mostly large, detached houses with hedges around their front gardens and iron gates into their driveways, she notices a few Halloween pumpkins already on doorsteps. A little early, maybe, but what does it matter? Kids enjoy these things, so why not let them? She's trick-or-treated with her own boys along this street many times over the years, although back when they were young it was nothing like it is now.

She wonders if anyone is watching her leave and how long it might be before someone remarks to a neighbour, 'Haven't seen Catie Mac for a while, have you?'

The neighbour might answer. 'Do you think she's, you know, gone away again?'

'What for? No! She can't have. Not like that, if that's what you mean.'

Someone else might say, 'It's terrible what happened to her.'

'Yes, but it's terrible what she did.'

She doesn't find the prospect of their speculation or suppressed horror particularly edifying, and nor does it make her feel guilty. She's had enough of that particular torment to last her a lifetime and, though she isn't fool enough to think she'd managed to lock it inside the house when she'd left, she isn't going to let it dominate her when she gets to where she's going.

'Which terminal?' the driver asks as they speed along the M4 towards Heathrow. Bristol Airport would have been more convenient, but at this time of year there are no flights to where she's headed.

'Five,' she replies, and continues to stare out at the passing landscape of misty, sun-drenched fields and autumn trees.

It isn't cold but, according to her weather app, it's a lot warmer at her destination. She'd chosen it randomly, a finger holding still as her father's old globe spun to a slow and steady stop beneath it. It had felt as though he was guiding her.

She'd been pleased with the results, thankful that she hadn't ended up landing on somewhere she'd hate to go. As it was, she'd had to perform another random pick over an unfolded map to narrow things down to a specific town.

She's never visited this island before, or even really given much thought to it. She knows no one there and doesn't speak the language, but that only adds to its appeal. No one will know her – or think to look for her – in this new small town of hers, and there won't be anyone to recognize her, apart from tourists, of course; but hopefully enough time has passed for anyone who might once have recognized her to have forgotten all about her.

The airport check-in is easy, the flight is on time, and not much more than three hours after take-off she is wheeling her suitcase into the busy Arrivals hall of another airport, Fontanarossa. She scans the nameboards held up to greet the passengers until she finds one that bears hers. How impressive of the driver to have spelled Catie correctly.

She hasn't changed her name, although she'd considered it. For a few wildly irrational days she'd even thought about cosmetic surgery, a new face for a new life, but thankfully the madness had passed.

The instant she steps outside the terminal, the sun embraces her like a friend who's long been waiting. Its warmth wraps gently around her and sinks all the way through to her bones. She takes off her coat, draping it over one arm, then unties her scarf as well, and her long legs seem to move more freely, a lightness in her step, as she follows the driver. All around there is noise and bustle, cars coming and going, people passing, children shouting, while the sky above is perfectly blue and serene, and the exquisite light, seeming both sharp and misty, is unmistakably Mediterranean. The sense of being in the right place at the right time brings a smile to her lips. If this is how she feels at the airport, she can hardly begin to imagine what it's going to be like when she reaches the small, hillside town fifty-five kilometres north of here.

The car is a Mercedes S-Class. She shouldn't be surprised, considering the cost of the transfer. Nor should she be surprised to find that Europe's most active volcanic mountain is right there, seeming close enough to touch, vast and magnificent, threatening and oddly beguiling.

Soon they are speeding along the autostrada with the Eagles' greatest hits on the sound system. It never matters where anyone is in the world, music is always the easiest connector, reaching across cultures, languages and generations in a way nothing else can.

'You like?' the driver asks, as 'One of These Nights' yields to 'Take It to the Limit'.

She smiles and nods. Yes, she likes. She's safe with the Eagles. In spite of how much she's always enjoyed them, they don't have part-ownership of her memories in the way others do.

'I see once, when they come to Milan,' the driver tells her. 'Very good time for me. My father take me. He big fan, and now me.'

Knowing all about a father's influence on musical tastes, she says, 'Are you from Milan?'

'No, no. I am born here, in Sicily.' The pride is so evident in his voice that she floods with affection for him. 'This your first time here?' he asks.

'Yes,' she admits, 'and I don't speak Italian. I'm sorry.'

'No sorry. Lots of people speak English in Taormina. Is a very beautiful town. Very historic and lots of shopping.'

Amused by the 'shopping', she considers what she's read about the place: a *comune* of Messina, more than eight hundred feet above sea level; a tourist destination since the nineteenth century; home to the magnificent San Domenica Monastery, now an exclusive hotel.

'How long you stay?' the driver asks, tearing past exits to places she's never heard of and will probably never visit. Belpasso, Santa Tecla, Giarre.

'I don't know,' she replies. She hadn't bought a return ticket. All she has is a hotel reservation for the next two weeks and a task to fulfil in that time. It might take longer, and she could end up moving on. Nothing is set in stone, and nothing lasts for ever, as she knows too well.

After a while, she lets her head fall back and closes her eyes. Already her old life feels far away, while the potential of this new one is beginning to feel overwhelming. She's tired, she realizes; things always seem more daunting then.

'Please look,' the driver says, gesturing to his left.

And there it is again, the famous volcano, rising darkly, mysteriously into the early evening sky, the burning glow of the sun sinking towards its open peak. She feels unaccountably moved by its grandeur, and half expects a flame to hurl itself into the air before night engulfs it.

She senses more anxiety and tension building, but only has to think of her father to become settled again. She pictures his face, his smile; hears his laughter, his music. He is with her in ways she can never see, but always feel. It's comforting to think he brought her here; it makes her seem less alone.

A phone starts to ring, and it's only when the driver glances at her in the rear-view mirror that she realizes it's hers.

Experiencing shock and alarm, she digs it out of her bag and checks the incoming ID. It isn't one she recognizes; certainly it's not the only person who has this number.

Is it you, Lawrence, she asks silently. Then, *Please God, let it be him with the news I crave.*

CHAPTER TWO

She could feel him watching her. Not the way everyone else was fixed on her, attentively, maybe a little fuzzily, even admiringly. The sensation of his gaze was different and almost making her breathless. She couldn't allow that to happen, not in the middle of a song. The bride and groom were counting on her, as was the groom's very wealthy father. But the intensity of his scrutiny seemed physical, encompassing, as though it were as close to her as the evening dress clinging so lovingly to her skin.

She moved across the stage, the mic clutched in her hand, as though it had never left, her head tipping back as she reached for the high notes, her hair tumbling in rich, natural curls. He was as distracting as if he were right here with her, touching her, filling every bit of space around her.

It should be creepy, but somehow it wasn't.

Outside, the night sky over Bristol was black and cold and glittered with stars. Inside this vast marquee, where two hundred guests were gathered for the big event, candles flickered at the centre of each table, while fairy lights looped between ivy-covered pillars and bouquets of sweetheart balloons.

The song was a special request from the happy couple. 'The First Time Ever I Saw Your Face', a massive hit some years ago for one of her all-time heroines, Roberta Flack. It was the version everyone had expected; they'd probably have been perplexed by the jazz interpretation the band usually performed. She loved that one too, had sung it many times, but she, and the Blue Notes Jazz Band, were always flexible.

Did it mean something that she'd never seen this guy before, the one who was watching her?

The First Time Ever I Saw Your Face.

She focused on the newlyweds swaying together before her, a flushed and happy couple at the heart of friends and family, joined for their first dance. As she sang, she could feel the lyrics, the romance, the soulful rhythm moving through her, as if it were the heat in her blood.

Eventually the song came to an end and, as the band segued seamlessly into the many other requests they'd been sent for this evening, guests began crowding onto the floor. There was everything from swing to Latin, blues, jazz, and plenty of pop. She'd rehearsed well, but none of it was hard for her. She'd been singing almost since she could talk. She loved the jazz tunes best, probably as much as she loved the guys who made up the band.

She couldn't be sure if *he* was still watching her; if he'd moved to the dance floor now, or maybe he was at the bar. He was no longer at the same table, so maybe he'd left? It didn't matter. She didn't know him, probably never would, and the thrill of singing, of surrendering her whole body to the music was so exhilarating that she rarely had a problem shutting out everything else.

It was well after midnight by the time she wound up the live music session with 'Love Is Here to Stay', and was treated to so much thunderous (and drunken) applause that she couldn't stop laughing.

Laughing too, Mac, the band's leader, came to put an arm around her shoulders. 'Thank you, everyone,' he said into the mic, 'it's been an honour to play for you tonight and we, the Blue Notes Jazz Band, want to wish Elaine and Simon all the happiness in the world. Are they still here?' He peered out through the crowd.

'Left an hour ago,' someone told him.

'Can you play "It's a Sunday Kind of Love",' someone else shouted.

'The DJ's ready to take over,' Mac informed them, 'but before we go, maybe you'd be kind enough to join us in a chorus of "Happy Birthday"? Catie here, our wonderful singer, who I'm sure you'll agree is exceptional, is eighteen today.'

Embarrassed, Catie gasped as a cheer erupted and the band struck up the age-old tune. Mac sang the loudest, while Rob blew every breath he had left into his trumpet and Hank crashed it out on the drums. It was raucous and hilarious and so much fun that they sang and played it all over again.

Finally, Catie bowed and waved her thanks, hot with pride and adrenalin. She had never felt so happy or elated. If it were possible, she'd have continued to sing till dawn. She didn't need sleep, or food, or drink; she only needed this feeling, this magic, to go on for ever. Not that it was the first time she'd fronted the band, far from it, she'd been doing it since she couldn't remember when, but no other gigs to date had been this big for her.

As soon as they were gathered in the side tent, she was swept into prideful hugs and told she was on her way to fame and fortune.

'I only ever want to sing with you guys,' she told them, glowing and tingling with their praise.

13

'That's what you say now,' Pete grinned, 'but you wait.'

'I'm not going anywhere,' she insisted.

'I am,' Hank grunted. 'Home. We're not all eighteen any more. Time for my bed.'

Minutes later, as Hank and Pete began carrying their instruments and equipment out to the Transit, an unfamiliar voice, clipped around the edges by breeding and privilege said, 'Mac, she's something else.'

Mac and Catie turned to find William Thurloe, the groom's father, had come into the tent.

Hank turned back from the exit flap. 'You're not stealing her,' he warned.

Thurloe's bushy eyebrows arched. 'Maybe not, but someone will,' he replied with a smile. 'You have a remarkable voice, young lady, but I'm sure you hear that all the time.'

'She does,' Mac assured him. 'Mostly from me.'

Thurloe's eyes twinkled. 'My company is hosting a dinner dance at the Town's Talk in May. I was going to book you anyway, Mac, but now I've heard your girl here, I have to insist she's with you.'

Catie's eyes grew wide. Town's Talk was a major venue in Bristol; even famous people played there. She beamed as Mac said, 'Don't worry, she'll be with us. You've got my number, so give me a call in the next couple of days and I'll make sure it's in the diary.'

'You can count on it, and don't be surprised if you get a lot more calls after tonight. You've made quite an impression, young lady, and here you are, only eighteen.'

'Come on,' Mac laughed, tweaking her nose, 'or we'll start turning into pumpkins.'

'But you'll definitely let me do the Town's Talk gig?' she insisted, her eyes bright with excitement already.

'By the sound of it, I'll have to.'

His dry tone didn't fool her; she knew he was as happy about it as she was. She was his discovery, after all.

Minutes later, she was wrapped in her fake sheepskin coat with a bright red bobble hat pulled down over her ears and her father's big leather gloves dwarfing her hands. She was humming 'I Get a Kick Out of You' while pushing a foot into a furry boot when someone wished her a happy birthday.

Starting, as she'd thought she was alone, she turned to find a stranger standing just inside the tent. It was him. The one who'd been watching her earlier. Up close and in full light he was . . . Actually, he was a bit like David Cassidy in *The Partridge Family*. Not that she was a fan, unlike most of her friends, but this stranger who definitely looked like him, with all that thick dark hair and the intense eyes, had to be one of the best-looking guys she'd ever stood this close to. He was young, although older than her, she reckoned, probably in his twenties, and he was easily as tall as Mac.

'Thank you,' she said, wishing she hadn't put the bobble hat on yet and was wearing boots on both feet instead of only one with a stiletto on the other.

'Will you see me again?' he asked.

Her eyes widened in amazement.

'I'm Lawrence Vaughan,' he told her. 'My family lives a couple of miles from here. I know you're Catie and that you're a seriously talented singer – and that you're someone I just have to see again. I'm sorry if that sounds weird, or heavy, it's just how . . . it is. I mean,' he went on awkwardly, 'if you're with the old bloke who plays the piano . . . He seems kind of nice, I suppose, but if you are, you're wasted on him. With your talent, you don't need someone like that to help you make it. I'm guessing your dream is to be a

15

professional . . . He'll just be using you to get his band noticed.'

'Catie, are you ready?' Mac said, re-entering the tent. Spotting Lawrence Vaughan, he came to a stop. 'Oh, hello, son. Are you lost?'

Colouring slightly, Lawrence said, 'No, I just wanted to talk to Catie before she left.'

Mac looked from one to the other. 'Do you two know each other?' he asked curiously.

'No,' Catie replied, barely able to hide her amusement.

'Not yet,' Lawrence informed him.

As understanding dawned in Mac's eyes he said, 'I get the feeling I'm interrupting something here.'

Like a young buck measuring up to an old stag, Lawrence said, a little belligerently, 'I was about to try and persuade her to go on a date with me.'

Mac cocked his head and, after assessing the newcomer, he said to Catie, 'And what do you think of that?'

Eyes still sparkling with laughter, Catie said, 'You should know that he thinks you're too old for me and you're using me to get the band noticed.'

Mac's eyebrows shot up, and when he replied it was clear, to Catie at least, that he was trying not to laugh. 'Is that right?' he said to Lawrence.

'No offence,' Lawrence insisted, holding up his hands in defence, 'I was just . . . I . . .' It was apparent Mac's amusement had wrongfooted him, but she wasn't sure she was ready to help him yet.

'You have to admit,' Lawrence continued to Mac, 'you're probably old enough to be her father, and somehow that's not right, when she's so . . . *young.*'

Talk about digging himself in deeper.

Clearly enjoying himself, Mac said, 'It's true, I am that old.

And what sort of age would you be . . .? Sorry, what was your name again?'

'He's Lawrence,' Catie told him, 'and Lawrence, this is David, but we call him Mac.'

Lawrence held out a hand to shake, which Mac readily took.

Becoming more awkward by the second, Lawrence said, 'OK, I get it. You're her dad, aren't you?'

Mac burst out laughing. 'I am, and very proud of it,' he said. 'And you, well, you're hoping to go on a date with her, are you?' He turned to Catie, gesturing for her to give a reply.

Knowing she'd like nothing more, she said, 'I might have to think about it.'

Lawrence and Mac exchanged glances. 'That's what you call playing hard to get,' Mac informed him.

'Dad!' Catie protested. 'What I'm saying is, I'm quite busy at the moment . . .'

'Tuesday night, under the clock on the Centre?' Lawrence said. 'Seven, or is that too early. Too late?'

Catie was about to reply when a dishevelled, clearly tipsy girl of about her own age stumbled in. 'There you are,' she said crossly to Lawrence. 'I've been looking all over . . .' Her eyes alighted on Catie and for a moment she seemed baffled. 'Are you the singer under that hat?' she asked.

Catie nodded.

'You were really good, but I expect everyone's told you that by now.' Turning back to Lawrence, she clutched his arm to begin dragging him away. 'Come on, everyone's wondering what happened to you.'

Removing his arm, Lawrence steered her back to the flap she'd come through, but before leaving he glanced over his shoulder. 'Tuesday, seven,' he said, and a moment later he'd gone.

Catie turned to her father.

Clearly still amused, Mac shrugged and then winced as Hank leaned on the horn to hurry them up.

Catie stooped to zip her boots and was about to follow Mac out when she realized the girl had come back into the tent.

'Is everything all right?' she asked, half-expecting Lawrence to reappear too.

The girl regarded her sourly, as if she were looking at someone who wasn't quite making the grade, at least in her eyes. Catie had seen the expression before. This girl was from a moneyed, maybe even an aristocratic background, while she, Catie, was not. Or maybe it was just the way Catie felt when confronted by someone who clearly came from this side of town.

'I don't know what he said to you,' the girl began, 'but best not go thinking you're anything special. OK? I'm saying this for your own sake, because you seem like a sweet girl. Good idea to stick to the singing. Like I said before, you're good and we wouldn't want anything spoiling things for you now, would we?'

Catie watched her leave, aware she hadn't spoken a word herself, and not entirely sure if she'd just been threatened, or put down, or what the heck had just happened?

CHAPTER THREE

Catie hadn't known the girl's name, the one who'd barged into the band's tent all those years ago, but she'd learned it soon after.

Jude Penrose-Fry, although the Fry was rarely used.

Even now she can picture the drunken hostility, the air of ownership, though whether of the place, or of Lawrence, it hadn't been clear – but it had probably been a bit of both.

Rather than dwell on it now, she lets the memory go, and focuses on the calming blue Ionian Sea spread out in front of her.

She inhales deeply and shifts to a more comfortable position in her chair, one of two on her spacious hotel balcony. How wonderful it is to be in this place that's so unlike anything she's left behind, that demands nothing of her, simply allows her to be anonymous and undisturbed and whatever else she might want to be while she's here.

A notebook and pen lie together on the table beside her, and pushed to one side is a finished cup of coffee and untouched biscotti.

Should she be writing by hand, she wonders, or typing into her laptop?

Does it matter?

She's slept a lot since arriving – not an intention, but it has probably been good for her. After only three nights and almost four days she can feel the restorative power of rest driving out the heaviness of despair and helplessness she'd reluctantly brought with her.

Gone too is the shock that had lingered like a bruise following the phone call she'd received while coming in from the airport.

It hadn't been Lawrence.

Of course it hadn't been him.

She'd known it even before clicking on, but the way she'd responded to the ringing, and the unknown number, was proof of where she was in her head, and ultimately of how badly she'd needed to get away.

The call had been from her new provider, asking if she'd like to add anything to her package. She hadn't, and that was the last time the phone had rung until a text arrived yesterday.

***188: *Are you settling in over there?*

CM: *I think so. How are you?*

***188: *It's me who should be asking you that.*

CM: *I'm fine.*

***188: *Have you started writing yet?*

CM: *A little.*

She inhales again, drawing in the fresh, salty air, along with the heady prospect of change; closing her eyes, she raises her face to the sun. The first thing she sees in the self-imposed darkness is Jude's face during the moments after that long-ago wedding. She'd always had a blowsy, red-lipped, tousled blonde look going on, even then.

Can more than forty years really have passed since that night when they'd first stared into each other's eyes, Jude's bleary and bloodshot, yet managing to emanate menace, while Catie's elation dimmed and yielded to confusion.

Does she really care about any of it now? No, not really, it's just where it all began, and every story must have a beginning.

Opening her eyes, she allows her new, exotic world to merge back into focus, sunlight eclipsing darkness, warmth pushing out cold. She spots a cruise ship on its way to Naxos and, much closer, right next to her, a tiny gecko darts across the balustrade.

After a while she looks down at the words she's written so far, her first attempt, her first chapter, and it makes her think of how many firsts there are in life. First smiles, first teeth, first steps, first days at school, right through to first love . . .

Is she really going to write about her life and, if she is, will it make a difference?

The therapist, in prison, whom she'd continued to see privately after, had advised her not to make any rules for herself.

'The order you tell your story in doesn't matter,' she'd said. 'It isn't a novel or a memoir. It's for you and only you. Write in the first, second or third person, whatever feels right at the time, and change if you have to. This is simply you purging, or maybe reassessing, what went before, emptying your heart and trying to see yourself with more tolerance and compassion. You're not a bad person, Catie.'

Catie had felt then, and still feels now, that the order in which she recounts the past *does* matter, and she gives a half-smile when she realizes the therapist would probably say, 'OK, that's fine. Whatever works.'

It's interesting to Catie now that she considers Lawrence to be the beginning, when of course he wasn't, not really.

Oh Dad, she sighs softly, as unexpected tears fill her eyes. *I know you remember that night too and how we stopped for curry sauce and chips on the way home and laughed at what all the posh wedding guests might have said if they'd known. Hank wondered if any of them had ever tried such a supreme delicacy and Johnnie said he'd eat his sax if they had.*

She can't recall Mac mentioning anything about Lawrence during the journey and midnight feast, and by the time they'd got home he'd been ready for his bed. She, on the other hand, had been so high on adrenalin that she'd wanted desperately to tell her best friend Lola all about it, but there had been no such thing as mobile phones back then, no one had even dreamt of them. There were just the big old rotary dial things most people kept in their hallways and that were guaranteed to wake up the whole house if anyone rang. If it hadn't been so late, she might have gone downstairs to the front room and poured her teenage exuberance – and trepidation – into their wonky and beloved old piano.

What would her mother have had to say if she had hit the keys that night, all those madly jubilant chords and crazy crescendos making the ceiling shake beneath her parents' bed.

Maybe not as much as she'd had to say about Lawrence the next day.

CHAPTER FOUR

'I despair of you two at times, I really do,' Patty sighed, wiping her hands on her pinny before going to check the roasters sizzling away in the top of the oven. 'You put all sorts of notions in her head, Mac, so she starts getting all these fancy ideas like she's going to be some world-famous singer, with more money than God and now this . . . this . . . What's his name?'

Behind her, at the kitchen table for four, with its red plastic cloth and padded back chairs, Mac's eyes were alight with laughter while Catie silently groaned and her best friend, Lola from next door, faked a swoon.

'Lawrence,' Lola answered dreamily. 'And I think it's the most romantic thing I've ever heard. Corny, but definitely romantic. I mean, you were actually singing "The First Time Ever I Saw Your Face" the *first time* you saw him. It's straight out of a film or a book. And then he comes up to you after and tells you he has to see you again. If you ask me, he fell in love at first sight.' Her round, spotty face – framed by a boyish bob and slightly protruding ears – was so flushed with excitement that her glasses were starting to steam over her chocolate-brown eyes.

'I told you, he seemed like a nice lad,' Mac declared, reaching to pull out a drawer behind him for a handful of cutlery. 'Are you staying for dinner?' he asked Lola.

'Oh, yes, please,' Lola replied eagerly. She spent more time here than in her own home next door, and was so slavishly adoring of Catie, so fannishly impressed by her, that even Catie found it a bit much at times. However, she loved Lola like a sister, and had been fiercely protective of her all through school, especially during the horrible episodes of ridicule and bullying.

Catie despised anyone who picked on those who were weaker, or who might look a bit different – they should all wish they were as clever as Lola.

'Maybe,' Patty commented archly, 'we should be calling it lunch now our Catie's going on a date with a posh boy?'

Catie groaned. 'Mum, you say the dumbest things sometimes,' she grumbled, irritated, but at the same time trying not to let her excitement show. It would only get further under her mother's skin. 'You don't know anything about him.'

'I know that everyone at that wedding last night comes from big houses on the other side of town, and you, Mac, shouldn't be egging her on with any of it. You know very well she's got A levels coming up. She needs to get through them, and she won't if she's gallivanting about with some toff who'll end up taking advantage of her.'

Pulling a face behind her mother's back, Catie looked imploringly at her father, who simply shook his head, telling her to let it go.

Lola said, boldly, 'I think she should go on the date. I mean, it would be rude just to stand him up, wouldn't it?' Seeming unsure about that now, she looked to Mac for help.

Giving her a wink, he said, 'Our girl has just turned eighteen, Patty, so she gets to make her own decisions. They won't always be the right ones – think about the bad one you made not so long ago . . .'

Catie clasped her hands over her ears. They weren't going to start on about Patty's vote for Margaret Thatcher again, were they? Please don't let it happen when it was too late now, the dreadful woman was already in office, and the last thing she wanted was her parents not speaking to one another again for a month.

'I know you regret it now,' Mac was saying, 'but it shows you don't have to be young to get things wrong, and gone are the times when we can make Catie's mind up for her.'

Patty scoffed. 'You've been doing it for so long she doesn't know what her own mind is any more.'

Amused by that, Mac said, 'She's always known it, and very proud I am of her for it. Now, set the table, you girls, and I'll start carving the chicken. Are your parents coming to the Old Duke with us later, Lola?'

'Oh yeah, they wouldn't miss it, especially if Catie's going to sing.'

Catie watched her father.

'No promises,' he cautioned. 'It'll depend on who's playing, but if it's someone I know, I reckon they'll be happy to share the stage for a number or two. Have you decided which songs yet? Just in case.'

'Oh, you've got to do "Blue Moon",' Lola insisted. 'I love it when you sing that, and my dad's a really big fan of Billie Holiday.'

'Isn't everyone?' Mac responded, shooting a mischievous glance at Patty, who played the old tunes any chance she got when she thought no one was listening.

'That's as may be,' Patty retorted, 'but it's a bit old fashioned . . .'

'It's jazz,' Catie cried indignantly, 'and that's what they play at the Old Duke. It's why we're going.'

'And what sort of eighteen-year-old wants to make her

25

first *legal* visit to a pub where old fogies, who've got nothing better to do with their time, bang out old tunes?'

Mac winced. 'Harsh, Patty,' he scolded, 'and you know you don't mean it, so let's hear what Catie's decided to sing, if she gets the chance.'

Loving her father with a devotion that knew no limits, Catie cast a fond look at Lola. 'I wasn't going to do "Blue Moon",' she said, 'but if your parents would like me to . . .'

'Oh, they would, they would,' Lola assured her.

'Then that's one,' Catie decided, 'and the other, if I get to do two,' she performed a drum roll on the table, and staring at her busy mother's back she announced, '"Too Young".'

Mac laughed and applauded, while Patty turned round with her eyebrows raised as if to say, 'You can't get round me that easily.' It was one of her favourite expressions, which Catie and her father could see right through. They knew how much she loved the song, mostly because Mac often sang it to her – it was their theme, he'd say, given they were barely out of their teens when they'd married. And when Catie was born, seven months later, she had, according to her father, come out singing. Patty had another way of describing it, but Mac would hear none of it.

You are truly gifted, he kept telling her throughout her childhood, as did just about everyone who heard her sing and play the piano, or the guitar, apart from her mother who was forever warning her not to let it go to her head. 'Music's all right for a hobby,' she'd scold, 'but you need proper qualifications behind you so you can get a proper job.'

Given that Mac – the best piano and trumpet player in the world, as far as Catie was concerned – earned his living as a factory worker over on Lodge Causeway, and the rest of the band all had day jobs too, it was hard to argue with her mother's determination.

'There are loads more opportunities out there for girls now,' Patty would chunter on and on, 'way more than in my day, and you need to take advantage of them. Look at Lola, she's studying hard, she's not up all hours watching her father's band.'

'Because he doesn't have one,' Catie would point out, but she usually left it there, as the only way to handle her mother was to let her think she'd won the argument. Mac had taught her that, secretly, over the years, and because he obviously loved Patty in spite of how awful she could be, Catie found it a little easier than she might have done otherwise to love her too.

She got to sing at the Old Duke that night with a band called the Donnington Dreamers, named after the village in Gloucestershire from which the three of them came. Mac had played with them several times in the past, filling in when someone couldn't make it, and once as a guest trumpeter, just because he was so good. He played that night too, and rendered the entire pub silent with his opening of 'Summertime'. Catie was so proud of him in those moments she could have burst with it, although it wasn't just those moments, it was how she always felt about him. How could she feel anything but blessed to be his daughter? Especially when she saw how popular and respected, even loved, he was by so many, including her mother, although Patty put on a good show of hiding it.

When Tuesday evening came round, he still had no problem with her going to meet Lawrence Vaughan; in fact, they were still enjoying the occasional laugh over the look on Lawrence's face when he'd realized Mac was her father. Catie hadn't told her mother about that, and nor had she mentioned anything to her dad, or Lola, about the girl who'd tried to warn her off Lawrence. Obviously Mac had seen her, but he hadn't heard what she'd come back into the tent to say.

Whoever she was, she was the last person on Catie's mind as she and Lola finally decided on what she should wear for the big date – brand-new blue check bell-bottoms from Chelsea Girl in Broadmead; a white peasant blouse from Wallis; her favourite dark red platforms from Ravel and the wooden chain necklace Lola had given her for her birthday.

She felt a bit anxious about what he might think of her outfit, given that the only other time he'd seen her she'd been dressed in a skin-tight black glittery number (from a second-hand shop in Redland that her mother had altered to fit). Obviously, he wouldn't be expecting her to wear anything like that tonight, but she couldn't help wondering what the girls from the wedding wore on dates, and if her own fashion choices were a bit . . . cheap? They probably shopped in expensive boutiques like Bus Stop, or the ones up in Clifton that she didn't even know the names of and had no way of affording.

'You look like a model,' Lola declared loyally as Catie performed a hesitant twirl in front of her wardrobe mirror. Her hair, thanks to Carmen rollers and Lola's expert brushing, looked just like Farrah Fawcett's, only dark, and her eye make-up was as blue as her eyes.

She attempted another turn. There wasn't a lot of space in her bedroom for fashion parades or assessing performances with an old mic, but she managed. Her most prized possessions were the record player on four legs, with the two speakers her dad had connected up, and a bookcase mostly full of vinyl, but also plenty of paperbacks.

Homework was done (to music) either lying on the bed, or sitting on the floor, or downstairs in the living room in front of the gas fire.

Hearing a car outside, she peeped out of the curtains and saw her dad's old Zephyr pulling up in front of their garden gate. He was just back from a quick half down the Full Moon with Lola's dad and, typical of him, he was in plenty of time to get her into town. Their arrangement was that he would stand outside the Hippodrome while she waited under the clock, about a hundred yards away, so if Lawrence Vaughan didn't turn up, Mac would be able to bring her home again.

'It doesn't matter if he doesn't come,' she told Lola as she led the way downstairs, gripping the banister so as not to go over in her platforms. 'I mean, I don't even know him, so why would I care?'

'He'll come,' Lola declared confidently. 'Where do you think you'll go?'

Catie had no idea, and wondered if Lawrence did.

Coming out of the kitchen into the hall, her mother looked her up and down and seeming, grudgingly, to approve, she said, 'Don't miss the last bus home. You know your father has to be up early, so he won't want to be driving in to get you at all hours of the night. Have you got enough for your fare?'

Catie nodded. 'And to buy a round if we go for a drink.'

'If he takes you to a pub, make sure you only have one, and whatever else you do, no going back to his place. Do you hear me?'

'Loud and clear.'

'Or anyone else's, come to that. We don't know anything about him, or the type of company he keeps. He might have a prison record, for all we know.'

'Bye, Mum, I promise not to get into any trouble, and if I do I've already written down the songs I want at my funeral.'

As Lola giggled, Patty's eyes narrowed crossly. 'You're not funny,' she chided. 'Are you going with them?' she asked Lola.

'Of course,' Lola replied, stuffing her arms into her coat. 'I want to see him for myself, so I'll be waiting outside the Hippodrome with Mac. I'll let you know what he's like when we get back.'

Half an hour later, hardly breathing properly she was so nervous, Catie parted from her father and Lola at the Hippodrome steps and walked on through the people milling about this side of the Centre. There were bus queues out by the kerb, and drinkers coming and going from the Drawbridge; the traffic was noisy and the night was dark. No moon, but headlamps and streetlights made everything bright.

It was two minutes past seven when she reached the clock and, though there were lots of people her age and older waiting for their dates, none of them was him.

She felt suddenly foolish and angry and ready to turn back to her dad, but quickly told herself that it was probably too soon to say he'd stood her up. She'd wait until five past; if he didn't show then, she'd leave.

At ten past she spotted her father and Lola strolling chattily towards her, and stupidly she wanted to cry. They'd obviously given up on him already, and so should she.

'Hi, Catie.'

She turned and gasped and broke into such an embarrassingly wide smile that there was no playing it cool from there.

'You're not going to believe this,' he said, looking a bit

harried and windswept, but grinning anyway, 'I know it sounds lame, but my car broke down on St Michael's Hill.'

Her eyes widened. 'You've got a car?'

He shrugged and laughed. 'I did, but I think it just died on me. If it's OK with you, before we go anywhere, I need to ring a couple of mates to ask them to take care of it. They should be able to bump-start it and get it somewhere safer. I'd have done it myself, but I couldn't risk being any later, or you might have left. Thanks for coming, by the way. Did I already say that?'

Aware of her dad and Lola walking nonchalantly by, she laughed as Lola gave a thumbs-up behind her back, and said, 'There are phone boxes, over there, by the taxi rank. Actually, I expect you already know that.'

Taking her arm, he tucked it under his and they headed off to make the call. As they stood in the small box together, their breath steaming the windows, and coats touching, she could feel the warmth of him mingling with her own, and somehow being so close didn't feel awkward at all.

After using up all the ten-pence pieces they had between them, he pushed the heavy door open and stepped out behind her. 'I owe them for this,' he declared, 'but most of all I owe you a drink for waiting. Is there anywhere particular you'd like to go?'

Wanting to appear decisive, and at least a little bit in the know, she said, 'How about the Mauritania on College Green? It shouldn't be crowded on a Tuesday night.' It was somewhere her father had suggested, along with a few others as backup. Everything seemed to be happening so fast, wildly even, which was strange when really nothing was happening at all.

'Maybe it's not your scene,' she said as he glanced off down the Centre towards the river.

'What? No, it's cool,' he assured her. 'I'm just working out which is the fastest way to get there, given it's about to rain.'

Happily allowing her hand to be grabbed, she ran with him across to Denmark Street, cut through to Unity Street, and they soon ended up, breathless and damp, in the porch of the Maurie.

Before opening the big glass and wood doors, he swung her round to face him, and gazed laughingly into her eyes. 'It's really good to see you,' he said. 'I can hardly believe you showed up.'

She tilted her head, hoping her grin wasn't making her look as daft and keen as she felt.

'I've been thinking about you ever since Saturday,' he told her, his dark eyes moving all over her face, as if drinking in every last drop of her. 'I can't get you or your amazing voice out of my head. You're something else, do you know that?'

She shrugged self-consciously, wishing she could think of something cool to say. This was as good as – maybe even better than – being on stage.

Standing aside for someone to come out of the pub, he caught the door before it closed and led the way in.

Minutes later they were at a corner table with a Bacardi and Coke for her and a pint of bitter for him. He'd also bought a bag of salt and vinegar crisps, which he tore open for them to share.

She listened attentively, even raptly, as he told her all about the pub's history: how the lovely art deco wall panels had been crafted out of wood salvaged from the famous ocean liner (she didn't admit she'd never heard of the ship, she didn't want to look stupid when he was obviously really clever). Apparently the building itself had been around since 1870, and all kinds of music acts had played here over the years.

'Have you ever?' he asked, pausing to take a sip of his drink.

She shook her head. 'But Mac has, my dad. Lots of times. They did a twenty-first birthday party here back in the summer. I wanted to come and watch, but the manager wouldn't allow me in because I was only seventeen.'

He grinned. 'But you're eighteen now, so we're perfectly legal . . .' He looked round as someone shouted his name.

'Lawrence Vaughan, as I live and breathe.'

Standing just inside the door was a group of student types, dripping with rain and clearly more than a little drunk.

'What the hell are you doing here?' Lawrence demanded, getting up from his chair. 'Sorry about this,' he murmured to Catie.

'Who are they?' she asked.

'It doesn't matter. I'll get rid of them.'

As she watched him go over, she realized that the girl from the wedding was amongst them and her glittery eyes were fixed on Catie as she slid her arms round Lawrence's neck.

Catie looked away. She had no idea why she felt embarrassed when she had no reason to, but a part of her would have liked to leave now. She might have done, if it hadn't meant going past them on her way out.

Eventually he managed to bundle them back through the door, but as he returned to the table she could see he was still trying to hide his annoyance. 'Sorry about that,' he said, sitting down and picking up his drink.

'Who are they?' she asked again.

'So-called mates,' he replied, 'who apparently thought it was a good craic to follow us here.'

'How do you know them?'

33

He shrugged. 'We're at university together. I share a house with a couple of them.'

It was no surprise to learn he was a student – she'd more or less expected it – but seeing that group just now had left her feeling a bit out of her depth. They really were from different worlds.

He smiled and reached for her hand.

She pulled back, afraid suddenly that he was only here for some sort of bet. Students were renowned for their pranks and cruelties, so what sort of prize was he up for if he got her into bed?

He regarded her worriedly. 'Ignore them,' he said. 'Don't let them ruin—'

'The girl who put her arms around you,' she interrupted. 'Is she your girlfriend?'

His eyes shot open. 'What? No! She's . . . just Jude, one of my housemates.'

A housemate? So they lived together?

'Last Saturday, after the wedding,' she said, 'she told me to leave you alone, for my own sake. Why would she say that?'

He looked flabbergasted and then nettled. 'She was drunk. Out of her mind, actually. It was a struggle getting her home, as a matter of fact. But listen, she's no one for you to worry about. I swear it. None of them are. When you meet them, properly, you'll see they're all essentially good blokes and she's, I guess she's a bit of a space cadet, but harmless really.'

Not at all sure she wanted to meet any of them, ever, especially not the space cadet, she considered finishing her drink and starting for the bus stop. But then he said, 'I really want to get to know you, Catie, more than anything. OK, I guess it's not cool to lay it out like that on a first date, but it's the way it is, so please don't let them put you off. If you do, I'll just have to kill them all to get them out of the way.'

Spluttering on a laugh, she shot him a meaningful look as she said, 'Just as long as I'm not the butt of one of your student jokes.'

He looked genuinely bewildered, even shocked, before seeming to get why she might think that. 'Just give me a chance to prove myself,' he urged. 'I promise I'll do everything I can to make sure you don't regret it.'

How could she refuse him when he asked like that, and when she didn't want to anyway?

CHAPTER FIVE

'So you want to know about me,' he said, over their second drink and another bag of crisps, smoky bacon this time. 'Well, I'm twenty-one, almost twenty-two, and not too keen on this song that's just come on.'

She smiled as she listened. It was 'Staying Alive', from the film her mum – and just about everyone else in the world – thought was the best they'd ever seen. Catie loved it too, but she'd only gone to see it twice when it came out last year, unlike Lola who'd sat through it at least a dozen times. And who cried actual tears over how much she loved John Travolta.

'Go on,' she prompted.

'Right, so I'm in my third year at Bristol studying English and Politics, and I'm currently working on my first novel.'

Fascinated, she said, 'You're a writer?'

With a nonchalant shrug, he said, 'Nothing published yet, but please don't let that stand in the way of any awe you might be feeling. Which, by the way, won't be anything compared to the awe I feel for you and your talent—'

'What's it about?' she interrupted.

Seeming surprised, but pleased by her interest, he said, 'It's a spy thriller, or it will be when I've finished. I've got as far as . . . chapter one.'

She burst out laughing.

'Well, I've got to start somewhere,' he protested, 'and I'm not getting a lot of time with finals coming up. I'm guessing you're looking at A's next year, if you're eighteen?'

She nodded and grimaced. 'So much revision,' she groaned.

'What are you taking?'

'Music, surprise, surprise – History and French.'

He was clearly interested. 'Why French?'

She shrugged. 'It's a lovely language, I like some of the books we've been set and they have some great jazz songs.'

He looked impressed. 'You sing in French?'

She shrugged, and tried not to look too pleased with herself – she actually only knew a couple of Edith Piaf songs, but they were French, so she wasn't making it up. '*De temps en temps*,' she said.

'Sing something for me.'

She gave a laugh of astonishment. 'What here? Now? No.'

He grinned. 'OK, but I'm going to hold you to it, so be prepared. Now tell me where you go to school.'

Wincing inwardly, simply for knowing it wouldn't be anything like as classy as where he'd no doubt been, she said, 'I'm at the local comprehensive in Fishponds, where we live. What about you? Where did you go?'

He grimaced. 'Clifton College. Do you know it?'

It was only one of the best private schools in the country. 'Did you board?' she asked, taking another sip of her drink.

He shook his head. 'I grew up in Abbots Leigh, so only a couple of miles away.'

'That's the other side of the Suspension Bridge.' *Seriously posh*.

Sighing he said, 'I know it's usual to move away from home when you go to university, but my dad died a

37

couple of years ago, and because my brother was already working in London – he's got a really good job – I agreed to change my application to Bristol so Mum wouldn't be on her own. I mean, she is, because I don't live there any more – it was definitely part of the deal that I'd get my own place – but I'm not far away, which makes her feel better.'

Riveted by the changing expressions in his eyes, the different tones of his voice that had no Bristolian at all in it, she said, 'I'm really sorry about your dad. I know I wouldn't be able to bear it if anything happened to mine. Was yours ill for a long time?'

His eyes stayed on hers, and she could see the sadness in their depths. 'A couple of years. He had stomach cancer. It was all pretty horrible, to be honest, especially for Mum. Then she had to put my grandma in a home soon after, just to pile it on.'

'Gosh, it sounds as though it's been a difficult time for your family,' she said sympathetically. 'Is your gran still in the home?'

'No, she died about six months ago. It was sad, but a bit of a blessing really. Do you have grandparents?'

Glancing up as a barman bustled a silver tinsel Christmas tree in from the back, she said, 'Only one. My mum's dad lives in the old people's bungalows near us. She goes in to see him most days, and I pop in when I can, but I'm not sure he's ever very pleased to see us. As my mum puts it, he's a grumpy old sod.' She wondered how small and ordinary her world was sounding in comparison to his, but she wasn't going to lie about it. She had nothing to feel ashamed of, she reminded herself, and if he was feeling put off by her lowly roots, well, she wouldn't want to know him anyway.

He was smiling over the rim of his pint glass, seeming, oddly, to like the sound of her gramps, or maybe something else was amusing him. It was hard to tell. 'Do you have brothers and sisters?' he prompted.

'No, I'm an only child. But you have a brother.'

'Graham. He's twenty-six, engaged to Fiona, and a really good guy. Dad would be dead chuffed to see him getting on so well in the City.'

Presuming that meant some kind of bank in London, she said, 'What did your dad do?'

'He was a lawyer – and yours is a far-out pianist and trumpeter. It must be so cool that, having an old man who's into music the way he is.'

She didn't mind admitting that it was, given she was really proud of her dad and had no problem with anyone knowing it. 'Unfortunately, it doesn't pay much,' she added, 'so he works in a factory on Lodge Causeway. My mum does shifts at the Van Dyck. It used to be a cinema, but it's a bingo hall now.'

'Wow. Does she call the numbers?'

'No, she just makes the tea and cleans up and stuff. What about your mum, does she work?'

He picked up his pint as he said, 'I'm not sure if helping out at the university library counts, because I don't think she gets paid for it. Anyway, tell me more about your dad. No, I want to know about you. I know you're a fantastic singer, but do you play any instruments?'

Enjoying how interested he seemed, even if it was only for show, she said, 'The piano, guitar, some clarinet, but not so good at that. Do you play anything?'

'Not really. I mean, I can strum out a tune on a banjo, I guess, but people would probably pay me not to. Do you write songs?'

She grimaced. 'I've worked on a couple, but they're not much good. My dad likes them, but he would, wouldn't he? What sort of music are you into?'

His eyes sparked with mischief as he said, 'Anything as long as you're singing it.'

She shot him a mean look. 'Seriously.'

'OK, I was being serious, but before I knew about you I was a big Hendrix fan; Pink Floyd, Cream, Led Zep, Deep Purple, that sort of thing . . . Am I turning you off yet?'

She quickly shook her head. 'No! All good choices in my book.'

'But really you're into blues and jazz?'

'I've grown up with so much of it that it's what I know best, and I kind of feel it, if you know what I mean.'

'I could see that when you were performing last Saturday. You blew me away.' His voice was soft and his eyes watching her in a way that made his words seem true. She couldn't stop herself smiling. 'Everyone was talking about you after. Do you know that?'

She didn't know what to say, so gave a simple shrug to try to hide her embarrassment, while thrilling to the idea that he'd heard people saying nice things about her.

'Are you going to do the dinner-dance gig at Town's Talk in May?' he asked.

With a flutter of nervous excitement she said, 'I think so. It'll be really cool to play somewhere like that.'

'Next stop the Colston Hall?' He slapped his head. 'What am I talking about? *Carnegie* Hall.'

She laughed with him, but spoke truthfully when she said, 'I'm not really turned on by big venues. I love pubs and clubs, private parties, that sort of thing.' And the reassurance of having her dad nearby, she didn't add. 'I know that might change, because I'm still young, but somewhere

40

I'd love to play one day is Ronnie Scott's in London. That would be amazing. My dad's played there a couple of times. He's even got a photo of himself with Miles Davis, can you believe it? Oh, did you know that it's where Hendrix did his last performance?'

His chin was resting on one hand as he nodded, appearing entranced. 'I don't know that I did,' he admitted, 'but I've got to tell you how much I'd love to see you sing again. I mean to see you, full stop. Are you doing anything at the weekend?'

Lighting up inside, she said, 'We're playing at the Star in Soundwell on Saturday night. I think it's a works Christmas do, but I'm sure it'd be OK for you to come, if you really want to.'

'I really do. I just need to know the time and I'll definitely be there.'

Feeling she might give a sudden laugh of happiness, she picked up her drink to try to stop herself seeming foolish.

'Can I have your phone number?' he asked. 'So I can call you tomorrow?'

He wanted to speak to her that soon! And the good thing was, they were on the phone, because not everyone on their street was. She dug into her bag for a pen and wrote the number on a beer mat.

'Don't you want mine?' he asked as she put her pen away.

'Give it to me on Saturday,' she said. That way, if he didn't ring or turn up, she wouldn't be in danger of making an idiot of herself by ringing up to find out what had happened to him.

CHAPTER SIX

Sitting here now, outside the Café Mocambo on Taormina's main piazza, high above the sea, almost two thousand miles from home and decades away from that time, Catie feels quietly amazed, even touched, by how much she remembers of their first date.

She'd found, once the memories had begun to unfold the day before, and she'd become so swept along by them, that writing them down by hand was too slow, so it's all on her laptop now. She hasn't read it back yet, and isn't sure that she will, but it feels kind of freeing to have released at least some of it. And, at last, she's ventured out of the hotel.

It feels good to be here, soaking up the glorious sunshine under the bluest of skies while sipping an espresso and watching the world ambling by. She smiles to herself as the music in the café changes to an old Chi-Lites number, 'Have You Seen Her?' Could there be a more appropriate song for right now?

She's never sung it herself, and doesn't suppose she ever will, but she's enjoying listening to it now. She wonders if anyone at home is asking that question about her yet, but doesn't dwell on it for long.

A while later, as a tour guide ushers her small party into the café, Catie pays her bill and sets off across the piazza, where half a dozen or more water-colourists are at work in the shade of oleander trees. An accordionist in a straw boater, red bow tie and matching trousers is playing a lively Italian folk song that gets a passing tourist dancing, and outside the Chiesa del Varo a juggler is making a small clutch of kids gasp and cheer.

On reaching the balustrade she rests her hands on it and leans slightly forward to gaze out at the sea. There is something so compelling about it, so irresistible and mesmerizing. The scent of it is in the air, along with warmth and lemons, and what feels like peace, in spite of the gentle cacophony of ongoing life.

That first date with Lawrence, so many years ago now, continues to resonate, making it seem as though time no longer has meaning. It's as though, if she took the right step, she'd be back there in that pub at the bottom of Park Street. She'd be eighteen again to his twenty-one. So young, so innocent, and soon to be very deeply in love.

He'd rung her the next day and they'd talked for over an hour. Her mother had despaired of how much the call must have cost him, 'He's obviously got money to throw away,' she'd snipped, 'and what on earth did you find to talk about for so long, sat out there in the cold, on the bottom of the stairs?'

Her father had called it romantic, 'And if you can't remember what that is, Patty MacAllister, it's high time I reminded you.'

Her mother had told him to get away with himself, but her flushed cheeks had shown how much she liked the idea, and it was clear she was quite intrigued by Lawrence, even if she didn't want to admit it.

He'd come to the gig the following Saturday night, the best-looking guy in the room, at least to Catie's eyes, and

Lola had agreed. She'd sat with him at the edge of the works Christmas party, almost like a couple, if he'd looked in Lola's direction.

Catie had been aware of him watching her sing as if no one else was there, and her performance had been all for him, in her head and her heart. Just as all her performances continued to be over the weeks and months that followed. He tried never to miss one, even if it meant listening from outside because the event was strictly private.

Her dad was as delighted with him as Lawrence was with Mac; it was as though they'd found in each other the father and son that was missing from their lives. Lawrence's hero-worship hit new heights when he learned that a twenty-year-old Mac had played trumpet with the Omega Brass Band as they'd led the last leg of an Easter CND march from Aldermaston to Trafalgar Square. They talked politics almost as much as they did music; they even began taking to the streets in support of movements as diverse as Reclaim the Night, Troops Out and Anti-Apartheid.

Catie had lost her virginity to him three months into their relationship, an awkward, fumbling affair in the back of his mother's Renault. At least the condom hadn't broken. Typically, he'd refused to be embarrassed, and had even made her laugh when he'd cheerfully assured her it would get better with practice – and of course it did.

By the time William Thurloe's dinner-dance do at the Town's Talk had come around, Catie had taken up several invitations to front other bands in the area. She was even being paid on occasion, and Mac kept jokingly saying that she needed an agent, a role that he, of course, was filling. Lola, who, like Lawrence, rarely missed a performance, started taking photos of Catie on stage that she got developed at Boots and sold for a pound each at the next gig.

Amazingly, some people actually bought them.

As her A levels drew closer, her mother, predictably, became less and less impressed by 'this infatuation with Lawrence', and Catie's increasing popularity as a singer. As far as she was concerned, education had to come first, because everyone knew that next to no one made it in the music business. Catie only had to look at her own father to see that.

'You're cruel,' Mac chided, hardly looking up from the trumpet he was cleaning at the kitchen table. Catie was next to him, standing on a chair, arms outstretched as her mother hemmed her dress, while Lola was perched on one of the cabinets watching proceedings.

'Just telling it like it is,' Patty retorted, reaching for her pincushion, made by Catie aged ten in sewing class. 'It's all very well for me to think you're talented and that madam here takes after you, but there's a big, ugly world out there that can't be depended on to treat either of you right. So, you'd better pass them exams when they start next week, my girl, or you'll likely end up over Parnall's along with your father. Now turn around so I can see what's going on at the back of this thing. It might be too low for decency, but I can put a few stitches in. Lucky I found it in Sara's last week, or you'd be going to Town's Talk in your underwear tonight.'

Lola giggled while Catie goose-bumped at the mere thought of it.

'She'll look like a royal princess,' Mac declared, glancing up from his labour of love.

'I wonder who had it before?' Lola mused. 'And why they'd throw out something so lush. I bet it cost a fortune when it was new.'

'Someone too rich for their own good, I expect,' Patty muttered through the pins clamped in her teeth.

'Ouch!' Catie shrieked as her mother jabbed her.

'Stop fussing,' Patty scolded. 'It's nearly done, and your father's right, you're going to look lovely, although I never thought emerald green would be a good colour for you. Are you doing her hair?' she asked Lola.

'That's why I'm here,' Lola replied. 'And I've got my camera all packed and ready in the hope they'll let me in.'

'They will,' Mac assured her. 'William Thurloe's a good bloke. I'll have a word if there's a problem.'

'If you ask me, you should be at the same table as Lawrence,' Patty stated sourly. 'I don't know why he didn't invite you . . .'

'He did,' Lola told her, 'I just don't want to sit with his mates or his mother, if she's going to be there.'

'Is she?' Patty asked Catie.

Catie shrugged. 'She's supposed to be, but she hardly ever goes out, so Lawrence doesn't think she'll come.'

'Are you sure you won't?' Mac said to Patty.

'You know how busy the bingo is on Saturday nights,' she retorted. 'I can't let them down now, can I?'

No one pointed out that she could have warned them weeks ago, because they all understood that no good ever came of trying to persuade Patty to do something she'd set herself against. Although she'd never really explained the real reason she never came to a gig, over the years Catie had come to wonder if she was afraid it would make her feel even more shut out of Catie and Mac's closeness than she already did.

Catie returns to the present, feeling a little like a time-traveller as she gazes down the Taormina mountainside to where train tracks snake along the shoreline and the echo of her parents' and Lola's voices fades into the wash of the waves, tiny drops of precious sound returning to the past.

She remembers that Marilyn, Lawrence's mother, hadn't come that night; but Jude Penrose had, as bold and bouncy and beautiful as Catie had ever seen her. She'd sat beside Lawrence at a table for ten, and preened as if she owned it and him and maybe the rest of the room. As William Thurloe's stepdaughter, maybe it could be said that she did own it all – except Lawrence, of course.

As always, he only had eyes for Catie that night, watching raptly as she sang straight from her heart – blues, jazz, swing, folk; they covered all the favourites and more – with her dad on trumpet, Hank on drums, Charlie on sax, and Flora Kidman, a dear friend from their gospel Sundays, on piano. How hauntingly Flora had played 'Killing Me Softly'. It was the first time Catie had performed the song in public and, though she would never claim to have anything like as beautiful a voice as Roberta Flack, her performance had brought the house down.

A burst of laughter somewhere nearby draws her back to the piazza and rescues her from what had come next that night.

She turns and sees three men standing outside the church. The one who's laughing is tall, distinguished, with dark, collar-length, silver-streaked hair, a closely shaved beard and the kind of features that make him seem almost patrician.

She decides, from his look, and the way he moves his hands as he speaks, that he could be a composer, or a conductor, maybe a singer, certainly a musician.

He laughs again, and she feels an unexpected sense of nostalgia welling up inside. It's like hearing a familiar tune, one that she suddenly wants to join in with and sing. How odd that someone she's never seen before, and who she doesn't even share a language with, can make her feel that way.

He appears entirely engrossed in the story he's being told, until something seems to alert him to her attention and he glances in her direction.

With an apologetic raise of her eyebrows, she turns away, and a few minutes later, as she begins wandering back to the hotel, she realizes she's experiencing a sense of loneliness for the first time since arriving. And yet she isn't alone. For better, or for worse, they're all here with her: Lawrence, her parents, the band, Lola, Jude and everyone else who'd meant so much to her – even those who didn't.

CHAPTER SEVEN

Catie was backstage at Town's Talk, jumping up and down with euphoria, beside herself with triumph and excitement as everyone hugged and kissed her, congratulating her on the most fantastic show.

Laughing, she fell into Lawrence's arms, and as she turned her face up to his everyone cheered.

'You were sensational,' he told her softly, and her father immediately began playing 'S'Wonderful, S'Marvellous' on his trumpet. A mere few bars in and he was drowned out by the raucous welcome of a waiter with two bottles of French champagne, courtesy of Mr Thurloe.

As the corks popped and glasses were filled, Lola muttered in Catie's ear, 'We've got a visitor.' Catie looked up and Lola nodded for her to turn around. To her amazement, Jude Penrose was standing at the door watching them.

Feeling nothing but love for everyone right now, Catie immediately went to pull her into the party, but Jude wrested her hand away.

'Can I have a word?' she asked quietly.

Catie blinked, not sure what to say.

'Please,' Jude added.

Feeling it would be wrong to refuse, Catie said, 'Of course. What is it?'

'I'll wait for you in the car park,' Jude told her, and left.

'What was that about?' Mac asked as Catie turned back to the room, baffled.

'What did she say?' Lawrence wanted to know.

Catie shrugged. 'Just that she wants to have a word. She's gone to wait outside.'

Passing his glass to Hank he said, 'I'll come with you.'

'It'll be fine,' she assured him, tilting her mouth for a kiss. 'But if I'm not back in five minutes, come and find me.'

Still wearing her flimsy silk evening dress and gold high heels, she tottered out along the corridor to reception, laughing and graciously accepting lavish praise from just about everyone she passed.

As soon as she stepped outside, she regretted not bringing a coat. It might be May, but the night was chilly; there was even the hint of rain in the air. She looked around, trying to spot Jude, but there was no sign of anyone, and the intermittent roar of traffic speeding up and down the A38 next to the club made the deserted car park seem quite creepy.

She was about to go back inside, when Jude called out, 'I'm over here.'

Following the direction of the voice, Catie saw her standing in the glow of an old-fashioned lamppost between a bronze-coloured Bentley and another equally fancy car.

Jude raised a hand, and the red tip of a cigarette went to her mouth before dipping down again.

Catie started towards her, not quite certain she wanted to do this, but she was here now. 'Is everything all right?' she asked, stopping a few feet away.

Jude shrugged and put her head back as she exhaled a cloud of smoke into the night air. 'It could be,' she answered, and her eyes flicked from Catie to the club and back again.

Catie glanced over her shoulder, wondering if others were about to appear, maybe to beat her up, or do something equally drastic. 'What do you want to talk to me about?' she asked, trying not to sound nervous.

'What do you think?' Jude retorted. She ground her cigarette underfoot and leaned against the high wall behind her. 'You know he's not going to stay with you, don't you?' she said. 'I tried to warn you—'

'Even if you're right, that's for Lawrence to tell me, not you,' Catie cut in sharply.

Jude's eyes turned glacial as a smirk curved her lips.

'If that's all this is about,' Catie said, starting to turn away.

'End your relationship tonight,' Jude said, 'and I promise not to tell anyone about your father molesting me.'

Catie froze, then turned back, dumbfounded. Had this vile girl really just said what she thought she had?

Jude raised an eyebrow, clearly waiting for an answer.

Catie tried to take a breath; so much fury was roaring through her that she was hardly aware of rushing forward and shoving Jude with all her might.

Jude's head cracked hard against the wall behind her, and Catie watched in horror as she slumped awkwardly onto the Bentley before sliding lifelessly to the ground.

'Oh my God!' Catie gasped in panic. She dropped to her knees, grabbed Jude's shoulders and tried to shake her awake. 'I'll get help,' she cried, more panicked than ever by the blood on her hands. As she stood, her heel ripped through her dress, trapping her there.

'Catie?' Lawrence called out.

'I'm over here,' she called back, struggling to free her foot and starting to shake uncontrollably. She looked down at Jude again. She still wasn't moving and Catie wanted to scream.

'Shit, what happened?' Lawrence cried as he reached them.

He threw himself down beside Jude and tried to sit her up. When he finally managed it, there was blood all over him too, and Catie wanted to be sick.

'Oh God, oh God,' she whimpered, staggering against the car behind.

'What the hell happened?' he repeated.

'She said . . . If you'd heard . . .'

'It doesn't matter. Go and call 999.'

Catie did as she was told, holding her dress high and kicking off her shoes as she went. She could hardly breathe through her terror, struggling to tell the manager what needed to be done.

He wasted no time, then sat her down, putting a blanket around her as someone went to find her father.

Less than half an hour later, Jude was in an ambulance being rushed to the Bristol Royal Infirmary, while Catie was in the back of a police car on her way to a police cell.

CHAPTER EIGHT

'*Salve, signora. Come sta?* How are you today?'

Catie smiles at the hotel's front-of-house manager as he comes around the desk to greet her with his usual warmth. There's a twinkle in his eyes that she can't help finding endearing, and even a little bit flattering. Although he probably turns it on for all the guests, at her age she's perfectly happy to be on the receiving end.

'I hope you don't mind but I have a suggestion,' he tells her, drawing her away from the main desk towards the silver and black art-deco bar that forms half of the reception area. A lively mix of old jazz and soul is played here each evening, but all too often she's the only audience, unless others arrive after she's gone to bed, which is highly likely. She usually vanishes around nine, in spite of knowing that it's the Italian way to get started around then.

'I'm intrigued,' she tells him, meaning it.

Clearly pleased, he says, 'You have been in Taormina for five days now, *sì*? I hope you enjoy our beautiful town, but I think you are not yet seeing all its hidden treasures. Am I correct?'

With a laugh, she says, 'I'm ashamed to admit that you're correct, Marcello, and I was just on my way to ask if you could recommend someone to show me around?'

His face lights up. 'This is my suggestion,' he tells her joyfully. 'I have the best guide in Taormina who I can call, right now. Please do not think he is my brother, or my cousin . . . Yes, I know what people think about Sicily.' He laughs good-naturedly, seeming not to mind the cliché. 'He is someone who lives here for many years, and he has very good soul and understanding of our special town. His name is Antonio, but we call him Tony in the English way. He prefers it. All of us who love him feel very – how you say – nourishing in our souls to know him.'

Not sure she's up for any spiritual enhancing just yet, although she probably ought to be, she waits for him to continue.

'Tony is also very much fun,' he says, 'and very knowledge-able about many things. So, if you require our literary trail, or our ancient theatre, our beaches, our wineries, our opera, or our shopping, he will be your excellent guide.' He quickly glances at his phone. 'Sorry, I will call this person back,' and whoever is on the other end of the line is treated to a firm 'reject'. Smiling again, he says, 'Please tell me if you would like me to call Tony . . .'

'I'd like that very much,' she assures him. She's more than ready for a tour of the town and, being so starved of company, she feels Tony could be ideal.

Wasting no time, Marcello makes the call. After several rapid, even impassioned-sounding exchanges that seem to border on actual anger, he rings off with several *ciaos*, more *ciaos*, and *ciao* again, before saying with a charming smile, 'Tony is very happy to meet you here, at the hotel, tomorrow morning at nine.'

Disappointed that it couldn't be today, she agrees, and because she hasn't had breakfast yet she decides to take her notebook – her *aide-mémoire* – to a different café this morning.

Time to treat herself to a *cannolo* – or two – she thinks.

Stepping out of the hotel directly onto the pedestrianized Corso Umberto, she turns left, away from the main piazza, to wander along the narrow street with its brick and pebble paving and colourful boutiques. She looks up and admires the beautiful filigree balconies adorning so many of the windows above. Some are too small for any more than a toweringly proud cactus, while others are bursting with bright ceramic pots, flowers, sculpted pine-cones, vintage glass lanterns, and even small olive trees. It's all so lavishly exotic, and perfect, and the staircases that rise between the buildings are as inviting as some of the restaurants that climb their steps.

She feels a wave of sadness as she realizes, once again, that it's harder being here alone than she'd expected. She has no one to talk to, to share the joy of new discoveries with, and she wonders who she'd most like to run into now, if it were possible. As the names start to clamour, she quickly closes it all down. There's no point tormenting herself with something that's not going to happen, especially when the people she would choose couldn't – or wouldn't – want to be here.

She soon reaches the Piazza Duomo, a small, cobbled square with a magnificent three-tiered fountain, and of course a cathedral (this one is very small). She chooses a café at random and sits down to watch the world go by. Her mind is like a badly tuned musical instrument as she wonders about this man, or that girl; where they might be going, who they might have left this morning, who could have upset them, who they detest and who they love. She's probably wrong in every guess, but it's a way of passing the time as she sits in the morning sunshine with a glimpse of blue sea between two nearby buildings and the delicious aroma of coffee as hers, with a cannolo, is brought to the table.

She takes a sip of the Americano, allows a moment for the enlivening bitterness of it to awaken her, and then, with no real intention, she opens her notebook.

She hasn't forgotten where she'd stopped typing into her laptop last night – *Town's Talk 1980*. Now, seeing the empty page waiting for her to go further, she feels an unsteadying mix of emotions rising up inside her. She'd been so young, so naive and impulsive back then . . .

She looks around the piazza, taking in more of its charm and history, as though needing its reality, its immediacy, its fragrances and music to ground her. Absorbing it all renews her sense of who she is today, of why she's here and what she needs to achieve before she can return to what she's left behind. It isn't long, however, before her memories begin to take her away again . . .

CHAPTER NINE

Though she no longer recalls much of the journey to Bridewell that night, only the terror of what was going to happen to her when she got there, she does remember asking the police, 'If I've killed Jude, will it make a difference that I didn't mean to?'

They hadn't answered, or maybe they'd reminded her she was under caution. Most probably they had. She recalls being taken into the station and looking around for her dad, or Lawrence, Lola even, but there was no sign of anyone she knew.

She was read her rights and put, sobbing, into a cell, still wearing her green sparkly dress with her dad's jacket around her shoulders, and a scratchy blanket over that. Her gold high heels were long gone; she had nothing on her feet.

Eventually the cell door opened and Charlie, the Blue Note's six-foot-four, baggy-eyed sax player came in. She didn't understand why it was him and not her dad, until she remembered that in his other life Charlie was a solicitor.

She threw herself into his arms, all her worst fears spilling out of her in an incoherent rush, until he gently held her still and told her, firmly, that Jude wasn't dead.

'You haven't killed anyone, Catie, so you can put that out of your head now.'

He took her to a room just off the custody area and closed the door behind them. He had a briefcase with him, a writing pad and pen.

'You need to tell me exactly what happened,' he said, sounding reassuring in spite of looking worried. 'Don't leave anything out.'

She told him everything, from how Jude had asked to have a word with her, which Charlie himself had witnessed, to going outside and finding Jude in the car park, smoking, to how Jude had threatened her if she didn't stop seeing Lawrence.

'Threatened? What did she say, exactly?' Charlie pressed.

Catie opened her mouth, but found herself unable to give voice to Jude's terrible words. It would be like destroying a beautiful song with the wrong chords, slicing her father apart with false words.

'Catie?' he prompted.

She shook her head and looked away. She knew her dad would never have done what Jude had accused him of, but if she repeated it Charlie would hear it, and then he'd tell the police and next thing it would be in the papers and no one would ever look at her dad the same way again. They might even arrest him.

By morning they'd learned that Jude had suffered a concussion, but was on her way home from the BRI now, with four stitches in the back of her head and bruises to her face.

Not long after that, Catie was released on police bail, and when Charlie took her outside the police station, she found her dad and Lawrence, pale-faced and unshaven, waiting to wrap her up in their arms.

Later that same day, William Thurloe rang to speak to Mac and told him that he and Jude's mother would not be asking the police to press charges.

Catie heard her dad ask, 'Do you know what happened? Catie's not saying anything. Has Jude told you why . . .?'

Mr Thurloe must have said he was also in the dark, because Mac came back into the living room where Catie was sitting in front of the gas fire with her mum and Lawrence. 'I know you wouldn't have hit her for no reason,' he said, 'so tell me, Catie Mac, why did you do it?'

Catie turned her face into Lawrence's shoulder, and felt his arm tighten around her, before she realized that he needed to leave. She couldn't tell anyone what Jude had said. No one at all. And if Jude wasn't repeating her filthy lie yet, no doubt because she was waiting to hear that Catie had broken up with Lawrence, then that was what Catie must do.

A week or more passed with Lawrence calling every day, and even turning up at the house trying to make her see him. He banged on the door until her parents let him in because they had no reason to keep him out. They had no explanation for him, only tea and sympathy, while Catie stayed upstairs in her room, the door blocked by the chest she'd shoved in front of it. She loved him with all her heart and soul, didn't even want to go on living without him, but she knew she had to do this for her dad.

She wouldn't even see or speak to Lola.

The only time she left the house was to go and sit her exams, and when she came home she returned to her room. She didn't want to eat, or talk, or see her parents, or even go on living.

In the end, unable to bear the misery of it all any longer, she somehow blurted it all out to her mother, the words tumbling over one another, catching on sobs and outrage and the wretched despair in her heart.

When she'd finished, her mother stared at her hard, her eyes glittering with anger, her fingers digging so hard into Catie's arm that bruises were already forming. Catie stared back and felt suddenly afraid of what her mother might be thinking, of what she was intending to do.

'Leave this to me,' Patty declared, getting abruptly to her feet, 'and don't breathe a word to anyone.'

CHAPTER TEN

They were seated around a table in a conference room on the second floor of Charlie, the sax-player's, law offices, just off Prince's Street in the centre of town. Catie was between her parents on one side, Jude was opposite with her mother and stepfather. Charlie was at one end, and the Thurloe's lawyer had set up camp at the other.

To Catie's mind it was her mother who ought to be heading the meeting, given that she was the one who'd made it happen, but as assertive (bossy) as Patty could be, she never relished the limelight.

Apparently Jude's stitches had been removed a week ago, but the bruise on her face, presumably from where she'd hit the car on her way down, was all yellow and purple, and impossible to miss. She could have covered it with make-up if she'd chosen to, but she hadn't, and Catie detested her almost as much for that as she did for everything else.

When Patty was satisfied that everyone was paying attention, she gave a nod for Charlie to start everything off. It was amazing to Catie just how many people obeyed her mother, as if it simply wasn't an option not to.

Charlie began by thanking the Thurloes for coming and, after informing them all that the conversation was being recorded, he gave a precis of why they were there.

When he'd finished, William Thurloe, clearly used to being the most important person in the room until he'd encountered Patty, said, 'I thought the fact that we decided not to press charges would put this to bed.'

Before Charlie, or anyone else, could respond, Patty said, 'Believe me, Mr Thurloe, no one wants that more than we do, but I don't think you're aware of what your daughter said to mine that provoked the attack.'

As Jude's eyes flashed with malice, Catie reached for her dad's hand and gave it a squeeze.

Patty was still speaking. 'I'm afraid your *step*daughter made up a wicked lie about my husband to try and stop our Catie from seeing Lawrence.' Her eyes moved to Jude and the normally smug and doughty Jude seemed to shrink a size.

Mrs Thurloe spoke up. 'Whatever she might have said, how do you know it's a lie?'

Unfazed Patty said, 'Because I know my husband, and if there was any truth in it, your girl wouldn't be backing down already.'

'She's backed down,' Catie seethed, 'because I've stopped seeing Lawrence. So she got what she wanted.'

Jude smirked, and too late Catie realized she hadn't helped her dad at all with her sudden outburst.

Charlie cleared his throat. 'I think we need to let Mac speak, as we agreed,' he said. 'Is everyone OK with that?'

Without consulting his wife, daughter or lawyer, William Thurloe gestured for Mac to go ahead.

Gently releasing his hand from Catie's, Mac leaned forward slightly and spoke quietly to Jude, almost as if they were the only ones in the room. 'You told Catie that I molested you,' he said, coming straight out with it.

Catie noticed William Thurloe stiffen, and suddenly she felt more afraid than she had before coming.

Jude said nothing, just kept her eyes fixed brazenly on Mac.

'We both know,' Mac continued, 'that what you said isn't true . . .'

'You would say that, wouldn't you?' she shouted in a sudden burst of temper.

Mac gave her a moment to calm down. 'Can you tell me when it's supposed to have happened?' he asked reasonably.

'That night! At the Town's Talk,' she cried as if it were obvious.

'Where, at Town's Talk?' he pressed.

'It was in a . . . corridor. If we went back there I could show you,' she told her mother.

Mac linked his hands together and continued to look at her as he said, 'You know what you're saying isn't true, but what I'm not sure of is whether you realize how much damage your lie could do to me if it ever went any further than this room.'

Jude's expression became pinched, mutinous. She knew, but apparently she didn't care.

Mac continued. 'I realize you probably don't mind too much about what happens to me, that all you really want is to come between Catie and Lawrence, but please try to understand that no matter what you say about me, or anyone else, it isn't going to change anything for him. If he wanted you as his girlfriend, that's what you would be.'

Jude flushed as her mouth opened, but whatever she'd been about to say didn't make it.

'I know it's hard,' Mac said, gently, 'when you're in love with someone who doesn't love you back, but destroying an innocent person's reputation with lies, especially the kind

63

you told about me, will never get you what you want. In the long run, it will only damage you.'

He fell silent and everyone looked at Jude, waiting for her to respond.

In the end Mrs Thurloe turned to her daughter. 'Was it a lie?' she asked quietly.

Jude didn't answer.

William Thurloe got to his feet. 'I think everything's been said that needs to be—'

'Not quite so fast,' Patty interrupted hotly. 'We need a proper admission that it was a lie before we leave here . . .'

'All right, it was a lie,' Jude shrieked furiously.

Thurloe looked at Patty to see if that was enough. It was, in a way, but Patty hadn't finished.

'I think some apologies are in order now,' she stated. 'You can go first, Catie. I know she provoked you, but lashing out like that isn't the way you've been brought up.'

'Mum!' Catie protested.

Patty glared at her.

Grudgingly, Catie turned to Jude and said, irritably, 'I'm sorry I pushed you.'

'Your turn,' Patty informed Jude. 'Apologize to my husband for your terrible accusation.'

Looking as though she'd rather pull out her teeth, Jude turned insolent eyes to Mac as she said, 'I might be sorry for what I said about you, but it doesn't change the fact that she stole Lawrence from me . . .'

'Sandra, take her to the car,' Thurloe instructed his wife. 'I'll be along in a few minutes.'

After the door closed behind them, Thurloe turned his attention to Mac. 'My apology has to come with a confession,' he said. 'I was afraid that something like this might have been behind the incident, which is why we didn't press charges. You see, she's done something like it before, when she was at school. A teacher almost lost his job over it. As it turned out, he didn't, but he ended up taking a position elsewhere anyway.'

Patty said, 'Poor bloke! Girls like that—'

'OK, Pats,' Mac interrupted.

Thurloe said, 'To be honest, I thought it might have been Lawrence she'd accused of something. It never crossed my mind it could be you.'

'You need to get her some help,' Patty told him sharply. 'She can't be allowed to go round saying that sort of thing about innocent people.'

'You're right,' he agreed, 'she can't. The only excuse I have for her behaviour is that her father walked out on them when she was ten. However, that's for the shrinks to deal with. Again, Mac, I'm sorry. And I'm sorry to you too, Catie. I hope you haven't let this come between you and Lawrence. He's a good lad, who I know has lost his father relatively recently. Luckily, it doesn't seem to have affected him quite the way it has Jude.'

Mac stood up and reached out a hand. 'Thanks for coming today,' he said. 'And good luck with everything.'

'You too,' Thurloe responded. 'And if there's ever anything . . . Well, you know where I am.'

That should have been the end of it, and in some ways it was, but in the ways that really mattered it wasn't. Mac had been so shaken by the accusation that he began suffering with anxiety in the run-up to a gig. He was afraid that somehow it had got out, and if someone in the audience believed it, how long would it be before everyone did?

Catie and her mother did everything they could to

persuade him out of the fear, but it was a good few months before he set foot on a stage again.

During that time, Catie and Lawrence reunited, and Lawrence moved out of the shared house into a bedsit, although he was in Fishponds more often than not. Since having Lawrence around was always a boost for Mac, it worked for Patty too. She didn't even lose her mind when Catie's abysmal A level results came in, or she did, but she blamed 'that dreadful girl' for the trauma she'd put Catie through at such a crucial time in her life.

And then along came *The Blues Brothers*.

Mac, Patty, Catie and Lawrence were at the cinema the night it opened in Bristol, and Mac and Lawrence loved it so much that when 'Jailhouse Rock' finished playing at the end, they stayed in their seats and watched the whole thing all over again. They did the same the next weekend, and the one after that. It wasn't long before they were playing out scenes together at home, proving they not only knew at least half the dialogue, but also the moves. And when they were invited to a silver wedding anniversary at the Staple Hill Legion just before Christmas, they hired black suits, dark glasses and pork-pie hats to go as Elwood and Jake. They even 'shook a tail feather' and brought the house down with their crazy dancing.

It was fair to say that *The Blues Brothers* really turned things around for Mac. The irreverence of it, the idiocy and exuberance, and all those famous faces in cameo roles, had him laughing and singing all the way back to the Mac they all knew and loved. There finally came a time when they'd more or less forgotten all about Jude Penrose. Certainly her name was never mentioned and, as far as Catie was aware, no one ever saw her.

Then Lawrence told them one night that she'd started visiting his mother.

CHAPTER ELEVEN

Jude, the stalker, Catie reflects as she wanders away from the Piazza Duomo to climb a stone stairway to . . . well, she's going to find out where. That was what they'd called Jude back then, and it wasn't as if she hadn't deserved it. The way she kept turning up at Lawrence's mother's house, Breemoor, no doubt doing her best to ingratiate herself while drip-dripping poison about 'the girlfriend' into Marilyn's ear was nothing short of creepy.

Catie still hadn't been inside the place, and nor did she want to while his mother was so set against meeting her. She knew it was all to do with snobbery – how could a girl from Fishponds, a *singer*, for heaven's sake, someone who apparently had no intention of going to university, or finding herself a proper job, ever be good enough for her precious youngest son? Of course, Catie had no idea if she actually expressed herself that way, but she was in no doubt that Marilyn Vaughan, probably helped by Jude Penrose, saw her as a nothing more, or less, than a social climber and money-grabber.

'Don't worry, she'll come round,' Lawrence kept promising, 'especially when I tell her we're getting married.'

Catie smiles as she catches the memory like the scent of something wonderful. She is passing a perfume shop and turns to explore inside. For the next few minutes she inhales all kinds of floral, fruity, nutty and woodland fragrances, examining soaps and diffusers, candles and sprays, salts and scrubs, all perfect gifts to take home with her . . .

She treats herself to a diffuser for her hotel room and goes on her way.

For the next several hours she makes an aimless tour of the town, winding up and down hidden flights of stone steps, crossing shady piazzas and soaking up the many different types of music that drift randomly from open windows and cafés. There's a tenor, a trombonist, a Motown medley, a guitarist, a mezzo-soprano and a pianist practising scales. She finds a small gem of a park close to the Ancient Theatre with a collection of delightful follies apparently constructed in the nineteenth century by an Englishwoman, Florence Trevelyan, for bird-watching and tea-drinking. She follows a map to the funicular on Via Pirandello, but doesn't take it. She'll go to the beach another day.

When she finally returns to the hotel, around six, she's tired and hungry, in need of a glass of wine and a shower. So, collecting her key, she's about to set off for her room when she hears someone say, 'Mrs Vaughan?'

Almost no one calls her that these days; she's Catie Mac and has been for so long . . .

Feeling a dull thud in her heart, she turns around expecting the worst. Someone has gone to the trouble of coming to find her.

'Hello, Mrs Vaughan, I am Tony.' He is short and wiry with a hesitant smile and earnest eyes, and is twirling a straw fedora hat between his hands.

'Do I know you?' she asks, politely.

'I am to be your guide tomorrow,' he replies, holding out a weathered hand to shake.

Relief makes her smile. 'Ah, yes, hello,' she says, taking his hand. 'It's nice to meet you.'

'You too, Mrs Vaughan . . .'

'Catie, please.'

His eyes show his pleasure. 'I am passing,' he explains, 'so I come to introduce myself if you are here. And to ask if there is anything special you would like to do during our time together?'

She gives a laugh as she throws out her hands. 'It's a good question, Tony, and I should be more prepared than I am to answer it.'

'It is no problem. I just like to know if we need a car to travel to Mount Etna, or maybe Siracusa. I can arrange this; everything is possible.'

She takes only a moment to decide on no car. 'There's so much in town I've still to see,' she admits.

'Then it will be my pleasure to show you.' He turns to take a book from a backpack he'd left on a chair. 'I bring you this,' he says, holding it out. 'Maybe you know it already?'

Taking it, she reads the title, *A House in Sicily*, and thinks, what a wonderful idea.

'It is written by an Englishwoman, Daphne Phelps,' he tells her, 'and the house is here in Taormina. The Casa Cuseni. I think you will find it very beautiful and interesting.'

'Is she there?' Catie asks, entranced and hopeful.

'Oh no, she dies in 2005, I think it was, but it is possible to visit the house and see how she lived. She had very many famous guests.'

'I'd love to see it,' she assures him, almost wanting to hug him for seeming to sense how much she'd enjoy it. 'It's so kind of you to think of it.'

Beaming, he says, 'I will leave you now and meet you at nine in the morning. Do you have all you need for this evening?

Maybe I can recommend a pizzeria, or if you prefer seafood . . .'

'Seafood,' she jumps in, and only just stops herself asking if he'd like to join her. It would be wonderful to have someone to chat to over dinner, someone who could tell her all about this magical place and wouldn't expect her to talk about herself.

'I get a map and show you a few nearby,' he says.

After he's collected one from the desk and circled his recommendations, he says, 'You know you are very safe here in Taormina. There is no problem to go out at night.'

'That's good to know,' she replies, touched by his concern.

'I give you my number,' he hands her a card, 'and if you need anything, or to change our arrangement for tomorrow, please just send a text.'

As she thanks him and watches him leave, she's struck by a sense of having seen him somewhere before. Then, as he puts on his hat, it comes to her: he was on the piazza yesterday with the distinguished-looking man she'd decided was a musician.

CHAPTER TWELVE

'Of course I'm serious about us getting married,' Lawrence declared, rolling onto his side and running a finger over Catie's flushed cheek, his sleepy eyes showing his own fulfilment following the past half an hour. 'Isn't it what you want too?'

It was, and it wasn't.

Mostly it was.

Stretching out her slender limbs, she gazed up at the skylight above their futon, seeing nothing beyond but darkness. During the day it allowed sunshine to flood into this wonderful top-floor bedsit, and sometimes, when it rained, they'd lie together watching droplets of water wriggling and streaming over the glass while feeling safe and snug inside.

'Earth to Catie,' he said, turning her to face him.

She looked into his searching brown eyes, and as they began to twinkle she felt her heart swell with the wonderful depth of her feelings.

'I can't be without you,' he said, smoothing back her silky curls.

She gave a laugh and tweaked his nose. 'Who's saying you have to be? I'm not going anywhere.' She frowned. 'Hang on! Does that mean you are?'

He arched an eyebrow. 'No plans right now, but if my book takes off . . .'

'No chance of that until you've finished it.'

He grimaced. Although he'd reached chapter five, and had even drafted an outline for where he saw things going, since he'd started at the *Western Daily Press* as a junior sub-editor, he only had evenings to work. And many of those were taken up with Catie's gigs, or getting together with friends, or working out to keep himself in shape. She often joined him for runs around the Downs, or for a bracing swim at the Lido, but most of her spare time, when she wasn't serving tables at Splinter's café on the corner of Boyce's Avenue – she was becoming a proper Clifton girl these days – was spent either with her voice coach, or in piano lessons, or rehearsing for an upcoming show.

'OK,' he said decisively. 'I want you to marry me because I think everyone needs to know that we're properly together.'

She treated him to a sidelong glance. This was sounding very much as though his mother had been trying, yet again, to talk him out of their relationship. Or more likely, into one with Jude Penrose, who was still visiting Marilyn as if she didn't have a mother of her own.

'It's not what you're thinking,' he said, cutting her off before she could draw breath. 'Well, I guess in part it is, but I just want it so that wherever I go, you're with me. Not literally, obviously, that would be weird, but you know what I'm saying.'

She did, more or less, but decided to let him go on.

'If something should ever happen with my book,' he explained, 'I'll want to introduce you as my wife so that people will know right away that you're the most important part of my life. Same if you hit the big time, and I know you will. I want to be there for you in a way that says we're more than just . . . Well, what we are now, which is brilliant, don't get me wrong, I just want us to be . . . Hell, I want you to be *my wife*.'

Inhaling the loveliness of his proposal, and sheer wonderfulness of how much they meant to one another, she smiled deeply into his eyes. His *wife*. Mrs Vaughan (no, no, *that* was his mother); but it was so romantic, so very much what she wanted too, that of course she was going to say yes. However . . .

When it came to her hitting the big time, why did everyone seem to think it was what she wanted? OK, it might happen, one day, but it probably wouldn't, and she was fine with that. What mattered most to her was performing with the Blue Notes and all the other bands she'd come to know well these past couple of years. They were their own community, family even, as were the people who regularly came to see her. She had quite a following now, albeit mostly West Country-based, but that was great. She loved the West Country, as much as she did the intimacy and flaws of live performances in pubs and clubs. Given how well she was being paid for some gigs these days, she saw no reason to try to turn it into something that could very easily run out of Mac's control.

'So, what do you say?' Lawrence prompted. 'Shall we do it?'

'What, and live here?' she teased.

He looked around as if to say, *what's wrong with it?*

She laughed and threw her arms around him. 'I love it here,' she told him, meaning it with all her heart.

Although she hadn't officially moved in, she was here six nights out of seven, and they'd become so close now, were so attuned to one another, that it often made them laugh and clutch their heads in crazed disbelief whenever they voiced each other's thoughts. They were meant to be, they knew that, so why not get married? They would eventually, anyway, so what was wrong with now?

'Your mother won't like it,' she pointed out, knowing he'd have considered this and already decided how to handle it.

'I'm not asking her,' he said. 'I'm asking you.'

She laughed, and as the turntable needle clicked back into place at the end of the Moody Blues album they'd been half-listening to, she rose gracefully from the bed, knowing he was watching, and went to put on something else. She chose an old Muddy Waters album they'd recently borrowed from her dad.

Though the bedsit wasn't exactly large, with the futon, an armchair, his desk, the music centre and small corner kitchen taking up most of the space, there was still room to dance and, as he came to pull her to him, she felt her heart flip over. She loved him so much and was always so immediately turned on by him that she knew very well where they'd be by the time this track ended. In fact, they were already on the way there.

'Tell you what,' she murmured after they'd made love again and were lying sprawled out on the futon. 'I'll say yes if your mum agrees to come to the wedding.'

He frowned, clearly not liking the sound of that. Sitting up, he reached for a half-smoked joint and lit it. 'And if she won't agree?' he countered, drawing in deeply.

Since she didn't have an answer ready she simply shrugged and wondered, would she really say no if Marilyn was against it? Which, of course, she would be.

As it turned out, the first resistance came when they went to break the news to Mac and Patty, who they'd imagined would be immediately onside.

Invited like guests into the living room, Patty brought in a tray of tea, took her time pouring, and after handing out cups and Jaffa cakes, she let it be known that she was not thrilled by the prospect of an imminent wedding. 'If you're in the family way, my girl—'

'I'm not pregnant,' Catie jumped in irritably. 'God, I knew you'd think that. You're so predictable.'

'Then what's the rush? You're only just twenty-one, for heaven's sake. No one gets married that young unless they have to.'

'You mean like you?'

Patty flushed and even Mac's eyes darkened.

'We're not talking about me,' Patty snapped, 'and I'll have less of that cheek, thank you very much.'

'I'd have married your mother anyway,' Mac informed her. 'You know that.'

Lawrence said, 'This is something we want to do. It feels right to us, but we want it to feel right for you too.'

'You're too young,' Patty pointed out stridently. 'And anyway, how are you going to afford a wedding, is what I'd like to know, because we don't have a big nest egg we can crack open for one of your whims—'

'It's not a *whim*,' Catie cried furiously. Her mother was the most maddening and hateful person on earth at times. 'We've been talking about it for a while,' she said, 'and now we've decided we want to do it.'

'If we make our commitment official,' Lawrence explained, 'then everyone will know that we're intending to spend the rest of our lives together.'

The words made Catie's heart sing, until she saw her mother treating him to one of her infamous put-down looks.

'OK, I get what's going on here,' Patty declared, putting down her teacup, 'even if my daughter doesn't. This is about your mother, isn't it, Lawrence? You want to prove to her that she's wrong about Catie and—'

'It's got nothing to do with her,' Lawrence broke in angrily. 'I don't care what she thinks. Catie and I have been together for over two years . . .'

'And your mother still hasn't invited her across the threshold of her very stately home, or given up on you finally coming to your senses and getting together with a girl from your own background.'

Stepping in here, Mac said, 'You know, Patty, you're as much of a snob as Marilyn Vaughan. These two don't care about backgrounds, or class, or trying to prove anyone right or wrong. They're in love, for God's sake. Anyone can see that. Yes, they're young to be getting hitched, but they're practically living together already. At least this way it'd be legal.'

Patty's lips pursed as she glared at him. 'I might have known you'd take their side,' she sniped. 'You always were a hopeless romantic, and I'm not a snob so you can take that back.'

'You need to look the word up,' he told her. To Lawrence he said, 'I presume you're intending to inform your mother before you go waltzing up the aisle?'

'Of course,' Lawrence assured him.

'And there won't be an aisle,' Catie added. 'We don't want anything fancy or big so we can pay for it ourselves. Just you two and Gramps, if he's up to it; the Blue Notes and their partners, obviously. Lawrence's brother and his fiancée, and his mum, if she'll come.'

'What about Lola?' Patty demanded, noting the omission straight away.

Catie felt a low note of sadness. 'Of course, her too, and her parents, if they want to come.' Since Lola and family had moved to Patchway about a year ago, with a tearful Catie and Lola promising to stay in touch for ever and visit all the time, they'd hardly seen anything of one another. Even their regular phone calls had eventually dropped off, with Lola being so busy studying business and photography at the polytechnic, and Catie getting so many more gigs, and of course being tied up with Lawrence.

'I'm glad to hear your brother will be there,' Mac said, leaning over to turn down the gas fire. 'Patty and I took a real liking to him when we met him and his girlfriend, back in the summer.'

Clearly pleased, Lawrence said, 'They've been Catie's biggest fans since they saw her at the festival. Yours too, of course,' he quickly added. 'Goes without saying.'

'I'll tell you what,' Patty said, picking up her cup again. 'If you can get your mother to go to this wedding of yours, I'll be there too.'

Catie's eyebrows shot up even as her heart sank. Damn her mother for coming up with the same condition she had, even if she'd cancelled hers now. 'And if we can't?' she said. 'Are you saying you won't come?'

'Of course she will,' Mac cut in.

'I can speak for myself, thank you,' Patty informed him. 'You heard what I said, Catie. If she'll go, I'll go, and that's my last word on it until you come back with an answer.'

CHAPTER THIRTEEN

Catie hasn't laughed like this in far too long. It's so wonderfully liberating and exhilarating that she could be shedding years off her age and lightening her soul. Tony, her personal tour guide, is laughing too, dear, sweet man that he is. He too seems to be loving their time together, and maybe, like her, he wouldn't mind staying right where they are for ever, perched so high above Taormina that they can see the toe of Italy across the Messina Straits. Even Etna looks smaller from up here, and lazy, with such a slow curl of smoke drifting from its open peak.

Their day together had started out more soberly, but also enjoyably, as they drank coffee at Wunderbar on the Piazza IX Aprile, known locally as Piazza Belvedere, before starting the climb to Casa Cuseni. Having read the first chapters of *A House in Sicily* last night, Catie had felt enchanted by the villa even before setting eyes on it. When she did, she was instantly captured by its quiet and yet stately elegance, set comfortably on the hillside at the heart of its exotic gardens. It seemed to retain the welcoming feel of a much-loved home, in spite of now being a fine arts museum and B&B.

It had affected Catie quite a lot to read about Daphne Phelps's life in Taormina, the adventures and fracas she'd become embroiled in, her passion for helping poor Sicilians, and the famous people who'd been inspired to great works whilst staying at Casa Cuseni. Most notably there was Hemingway, who'd apparently written his first short story here; Bertrand Russell, who'd conceived one of his great philosophical works while visiting; plus the artist Henry Faulkner, author Roald Dahl, Dylan Thomas's widow Caitlin and apparently the actress Greta Garbo too had come here to be alone.

It is while Catie and Tony are roaming the villa's spiritual garden, and he is telling her about the small concerts that are sometimes held on one of the large terraces that she confesses to once being a jazz and blues singer.

It is as if a light has suddenly switched on inside him. 'I know I see you before,' he cries excitedly. 'And your name when I hear it . . . You are Catie Mac. I see you one time at the Umbria jazz festival, or was it Venezia? That was you?' He is so thrilled that he actually throws up his arms and spins around. 'I am,' he told her, proudly, 'Italy's biggest jazz fan.'

Apparently, he travels all over to watch his favourite bands at clubs, bars, festivals and concerts. Moreover, he knows all the old songs. As he reels them off, he can't stop himself singing them, and his lack of embarrassment over lurching off-key or bungling a lyric is nothing short of hilarious – and possibly deliberate, she thinks, given the way he keeps stealing secret glances at her response.

Now they are on top of the world, sitting with their legs dangling over a wall at the edge of this mountain village, Castelmola, him still singing, her laughing and cheering as they eat ice-cream and absorb the magnificent vista. He'd implored her to sing with him at first, but when she'd gently refused, he hadn't insisted.

He's clearly a sensitive soul and she can't help thinking of how much her father would have loved him, with his old straw hat and encyclopaedic knowledge of jazz. Only Mac would know the names and tunes this dear, sweet man keeps coming up with – Muggsy Spanier, Scrapper Blackwell, 'Your Feet's Too Big', 'One Sweet Letter from You', and only Mac would be able to sing along with him.

Dad, she sighs silently to herself, as she gazes out at the endless blue sea and sky, *oh dad*.

By the time they make the steep descent back to Taormina, via Madonna della Rocca, a tiny, exquisite church carved into a cave, the sun is going down and the cafés are filling up with people sipping aperitifs. She's tempted to invite Tony to join her for a glass of Prosecco, either at the hotel or on the piazza, but is worried that it'll embarrass him if he has to refuse. So, instead she thanks him for such a lovely day, and is about to ask if he might be free for more exploration and singing tomorrow, when someone behind her says, 'Tony. *Ti stavo cercando*.'

She turns and is momentarily thrown to see the man she'd decided was a musician bearing down on them with a very determined look on his face. He is, she notes, even more striking close up than she'd considered before, with his abundant dark hair, high forehead and perfectly Roman nose.

'*Mi scusi per l'interruzione*,' he says to her, not impatiently, but not exactly friendly either.

'Giancarlo,' Tony says quickly, 'please let me introduce you to Catie Mac. She is famous jazz and blues singer—'

'Not famous at all,' Catie corrects.

'Catie,' he continues as if she hasn't spoken, 'this is *Giancarlo Santori*.' The way he emphasizes the name seems to suggest that Signor Santori is a person of note. So, yes, maybe a musician.

'I am pleased to meet you,' Giancarlo says, taking her outstretched hand and regarding her more closely now. 'I'm afraid I am not familiar with your name.'

'Not many are,' she assures him, and changing the subject, 'Tony has been showing me around today.'

Santori's smile almost makes her blink it's so transformatively appealing. 'Tony is one of our best tour guides,' he declares, slapping Tony on the shoulder. 'There is nothing he doesn't know about Taormina.'

Impressed by his almost accentless English, she says, 'Or about jazz, it would seem.'

Tony draws breath as if about to burst into song, but laughs instead. 'You have suffer enough today,' he tells her.

Giancarlo says, 'I don't wish to be rude, Mrs Mac, but I need to speak to Tony . . .'

'Please, go ahead,' she insists, taking a step back.

'No, don't go.' He stares at her hard for a moment, seeming to think something through, then says, 'Are you in Taormina alone?'

Startled, she admits that she is.

'Then maybe you will have dinner with me later?'

She balks in astonishment, and starts to remind him that they've only just met, but he cuts her off.

'Where are you staying?'

'At the Metropole,' Tony replies for her.

Santori nods and says, 'I will pick you up there at nine, but for now I'm afraid I must take Tony away from you.'

As the two men head off along the Corso Umberto in the direction of Porta Catania, one sprightly and short in his check shirt and straw hat, the other very tall and lithe, Catie remains where she is, watching them go. Of course, she has no intention of meeting a complete stranger for dinner tonight, even if she is lonely, and a little bit intrigued by him.

No, she won't be there at nine. She's going to eat early at the hotel restaurant, then sit on the balcony of her room, soaking up the balmy night air while getting on with the reason she's here.

Or maybe she'll read more of *The House in Sicily*.

CHAPTER FOURTEEN

'Oh!'

Catie looked up from where she was sitting, her heartbeat faltering as Lawrence's mother, Marilyn Vaughan, came to a stop on the threshold of her own very posh drawing room. She was a rangy, middle-aged woman, with neat, salt-and-pepper hair pinned back by an Alice band, and the kind of air that exuded class and money. Her shocked and instantly hostile expression left Catie in no doubt that this had been a very bad idea. Not that she hadn't known it before coming; she had, and she'd been arguing with Lawrence about it for days. She should have stuck to her guns. Trapping his mother in her own home was not going to get them the outcome they wanted.

'She might not let you through the door otherwise,' he'd tried to reason.

'That's OK, because I don't want to go.'

'You have to.'

'I do not.'

'We need to stand up to her and I just know that once she meets you, she'll love you as much as I do. Well, maybe not that much, and it might not happen straight away, but you get what I'm saying. This is something we should have done a long time ago.'

Catie could only berate herself now for finally giving in; what a fool, what a horrible and humiliating mistake.

'Hi, Mum,' he said, completely failing to be daunted by her intimidating manner as he got up to greet her.

Marilyn raised a hand to stop him. 'A word please,' she said shortly, and without another glance in Catie's direction, she turned and walked away.

'Catie and I don't have secrets,' he called after her, 'so whatever you have to say you can say it here.'

Marilyn didn't return.

'Go and talk to her,' Catie said quietly.

'No way,' he retorted, loud enough for his mother to hear. The house was big, but she was very probably still in earshot. 'She has to deal with this like a grown-up, or . . .'

'You be the grown-up,' Catie whispered, 'and go and explain that this was your stupid idea, but now we're here can we at least try to be civil to one another.'

Says the girl from the council house, to the boy from an amazing double-fronted mansion at the end of a private cul-de-sac with acres of garden, and a cottage somewhere in the grounds, apparently. It made her parents' weary patch for cabbages, leeks and rhubarb, along with shed, washing line and rusty bonfire bin, look humble indeed.

Actually, Breemoor was a truly lovely redbrick house, with white-framed sash windows along the upper level and either side of the glossy, navy-blue front door. When she and Lawrence had pulled up outside, it had seemed so relaxed and welcoming, so settled in its space and ready to invite others in. No one would ever believe it could be home to someone so unfriendly. Although, for all Catie knew, Marilyn was perfectly charming, and sweet-natured with everyone else. The nostril-flaring hostility could be reserved solely for her, the girl who was ruining her son's life.

'Look, this is making me more nervous than ever,' she said as Lawrence sat back down and stubbornly folded his arms. 'I know she doesn't want to meet me, but we can't get married without at least telling her first.'

'We can,' he argued.

'No, *you* can't if I'm not there, and I won't be if we don't try to work this out.' She didn't add, although she felt she should, that she didn't want to end up in a situation where her own mum didn't come to the wedding because this Jude-loving battleaxe wouldn't.

'She'll come round,' he insisted.

'Not while we're sitting in here like this. Actually, maybe I should leave . . .'

He caught her hand as she started to get up. 'All right, I'll go and talk to her, *but* . . . only to tell her that she has to come right back in here and at least have the good manners to meet you.'

'I heard that,' Marilyn said from the door, 'and you're right, Lawrence, my manners were not acceptable. I'm sorry . . . What was your name again?' Her smile was glacial.

'For God's sake, Mum!' Lawrence growled. 'You know exactly who she is, so stop being such a pain.'

Marilyn came further into the room. 'Why have you brought her here?' she asked as if Catie had now ceased to exist.

'Because,' Lawrence replied, 'we're going to get married and we thought—'

'No! I'm afraid that won't be possible.'

'There's nothing you can do to stop it,' he pointed out, 'so either accept Catie, or lose me. It's as simple as that. She is your daughter-in-law, or I am no longer your son.'

Marilyn's jaw tightened; her cool eyes remained fixed on his. 'You'll regret this one day,' she told him, 'not only because you're too young for such a monumental, and frankly ridiculous decision, but because all the opportunities that are coming your way now will have passed you by.'

She left them in stunned silence, and a moment later they heard her car start, telling them that she was no longer around to discuss this any further.

CHAPTER FIFTEEN

Giancarlo grimaces as he tops up their wine glasses with a perfectly chilled, zesty Grillo before sitting back in his chair and regarding her curiously. 'So what did you do after the terrible woman walked out?' he asks, sounding genuinely interested in her story.

'We got married,' Catie replies simply, and picks up her drink to take a sip.

She can't quite believe she's here in this quaint trattoria, close to the piazza, when she'd had no intention of coming. And how on earth has she got into telling him about Marilyn, about anything to do with her life at all, come to that? She's clearly had a little too much wine, or maybe he's just incredibly skilful at getting people to open up.

Just as likely is that she's been so starved of company, even before coming here, and is needing to share her thoughts with someone so badly that when he asked, over their first glass, what she would be doing this evening if she'd been spending it alone, she'd actually told him. 'I'd be going back over my life,' she'd said. 'A therapist recommended I should, so I'm making notes and typing it into a laptop.'

That, she remembers now, is how they'd got into it.

'And did she keep to her word and stay away from the wedding?' he wants to know, picking up his drink.

'She did,' she confirms.

'And what about your own mother, did she come?'

She watches him cut another slice of the most delicious pizza and tip it onto her plate. 'She did and she didn't,' she replies, 'which means she stuck to her word that she wouldn't come if Marilyn didn't.' She leans in as if not to be overheard, 'Between us, I know she regretted making that decision, but she was always a proud woman, and very stubborn. Anyway, she didn't come into the register office, but she was waiting outside all dressed up in a brand-new suit, like a real mother of the bride . . . Actually a bit like the Queen, with a handbag over one arm and a very fancy hat on her head.'

His blue eyes crinkle at the corners as he smiles. 'She sounds something of a character,' he comments.

'You're right about that,' she confirms, and for a distracting moment she finds herself back on the steps of Quakers Friars in the centre of Bristol, reliving the instant she'd spotted Patty standing, like a statue, amongst the passing crowds, waiting for her. It had made her laugh and cry.

Then suddenly, out of nowhere, Jude Penrose was right there, digging a hand into her bag . . . Patty ran forward, Mac began to shout and Catie shrank back into Lawrence . . .

Jude's hand reappeared and with a big, wide-eyed grin, she'd cried, 'Boom!' and tossed a handful of confetti into the air.

It had been a terrifying moment that had taken some getting over at the time. Not worth mentioning now though.

'And your father?' Giancarlo prompts. 'Did *he* come into the register office?'

'Oh yes,' she smiles. 'He already loved Lawrence like a son, so he was happy to give me away. He looked so smart in his navy-blue suit and jazz-themed tie. Actually, I was half afraid the two of them would turn up as *The Blues Brothers*. Do you know the film?'

'Of course,' he laughs.

'They had a thing about it,' she explains. 'Any chance they got to dress up as Jake and Elwood, they took it, and actually they did change into the outfits later, at the reception. As did the whole band. Even Lawrence's brother Graham, who was best man, had got himself a pork-pie hat and dark glasses.'

'It sounds like a very special day,' he comments, seeming to be genuinely enjoying her reflections.

She nods, and thinks of how true his words are. 'We partied until the wee small hours.'

'At your home?'

'No, at a place called the Inner Man. It doesn't exist any more – actually, it's called something else now – but back then it was a cellar restaurant with dance-floor and bar. Perfect for weddings, especially when we had so many guests wanting to perform.'

'Including you?'

She laughs. 'I only did one song that night, just for Lawrence, because it was one of his favourites.'

'Can I ask what it was?'

She inhales, takes another sip of wine, and says, 'He was mostly into rock, or new wave, or even heavy metal . . . some blues, actually a lot of blues, but I knew exactly what he would want me to sing, so I did. It was "The First Time Ever I Saw Your Face". The Roberta Flack version. Do you know it?'

He smiles and nods.

'I sang it the first night we met,' she explains, 'and he always said it was why he fell in love with me.'

'It is a very romantic song,' he agrees, and gestures to a

waiter to bring more wine. She knows she shouldn't, but she does anyway, and after the waiter has left, she says, 'You know, I don't normally talk this much about myself, especially to strangers.'

He seems amused by that. 'Sometimes it's easier with people we don't know. There is, perhaps, less expectation, less judgement?'

He's right of course, but it really is time to change the subject. So, resting her chin on one hand, she says, 'Tell me about you.' His eyes might be the bluest she's ever seen and the long dark lashes surely are wasted on a man. She smiles at the observation and he regards her quizzically.

'What's funny?' he asks.

'Nothing,' she says, still looking at him. Then changing her mind, 'How come your eyes are so blue?'

He's clearly amused by the question. 'I have Norman ancestry.'

Surprised, she says, 'The Normans were in Sicily?'

'They were, but I'm Italian. Now tell me, how come your eyes are so blue?'

Enjoying the tease in his voice, she says, 'They're the same colour as my dad's, and his before him, I believe, but any further back than that ... Maybe I have Viking ancestry, although I think it's a myth about their eyes being blue. Anyway, I'm afraid history and genealogy aren't my strong points.'

He shrugs. 'But music is.'

'You know, I think you're a musician,' she tells him. 'A composer? Conductor? Maybe a baritone?'

Apparently enjoying her guesswork, he says, 'Nothing so glamorous, I'm afraid. In fact, I am a simple businessman, but one who enjoys music very much.'

'What kind of music?'

'All kinds. I have no real preference, but I'm keen on opera. Is this something you enjoy too?'

Sighing she says, 'I'm afraid the only one I've seen all the way through is *Aida*, at the Hollywood Bowl.'

He looks surprised and intrigued. 'I'm not sure what to ask next about that,' he confesses. 'Maybe let's start with what you thought of the performance.'

With no hesitation she says, 'It was magnificent, in every imaginable way, but for someone who knew – *knows* – nothing about opera, it was a little overwhelming.' She sighs again and says, 'I feel disappointed in myself that I haven't been to more.'

He frowns. 'That sounds as though you're giving up on it and I have no idea why you would. In fact, it's a shame that performances at the Ancient Theatre are at an end for the season, but there is still opera in Taormina, at Teatro Nazarena. There are posters all over town.'

'Really? I haven't seen them.'

'Then you are not looking; but if you're interested we shall get some tickets for this weekend. Will you be my guest?' He puts up a hand to stop her from responding. 'Maybe first I should ask if you will still be here?'

Wondering just how brightly her eyes are shining, and suspecting quite a lot, she says, 'I'm booked into the Metropole until the end of next week and after that . . . I'm not sure what I will do, or where I will go, but the answer to your question is, yes, I'd love to be your guest at the Teatro Nazarena. Thank you.'

He picks up his glass and clinks it to hers.

'Don't think I haven't noticed,' she says, putting her glass down again, 'that you've managed to turn the subject back to me, but I'll have no more of it. I want to know what kind of business you're in, because I am absolutely certain you're a pianist really. You have the hands.'

Laughing, he turns them over and back again, almost as though seeing them for the first time. They are so masculine and large and yet also elegant that it's impossible to believe he's not some sort of artist or artisan. 'I am sorry to disappoint you,' he says, 'but I cannot play a note. My mother, however, is very talented, or she was until arthritis put an end to her career.'

'Oh no, that's awful. Was she a professional?'

'No, strictly amateur, but she enjoyed playing very much. Now she is of an age where she is happy simply to listen to others performing. She is quite the jazz fan, as a matter of fact.' His eyes twinkle in a way that almost makes her want to laugh with delight. She really is drunk.

'So, you have a mother,' she states, feeling pleased for him as it was never a given at their age.

'And a brother, and a son and a daughter,' he adds.

She waits for him to mention a wife, but he doesn't, and as he isn't wearing a ring, she decides to assume, for now, that he doesn't have one. 'Are your family here, in Taormina?'

'Oh no, none of us actually live here. My brother, my mother and I are all based in Turin, my son is in Beijing and my daughter is in Milan. So, as you English would say, we are a little spread out.'

Realizing he's just countered the cliché of Italian families staying together to look after one another, she says, 'So, what brings you to Taormina?'

He shrugs dismissively. 'There are some matters I have to attend to that will keep me here, I think, at least until the end of the month.'

Pleased to hear he's not leaving right away, she wonders

if she's already asked what sort of business he's in, but can't quite remember now.

Definitely no more wine.

'Are you staying at a hotel while you're here?' she asks.

'No, my family – we have an apartment not far from the Casa Cuseni that used to belong to my grandmother. She was Sicilian, but after she married my grandfather she moved to Turin. They kept the apartment; there is also *una fattoria* – an old farmhouse – in the countryside not too far away. Ever since we were very young, we have come each year for a holiday. My children too, but of course they are grown-up now and living their own lives. Do you have children?'

Pushing past the pang that burns her heart, she playfully narrows her eyes as she says, 'You're trying to turn things back to me again, but I haven't finished asking my questions.'

He laughs, and gestures for her to continue.

'What does your son do in Beijing?'

'He is something very grand in tech, please don't ask me to explain. He is also, so he tells me, currently dating a supermodel.'

She smiles at his irony.

'And my daughter, she is the director of a famous fashion brand that I have never heard of. She is married to a plumber. '

Her eyes widen in surprise.

'He owns the company,' he explains, 'but that is how he likes to be called. Actually, he is quite admirable, because he learned the job of his workers before taking over from his father. Now, can we talk about you again? I am eager to know what happened after you and Lawrence were married? Did his mother ever speak to you?'

She shakes her head. 'Not until she had to, but you haven't told me yet what sort of business you're in.' He hasn't, she's sure of it.

'That is because it's really not very interesting. We manufacture parts, mostly for cars, but also for domestic appliances. You know, perhaps I prefer it if you continue to think of me as a musician, just as long as you don't ask me to sing or play.'

She laughs and raises her glass, as if to concur. 'When you say *we*,' she prompts.

'Ah yes, my brother and I, and of course our workforce. My grandfather started the company with his father back in the Fifties, and since then we have grown to be one of the major manufacturers in Turin. I am boasting, but I hope I'm allowed to be proud of what we have achieved.' As he finishes speaking, he is checking his phone. 'It is Tony,' he tells her. 'I have been waiting for the call, so if you will excuse me.'

She gestures for him to go ahead, and half-expects him to leave the table, but he simply clicks on, and says, 'Tony,' before continuing in Italian.

She sits quietly, enjoying the sound of his voice as she gazes absently out of the open windows to where, in the far distance across the night-darkened sea, the lights of Naxos are glittering like fallen stars. She wonders what the time is, although doesn't actually care. She could happily sit here all night, listening to him, talking to him, drinking more wine, and maybe when the sun comes up they could wander into the piazza for coffee.

As his call ends he says, 'I am very sorry, but I must leave. Tony has . . .' He starts again, 'His mother, Olivia – she lives with him – was taken to the hospital earlier. She fell down the steps outside their apartment.'

'Oh no, is she badly injured?'

'A broken wrist, apparently, and a lot of bruising. She was lucky it wasn't a lot worse.'

Curiously she says, 'They called you when it happened, and not Tony?'

His smile is ironic. 'I think Tony was having such a good time with you that he turned off his phone. That's why they called me. I asked him to let me know the news when he had some, and apparently she can leave the hospital now. He says he will take a taxi, but I shall go to collect them.'

'Of course. Is the hospital far?'

'Fifteen or twenty minutes by car, but of course I must fetch the car first. My driver is off this evening, so it's in the garage. I am so sorry to end our evening like this. Please let me walk you back to your hotel before I leave.'

'No, no you must go right away. I'll sort out the bill.'

He regards her as if she's said something truly astonishing. 'You will not,' he informs her, 'and Federico, the owner, knows better than to let you. I will settle with him tomorrow. If it's permissible I will call you in the morning, at your hotel, and if we are able to meet later in the day I shall look forward to hearing what happened to you and Lawrence after you were married.'

CHAPTER SIXTEEN

It was their *fourth* wedding anniversary. Totally amazing! Almost impossible to believe that so much time had gone by, never mind all that had happened . . .! It was a whirlwind! A sensation!

Tonight's plan had been to go and watch the Blue Notes at the Old Duke, before going on to a club with friends, but as they were leaving home Lawrence had received a call from his literary agent. Apparently, his number one bestselling spy-thriller *The Wrong Way Round* had been optioned by a Hollywood producer.

It was so far out, so totally unexpected, that for a long moment he and Catie could only stand staring at one another. Then suddenly they erupted in ecstatic, wild celebration, leaping up and down, hugging, kissing, dancing, hugging and kissing again, before falling into a laughing, breathless heap on the sofa.

'We've got to tell your dad,' he declared, heading back to the phone.

'We're about to see him at the pub,' Catie reminded him with a laugh. 'Everyone's going to be blown away by this news. Drinks all round on us!'

So many great things had happened since they'd got married that sometimes it felt crazy trying to remember them all. It had started with Lawrence's sudden burst of creativity when they'd returned from their honeymoon in Paris. He'd found himself able to write, not just in fits and starts, but in a seriously committed way that had him at the typewriter virtually every minute he wasn't working.

He'd finished his thriller by their first anniversary and, amazingly (to him, not to Catie, who'd found it impossible to put down when she'd read it), it was accepted by the first agent he sent it to. Three weeks later there was a bidding war going on between two London publishing houses that ended up making them millionaires overnight. True, they didn't get it all at once, but the whopping signing-on fee had been more than enough to start changing things in significant ways.

Although it had been harder than they'd expected, saying goodbye to their beloved bedsit after all the happy times they'd shared there, at least they were in the same building when they moved. Now they were in the two-bed ground-floor apartment with its own entrance and tiny garden. This meant Lawrence had an office where he could work on his next book, and the sitting room was plenty big enough for Catie's brand-new piano.

Though she was still singing at clubs and pubs all over the West Country, and beyond, and she even had a fan club of sorts these days, there were often spells when there was no paid work. This didn't matter too much financially, she had a job at an estate agent's now, and actually it gave her more time to perform with her dad and the Blue Notes.

'You need to get a booking agent,' Lawrence was constantly telling her. 'And we should do as your dad says and hire a recording studio. You need a demo tape, babe, something we can send to the record companies.'

'You know the band will do the session for free,' Mac assured her – they were still a bit of a double-act, he and Lawrence. 'Of course, once you hit the big time, we'll be expecting some royalties, but you've got real talent, Catie girl. You should be putting it out there more.'

Although she wasn't against it, as such, she really didn't like the idea of someone else taking over her life, and she just knew that a record company would. That's if she could even get signed by one, and the competition was so fierce that the chances, in reality, were close to nil. She was good, she knew that, but she wasn't anywhere near as good as her loyal little fan club tried to make out.

Anyway, as it turned out, it was just as well she didn't have any serious career commitments, because four months after the movie option was taken up, Lawrence was invited to go and consult on the screenplay. All expenses paid, including club-class flights, a house in the hills and a car.

When they got the news, Lawrence looked as though he might pass out. 'We're going to Hollywood,' he murmured incredulously, resting his head against hers.

'Your name is going to be up in lights,' she teased. 'Based on the bestselling novel by *Lawrence Vaughan*.'

He inhaled the dream of it, and pressed a kiss into her hair. 'You know, none of it would be happening without you,' he told her. 'I don't know what got into me after our wedding, but the way I started to write then . . . Just having you there, knowing you're properly in my life, it was like nothing could stop me. And now . . .' he was gazing searchingly, even worriedly into her eyes. 'Are you sure about coming with me?' he asked gently. 'You know I won't go without you . . .'

Lifting a hand to his face, she said, 'I'm sure.'

Her mother, predictably, when they broke the news, wasn't at all sure. 'It's too far,' she protested, banging a teapot down on the table so hard everyone winced. 'We won't ever see you, and you know your father won't be able to cope with that.'

'Speak for yourself,' Mac argued. 'I think it's the most wonderful opportunity, for you both. A house in Los Angeles, paid for by the studio, or production company, whatever it is; Lawrence getting involved in the script, and you, Catie, just think of all the contacts you'll make.'

Though it was exciting, and absolutely what she wanted for Lawrence, Catie's eyes suddenly filled with tears. 'Mum's right, it's a hell of a long way,' she said, 'and with the time difference, and cost of phone calls . . .'

'Why don't you let Lawrence go and you stay here until he's sure it's going to work out over there?' Patty suggested.

Catie and Lawrence stared at her uncomprehendingly. It had never crossed their minds to be parted, and one glance at each other was enough to confirm that they weren't going to start considering it now.

'What *I'm* thinking about,' Mac said, rubbing his hands together, 'is how soon we can come to visit. How long did you say the flight is?'

'I don't care how long it is,' Patty put in, quickly, 'you're not getting me on a plane, not for love nor money.'

As if she hadn't spoken, Mac said, 'We'll have to give you some time to settle in, of course, but where are we now? July. You're flying out in September, so I reckon we could come for Christmas. If you'll have us, of course. You'll probably have made lots of new friends by then, and we wouldn't want to be in the way . . .'

'That could never happen,' Catie and Lawrence said together.

'You'll always be welcome,' Lawrence told him earnestly. 'If we could we'd take you with us.'

'Not me you wouldn't,' Patty informed him tartly.

Still ignoring her, Mac got up and pulled Catie into his arms. 'I won't lie,' he said tenderly, 'I'll miss you like hell, we all will, but this is something special, for you both, and what's really great about it – as if it's not fantastic enough – is that you're still young enough to really make something of it. There's nothing to hold you back.'

'Apart from me,' Patty stated. 'That's what you're saying, isn't it? That I'll try and stand in their way while you'll just wave them off with stars in your eyes as if nothing could possibly go wrong.'

Mac laughed. 'And that, right there, Patty MacAllister,' he said, 'is why I love you so much.'

'What?' she said confused.

He winked at Catie and Lawrence and, going to the fridge, he took out a bottle of real champagne.

Catie almost choked. 'Where did you get that?' she cried. 'I've never seen anything like it in this house before.'

'Your mother won it at bingo a few months back,' he replied, 'we've been waiting for the right occasion.'

Taking glasses from the dresser behind him, Lawrence said, 'I hope you're going to have one, Patty.'

'Well, it's mine, so I think so,' she retorted. 'Now tell me what you reckon your mother's going to say when she hears about all this, Lawrence.'

He grimaced and shrugged. 'I'm sure she won't be any more thrilled about it than you are, and she definitely won't be planning to visit.'

'Well, there's one good thing at least,' Patty snipped, starting as Mac popped the cork, 'you won't want someone hanging around the house who's not speaking to you.'

As they all laughed, Mac filled the glasses and raised his own to make a toast. 'To Catie and Lawrence,' he said, his voice thick with affection, 'and to all their dreams coming true in the great US of A.'

CHAPTER SEVENTEEN

'So you went to Hollywood,' Giancarlo remarks as he and Catie make themselves comfortable at a table in the lavish courtyard of the Palazzo San Domenico. All around them the arcaded loggias of the centuries-old monastery, restored to magnificent glory now, and the succulent greenery in specially constructed beds and vast marble pots are as exotically Mediterranean as the intricate terrazzo floor and blazing blue sky above.

'We did,' she confirms, and glances up as a waiter appears with a loaded tray of coffee and delicious-looking pastries. 'Did you order this?' she asks Giancarlo.

'I called earlier,' he admits, 'to let them know that I might stop by with a guest. Someone obviously saw us come in through the lobby.'

She's impressed, not only by the speed at which the coffee has been brought, but that he should have such influence in this exclusive five-star hotel. 'I'll take mine black, thank you,' she tells the waiter, who is holding two pots ready to pour.

Giancarlo takes his the same, something the waiter already seems to know since he's given no instruction.

'I can never say these words without groaning or laughing,' she whispers as Giancarlo nods a friendly greeting to someone behind her, 'but do you come here often?'

He laughs and picks up his cup. 'From time to time,' he replies. 'This is where they filmed *The White Lotus*. Did you know that?'

'The TV series? I've read about it, but I haven't seen it.'

'It's very good. Strange and comical, definitely absurd, but an excellent showcase for Taormina.'

If you could afford to stay somewhere like this, she thinks but doesn't comment out loud, because it seems he probably can; she knows the rooms start at around eighteen hundred pounds a night.

'Ah, this is Tony,' he says as his phone rings. 'I asked him to call and let me know when he gets there. *Salve, amico mio.*'

Knowing that Tony is driving his mother to stay with her sister near Catania for rehabilitation, Catie sips her coffee and takes in more of the stupendously splendid surroundings. It's as luxurious as any hotel she ever visited in LA, and God knows they were beyond anything she'd ever seen before in her life. And she can't help noticing how truly at ease Giancarlo is here, with a bare ankle resting on one knee and an arm hooked over the back of the padded bamboo seat as he speaks on the phone. It's almost as if he's sitting in his own courtyard with his own staff around him. For a moment she wonders if the place actually is his, but then dismisses it when she remembers reading something about American owners.

'They have arrived safely,' he tells her as he ends the call. 'Tony will return later today and will, he wants you to know, be at your disposal for more exploration tomorrow. Meantime, I'm afraid you have to make do with me.'

She laughs, surprised and pleased that she is being considered at all. 'I'm sure you've got much better things to do than be my tour guide,' she tells him, 'and to listen to me banging on about my very ordinary young life.'

He shrugs. 'I can assure you I don't find it ordinary. In fact, I find it compelling, but I have to admit I will have certain limitations as a guide. Tony is much more knowledgeable when it comes to the hotspots and history of Taormina.'

She sips her coffee. 'But you've been coming here all your life . . .'

'And I didn't pay enough attention to what I was being told. However, I do know one of the best places to watch the sun set.'

Interested, she says, wittily she thinks, 'But it's only 11 o'clock.'

He laughs. 'I will take you to it when the time is right. For now, I am eager to know more about your life in Los Angeles. Actually, before we go there, someone you didn't mention while we were walking here is Jude. Did she disappear after you and Lawrence were married?'

Impressed that he not only remembered Jude's name, but that he'd realized she was missing from the narrative, she says, 'Not a bit of it. Not only did she carry on seeing Lawrence's mother, she started turning up at my gigs. Lawrence wasn't coming as often then because he was writing, and not all the bands I sang with knew her, so she came and went without anyone but me noticing.'

'Did she speak to you?'

'No, never.'

'Was she alone?'

'She seemed to be. She didn't sit at a table, or at the bar, nothing so normal. She'd just stand at the back of the room staring at me.'

He frowns.

'It was as though she was waiting for me to notice her and, as soon as I did, she'd leave.'

'So her intention was?'

'To spook me, I guess, and believe me it worked. I started asking one of the band to walk me to my car when the gigs were over, I was so afraid she was out there somewhere.'

'And was she ever?'

'I only saw her once, watching me from behind the wheel of her car. I was already in mine by then, so I made sure the doors were locked and drove away. I don't know if she followed. If she did, she didn't catch me up.'

He seems as puzzled by the odd behaviour as she'd been at the time. 'Did you tell Lawrence about it?'

'Of course. He even went to see her to ask her to stop, but she claimed to have no idea what he was talking about. She accused me of being crazy and paranoid, said I was making things up to try and turn him against her, and actually she had better things to do with her life than to follow me around like some sort of groupie.'

With a slight move of one hand to acknowledge, or summon, someone nearby, he says, 'So why was she doing it? Surely, she didn't think she was going to win Lawrence back that way?'

Noticing the waiter hovering, she waits for their cups to be refilled and says, 'God knows what was in her mind back then, because she never called him, or tried to see him. She even stopped visiting his mother after a while, although Marilyn admitted to Lawrence that she'd told Jude she needed to put everything behind her and get on with her life.'

'*Da vero?* That sounds as though Lawrence's mother had come to accept that you were married?'

Her tone is sardonic. 'She didn't have much choice given it had already happened, but she still didn't want to meet me.

104

I think pride was her biggest enemy by then; she'd taken a stand and wasn't going to back down from it. She was so like my own mother at times it was scary.'

He smiles, and for the first time she notices a dimple in his right cheek, mostly hidden by his shadow beard. 'How did she take your departure to LA?' he asks.

With raised brows she says, 'Pretty badly. I wasn't there, of course, but apparently she begged Lawrence not to go. She even offered him money to stay, as if he needed it, which of course he didn't by then. I think she said some horrible things about me. He wouldn't tell me what they were, but I expect it was her usual scheming, gold-digger, wrong-side-of-the-tracks sort of thing.'

He frowns. 'Are the English still so snobbish?'

She shrugs. 'Some, yes. It's not one of our best traits. Is it the same in Italy?'

With a sigh he admits that it is, but doesn't go into it as he's distracted by a dark-haired, willowy woman who appears at his side.

'*Mi scusi,*' she says softly to Catie, and continues in rapid Italian as she speaks to Giancarlo.

When she's finished he nods and says, '*Sì, eccellente, grazie,*' and turns back to Catie as the woman sashays away. 'She is one of the restaurant managers here,' he explains. 'She asked if we will stay for lunch and I told her yes. I hope this is OK for you?'

Surprised and thrilled, Catie says, 'Thank you. I'd love to.' Eating here is surely an experience not to be missed, especially if it's with him.

His hypnotic blue eyes smile, and as if the interruption never occurred, he says, 'So in spite of your mother-in-law and your mother's objections, you and Lawrence went to Los Angeles anyway – and you were how old by then?'

'I was twenty-five, almost twenty-six. Lawrence twenty-eight – and when we got there . . . Have you ever been to LA?'

He nods. 'Just a few times.'

'Then you know what it's like. We could hardly believe our eyes. Everything was on another scale, so big and glamorous and *exotic*, with all the palm trees and boulevards, the Spanish-style architecture – actually *every* style of architecture, with houses as big as palaces, one after the other after the other. Obviously I'm talking about Beverly Hills, Bel Air, Santa Monica, those sorts of areas. Our house, the one that was rented for us, was just off Mulholland Drive, overlooking the San Fernando Valley and San Bernadino mountains beyond. It was spectacular, like stepping into a movie set. Not huge, you understand, at least not by Hollywood standards, but it had its own pool, a massive sitting room, four bedrooms, and a kitchen with more gadgets and mod-cons than we even knew existed. For two youngsters fresh out of Bristol, it was mind-blowing.'

He's clearly amused, and gives a small movement of his fingers, something he does quite a lot, she's noticed. This time it's for her to continue.

'Well, obviously,' she says, sipping her coffee, 'we had a ball settling in and getting to know Lawrence's new team. Everyone was so welcoming and friendly. We were at parties almost every night, and even started to throw them ourselves. We spent weekends at the beach, usually at someone's house in Malibu, or further up the coast in Santa Barbara . . . Don't get me wrong, Lawrence worked hard and sometimes it was pretty stressful, but mostly it was like we were living in a dream. Obviously, we knew LA had its problems, areas like downtown where it wasn't safe to go, but I have to admit we had no idea how bad it was until the Rodney King episode a few years later and the riots that followed. We'd already left by then, but we watched it on TV, and we were constantly on the phone to friends who were still there. It was terrifying.'

He nods agreement. 'It was an unspeakable crime,' he reflects gravely, 'and a tragedy that so many lost their lives and their homes. It's what can happen if you don't treat people right.'

She thinks back to the riots in Bristol when she and Lawrence were first together, and how so many of their black friends had been treated then. During the days that followed, Mac had gone to check on the musicians he'd known for years and considered family. It had been a horrible, wretched and shameful time for their city; luckily for them no one had been killed, but nevertheless . . .

Giancarlo says, 'So you were in Los Angeles for how long?'

'A little under four years. I'm afraid it didn't go well for Lawrence in the end. The movie got shelved, and he found it difficult to write anything else. He'd connected with a lot of people by then, other writers, actors, directors, self-styled producers. They used to come and go from the house as if it were theirs, sitting around talking about the next big project, how to get financing, the agents who'd be crazy about Lawrence's book if they could get it to him, or her. They smoked dope like it was simple tobacco, and snorted tons of cocaine off our glass-topped tables. Girls I didn't know would come and hang out around the pool . . .' She shudders as she recalls arriving home one evening to find a semi-conscious blonde being stretchered out of the house by paramedics. The girl's overdose didn't turn out to be serious, but it was a truly scary few hours, and it was weeks before Catie could even look at Lawrence again.

'I had nothing to do with it,' he kept telling her. 'She came with Baxter and they were out by the pool . . .'

'And where were you?'

'In here working through some scenes with Jenny and Bo.'

'But you were high too. No, Lawrence, don't deny it, I could see it the instant I walked in. What's the matter with you? Why are you doing this stuff?'

His eyes sparked with anger, but he couldn't hide his sense of failure and the overpowering need to escape it. 'Maybe if you were here more often, I wouldn't want to,' he shot back.

Incensed, she cried, 'Oh no! You're not going to make me feel guilty about getting my life together. You could too if you hung out with the right people. It doesn't have to be like this.'

The arguments were always the same, over and over, firing them up, wearing them down, sometimes even turning them into outright enemies. The good times were becoming fewer and fewer.

'So what were you doing while he was mixing with the wrong sort?' Giancarlo asks.

She takes a breath and smiles. 'Me, well, actually things were going quite well for me. I met a wonderful woman called Abbie Cross, about six months after we arrived. I was walking in one of the canyons at the time and I heard her practising scales. We got talking, she invited me to one of her gigs, and the next thing I knew I was up on stage singing with her.

'I guess you could say it all snowballed from there. Her booking agent took me on, the two of us became great friends, and before long we weren't only performing around the clubs and bars of LA, we were going to Vegas, San Diego,

Chicago, even New Orleans. My dad was beside himself with excitement over it all, and obviously when he and Mum came to visit, they were at every gig.'

'So your mum did visit?'

'Of course, she wouldn't have let Dad go without her, and no way would he have left her behind.' She pauses as she recalls them in LA, their almost childlike enthusiasm for the Walk of Fame, the movie-star home tours, photographing themselves in crazy wigs at Universal Studios. They could hardly get enough of it all, and were totally dazzled when she got them tickets for a movie premiere complete with attending stars and red carpet. But best of all, certainly for Mac, was coming to her shows. 'He had great ambitions for me to sing at The House of Blues on Sunset Strip,' she continues, 'of course he would have, but can you believe the first one of us on stage in that revered venue was Mum?'

He blinks in surprise.

She laughs. 'I'm serious. We were at a gospel brunch one Sunday morning – actually it was during their very first visit – and audience members were invited up to take part in a kind of boogie-woogie dance skit. We sat, open-mouthed, me, Lawrence and Dad, as she got stuck right into it. It was the funniest and most fabulous thing I ever saw her do.'

Enjoying the image, he says, 'And did you ever sing at The House of Blues?'

'I did,' she admits, 'but even better than that, Dad got to play trumpet with a band from Tennessee. He knew the double-bassist, Deso Crimes, from a tour Deso had done of the UK a couple of years before. And as soon as he found out Dad was in the audience – I'm sure it was Mum who sent word – Dad was up there. It was truly magical to watch him living his dream. I just wish we'd had mobile phones with cameras then so I could have recorded it.'

'But you did get into recording?'

She regards him quizzically.

'I looked you up,' he confesses, 'and you have a beautiful voice. The Anita O'Day of your time?'

Her eyes narrow. 'You read that somewhere,' she accuses.

'Guilty, but it's true. The duets with Carlin Monroe are hard to stop watching.'

She looks away and seems to lose a sense of where she is for a moment. Simply hearing Carlin's name brings it all back in a way that's as gently insistent as the waves lapping the rocks in the bay below. She can picture his beautiful, mischievous brown eyes gazing into hers as they sang duets in smoky lounge bars and late-night jazz clubs: 'You Can't Lose a Broken Heart'; 'Let's Do It'; 'Summertime'; 'Dream a Little Dream'.

Giancarlo says, 'Are you going to tell me about him?'

Her eyes return to his and she knows in her heart that she's not ready to talk about Carlin yet. She will, because she has to, but maybe not today.

CHAPTER EIGHTEEN

'You don't want to leave, do you?' Lawrence's voice was gruff, breaking raggedly through the cracks of his anguish.

Catie remained where she was, standing on the deck of their Mulholland home, gazing out at the faraway mountains washed pink by the setting sun. Though she'd heard him, she wasn't sure how to answer.

'It's because of him, isn't it?' he said, hoarsely.

She swallowed and forced herself to turn around. He was standing only a few feet away, at the end of the pool, his reflection wavering in the pale blue water, his expression as tortured as she knew his heart to be.

'Are you fucking him?' he asked, wretchedly.

'Lawrence, don't . . .'

'I said, *are you fucking him*?'

Angry, she said, 'This isn't how we speak to one another . . .'

'Just answer my question, goddammit. I need to know.'

'I am not,' she told him harshly.

'I don't believe you.'

She stared at him hard, letting the truth in her expression speak for her.

'But you want to,' he said. 'Please don't deny it. I've seen you together, the way you look at him, and he looks at you. It's like you're having fucking sex right in front of everyone.'

She couldn't, wouldn't tell him that it was sometimes how it felt, that when Carlin Monroe looked into her eyes, his words felt as intimate as if they were reaching all the way inside her. It would just be cruel.

Carlin. Her breath caught on the mere thought of his name, her senses came alive simply to imagine him.

'He's the reason you don't want to leave LA,' Lawrence stated, and the devastation in his eyes was so deep that she almost couldn't bear it.

'He's already left for Chicago,' she told him quietly.

Lawrence lowered his head and, though she felt a mix of tenderness and pity for him, there was a surge of anger too that she needed a moment to control. Everyone made mistakes, including her, and it wasn't his fault everything had turned sour on him, or that he was being forced to return to England now. And in spite of everything, she really did love him.

Going to him, she pulled him into her arms. For a long moment, as she held him, and felt the immensity of his grief, she detached from her own feelings while watching a humming bird flitting around a feeder they'd hung on a yucca. Next to it the evening light had turned their bedroom window into a painting of the setting sun and parasols at the edge of the pool. It was so beautiful here, and there was so much about LA that they loved. She desperately didn't want to leave . . .

In the end, she said, 'We belong together. We've always known that and, in spite of everything, we still do.'

His head came up, his eyes full of tears. 'You mean in spite of you falling for another man?'

She held his stare as she shook her head. Speaking frankly, while trying to keep an edge out of her voice, she said, 'I mean in spite of the booze and drugs and all the money you've gone through. And in spite of the girls who keep coming here.'

He flushed, and for a fleeting moment she wanted to slap him.

They'd argued so often and bitterly over his 'failings', as she called them; she'd come close to despising him for how delusional he could be, so easily led by his wannabe cronies and insanely reckless with money. He had almost nothing to show for his time here, apart from a marijuana and cocaine habit, and a catalogue of failed projects.

'I've never slept with any of them,' he said quietly.

For some reason she believed him, probably because it was easier to, but he was guilty of everything else and ashamed of it, she could tell.

'And I never slept with Carlin,' she said, but God knew she'd wanted to, so badly at times it had almost driven her out of her mind. His huge, muscular body, his sensual mouth, his hands, his skin, his eyes . . . Their voices fused with an intimacy that almost transcended the physical. They were so good together, the connection, the chemistry . . .

She'd seen the latest recordings that had been made of them in a Westwood studio and had almost felt shame at so much carnality on full display. It was what the producers craved, but there was no acting involved. Only last night he'd whispered huskily in her ear, 'I want you, Catie Mac, you know that,' and she'd felt the sweet warmth of his breath on her cheek like a kiss, and the solidity of his body grazing against hers as if it were an embrace. 'Don't walk away from me,' he said.

She hadn't wanted to, had been desperate not to, while wondering how an attraction could be so strong, so compelling that it could take her over completely. It was as though it had its own magnetic force, invisible currents impossible to resist. If she didn't love Lawrence so much, she knew she'd have become a willing slave to its power.

She had walked away, and he'd flown out this morning without saying goodbye.

Taking Lawrence's hand, she drew him to one of the loungers and sat down with an arm around him. 'We'll get through this,' she told him softly, 'and what's happening to your mum. She'll be OK too. I'm sure of it.'

He didn't answer, and she realized he wasn't quite ready to talk about what was summoning them home. The shock of his mother's cancer would be dealt with when they got there. For now, he needed to try to get a grip on what was happening between them.

After a long time he said, brokenly, 'I know I should let you go—'

'Sssh,' she interrupted, unable to stop herself wondering what she'd do if he did.

'You have a good life here,' he went on. 'You're making it, Catie. People are buying your music. Audiences want you . . .'

'And I want *you* . . . None of it will mean anything without you,' and that was the truth, regardless of how desperately she'd wanted Carlin. She and Lawrence still meant everything to one another, and there was no denying that being here, in LA, had started to pull them apart. She couldn't, wouldn't allow that to happen for the sake of a few nights, maybe even a few months, with another man. Besides, Lawrence's mother needed them now, and though the reason was awful for Marilyn, for them it could be what ended up saving their marriage.

What a striking irony that would be, when Marilyn probably still hoped her son would 'come to his senses' and find the right wife. It was hard to know for certain what Marilyn wanted these days, given how little contact they'd had with her these past few years. However, there was no doubt she was keen for her youngest son to come home in her hour of need. So, no matter how hard Catie was going to find it to leave LA and all it had come to mean to her, she was willing to do it for the sake of their marriage.

CHAPTER NINETEEN

'And did it save your marriage?' Giancarlo asks, after she finishes telling all she's prepared to tell at this stage. Best to leave it as though Carlin never re-entered her life, at least for now.

'Yes, it did,' she replies, and twirls her fork through the delicious spaghetti tangle in front of her that's filled with lobster and zucchini. She can't help reflecting on how fitting a setting this is while talking about LA: a luxury hotel, with a hot sun beating down on a sea-view terrace, and a stunning aquamarine pool that seems to flow into the waves. All the opulence and style, exclusivity, fine cuisine, exotic cocktails and beautiful people . . .

'You're smiling,' Giancarlo tells her as he takes a little more of his Caprese salad.

'No real reason,' she replies. 'I'm just enjoying being here.' She looks around to take in more of the impossibly blue sea and cloudless sky, and says, 'It's been too long since I was somewhere this lovely,' and, after a beat, 'I'm glad I came.'

His eyebrows arch as if to say he's glad too, and as a waiter comes to top up their glasses, he turns to watch a speedboat cutting and bouncing through the waves heading towards Naxos.

'Someone you know?' she asks, reaching for her drink.

He turns back, and as he meets her eyes she's struck, not for the first time, by how encompassing his attention feels, and how much she likes it, although she's unnerved by it too. He's the kind of man it would be easy to fall for, but she can't let that happen, especially when she has no idea who he really is. Or why he seems so interested in her.

'I have an idea,' he tells her, picking up his own glass. 'It is not for today, as I have things I must attend to when we leave here, but it's something I think you will like.'

Intrigued, she says, 'Can you at least give me a hint?'

He shakes his head. 'It will be a surprise. And now, please select a very wicked dessert for us to enjoy while you tell me what happened when you and Lawrence returned to England. I hope his mother was fully appreciative of what *you* had given up for her.'

CHAPTER TWENTY

Mac was waiting at the airport when they flew in from LA and, as he swept Catie into his arms, it was all she could do to stop herself bursting into tears, mostly with the joy of seeing him. In spite of his yearly visits to LA, she'd missed him so much, and with her heart, her life, in so much turmoil now, she'd never needed him more.

Laughing, and half sobbing himself, he opened his arms to draw Lawrence into the embrace, and Catie wondered if just being near Mac made him feel secure and loved as well. Certainly he seemed unable to let Mac go, and when he did Catie saw the tears on his cheeks. This was exactly where they needed to be right now, she realized; back in England, with her father nearby and all the chaos and temptations of Hollywood behind them.

As they journeyed down the M4 to Bristol, she sat in the back of the car, gazing out at the hopelessly drear countryside, as mile after relentless mile of it unfolded. It was at its February worst: low grey skies, icy winds cutting through the desolate trees and empty fields. She knew she shouldn't make comparisons with the lush canyons and sunny boulevards they'd left behind, but it was hard not to when they still held such a special place in her heart. She shouldn't allow herself to think about Carlin either, or imagine him in Chicago, playing at some of the clubs she knew, with bands both familiar and new, duetting with other singers and maybe thinking of her . . .

'Are you OK, Catie girl?' Mac asked, glancing at her in the rear-view mirror.

Knowing he'd sensed she wasn't, and that it was probably more than her dread of what lay ahead now she was back, she smiled. 'A bit jet-lagged,' she replied. Then added, because it was true, 'It's so good to see you.'

He grinned. 'I can tell you it feels like all my dreams coming true, having you guys back, but I know it won't be the same for you, especially given the reason you're here.' Seeming to realize that might have been clumsy, he said to Lawrence, 'Patty has been to see your mother a couple of times lately and, the miracle is, they both lived to tell the tale.'

Though the joke was a little awkward, Lawrence laughed, and Catie loved him for it. 'That was good of Patty,' Lawrence said. 'Did she say how Mum seemed?'

'As good as can be expected,' Mac replied, 'whatever that means. I think she's looking forward to seeing you.' He meant Lawrence of course, not the two of them. 'I've promised to take you straight there.'

Since they had nowhere else to go, apart from to her parents which wouldn't make any sense at all in the circumstances, this was what Catie had expected. Breemoor was going to be her and Lawrence's new home for . . . Actually, she had no idea how long they'd be there, but it was hard to imagine them being able to leave any time soon. There was Marilyn to take care of, of course, but neither of them had a job, and thanks to Lawrence blowing all his money on high living, plus rash investments in projects that were doomed long before they got off the ground, he had no backup at all.

Thankfully, she had her own little nest egg having earned quite well in recent times, but even if it could afford them a flat of their own, they'd already committed to staying with Marilyn.

Realizing her father was watching her again, she attempted another smile.

He said, '*One fine day in the middle of the night,*
Two dead men got up to fight.
Back to back they faced each other,
Drew their swords and shot each other.'

Catie found herself laughing and shaking her head. She loved him so much she could burst with it. She hadn't heard that since she was a small child, when he'd quoted all sorts of nonsense to try to cheer her up if she was sad.

It was approaching midday by the time Mac steered his three-year-old Ford Fiesta into the drive of Breemoor and came to a stop in front of the house. As picturesque as it remained, and seemingly benign, Catie could feel her spirits sinking. How the hell was she going to live with a mother-in-law who was sick, and who couldn't stand her?

Why did Marilyn even want her here?

Presumably because she'd been afraid Lawrence wouldn't come without her.

'I wonder who these other cars belong to,' Lawrence remarked as they climbed out of the Fiesta. There were three, in a row, beneath the old oak where a rope swing still hung, and as if in answer to at least part of the question, the front door opened and Graham, his older brother, came out.

'Welcome! Welcome!' he cried, throwing his arms wide as he hastened first to Catie, then to Lawrence, to embrace them hard. 'God it's good to see you two,' he declared, standing back to get a serious look at them. Though he and Lawrence were alike in many ways, colouring, build, sound of their voices, Graham wasn't as tall as Lawrence or as sharp featured. His dear face was fuller, and faintly scarred by old acne; however, his smile was every bit as winning as his inherent good nature.

What memorable times they'd shared in LA when Graham and Fiona had come to visit, the best being their small but very glamorous wedding at the Beverly Hills Hotel last year.

'Go on in,' Graham instructed. 'Fiona's here. Mac, let me help you with the luggage.'

Since most of their belongings were being shipped from LA, due to arrive sometime in the next six weeks, there were only a few bags to retrieve from the boot. Catie stood watching for a moment, leaning into Lawrence as he put an arm around her.

'Ready?' he whispered.

'As I'll ever be,' she replied, and holding hands they walked in together.

'Hi, you two,' Fiona cried, turning from the log she'd just added to the fire as they entered the sitting room. 'Come in, come in. It's so cold out there. Oh, Catie, how do you manage to look so lovely after such an interminable flight?'

Catie had to laugh, for she knew she looked as wretched as she felt, but it was typical of Fiona to try to make someone feel good. As they hugged, Catie saw Marilyn get up from her fireside chair and, in spite of her dislike of the woman, and the trepidation she felt about living here, she couldn't help but feel glad for her that Lawrence had come. It must have been terrifying to be told she had breast cancer, only then to learn it was necessary to undergo a double mastectomy. She needed her family around her, even if it did include the despised daughter-in-law.

As she turned from Lawrence, Catie was struck by how well she looked, although as far as Catie knew no follow-up treatment to the mastectomy had yet begun. So she still had her luxuriant hair, held in place by its usual Alice band, and her weight was just right for a woman of her height and age.

'Catie,' she said, and there was a warmth to her tone that Catie immediately mistrusted. OK, brushes with mortality could do things to people, like changing them for the better, but this was Marilyn . . .

She watched her come forward and, because it would seem wrong not to, she allowed her hands to be enfolded in a gentle clasp. 'I don't know whether I should thank you first,' Marilyn said, her grey eyes looking right into Catie's, 'or apologize. I know I've treated you badly in the past, and I'm truly sorry for it. I realize I don't deserve your forgiveness, and I really don't expect it, but I still appreciate you coming here to support Lawrence at this difficult time.'

Because she had to, Catie said, 'Of course we're here for you. No one would want you to go through this alone.'

Marilyn smiled in a way that seemed both tender and grateful, then turned to greet Mac as he came into the room. Catie watched them exchange a friendly embrace and realized that he must have visited with Patty, for it didn't appear to be the first time they'd met.

Marilyn was reaching for her hand again. 'Catie dear, and Lawrence,' she said. 'I have some news that I hope will help your homecoming feel a little less . . . burdensome.'

'It's not—' Lawrence started.

'Ssh,' she chided. 'Graham and Fiona have very kindly invited me to stay with them for the next few months, while I'm undergoing chemotherapy. This means you will have Breemoor to yourselves.'

'What?' Lawrence cried, looking at his brother and back to his mother.

So they hadn't needed to come? Catie couldn't stop herself thinking. And why hadn't Graham and Fiona offered before? Then it dawned on her that they probably had, but Marilyn had delayed telling her and Lawrence in order to get Lawrence home.

Marilyn was still speaking. 'I've decided it will be easier for us all if I accept the invitation, at least until you and I can get to know one another better, Catie. And with Graham and Fiona living near Malmesbury now, we won't be too far away from the clinic in Bath.'

'Mum, we're not going to push you out of your own home,' Lawrence objected. 'We can take care of you . . .'

'It's all settled,' Marilyn told him, patting his hand. 'In fact, we've already changed things around for you. My bed and a few other things were moved to Wiltshire this morning, so you'll be able to take over the master suite as soon as you've found a bed of your own. And anything else you'd like to change here will be fine with me. Most of it is quite old now and the place could do with a freshen-up, but there are a few items I'd like you to keep. I've put little notes on them; they're mostly paintings and pieces of furniture that Dad and I collected during our travels.'

'For God's sake, Mum, this is—'

She put up a hand to silence him. 'My personal effects, those I'm not taking with me, have already been locked in the safe, and bigger items have been taken over to the cottage for storage. I just ask that you make sure the place is properly ventilated and cleaned from time to time.'

Lawrence turned to his brother, clearly still needing more, but Graham only shrugged.

'She's made up her mind,' Graham said, 'and we're happy for her to be with us. We've got plenty of room and you guys are going to need some time and space to settle in now you're back.'

'You don't want to be forced to work your commitments around me,' Marilyn added, 'so I think this is a good solution.'

Catie looked at Fiona, who gave her an 'eek' sort of smile, though Catie knew that she and Marilyn had always been close.

Stepping into an awkward silence, Mac said, 'Well, that's not what any of us were expecting, but I guess what really matters is that you are comfortable, Marilyn . . .'

'And somewhere I won't be in the way,' she added, with no rancour that Catie could detect, only self-effacement and gratitude. She was either a gifted actress, or she'd taken holy vows.

'You wouldn't be in the way here,' Lawrence started to say, but she stopped him again.

'I don't think we need to discuss this any further,' she said. 'So why don't we all sit down and have a nice cup of tea before we leave these two to sleep off their jet-lag and get on with all they need to do . . . Ah, here we are, right on cue,' and Catie looked up as a door adjoining the kitchen banged open and a woman, a nurse maybe, wheeled in a laden tea trolley.

Except it wasn't a nurse, or just any woman . . .

'Hello, Catie,' Jude said with a beaming smile. 'Welcome home.'

CHAPTER TWENTY-ONE

***188: *How are you? Haven't had a text from you in a while. Hope this is a good thing.*

CM: *Actually, it might be. I've been quite busy. How are you?*

***188: *Fine. Busy doing what? Are you writing things down?*

CM: *I am, but you'll probably be interested to hear that I've made a friend.*

***188: *Go on.*

CM: *He's very charming.*

***188: *He?*

CM: *Yes, he.*

***188: *Are you going to tell me more about him?*

CM: *He's Italian, around my age, seems very well connected. I think you'd like him.*

***188: *I'm hardly the one who matters. How are you coping emotionally? Not with him, with everything else?*

CM: *Not too badly so far, haven't hit the worst bits yet. Has anyone got in touch with you, trying to find me?*

***188: *No, not yet.*

Catie is in a small, darkened room deep inside the Metropole Hotel, with a sweet-smelling seaweed mask coating her face and Zen music drifting its relaxing rhythms over her senses.

She has been in Taormina for ten slightly turbulent days of moving between then and now and feeling sometimes as if they are blending into one.

She hasn't seen Giancarlo for the past two days – actually since their lunch at San Domenica. However, he sent a message yesterday, via Tony, to assure her he'd be back soon. She didn't ask Tony where he was, she'd simply assumed from the wording that he was no longer in Taormina. Curiously, and very generously, he'd left his car and Ricardo, his driver, at her and Tony's disposal.

Why is he being so kind to her? Should she be worried, or just accept and enjoy it? After all, what does she have to lose?

Yesterday she, Tony and Ricardo made a trip south to Punta Secca, a rustic seaside village near Santa Croce Camerina, where *Montalbano* was filmed. Though she isn't familiar with the detective series, she knows it's popular in

England, and Tony and Ricardo were so excited to show her this jewel on their island's coast that she'd happily gone along with them.

And what a jewel it was, with its sun-scorched cobbled streets and endless stretches of hot white sand. She couldn't help thinking of how she might have enjoyed it even more if Giancarlo had been there, but had gently pushed it out of her mind. Though she couldn't deny she was attracted to him, and spent far more time thinking about him than she should, a romantic attachment at this time in her life was the last thing she needed.

It was during the return journey from Punta Secca that Tony had let slip that the excursion had, in fact, been Giancarlo's suggestion.

Catie had looked at him askance, allowing her curiosity to show.

'There are places he wishes to take you himself,' Tony admitted, 'and he knows that Ricardo and I always enjoy a visit to Ragusa. You enjoy too, I hope.'

'*Ovviamente!*' Ricardo exclaimed from the front seat, tilting his ruddy face to the rear-view mirror to see her better. His eyes were hidden behind dark glasses, but she knew they were watchful and somehow suspicious, which made the humour in his tone all the more welcome as he said, 'It is your singing she does not enjoy, *e chi le può dare torto?*'

Tony and Catie laughed, and were still laughing – about other things by then – after Ricardo dropped them close to Porta Catania at the end of the day. Traffic was forbidden in town, so they'd strolled along to the hotel, where Tony had left her saying, 'there is someone I need to see about something important, but I will be in touch tomorrow.' He'd then kissed her hand, removed his hat to make a flourishing bow, and hurried away.

127

It's tomorrow now, late afternoon and, as there has been no word from him, or Giancarlo, she's treating herself to a facial in the hotel spa. She'll need to decide soon where to go when she leaves the Metropole, as her stay is due to come to an end on Friday and the place is full after that. Of course, there are plenty of other hotels in town, should she decide to remain in Taormina, and she thinks she probably will, at least for now. Perhaps Tony, as a tour guide, can recommend somewhere for her to try next.

She continues to lie quietly in the darkness, lulled by haunting music and musky essential oils, and soon finds her thoughts full of Giancarlo again. It had been tempting, yesterday, to ask Tony and Ricardo to tell her more about him, but she'd resisted, certain they'd report everything back to him.

She'd googled him, of course, and had discovered that he was indeed the head of what appeared to be (it was all in Italian) an engineering company headquartered in Turin. However, there was no picture of him on the site, but none of the other Giancarlo Santoris that had come up in her search had been him. There could be, bizarrely and even amusingly, a possible – though convoluted – family connection to the dukes of Milan. (How can she really know when she doesn't speak the language?) Certainly his looks and manner could be described as aristocratic, and there's no doubt he has an air of authority, but she'd never embarrass herself by asking.

More worrying, albeit fascinating and fantastical, is the question that was given some momentum last night by what she'd read in Daphne Phelps's book.

Apparently, amongst Daphne's many famous and colourful friends, there had been a Mafia don who'd given the Englishwoman a certain amount of protection at the times she'd needed it most.

Of course, Catie has only to picture Giancarlo in her mind's eye to feel certain he has nothing at all to do with one of Sicily's most notorious syndicates. Although she has to admit she has no idea what a Mafia don is supposed to look like – and Giancarlo is such a mystery. She can't decide how bothered she is by that; on the one hand it holds her back from getting too involved, while on the other she has to admit to how much she enjoys thinking about him.

The treatment room door opens and a diminutive therapist wafts in as quietly and gently as a summer breeze.

'OK, *tutto finito*,' she announces and begins the process of removing the mask, before applying a heavenly scented moisturizer and ending with a gentle massage.

Eventually, fully dressed and feeling faintly light-headed, Catie is signing a bill at the salon's reception desk when the therapist says, in English, 'There is a gentleman waiting for you in the bar.'

There is nothing Catie can do to stop her hopes rushing to Giancarlo, but if it is him she can't go straight upstairs like this. Post-facial is never a good look, especially at her age, so turning right instead of left as she leaves the salon, she returns to her room to try to make herself presentable.

It turns out to be Tony waiting in the bar, and she hates herself for feeling disappointed when she's so fond of him.

'I take the liberation of ordering you a Prosecco,' he declares, standing as she approaches the table.

'*Grazie mille*,' she smiles, practising two of her five words of Italian. 'Have you had a good day?'

'*Sì, sì, molto bene*. First, I tell you that Giancarlo has tickets for the opera at Teatro Nazarena this evening at nine p.m. He wishes to know if you would like to eat dinner first, or after?'

Feeling faintly dazzled, and ludicrously pleased, she's about to say after, when she realizes how late it's likely to be. The Catie of old would have had little problem staying up all night, but she isn't that Catie any more. 'Perhaps we can meet at seven?' she suggests.

Apparently having no issue with that, Tony says, 'Absolutely. The boss think you might say that so he has already make a reservation for you at the Raya Ristorante, where you will enjoy delicious Sicilian cuisine.'

The boss?

She can't be sure whether she's a little worried now, or simply intrigued, and decides to make it the latter.

'I will walk you there,' Tony is saying, as her Prosecco arrives, 'but it is not difficult to find. And now I have other news. You mention yesterday, while we are at Punta Secca, that your stay at the Metropole is soon finished. *Sì?*'

'It's full after Friday,' she confirms, 'and actually I was going to ask if there's somewhere else you can recommend. The Paradiso looks very nice . . .'

'*Sì, sì,* very good hotel, and I can make enquiries for you, but I have another suggestion if it interests you. My cousin, Isabella, has an apartment not far from the Paradiso, with lovely big terrace and sea views. Two bedrooms, very special place – my cousin is very proud of it. She leave for Rome this morning – this is where she live most of the time – but I see her last night and tell her about you and she is very happy for you to stay at her apartment if you would like to.'

Catie blinks, needing a moment to take it in. An apartment, not a hotel? Although she's not against the idea in principle, will it make her feel more lonely – or more independent? Probably both, and actually there's something appealing about the thought of living a little like a local for a while.

'How long would she be prepared to rent it to me?' she asks, and thinks to add, 'and can I afford it?'

He laughs. '*Sì, sì*, she will make you a good price, and she is not coming back until March, so she will be very happy to have someone to take care of it.'

Catie smiles. 'I'm not sure I'll be staying that long, but I can promise to take good care of it while I'm there.'

He claps his hands in delight. 'I will take you there tomorrow so you can see if it is suitable. If it is, Ricardo and I will help you to move from here on Friday. Ah, here is Giancarlo,' he says as his phone rings. 'I think he will be pleased by this news. *Salve*,' he says, answering the call.

Catie picks up her Prosecco and, as she looks around the bar where others are sipping cocktails and seeming very contented in this romantic setting, she tries to assimilate this surprising turn of events. On the surface she's feeling quite excited about it, and maybe she'll find it easier to write her thoughts down if she's in a place where there are no interruptions, and no one noticing her coming and going.

Realizing Tony is speaking in English now, she turns back to him as he says into the phone, '*Sì*, she is here, I am passing you over,' and holding out the mobile he says to Catie, 'Giancarlo would like to speak to you.'

Pleased, she takes the phone and says, 'Hello.'

'Caterina,' and the surprising use of her name stalls her for a moment. He has such a beautiful voice. 'I am sorry,' he says, 'but I must let you down this evening. It is a great disappointment to me, but things have happened at this end to delay my return to Taormina.'

Sharing in the disappointment, she says, 'Is everything all right?'

'*Sì*, it will be, and is nothing for you to worry about. I hope we can go to the restaurant and to the opera

131

another time. Tony tells me you are moving into Isabella's apartment?'

'Uh, yes, it's possible. I'm going to see it tomorrow.'

'I think you will like it. And did you enjoy your day in Ragusa yesterday?'

'It was lovely, and thank you for letting us use your car.'

There's a smile in his voice as he says, 'You are welcome. I hope Ricardo did not drive too fast for you.'

He had, but Catie says, 'Are you sure everything's all right. You sound . . . tired?'

He sighs as he says, 'Unfortunately I am not so young any more.'

She laughs, knowing she's meant to. 'I guess that makes two of us,' she says.

'If you would like it, Tony will escort you to a different restaurant this evening,' he tells her, 'and we will save the Raya for another time. And maybe, when we are next together, you will continue to tell me about what happened when you returned to the UK at the age of thirty. I was very regretful to leave the story at the point where Jude brought in the tea. What a shock for you, and what, I keep asking myself, was she doing there?'

Recalling how much the moment had appalled her, Catie smiles and says, with no small irony, 'It's a very good question, which I will be happy to answer when you're back. And maybe you'll tell me a little more about you?'

There is no hesitation before he says, softly. 'I will.' Then he adds, 'I am looking forward to seeing you again.'

CHAPTER TWENTY-TWO

'I have good news and bad news,' Lawrence declared, unwinding his scarf as he came into the kitchen where Catie was sloshing brandy over the ingredients for a plum pudding. 'Mm, that smells good,' he murmured, going to peer over her shoulder, 'and so, Mrs Vaughan, do you.'

'You know you're not supposed to call me that,' she protested with a scowl.

'But it's who you are.'

'I know, it just seems to belong more to your mother, especially as we're in her house. Anyway, before you tell me your news, I've heard from the decorator and he can start on the other bedrooms as early as next week.'

'Cool. Can we afford it?'

'Just about, I think. He's only painting, no fancy wall-paper or jazzy frescoes.' *No baby's room yet*, she didn't add, *we don't want to jinx things*. 'He's going to repair all the broken cornices, and we know he's good at that because of what he did in our room.' The fact that Marilyn really had seemed to mean it when she'd told them to do whatever they wanted to freshen up the place was, so far, bearing out. Not that they'd done much in the past year, they'd had many other priorities, but after they'd finally finished making the spacious master suite their own a few weeks ago, Marilyn had come for a viewing and declared it to be exactly what she would have done if she only had Catie's sense of colour and style. It was a compliment that had thrown Catie so completely that she'd hardly spoken for the rest of the visit.

One day she might understand her mother-in-law, maybe even trust her – and one day they'd be able to update the kitchen and bathrooms, and even get a landscaper to redesign parts of the garden. For now, though, they were happy with the sprawling lawns and flowering beds as they were. After all, it was a beautiful property that they could never have afforded any other way and, if everything went to plan, there might soon be an additional little person whose needs would have to be taken into consideration.

'So, who's the pudding for?' Lawrence asked, dipping a finger into the fruity mix and hooking out a good helping.

'Dad, of course,' she replied, tapping his hand with a wooden spoon. 'Remember I promised I'd make one for Christmas, so Mum gave me her recipe.'

'Great, just the way I want you, barefoot and pregnant in the kitchen,' and wrapping his arms around her from behind, he planted a kiss on her neck.

She grimaced as her heart contracted. 'Still only two of us,' she told him, fighting back the tears that had begun with an unwelcome showing that morning. 'Sorry.'

'Hey, don't say that,' he admonished, and turned her to face him. 'We knew it probably wouldn't happen right away, and we're having fun trying, aren't we?'

She had to smile at that, because yes, they were, and gazing lovingly into his eyes she sang along softly with the tape she had been playing – Aretha Franklin's 'You and Me'. One of the best things about this house was that she had her own music room where she could write and rehearse with the piano and create compilations on cassette from their enormous vinyl collection.

Smiling at the timeliness of the song, he pulled her closer and moved with her in a slow smooch that continued through the next, less appropriate but no less loved track, Gary Moore's 'Still Got the Blues'.

'So,' she said, when they finally parted and she went back to her pudding, 'what's your good news? We'll let the bad wait, mm?'

'Mm,' he agreed, taking a beer from the fridge. 'The good,' he said, searching for a bottle opener, 'is that I ran into William Thurloe earlier. Jude's stepfather?'

Frowning, she said, 'Yes, I remember who he is. Where did you see him?'

'Coming out of Dingles, would you believe, and yes, I was in there getting your birthday present. Anyway, it turns out Jude got married last year to Henry Clarke. Did you ever know him?'

Amazed she turned to look at him, forgetting her task for the moment. 'Jude's married?' she echoed incredulously. 'To Henry Clarke. Actually, I don't remember him. Who is he?'

'He was a year ahead of me at uni, studying physics, I think. I didn't know him well. Anyway, apparently, they got hitched about eighteen months ago, and they have a little girl.'

Catie swallowed as a surge of envy crawled all over her sense of failure. Jude could get pregnant, but apparently Catie herself couldn't. 'I wonder why she didn't say she was married when she popped up like a Halloween spook at our welcome home party?' she commented tartly.

He shrugged. 'I guess she didn't feel it was the right time to go banging on about herself. Anyway, I was thinking that it explains why she hasn't been turning up at any of your gigs the way she used to. And now you can stop worrying that she might. She's obviously got other things to do.'

Catie nodded slowly, still not sure what to make of this, although it had to be good, didn't it, that Jude no longer had some deluded reason to be a stalker? 'Do you know where they're living?' she asked, returning to her mixing.

'Actually, not far from here, in Leigh Woods. Henry's parents are loaded, it's the only way they could afford somewhere there, unless teacher's pay has gone up. Apparently, he's deputy head of physics at the Cathedral School. Or maybe it's the grammar. Whichever.'

'And they've got a little girl?' Catie mumbled. How could she not feel insanely jealous of that when she and Lawrence had been trying for over a year and still nothing had happened? Maybe it was time to go and talk to a doctor.

'Did you bring in the mail earlier?' Lawrence asked, looking around.

'I checked the box but there was nothing,' she replied, and dumped her pudding mix into a bowl lined with greaseproof paper. She was annoyed that the news about Jude had shaken her so much, not only because of the pregnancy, but it made her seem foolish for having worried all this time about Jude stalking her again. As Lawrence had said, she had other things to do, so her silence wasn't some sort of sinister calm before a storm. It was just a happy, well-balanced wife and mother-to-be getting on with her life.

'OK, time for the bad news,' he announced, and perched on a stool at the breakfast counter. 'Although it's not as bad as you might think, you just have to promise to hear me out.'

Already not keen to hear it, she delayed by insisting on getting the pudding on to steam so she could give him her full attention. By the time it was done, he'd poured her a glass of wine and taken it into the sitting room, 'so there'll be no sharp objects to hand,' he'd joked as he left.

'OK,' she said, settling into the fireside chair that had become hers, while he generally used the one that was Marilyn's, unless they were snuggled up together on the old damask sofa that they actually loved. He'd lit the fire while he was waiting and the TV news was on, but he went to turn down the sound.

'Please don't tell me you've lost your job,' she warned, although it couldn't be that or he'd surely look a lot more worried than he did. They'd actually been doing surprisingly well since returning – not so difficult for her when she had Mac's support, and also a UK booking agent now. She'd even had several sessions with a producer in a West London recording studio. Her CDs might not be selling in chart-topping quantities, but they rarely had any left over after a gig.

For Lawrence things had been a little trickier. However, after a short spell as a sales rep for Allied Carpets, combined with shifts as a barman at the Old Duke, he'd finally been offered a position at the BBC on their local news programme.

'No, I haven't lost my job,' he told her, 'in fact there could be a promotion in the offing, but I'll tell you about that after. No, my bad news is actually good in that Mum's scans are still coming up clear and she says she's feeling more like her old self.'

Catie stopped breathing. She had a fair idea of where this was going now, and needing to know if she was right, she said, 'She wants to come back here?'

He looked surprised, then grimaced in a way that confirmed her suspicion.

'I'm sorry, Lawrence,' she said, 'but I can't live with your mother. I know we've been getting along quite well since she went to Graham and Fiona's, but that's because we hardly see one another. She still hates me, I can feel it—'

'She does not,' he cut in forcefully, 'and if you'd kept your promise to hear me out, you'd know that she isn't proposing to move back into the house. She wants us to get the cottage ready for her.'

Catie gaped at him in disbelief. 'You mean she's going to live at the end of the garden like some nasty little gnome watching our every move?'

'Don't be cruel,' he objected. 'She's been through a lot, you know that, and why don't we just be thankful she's in remission?'

Yes, thank God, indeed. Catie couldn't wish the alternative on her, but the thought of having her *here* . . .

'She misses her friends,' Lawrence pointed out, 'and she's promised not to get in our way. It's got its own separate drive, you know that, and she'll only come to the house when invited.'

'And how long will that last?' Catie cried, looking up at the sound of a car turning into their drive.

'It'll be your parents,' he told her, getting to his feet. 'I invited them for supper *before* I knew about Mum's decision, so no, they're not here to give me moral support.'

'But they will,' Catie muttered as he went to let them in. And they would, because anyone with any sense of compassion and decency would allow the woman who'd survived cancer and owned the roof over their heads to have a little part of what was actually hers.

Except it wouldn't stop at a little part, Catie felt as sure of that as she did of her pudding being a disaster – actually as she did of never being able to get pregnant, especially if her mother-in-law was in the vicinity.

As it turned out Catie was wrong about the pudding. It went down a treat on Christmas Day, and even the weirdly tame Marilyn, who'd installed herself in the cottage a week ago, asked for a second helping. Patty gave it a generous nod of approval, while Mac, of course, waxed lyrical simply because she'd made it. (He'd eaten some terrible stuff over the years to keep his daughter happy, and Catie had no doubt he'd continue to for ever, although she had to admit, this pudding wasn't bad.)

By the end of the day, it was clear to Catie that everyone had stopped waiting for the news they'd hoped for, and because she couldn't bear it, she took herself off to the kitchen to burst into tears.

It was her father who found her and pulled her into his arms. 'It'll happen, sweetheart,' he assured her, stroking her hair. 'Sometimes it just takes a little longer than we'd like.'

'But I'm thirty-one, Dad. Everyone I know has had a baby by now.'

He smiled. 'It's not that old, and Lola still isn't a mother.'

Lifting her teary face, she said, 'Have you seen her?' Funny how much she'd been missing Lola lately; their only contact now was through birthday and Christmas cards.

'No. Apparently, she's still travelling the world as an air hostess, so even her parents don't see much of her. I ran into them last weekend after a gig at the Bendix social club.'

Knowing it would have been some sort of seasonal knees-up, she said, 'How are they?'

'They seem to be doing fine. Asked me to send their love.'

She managed a smile. 'So, none of you are grandparents yet,' she said dolefully, while wondering if it mattered as much to Lola as it did to her.

He raised an ironic eyebrow as he said, 'We count our other blessings.'

'But I know how much you want to be a grandpa, and you'd be wonderful . . .'

'She's right, you would,' Lawrence said, coming to join them, 'and we'll make it happen, babe. I promise. We'll go to see someone in the new year, find out if there's something we're doing wrong.'

Catie spluttered on a laugh, as Mac tugged his son-in-law into an embrace. 'I've every confidence you know what you're doing, son,' he said, 'but if you need any pointers . . .'

'No Dad,' Catie quickly protested, 'please, just no.'

Another year passed but, in spite of being assured by the professionals that there was no reason for her not to conceive, Catie still hadn't. It began to weigh so heavily on her that she found it difficult to think of anything else. And matters weren't helped by Marilyn's frequent recommendations that she should give up her career for a while.

'All those late nights and smoky clubs,' she'd say, 'it can't be good for you. You probably just need to get your health and metabolism into the right place.'

Catie didn't argue; she'd learned not to with Marilyn, as it never ended well. She simply continued performing up and down the country, often as a support act for much bigger names, other times topping the bill herself, albeit in much smaller venues. Naturally she still played with Mac and the Blue Notes whenever possible; she couldn't imagine a time when she wouldn't, and the intimate settings and familiar audiences were still her favourite gigs.

Then the day arrived when Marilyn couldn't wait to break the news that Jude had just given birth to her *second* child.

'Apparently it's another girl,' she declared, so happily that it might have been her own grandchild she was announcing.

'Mum, you're not helpful,' Lawrence scolded as he put an arm around Catie. 'And what the hell has Jude got to do with anything? Why are we even talking about her?'

'I'm just saying,' Marilyn replied, frostily. 'Jude and her husband live more . . . well, more regulated lives, whereas you two are dashing around all over the place, you reporting your stories, and Catie flitting from pub to club at all hours of the night. It's a miracle you ever get to see one another. Now, if you, Lawrence, were to take my advice and be at home more, and Catie, if maybe you found a different sort of job, you might be surprised by what happens.'

Furious, Catie said, 'I notice you're not suggesting Lawrence should change career.'

Appearing astonished, Marilyn said, 'Well that would just be silly when he's the main breadwinner and, anyway, you're the one who'll have to stay at home when the baby eventually comes.'

Catie didn't bother to point out that actually she earned more than Lawrence. Marilyn wouldn't want to hear it, and even if she did, she'd most likely refuse to believe it. 'When exactly did you see Jude?' she asked, the words coming out in spite of how much she didn't want to continue the conversation. 'I mean, I presume you've seen her if you know she's just given birth.'

Marilyn waved a hand. 'Oh, she drops in from time to time,' she said airily. 'Her little girl, Harriet, the one she already has, is an absolute poppet.'

As Catie turned to Lawrence, he got to his feet. 'I think it's time you went home now, Mum,' he said, going to help her up and ignoring the fact that she hadn't yet finished her meal.

Marilyn looked about to protest, until seeming to realize she'd gone too far, she dabbed her mouth with a napkin and went for her coat.

'I'm sorry,' Lawrence said, looking wretched as he closed the door behind his mother. 'We try to do the right thing by inviting her over and this is what she does. I could throttle her.'

'Do you know what I think?' Catie said, reaching for the wine and hating that she could. 'I think it's a not-so-subtle attempt to get us to move out of here. She wants the house back. Of course she does, it's her home, and she's stuck over there in that cottage . . .'

'Which happens to have three bedrooms, a state-of-the-art kitchen and its own garden,' Lawrence put in angrily. 'All paid for by us!'

By me, Catie thought but didn't say.

'It doesn't matter how lovely it is,' she countered, 'in her eyes it's a granny annexe and she isn't a granny. You see, it's really not that difficult to work out what's going on with her – apart from the fact that she's always hated me anyway.'

For once he didn't deny it and, sighing, he came to fold her in his arms. 'If it doesn't work out,' he said, his voice thick with emotion, 'if we don't become parents, I'll still never want to be with anyone but you. I hope you know that.'

CHAPTER TWENTY-THREE

'And did you?' Giancarlo prompts as she trails to a stop. 'Become parents?'

Catie nods and fleetingly recalls the joyful moment when she'd first learned she was pregnant, and how she'd immediately picked up the phone to call Lawrence.

Shutting it down, she goes inside the apartment to fetch more wine.

Only two days have passed since she moved in, but it's already starting to feel like home. With its large open-plan sitting room, filled with pastel-coloured sofas and lounge chairs, and sea-facing terrace ornamented with vibrant ceramics and flowering succulents, there's nothing about it not to love. There's even a turntable and small collection of vinyl, the Doors, Carole King, the Beatles; various Italian bands she'd never heard of but was enjoying anyway.

The best part of being here though, at least so far, was Giancarlo turning up unexpectedly just over an hour ago, laden with grocery bags, flowers and two bottles of Nerello Mascalese. And almost as if the place were his, he'd set out a plate of succulent *arancini al pistacchio* for them to enjoy while he prepared a *parmigiana di melanzane*.

More than happy for him to take over, she'd flitted about the place lighting candles in tall glass vases, before laying the long marquetry-topped table outside. She couldn't remember when she'd last set a scene for a relaxing evening at home, nor was she going to try. Much better to feel almost teenager-ish as she stepped back to admire it all.

They ate on the terrace that overlooked a cluster of rooftops and the sea beyond, and occasionally, as they talked, the sound of voices and music carried up from the street below. By the time they'd finished the meal, she'd kept her promise to tell him about Jude and everything else that had happened during those early years after returning from LA.

Of course, he'd been bound to ask her about becoming a parent, and she had become one . . .

She glances up as he comes into the kitchen and, taking the wine bottle to open himself, he says, 'I sense that you don't want to talk any more, so maybe we can just enjoy being together?'

Her heart turns over. He makes it sound so simple, so natural, and it's all she wants to do, but with Chet Baker singing 'I Fall in Love Too Easily' on the sound system, she can't help recalling Carlin Monroe performing the song. His voice was more mellow and languid, maybe richer than Baker's . . . He'd been good, everyone was always agreed on that.

She turns to Giancarlo, not sure what she wants to say now, until the words start to spill out in a sudden, irrational surge of anger. 'I don't understand,' she tells him. 'You hardly know me and you surely can't really be interested in everything I'm telling you, so I'd like to know what's going on. Why did you invite me for dinner that first evening, and why are you here now?'

Seeming both surprised and bemused by her sudden change of mood, he puts down the wine and turns to lean against the countertop, folding his arms. 'The reason I invited you for dinner the first night,' he replies, evenly, 'is because I am alone here in Taormina, and you told me that you were too. I thought, I hoped, that we might enjoy one another's company, and I think we are doing that?'

How can she deny it? But how can she trust him when she doesn't even know him?

She feels confused, slightly panicked and momentarily lost for words.

He reaches out to tilt her chin so he can look into her eyes. There is a smile in his own as he says, 'There is nothing sinister in my motives, Caterina, if that is what you're thinking. And you're wrong to say I can't be interested in what you're telling me, because I am. It's helping me get to know you . . .'

'But it can't be all about me.'

He laughs and she says, 'You hardly ever talk about yourself.'

He seems surprised by that, as if he genuinely hadn't noticed. 'You can ask me anything,' he tells her, 'and I am happy to answer.'

She swallows and looks away, embarrassed by her ridiculous outburst now and searching for a way to make up for it.

'Relax,' he says softly.

She inhales, and as the build-up of unsteadying emotion starts to fade, she becomes aware of his cologne, the natural male scent of him, his nearness, and it's all as intoxicating as the wine. She wonders, somewhere at the back of her mind, what it would be like to dance with him, to feel his arms around her, but he's already turning away, going back to the table on the terrace.

She follows and sits as he refills their glasses. She isn't

sure if it's a good idea for him to stay any longer, but nor does she want to ask him to leave.

In the end, she says, 'You never mention your wife.'

He glances at her and sits back in his chair, stretching out his legs as he stares out at the moonlit night. 'No,' he agrees, 'I don't.'

When he doesn't elaborate, she wants to prompt him, but in the end, he says, 'She is in Turin. Her name is Luisa.'

Too late she realizes she might have preferred not to know this, because now she can't allow herself to imagine he is free to be here, that there is no harm in their friendship. Nor can she stop herself wondering what Luisa might be like, and pictures someone as beautiful as only an Italian woman can be.

'Is that where you've been this week?' she asks, picking up her glass.

He nods. 'For part of the time.' He reaches for his own wine, but doesn't lift it. 'We are estranged,' he tells her. 'For the moment she continues to reside in my house, but we are no longer living as husband and wife.'

Unable not to feel relieved about that, even if the split is causing him pain, she says, 'Is she the mother of your children?'

He shakes his head. 'No, she is not.' He drinks and puts his glass down again. 'Vittoria, my first wife, the children's mother, died six years ago,' he tells her. 'Luisa agrees with me that our marriage was a mistake made too soon after the death.'

The air suddenly feels charged with the mistake, as though it's troubling him in more ways than he might want to admit. After a while, Catie says, softly, 'How did Vittoria die?'

His eyes are fixed on the middle-distance as he says, 'There was an accident. I was driving – and my daughter has never forgiven me.' His tone suggests that he's probably never forgiven himself. She wants to ask more about it, but senses now isn't the right time to go any deeper.

In the end, she says, 'I'm sorry. That's such a terrible thing to happen. It must be very hard.'

He doesn't deny it, simply raises his glass again and finishes his wine.

She lets the silence run, wondering what's in his mind now, if he's sorry he mentioned the accident, if he's thinking back to it, feeling all those terrible emotions again. He seems shut off, making him impossible to fathom, and she's reminded that they're really little more than strangers. And yet, even in this quiet impasse, with the ghosts of his past so close, she can still sense an instinctive connection holding them in place.

The intro to 'What a Little Moonlight Can Do' starts to play inside the apartment, and when the vocals begin he seems surprised as he says, 'Is this Diana Ross?'

She smiles. 'It's a track from *Lady Sings the Blues*.'

He nods. 'Yes, of course.' Then, 'Have you ever performed this song yourself?'

Going with the change of subject, she says, 'Yes, I have, but not nearly as well as Diana Ross, or Billie Holiday.'

He regards her closely as he says, 'I'd like to hear you sing.'

'You already have, on YouTube,' she reminds him.

'Yes, but you know that's not what I mean.'

She'd guessed it was coming and can feel the resistance starting to build inside as she looks out at the darkness, not sure what to say now.

'When did you stop?' he asks gently.

She swallows, but still doesn't answer.

'You don't have to tell me,' he says.

'I had children,' she suddenly blurts, 'but that isn't what comes next.' Her head is starting to spin with too much wine and too many memories. 'I'm just not sure if I can tell you what does.'

CHAPTER TWENTY-FOUR

'Catie! Thank God!' Lawrence shouted down the line. 'I've been trying to get hold of you. Where are you?'

'You'll never guess,' she laughed excitedly while glancing over her shoulder. 'I'm at Lola's, in London. She came to the show last night, and . . .'

'That's great, babe, but you need to listen . . .'

'No, no, you do. Oh God, Lawrence, you're not going to believe this. I just did a test and it's only *positive*. I swear it! Everyone knows they're completely reliable these days, so it means we're going to have a baby. Isn't that fantastic! I wish you were here. Lola's just made us a cup of tea to celebrate. No wine for me for a while.'

'Oh Christ, Catie,' he groaned wretchedly.

Her smile started to fade. This wasn't the response she'd expected – nothing like it, in fact. 'What is it?' she asked, turning to look at Lola again. Her oldest, dearest friend was so sophisticated now, so chic with her Jennifer Aniston hair and super-trim figure. Gone were the glasses and crooked teeth, even her skin looked flawless, and it had been so good to see her after all this time, had actually been totally wonderful her turning up at Ronnie Scott's out of the blue last night.

'Catie, I want you to stay where you are,' Lawrence said quietly. 'I'm going to come and get you.'

Her heart lurched as she blinked. 'What? Why? I don't understand. I can drive myself home.'

'No, you can't . . .'

'Lawrence! You're scaring me. What's happened? Is it your mum?'

He took a breath and Catie suddenly knew what he was going to say. She started to back away from the phone, the coil stretching as she kept the receiver to her ear. 'No!' she said raggedly. 'No, Lawrence. Please, *no*!'

'What is it?' Lola asked, clearly alarmed.

'Lawrence, please tell me it's not Dad,' Catie implored, her throat so tight she could barely get the words out. 'You have to tell me it's not him.'

Lawrence's voice was strangled by tears as he said, 'I'm sorry, babe. I'm so sorry . . .'

'But he's all right, isn't he?' she urged desperately. 'It's not serious.'

'Oh, Catie,' he sobbed.

She turned to Lola, staring at her in horror.

'He had a heart attack just after he arrived at work this morning,' Lawrence explained, 'and the ambulance didn't get there in time.'

As the words reached her, Catie began sinking to her knees. 'No, Lawrence, please! *No!*'

Going down with her, Lola took the phone and said to Lawrence, 'It's me. I think I get what's happened. What can I do?'

'Just stay with her until I can get there.'

'It's OK, I can bring her. I'm not working again until the weekend.'

Taking a moment to process this, he said, 'OK, I'm at work now, but I'll go home . . . Actually, if you can bring Catie, I'll go to Patty's.'

'I'll call my parents. They'll want to know and . . .' She started to break down, but managed to steady herself. 'You should have someone to take care of you,' she said, brokenly.

'I'll be fine. Can you put Catie back on?'

Lola tried to give Catie the phone, but Catie shook her head, over and over. Her face was buried in her hands, her whole body was shaking. 'I can't speak to him,' she whispered raggedly. It wasn't possible to have a world without her dad in it, so she wasn't going to let this be real.

Lola said to Lawrence, 'I'll take care of her and bring her home as soon as I can.'

'OK, thanks. I've been trying to ring Patty but she isn't answering. Maybe she's at the hospital, I'll try to find out. Meantime, I guess it would make sense to go straight to ours and I can meet you there. Do you have the address?'

'Of course. Let me give you this number in case you need to ring again before we leave.'

After he'd written it down, he said, 'This is going to be hard for her, Lola.'

'I know,' she said, looking desperately at Catie. Then, 'Please give Patty my love when you see her.'

'I will. I'm going to call my brother now. I think we could do with him being around.'

As Lola replaced the receiver, she wrapped Catie tightly in her arms, but Catie pulled away.

'It can't be true,' she said, her face ashen and ravaged by shock, her eyes glassy with disbelief. 'He's only fifty-two.'

'I can't believe it either,' Lola agreed, dabbing away a tear. 'Just thank God you're with me this morning and not on your own.'

Catie looked around the Battersea flat as if seeing it for the first time, as if she had no idea where she was. 'Before he goes anywhere,' she said faintly, 'I need to call and tell him about the baby. He'll want to know.'

Lola regarded her helplessly.

'He'll be at work now, so I'll have to do it later,' Catie decided.

As she started to get up, Lola held out her hands just in case she toppled. 'Can you walk?' she asked.

Catie nodded, as if it were a question she was often asked.

Once certain she was steady on her feet, Lola said, 'I'll get your coat. My car's parked just down the street. Not far.'

Catie said, 'He usually finishes at five, but sometimes he does an hour's overtime.' After a beat she added, 'He works at Fry's in Keynsham now. Parnall's closed down.'

Lola started to say that he'd been at Fry's for over ten years, but stopped herself. 'You just stay there a moment,' she said, easing Catie into a chair, 'I'll be right back.'

She was in the hall for only a moment when she heard the start of a terrible, wrenching keening coming from the sitting room and, sobbing herself, she raced back to Catie's side to find her clutching the positive pregnancy test.

All the way back to Bristol, Catie kept experiencing sudden and overwhelming urges to get in touch with her father so he could tell her everything was all right. He was who she called when she was confused and afraid, when she didn't know what to do, and he always had an answer. He would show her how to be calm about this, how to be strong and brave, and he'd know just the right song to bring a smile back to her face.

One fine day in the middle of the night . . .

They stopped at a services to call Lawrence. Lola went

inside while Catie stayed in the car, still clutching her pregnancy test and gazing around at what felt like an alien world.

There was no reply from Breemoor, or from Patty's, so Lola drove them on.

Lawrence was waiting when they got to the house, and came straight to take Catie in his arms. She didn't want him to hold her, it was making it real, and when Marilyn came to offer her sympathies she turned away.

Graham was there, and Fiona – and back in her role as tea-maker was Jude.

'I'm so sorry,' she said, taking Catie's hands between her own.

Catie looked down at them and tried to recall who this woman was and why she didn't like her.

'Where's Mum?' she asked, turning to Lawrence.

'At home,' he replied. 'Lola's parents are with her.'

She thought about this for a moment, and said, 'That's good. Dad will be pleased to see them when he gets home.'

More than two hundred people turned up for the funeral, travelling from all over, crowding the church and spilling outside into the graveyard. At the wake, the Blue Notes played lively swing numbers, nothing too soulful or morbid, because Mac wouldn't have wanted that. Someone else had made the decision, and neither Catie nor Patty had objected, because this person was probably right.

Catie sensed that everyone expected her to sing, but it was too soon, too hard. She knew that with each breath, each note, the pain of loss would only get worse, so that her voice would be shredded and destroyed by the depth of her grief.

She spoke to people, thanked them for coming and at the same time wished they would stop offering condolences.

She didn't want to know how sorry they were, or even how loved her father had been, she just wanted it all to stop.

In the end Lawrence took her home early. Patty refused to join them; she wanted to stay awhile amongst Mac's friends and with Lola and her parents.

'They'll see me home,' she told Lawrence, her pale eyes shadowed by grief, the shock of her loss still plain to see. 'No need to worry about me. Just take care of Catie. That's what Mac would want, to know his girl is all right.'

Back at the house, Lawrence and Catie lay down on the bed together, still in their coats, and Catie, dry-eyed and aching, held him as he sobbed. She had no idea how they were going to get over this, how it would be possible to feel happy again, how anything would ever feel worthwhile if her father wasn't there to share in it.

CHAPTER TWENTY-FIVE

'And now, here I am, thirty years later,' Catie tries to smile through her tears, 'still unable to talk about him without crying.' She dabs her eyes with a paper napkin and gives a resigned sort of laugh. 'Actually, it doesn't happen every time, but I still miss him so much. Who'd have thought that was possible after so long?'

Giancarlo's eyes are dark with understanding as he says, 'Grief doesn't have an end point, and from everything you've told me about him, he was an exceptional man.'

She nods and exhales a sigh. 'I was very lucky. Not everyone is as blessed when it comes to a father.'

'That,' he agrees, 'is true.'

'What about yours?' she asks, watching his hand as he reaches for his coffee cup. 'Is he still alive?'

He shakes his head and puts the cup down. 'We lost him about fifteen years ago. It was a very sad time. He was a good man. Stern, some might even describe him as aloof, but I always found him to be fair. I had a lot of respect for him, but I won't claim to have been as close to him as you were to Mac.'

Liking the way he has used her father's name, she finishes her own coffee and, as the nearby church clocks start to chime the half-hour, she realizes she can't remember if midnight has come and gone, or is still to happen.

Getting up from the table he carries their cups inside. 'Do you recall?' he says, over his shoulder, 'when we were at San Domenica, I told you I had an idea that I thought you would like?'

Following him in with a small tray of untouched almond cakes, she chides, 'And you wouldn't even give me a hint.'

He smiles, his teeth flashing white in the semi-darkness. 'Are you free tomorrow?' he asks.

Startled, she laughs. 'I'm always free.'

'Then I'll pick you up at ten. Make sure you're wearing shorts and flip-flops, if you have them, don't worry if not. You might also want to bring a swimsuit, but that is entirely optional.'

Her eyes widen. 'Optional, as in . . .?'

Catching her meaning, his head goes back as he laughs. 'I meant you can swim if you like, or not. But if you would prefer to do it in the nude . . .' He shrugs, and meets her eyes as he says, 'There will be no one to stop you.'

The following morning, with a tankini swimsuit under her sun top and knee-length shorts (she might be in reasonable shape for her age, but she definitely isn't up for skinny-dipping), Catie goes to sit on a wall outside the apartment building to wait in the sun.

A few minutes after the clocks begin their erratic chime of ten, she spots Giancarlo coming along the narrow, cobbled street, which is lined with shops and cafés. With him is a portly man who is gesticulating wildly as he speaks, and appearing very earnest about whatever he is saying.

As they reach her, Giancarlo smiles into her eyes and puts a hand on the man's shoulder to stop him. 'Paolo,' he says, swivelling the man in her direction, 'let me introduce you to my good friend Caterina. Caterina, this is Paolo

Lombardo, a very fine *consigliere* who is hoping to become mayor at the next election.'

Consigliere? Didn't they feature in *The Godfather*?

Apparently unfazed by suddenly being spoken to in English, Lombardo gives a charming smile and takes Catie's hand as he makes a friendly little bow. 'It is a pleasure to meet you, *signora*,' he says in heavily accented English. 'May I h'ask, are you resident of Taormina?'

'No, she is not,' Giancarlo replies in a decidedly droll tone, 'so no good trying to win a vote.'

Lombardo grins good-naturedly and shrugs as if to say, *Can't blame me for trying.*

'You will need to excuse me now,' Giancarlo tells him bluntly, 'but I have enjoyed our chat.'

'Ah, *sì, sì*,' Lombardo responds with alacrity and, clasping one of Giancarlo's hands in both of his, he says, 'It was good to see you too, *amico mio*. I will certainly follow your advice.' To Catie he says, 'I wish you a delightful day, *signora*. Very good sunshine for this time of year. Like summer.'

Catie smiles. 'I've certainly chosen the right time to come,' she remarks, and realizes she's managed to give a double-meaning to her words by glancing at Giancarlo.

His raised eyebrows tell her that he's recognized it too.

After Lombardo has gone, Giancarlo takes her towel bag and, hooking it over one shoulder, gestures for her to start walking with him.

'That was polite of Signor Lombardo to continue speaking in English,' she observes as they stroll towards the piazza where she'd enjoyed an early morning coffee an hour ago.

'He is a good man, and an astute politician,' Giancarlo responds, his amused tone causing her to glance at him.

'You might not be a resident,' he says by way of explanation, 'but you are a friend of mine and I do have a vote.'

Catching on, she laughs, and adds – because why not? – 'You said he's a *consigliere*?'

'Mm, mm,' he replies, nodding to the florist who's filling vases in his shop window.

'Isn't that something to do with the Mafia?' she asks, and even as she says the word she feels foolish – even more so when he starts to laugh.

'A *consigliere* is a councillor,' he explains, 'but I think you have seen *The Godfather* movies?' Without waiting for an answer, he adds, 'I'm sure you must know by now that there is no Mafia in Sicily any more.'

As his tone is loaded with irony, she can only assume that there is still a presence; however, she goes along with it saying, 'Of course, there isn't. I can't imagine what I was thinking.'

'Nor can I,' he grins, and cupping her elbow he turns their direction to the steps that rise to the Via Pirandello.

When they reach the top, she says, a little breathlessly, 'Can I ask where we're going?'

There's more traffic now, so they're clearly outside of the old town.

'To the *funivia*,' he replies, waiting for a couple of tourist coaches to pass before crossing them over the road. 'Have you ever ridden in one?'

'Yes, once, in Lucerne,' she tells him as they reach the other side.

Relaxing into a steadier pace he says, 'Ah, Lucerne, a beautiful city. Were you there for a holiday?'

'Actually no, it was a wedding. The happy couple flew us out there to play at the reception, and you're right, it's a beautiful city.'

'As is most of Switzerland. It is my favourite place to ski. Do you ski?'

Though she falters at the question, she quickly pushes the image of Alps, snow, anything to do with the sport, out of her mind, and says, 'Not really, I prefer the beach, which I presume is where we're going?'

He comes to a stop, and hits a hand to his head as he cries, 'How did you guess?'

She has to laugh. 'Because that's the only place the cable car goes?'

As they board with several tourists, he takes her hand and draws her to the front where they can enjoy the slow-motion feel of a fairground ride. As they descend the mountainside, he points out the football field where his son often played as a boy; the scattering of residences descending like steps in the rocks . . . And, of course, spread out in front of them like a whole other world is the gentle aquamarine sea and endless expanse of blue, blue sky.

At the bottom they walk through to a small, crescent-shaped beach where dozens of sunbathers are already laid out on loungers or paddling in the waves.

'*Giancarlo! Da questa parte, per favore.*'

Understanding the words, mainly because the scrawny man who's just stepped out of a small hut is pointing along the pontoon that circles behind the beach, Catie looks up at Giancarlo.

'You will see,' he murmurs, and puts a hand gently on her back as they follow the man. Catie looks down at the beach-lovers and, not for the first time in her life, admires the Italian lack of inhibition.

Soon they come to another part of the beach with no sunworshippers on the pebbles, just ten or more small boats bobbing close to the shore. A young lad with a shock of inky curls and a dazzling smile comes to greet them.

'Buongiorno, *Dottore*,' he says, holding out a hand to shake.

'Tomasso,' Giancarlo smiles warmly, and pulls the boy into an avuncular embrace. '*Come stai. E come sta la famiglia?*'

The boy answers in Italian, but it's clear to Catie that Giancarlo knows the lad, and, by the sound of it, is asking after his family.

'Tomasso speaks only a little English,' Giancarlo explains, turning to Catie, 'but he would like me to tell you that you are very safe in my hands, or he would not be allowing us to use his boat.'

Catie shoots him a look, fairly certain this isn't exactly what Tomasso said. Nevertheless, she holds out a hand to shake the boy's, saying, '*Mi scusi, non parlo italiano* but *grazie mille* for the boat.'

Tomasso beams and she doesn't miss the small bundle of euros being pressed into the lad's shirt pocket.

'*Dottore?*' she asks quietly as Tomasso turns to speak to someone behind him.

'It is a title of respect, no more,' Giancarlo explains, 'although I am a doctor of engineering, so in this case he is correct.'

'You leave shoes here?' Tomasso suggests, pointing to Catie's sandals.

Seeing Giancarlo kicking off his, she follows suit, then wades into the water after him to a small green wooden vessel with an outboard motor at the stern and a pale blue canopy, held up by a metal frame, protecting the helm.

She's aware that her climb aboard is not the most elegant manoeuvre she's ever made; however she lands without tipping into the sea, and decides to ignore the fact that Giancarlo is trying not to laugh.

He, of course, steps easily aboard, gets behind the wheel and, after Tomasso has started the engine, he begins steering them wide of the nearby rocks.

For the next half an hour, maybe longer, they putter around the coastline, never far from shore, going first to Baia delle Sirene – Mermaid Cove, he translates – before motoring gently in and out of an enthralling grotto of hidden smugglers' caves. The sun blazes through gaps in the rocks and the water is so translucent that it's possible to see to the bottom, where fish swim lazily around islands of pebbles and seaweed stretches its tangled limbs into the current.

From her bench seat, happily exposed to the late morning sun, Catie looks back to Giancarlo and smiles to see how absorbed he seems in his task. His long, dark hair is ruffled by the breeze, his white linen shirt billows softly against his skin. She wonders what he's thinking, what this small, exotic part of the world really means to him.

Apparently sensing her watching him, his eyes come to hers and he smiles.

Her heart flutters with pleasure, and though she knows he won't be able to hear her above the engine, she says, 'It was a good idea.'

And it was, because she's feeling so relaxed and happy, so free of everything that could weigh her down, so glad she took the risk in coming here, that she'd stop time right now if she could. No more past, no future even, just this.

Eventually, still not far from shore, with white-topped waves licking at the nearby rocks, he kills the boat's engine and drags an ice chest from beneath the helm.

She laughs in surprise as he takes out a dripping bottle of Prosecco, two glasses, and a mix of almond cakes and tiny biscotti.

'This here,' he says, when they are sitting opposite one another enjoying their unexpected (at least for her) refreshment, 'is Isola Bella.' He is pointing towards a large tree-covered outcrop of rock just ahead of them. 'You know that means "beautiful island".'

She nods, taking a sip of her drink.

'It's possible to walk there from the shore when the tide is in,' he tells her. 'It is full of exotic plants, mostly brought in by Florence Trevelyan, the Englishwoman who once owned it.'

Recognizing the name, she says, 'Didn't she create the Communal Gardens?'

He nods. 'But here is a very special place. Florence built a house, you can see it, yes?'

She can, at least the roof of one; the rest is hidden by rocks and greenery.

'It's said that she allowed lovers to meet here, and because of this the whole island is enchanted.'

For a moment Catie is rapt, imagining who the lovers might have been, how star-crossed, or happy, how illicit or unlucky until – realizing he's probably making it up – she turns to look at him.

He laughs and, stripping off his shirt, suddenly tips himself backwards into the sea.

He resurfaces, moments later, olive-skinned, strong, seeming half his age, and calls for her to join him.

So, putting aside her glass, she removes her own top and shorts and launches herself off the boat in a joyous leap.

An hour later, their hair and clothes still wet from their swim, Giancarlo and Catie are shown to a beachside table in a local restaurant, where, of course, Giancarlo knows the owner.

162

Is there anyone he doesn't know?

They are served more Prosecco and a plate each of the most succulent *gamberoni*, the shells and whiskery heads glistening in olive oil, garlic and flakes of chilli.

After breaking one open, he closes his eyes in ecstasy as he eats it, and encourages her to follow suit.

She's already there and gives a quiet moan of pleasure as the flavours and texture fill her senses.

'You are a good swimmer,' he tells her, tearing open a second prawn.

Her eyes sparkle. 'I know you let me win the race,' she counters, 'but I'm sure I could have beaten you anyway.'

He cocks a sceptical eyebrow. 'Mm, maybe. We shall put it to the test the next time.'

Liking the thought of a 'next time', she licks the delicious oil from her fingers, then dips them in a bowl. 'It makes me feel so young, being here,' she sighs, picking up her glass and taking in the picture-postcard scene of beach, boats and bay. 'When I was young, I'd have imagined feeling old at sixty-three, but now . . . It doesn't feel old at all, does it?'

He shrugs. 'I don't know, I'm only forty.'

She splutters on a laugh.

'Let me tell you,' he says softly, 'you look only forty-three, and you are making me, a sixty-five-year-old, feel that age too.'

A small rush of warmth colours her cheeks, and she holds up her glass for him to clink his own against it. 'To us youngsters,' she smiles.

'To us,' he echoes, 'and to whatever you wish to achieve while you're in Taormina.'

Her eyes drift as she considers his words. What is she trying to achieve, really? What is the point in reliving her life when there is no way to change any of it now? And yet she can't get away from the fact that it's the reason she came, to try to figure out where she went wrong, what she might have done differently, and how, when the time comes, to take the next steps forward.

Moving on from here feels like an impossible task right now, and one she isn't willing even to think about.

Turning back to him, she says, 'You've never really told me about your mother.'

A slightly comical light comes into his eyes as he says, '*Ah, mia madre.* Well, she lives about a mile from me in Turin, in a house that she insists on running herself with the help of only a housekeeper. Next month she will be ninety-two. She still drives her car, though many of us wish she would not. She hosts aperitifs for her friends at six every evening – there are far fewer of them now than there used to be – and she goes to mass on Sundays. She likes to paint when her hands aren't too painful, usually water-colours, sometimes in oil, and occasionally she has an exhibition. She loves her family, but will not allow any of us to interfere in her life. She enjoys yoga and tai chi and recently I heard from her housekeeper, Cara, that she is considering Internet dating.'

Catie chokes on a laugh. 'Seriously?'

'Knowing her as I do, I'm sure she is having some fun at Cara's expense, or maybe at mine, because she knows Cara will tell me.'

Entranced by the thought of this eccentric old woman, whom he clearly adores, Catie says, 'She sounds delightful.'

'She is, in many ways. We are all extremely fond of her, but she is also formidable, stubborn, opinionated and, I'm afraid, a little too Catholic.'

Catie frowns her confusion.

'One of my nephews is gay, and every now and again she tries to talk my brother into getting his son some treatment.'

'Ah, I see.' Then, 'I guess she's too set in her ways, her beliefs, to change them now?'

'She is, but over the years many of us have tried.' He waits as their plates are cleared and, refilling their glasses, he says, 'So that is my mother. Will you tell me more about yours now?'

As Catie looks out across the bay, she feels a dip in her spirits to think of what happened after her father died. It's as if the sun has suddenly gone in and the day has become a tiny bit colder.

CHAPTER TWENTY-SIX

It was a chilly, starry night, around five months after her father's death, that Catie arrived at her parents' house – she still couldn't think of it solely as her mother's – to find the front door on the latch and no sign of Patty outside.

Unbuttoning her coat, she pushed the door open and stepped inside. The familiar smell instantly overwhelmed her, almost crushing her heart. It was as if her father was still here, his presence so strong it felt tangible. Maybe he was in the kitchen, or the front room listening to music, or outside somewhere seeing to his vegetable patch. If she called out she was sure he'd appear from wherever he was and laughingly pull her into his arms. He'd make a joke about not being able to get so close these days with the baby swelling out her belly. *Really, another two months to go?* he'd cry incredulously. *Are you sure you're not carrying twins?*

But he wasn't here, he'd never say it, and it didn't matter how many months or years went by, she knew she'd never be able to bear it.

'Mum!' she called out. 'It's me!'

She closed the front door, switched on the hall light and went through to the kitchen. Although there was no sign of her mother, someone had to be here because the light was on and she could smell something . . . burning? She quickly checked the oven, then the fire in the living room, but both were off, and the house, she realized, was cold. She put a hand on a radiator and wondered why the heating was so low when it was the end of November.

'Mum!' she called again. Where was she?

Feeling the wrenching guilt of not coming more often, for failing to be more understanding of her mother's grief when she was so wrapped up in her own, she returned to the kitchen.

It wasn't as if Patty had made things easy since Mac's passing. She kept saying she didn't want visitors, she was fine on her own, and it was too far to come to Abbots Leigh when she didn't have a car.

'I don't want to make a fuss,' she'd tell Lawrence when he offered to pick her up.

'It's no trouble,' he'd insist. 'We want to see you.'

'Well, that's as maybe, but I'd rather stay here, thanks very much.'

Catie didn't try as hard to persuade her, knowing better than Lawrence how stubborn her mother could be. She'd never admit it to anyone, but it was easier not seeing Patty too often, and she suspected the feeling was mutual. Their grief was so terrible that neither of them could bear to see the other suffering; it was too harsh a reminder of what they'd lost; too horrible to know that they could never fill the gaping hole for one another.

Going to the foot of the stairs, Catie shouted, 'Mum! Are you up there?'

Still no reply, and all was in darkness.

Starting to feel afraid of what she might find if she went up to the bedrooms, she forced herself to do it anyway.

To her relief, everything seemed to be as it should, and no one was in the bathroom.

She wondered if her mother had gone to work and left the door on the latch. She did two evenings a week at the local Co-op now, and during the day she was, as she called it, a 'good-old-fashioned home-help'. Gramps had passed on several years ago, but her mother continued to look after the elderly who came and went from the bungalows, so maybe one of them had taken sick.

Whatever, it was unlike her mother not to lock the door if she was going to be out for a while, although everyone was forgetful at times, even the assiduous Patty.

Maybe she should just take what she'd come for and leave a note to let her mother know that she had it. Would it be wrong to help herself to her father's music without asking first? Didn't it belong to her as much as it did her mother? More even? Though she wasn't sure what she'd do with it yet, she was hoping that after the baby was born, she'd find the heart to sing again. And one of the first things she wanted to do was play, sing and record everything Mac had written. It might not be very good in most people's views – he'd endured a lot of good-natured joshing from the band over the corniness of some of his lyrics – but it would mean everything to her to be able to lift it from the music sheets and give it life.

It wouldn't bring him back, of course, but lately she'd developed a visceral, inescapable need to do it.

'Then go and get it,' Lawrence had said last night. 'Patty will understand. She's probably expecting you to take it.'

Going to her parents' bedroom window, she pulled aside one of the closed curtains and looked down into the small back garden. It took a moment for her to understand what she was seeing – her mother was standing over the old metal dustbin that Mac had used for bonfires, and the flames springing out of it were so high that it almost looked as though Patty was in them.

Running awkwardly down the stairs, one hand supporting the bulge of the baby, the other clutching the banister, she hurried through to the back door and out into the garden.

'Mum! What are you doing?' she cried over the roar and crackle of flames.

Patty didn't look up, simply continued to feed the fire from a box she was holding under one arm, as if nothing else in the world mattered more than what she was doing.

'Mum! For God's sake!' Catie shouted and, picking her way round the dead cabbages and a wheelbarrow full of dirt, she came to the other side of the fire. 'What are you burning?' she shouted.

'I have to get rid of it,' Patty said fiercely. 'He's gone, so there's no point hanging on to any of it.'

Catie's eyes rounded in horror as she registered what her mother was destroying. 'No!' she cried, frantically, almost stumbling into the flames as she tried to get to Patty. 'Mum! You have to stop,' she screamed. 'It's his music, the songs he wrote . . .'

'I know what it is and he won't be needing it any more, so . . .'

'But I will! *Mum! Please! You have to stop!*'

'Get away from me, Catie.'

Catie tried to grab the box, but Patty snatched it clear and upended it so fast that everything was swallowed into the heat of the flames before Catie could save it.

'I can't believe this,' Catie sobbed despairingly and, grabbing a stick, she tried to rescue something, anything, but it was no use, the fire was too hot and if she got any closer she'd go up in flames too. As it was, her sleeves were scorched and maybe her hair was too.

Patty was dumping his clothes and shoes into the inferno now.

'Mum! Oh God,' Catie wailed, covering her face with her hands. 'This isn't what he'd want. You know that.'

'It doesn't matter what he wants, does it?' Patty shot back.

Catie's breath was coming too fast, her head was swirling and she felt sick. Her dad's music, the tunes he'd composed for the band, the arrangements of old numbers, the ballads, the half-written lyrics, the collection of vintage manuscripts . . . How could her mother do this? What the hell had possessed her? She would know more than anyone how much Catie would treasure it all.

She looked at her mother's face in the firelight, half demented with grief, and shouted, 'I'm never going to forgive you for this, I hope you know that.'

Patty rounded on her. 'And I'm never going to forgive you,' she snarled furiously. 'He died because of you, you selfish cow. He'd do anything for you – and in the end he gave up his bloody life for you so that baby could be born. God gives and He takes away. So don't come here telling me you'll never forgive me. Your precious father is dead because of you and nothing, *nothing* means anything without him, not even you.'

Catie took a step back, knocked into an old wooden bench and picked herself up again. She clutched the washing line and then the post to propel herself back to the house. She needed to get out of here, to be as far away from her mother as she could get.

Patty was shouting again, but Catie could no longer hear her. She pushed into the kitchen and out along the hall. Minutes later she was in her car, reeking of smoke and hardly able to catch her breath.

So, her mother believed the same as she did, that for every death there was a birth, and if she hadn't wanted so desperately to have a baby, her dad might still be here. It was the kind of selfless thing Mac would do.

Matthew David MacAllister Vaughan came squalling into the world ten weeks later, all nine pounds three ounces of him, red-faced, angry, and wanting nothing to do with his mother. Not then, and not when they got home either.

Though Catie tried hard with her feelings, her heart was empty, and the feeding was so painful and horribly distressing for them both that she longed to stop. The awful, shameful truth of it was that she didn't want to breastfeed at all. She just wished someone would take him away and give him whatever he needed, because she simply couldn't. Every time she heard him cry, and he hardly stopped, she wanted to clap her hands over her ears and scream with bitter frustration and resentment. She knew she was the worst person in the world, that she'd done this to herself and to her baby by wanting him too much, and now they were stuck with one another.

As the weeks passed, she continued trying to bond with him, knowing she had to, but the way he bawled if she went near him, or became hysterical if she attempted to pick him up was terrifying. His takeover of their lives felt like a horrendous punishment, although she couldn't be clear about what she was being punished for. If her father really had given up his life for his grandson, wouldn't the baby be sweet and gentle and full of love, just like Mac?

She'd never told anyone about the 'death for a birth' fear that she and her mother had become tangled up in. No one, not even Lawrence knew what Patty had said to her on that terrible night. He thought their estrangement was caused by Patty's burning of Mac's music, and he wasn't wrong about that, it just wasn't the whole story.

Lawrence, thank God, was a wonderful father. Matthew rarely cried while in his arms and, if he did, it took Lawrence next to no time to settle him. He changed nappies, made up the formula, bathed and dressed him, walked him around the neighbourhood in his baby-sling, and spent hours reading to him even when he was asleep. While he was at work Marilyn, the ever-doting granny and disapproving mother-in-law who'd all but moved back into the house, was as able, it seemed, to handle her demanding grandson as Lawrence. No baby tantrums for Marilyn; no refusing to eat or to lie still in the magnificent 3-in-1 pram-carrycot-pushchair Granny had bought him.

His other granny, Patty, never came to see him. She didn't even send a card after Lawrence called from the hospital to tell her that the birth had been difficult, but mother and baby were doing fine.

'That's good,' Patty had said shortly. 'Thanks for letting me know.'

That was it. No communication since, and it was tearing Catie apart to realize how much her mother resented her; that she probably had for years, maybe since birth, and that she'd truly meant it when she'd said she was never going to forgive her.

It didn't seem Matthew was going to either. Was he able, on some level, to sense that she didn't really want him? Sometimes, if he was sleeping, she'd stand over him and try to feel something more than just sorry that she was his mother. And wretched that she'd deprived him of the best grandpa in the world.

Throughout this terrible time Lawrence tried to coax her to take care of herself, even if it was too hard right now to cope with the baby. Maybe she should listen to some music, or get in touch with her agent to talk about taking on some gigs again.

She couldn't face any of it, and sensed that Lawrence was becoming deeply worried and frustrated. Though he never shouted at her, she could tell he wanted to, and sometimes she wished he would. Whether it would make a difference she had no idea, but she did know that even his tears of despair never seemed to move her. She didn't want him to be sad, any more than she wanted the baby to be angry, and she hated being the cause of it, but there seemed nothing she could do to change it.

She wasn't sure at what point Jude started coming to the house; maybe she'd been helping out for months while Catie lay upstairs in bed, unable to confront the world. She knew she should mind about her old nemesis being in her home, interfering in her family life, but Lawrence had to work and Marilyn couldn't do everything on her own. And it seemed the baby was happy to be with Jude. Catie never heard him crying or throwing a temper when she was around. All the anger and rejection were reserved for her.

He was seven months old by the time Lawrence and the health visitor finally persuaded Catie to get a referral from the GP to see a counsellor.

'You don't have to do it alone,' Lawrence told her, holding her hand and gazing anxiously into her pale face. 'I'll be with you every step of the way, if you want me to be, and whatever it takes we'll get you back to your old self.'

Catie simply stared at him from the depths of her misery, not knowing what to say.

'Janice, the health visitor,' he went on, 'has already made an appointment with Dr Gordon. I know you've seen him before and he prescribed antidepressants, but you haven't taken them so we need to find out what else can be done.'

So, for Lawrence's sake more than her own, she began a course of cognitive behaviour therapy and agreed to take the antidepressants. Lawrence made sure of it by handing her the pills and water himself. She could have cheated and spat them out when he wasn't looking, but he didn't deserve that. He needed to know she had the will to get better, and maybe, one day soon, she'd start to find it.

'I want Jude to stop coming here,' she told him one night after standing at her bedroom window during the afternoon, watching Jude with her own two daughters and Matthew in the garden. They'd looked like a happy, bonded family, presided over by an adoring granny, and Catie, in a sudden surge of protectiveness, had almost rushed out there to grab Matthew away from them. He was her son, not Jude's, or Marilyn's, and if either of those scheming witches thought Jude was going to insinuate her way into Lawrence's life this way, they had another think coming.

'She's been quite worried about you,' Lawrence said gently, 'and Matthew likes playing with the girls.'

'I'm sure he does, but he's still young, he won't know any different if they stop coming.'

When Lawrence didn't answer, she turned to look at him and saw how torn and awkward he felt.

'You have to know what's going on here,' she cried, throwing out her hands. 'She's helping out, yes, and your mother's allowing it because they think you'll eventually give up on me and turn to Jude.'

'Jude's happily married!' he protested. 'She doesn't have any designs on me.'

'You can tell yourself that, but believe me, that's what's

happening here. So unless you want her to take over as Matthew's mother, you need to tell her to stop coming.'

'Of course I don't want that. *You* are his mother and you could be a damned good mother if you'd just let yourself try.'

'You mean if he'd let me try.'

'Catie, he's a baby. He doesn't know how to make things happen on the kind of level you're meaning it.'

'He's acting on his instincts and they're telling him to reject me.'

Sighing, he pushed a hand through his hair, clearly at a loss for what to say or do. 'Listen, the therapist has already told you you're the one doing the rejecting and you don't have to. You can accept him and love him the way I know you want to.'

Stiffly she said, 'Maybe I'm more like my own mother than I realized.'

'No! You are your father's daughter. You are more like him than anyone else alive, and that's why Matthew needs you, because only you can give him the kind of love that Mac would if he were here.'

With tears burning her eyes, Catie turned away. She wanted to remind him that Mac would be here if there was no Matthew, but since admitting to that fear in therapy with Lawrence in the room, she was trying to accept the nonsense of it.

'I have a surprise,' Lawrence said. 'I think you're going to like it and it'll mean Jude won't need to come so often to help Mum out. At least not for the next couple of weeks, anyway.'

Couple of weeks! That was hardly any time at all when she wanted Jude out of their lives completely.

'She's already here,' he said with a smile, and taking her

hand he tried to lead her out of the bedroom, until suddenly horrified she pulled away. 'If it's my mother. I'm not . . .'

'It isn't your mother, I promise. It's Lola.'

Catie almost gasped, clapped her hands to her mouth and regarded him disbelievingly.

'She's devoting her entire fortnight's leave to you,' he said tenderly. 'I thought you'd be pleased.'

Catie was starting to choke on a sob. 'I have to see her,' she cried, looking at the door. 'Is she really here?'

'Why don't you go and see for yourself?'

She raced down the stairs, almost stumbling and catching the banister to steady herself. It felt as if she didn't get there in the next couple of minutes, Lola would be gone.

But she was still there, in the kitchen, and the instant Cate saw her beloved face, her best friend for ever, she fell sobbing into her arms.

She knew it made no sense, and she wouldn't say it to anyone, but it was as if Mac had sent Lola, and because of that Catie knew everything was going to be all right.

CHAPTER TWENTY-SEVEN

***188: *How are things going with your friend?*

CM: *I haven't seen him for the past five days.*

***188: *Is this making the heart grow fonder?*

CM:

***188: *Are you afraid of having a relationship?*

CM: *Maybe. I don't want to complicate things for myself, or for him.*

***188: *Where is he?*

CM: *I don't know.*

***188: *Are you making some headway with the writing?*

CM: *Yes, some. I've reached the part where Lola came to the rescue after Matthew's birth. Do you have any news for me?*

***188: *No word from anyone. Are you finding the writing helpful?*

CM: *I'm still not sure yet.*

Catie is wandering along the Corso Umberto to find Giancarlo when she spots him outside the police station on Piazza Duomo. He appears to be in a heated exchange with a red-faced man whose fists are held up like a boxer's meaning business.

People are stopping to watch and listen, and as Giancarlo turns to walk away and immediately turns back again, this time standing so close to the smaller man that he might tread on him, there's a gasp.

Having never seen Giancarlo angry before, Catie merges with the tourists around the fountain, bracing herself worriedly for what might happen next.

To her astonishment, after some muttering, both men laugh and start slapping one another on the back, as if some sort of bizarre male ritual has just been concluded. People around her mutter and shake their heads, apparently disappointed to be denied some sport, and continue on with their day.

It isn't until Giancarlo spots her waiting on the fountain wall and comes to greet her that she notices how pale he is. His beautiful blue eyes look sore and shadowed.

'Are you OK?' she asks as he brushes a kiss to both her cheeks.

'I am excellent,' he assures her, 'but I hope I will not have to go to Palermo again for a while.' He adds, tenderly, as he takes in her suntanned face, 'Am I allowed to tell you I've missed you?'

Experiencing a pleasing lift in her heart she says, even

though she knows she shouldn't, 'I've missed you too.' Then, 'Why was Palermo so difficult?'

With a sigh, he slips an arm around her shoulders and turns them towards the Porta Catania. 'I can give you an answer,' he replies, 'but it is very tedious, all to do with microchip supply, so why don't we talk about something else? I was very happy to hear from Tony that you are taking a course in Sicilian cooking?'

She has to laugh. 'I've had one lesson,' she corrects, 'however, I think I might be able to conjure up a reasonable *occhi di lupo* with pistachios and ricotta – should you feel brave enough to try.'

'I am a very brave man,' he assures her, 'so maybe, when we return later, we can shop for what you need and take it back to your apartment?'

Liking the idea of that very much, she casually links her hand with the one of his that's dangling over her shoulder, and says, 'Am I allowed to ask what all that was about back there on the piazza?'

He chuckles, and twines his fingers more securely around hers. 'That was Alfredo Costa, from the *polizia municipale*, and what you saw was him challenging me to a boxing match, and me declining.'

'Seriously? And that's how it's done?'

'If you're Alfredo Costa it is. He is a little . . . eccentric, but a very good fellow, as you English would say. Now, today Ricardo is going to drive us to Mount Etna so you can see the great volcano at close quarters. I believe everyone who comes to Taormina should make this visit, but it is not all we will do. My housekeeper has prepared a picnic for us, which Ricardo has already taken to the car.'

Ducking with him as they pass two workmen coming through the ancient stone gate carrying an enormous ladder, she says, 'And are we going to a winery? I've read that there are quite a few on the slopes of Etna.'

'It's true, there are, and yes, we will visit one, but you won't have read about it. It's very small, quite exclusive in fact, and it produces some excellent wines which we shall taste. It's possible you'll meet Lorenzo, the *enologo*, and maybe his wife, Rina, will also be there. They are quite an old couple – even older than us,' he grins and she has to laugh. 'And they don't get many visitors, so I think they'll be happy to see us. Ah, there is Ricardo with the car,' and raising a hand to wave the driver over he opens the back door for her to get in.

'*Buongiorno*, Signora Catie,' Ricardo grunts as she slides into the cool leather seat. '*Come sta?*'

'*Sto bene, grazie,*' she replies fluently. 'It's nice to see you again.'

'*Sì, sì,*' he responds. '*Altrettanto.*'

Giancarlo slips in beside her and speaks first to Ricardo in Italian, then says to her, 'I would have driven us myself today, but if I do, I will not be able to drink the wine.'

She says, mischievously, 'I thought we were only supposed to taste at a vineyard.'

'You are in Sicily now,' he responds, pretending to be serious, and reaches for his seatbelt as Ricardo manoeuvres them out of the snarl-up between the post office, the old gate and a busy pizzeria.

For the next half an hour he is engrossed in replying to emails on his phone – 'I am sorry,' he apologizes, 'but I am very behind with everything' – so she rests her head on the seat-back and enjoys the passing scenery. She feels so glad to be here, and with him again, that her heart is swelling with the pleasure of it. Every now and again, she turns to him and they exchange smiles, though she can tell he's distracted. She wonders, idly, where this friendship of theirs is going, while knowing it should be nowhere. Whether she has that sort of willpower, she isn't yet sure, although he's never said, or done, anything to make her think that he wants any more than what they already share.

At last, he puts his phone aside and reaches for her hand. He hasn't been this intimate before, kissing her cheek on meeting, touching her hand, and now it's happened for the second time in as many hours. 'Do you feel like talking today?' he asks, turning towards her. 'I mean about you.'

She smiles and shakes her head. 'While you were away, I managed to write quite a lot down. If you'd like to read it . . .'

'Did you bring it with you?'

'No, I just wanted to enjoy today.'

He holds her eyes, searching them with his own, until finally he says, 'We shall do that.' His phone buzzes and, checking the message, he quickly replies before turning the phone off. 'My mother,' he tells her. 'She's heard where I am going today, and wants me to send her best wishes to Lorenzo and Rina.'

Amused, Catie says, 'How has she heard?'

'Fiorella,' he replies drily, 'this is my mother, she knows everything. We are not always sure how, but this time I expect she has spoken to my brother.'

'You told your brother where you're going today?'

'He called last night to make sure I am planning to check on *la fattoria* – our grandmother's old house – while I'm in Taormina. It is in the countryside, outside Linguaglossa, on the slopes of Etna. I'm afraid it is a little run-down now, but Lorenzo and Rina live less than a kilometre away and they are there most days, repairing or cleaning and taking care of the vines.'

She's thinking of Daphne Phelps's Sicilian house, Casa Cuseni, as she stares down at their joined hands, his fingers, large and strong around hers, making them seem almost fragile in his loose grip, and pale – in spite of her tan – next to his Mediterranean colouring.

When she looks up she finds him watching her, and as his eyes drop to her mouth she feels, for a stirring moment, as though he has kissed her.

She wants to ask how he did that, how it's possible to feel as though he touched her when he didn't, but she isn't willing to break the moment, simply wants to carry on looking at him and feeling the breathlessness seeming to tighten the space between them.

In the front Ricardo starts to speak, and Giancarlo turns away, gently releasing her hand as he tells her to look out at the volcanic territory they are now driving through.

It is spectacular in its own unique way, an undulating and towering landscape of porous black and grey rock, with enormous craters and gullies carved into the mountainside. He tells her about the explosions that have occurred during her lifetime, one as recently as the previous June, though none major enough to cause serious damage.

'The last devastating eruption,' he continues, 'was in 1928, when the city of Mascali was destroyed.'

'I've read about it,' she tells him. 'Daphne Phelps's uncle, the one who built Casa Cuseni, helped rescue people. It's part of what made him a hero in Taormina.'

'Yes, Robert Kitson did many things for Taormina and surrounding areas to earn himself great affection and respect. My Sicilian grandmother knew him back in the 1920s and 1930s, and my mother has inherited a few of his paintings.'

Catie says, 'I'm impressed – and oddly pleased by the thought of your two families being linked.'

He smiles and speaks to Ricardo, giving him directions, it seems, for they soon break away from the tourist traffic climbing to the crater, and start to wind a descent through more volcanic terrain until they reach the lushly verdant slopes of orchards and vineyards.

'I hope you didn't want to go all the way to the top,' he says as they pull up outside a ramshackle cottage. 'It is a very steep walk and can be icy cold and we don't have the right shoes or coats.'

'I can live without visiting a crater,' she assures him, and noticing him wincing as he unfastens his seatbelt, she adds, 'Are you sure you're all right? You look as though you accepted the boxing match – and lost.'

He grins and says, 'I probably would against Alfredo. He is, how do you say, *un mostro nell'arena*. A monster in the ring. Come on, let me introduce you to Lorenzo and Rina.'

As they step out of the car into the warm sulphurous air, she breaks into a smile as an elderly Italian couple bustle forward to greet them. They are so pleased to see Giancarlo that they are both clutching their hearts, his hands, their own faces, with loud exclamations of joy.

Catie coughs down a laugh as Giancarlo tells her, in English, 'I was here last week.'

It's only when they treat her to a similarly rapturous welcome that she thinks he might have been serious. Though they speak no English, the way they look from her to Giancarlo, gesticulating and urging her to come in – '*Entrare, prego*' – more or less speaks for them.

They make their way around the side of the house, which turns out to be much larger and grander than it appears from the front. They descend two flights of stone steps adjoining many tiers of harvested vines, to a terrace that overlooks the vast and enchanting valley of Linguaglossa, all the way down to the sea. Every part of it, from the tumbling terraces of yet more vineyards and fruit trees to the tantalizing glimpses of other properties further afield, to the magnificent rise of the mountains opposite, the stateliness of Etna behind and the scattered rooftops of the town in the valley, makes her heart soar with so much emotion she feels it might take flight. The light is magical, pure, seeming to transcend reality to create its own dream-like world.

'This,' she says, softly, as Giancarlo comes to stand with her at one of *la fattoria*'s balustrades, two glasses of wine in his hands, 'is where you spent your summers as a child?' She can't help contrasting it with her own family's week-long caravan breaks in Croyde, in March, because it was cheaper at that time of year. Or at the Lido in Fishponds, which didn't involve the expense of going away. And once, after Patty won fifty quid on the bingo, a chalet near Dawlish.

'Mostly,' he replies and, after holding his glass up to the light, he twirls it gently before tipping the rich, amber wine into his mouth. 'This is our best Carricante. I think you will find it fruity at first, with an undertone of mineral, to be expected from this region.'

She drinks and finds he's described it perfectly, for she easily picks up the flavours, and then she isn't sure if she likes the wine for its taste, or simply because it's his.

Keeping his voice low he says, 'I'm afraid our picnic must wait. Rina was warned we were coming and so she has baked us a lasagne. It will offend her if we refuse.'

Loving the promise of a home-cooked Sicilian meal, she turns her back to the view and gazes up at the house. Its high, sun-baked walls are a mix of old pale and russet stones, and most of its tall, mullion windows, some hugged by filigree balconies, are topped with decorative architraves. Although the shutters are closed, giving the impression the whole place is sleeping, its charm, its quiet grandeur, is utterly captivating.

'It has so much character,' she says, her gaze moving along to the tower at one end where large French doors (she suspects they're called something else here) are opened up wide to the terrace, and a castellated roof is crumbling with age. 'I almost feel like it could speak if we listened hard enough. Maybe it can sense we're here.'

He smiles and gazes up at it too. 'It will be hard to let it go when we find a buyer,' he sighs, 'but it is better for it to have a family who visits often, or even someone who lives here.'

She thinks of how much she'd love to be that person; how completely wonderful it would be to spend her days bringing the old place back to life and waking up each morning to this magnificent view. She could learn everything Sicilian, from cooking, to wine-making, to harvesting, to making honey in the abandoned hives.

'What are you thinking?' he asks, taking another sip of his wine.

She tells him, and adds, 'I'm not sure how good it is to dream when you know it can never come true. It ends up feeling like a loss.'

He considers this and says, 'Maybe it is more beneficial to live in the moment, but dreams matter, even at our age.'

Laughing, she treats him to a baleful look, and wanders towards the table that has been set for them in a gazebo surrounded by flowering oleanders and almond trees.

When Rina brings the food, the dish is so large that Giancarlo insists everyone must eat with them. So, Ricardo is summoned from the car, and Lorenzo carries out many bottles of wine, while Rina happily serves them the most delicious lasagne Catie has ever tasted.

It isn't long before they fall into easy chatter and hilarious translations, and when they learn that Catie is a singer, they plead with her to sing for them. Giancarlo steps in to the rescue, and a moment later Lorenzo is treating them to a full-throated and entirely tuneful version of '*Volare*'.

When he comes to the end, his small audience breaks into rapturous applause and cheers, as red-faced, he beams and bows, saying, '*Sono migliore di Dean Martin. Giusto?*'

'Better than Dean Martin,' Giancarlo translates quietly.

'*Sì, sì,*' Catie cries, still applauding and only wishing she'd been able to duet with him, but she no longer has the voice, or the heart.

Finally, it is time to leave, and Rina embraces her warmly, urging her to come again, before holding Giancarlo back for a moment to speak privately. Catie has no idea what they're saying, but after a while suspects it's about her from the way they keep looking at her and smiling. Or in Giancarlo's case, shaking his head and nodding. Then Lorenzo comes to say goodbye and, as he plants a hand firmly on Giancarlo's shoulder, Catie hears Giancarlo's sharp intake of breath, as if the fond gesture has caused him pain.

Minutes later they are travelling back down the mountain, passing hikers and sightseers, more lunar-type landscapes and olive groves, when Catie says, 'I saw what happened when Lorenzo put a hand . . .' She stops as he touches a finger to his lips and nods towards the front of the car.

Understanding that he doesn't want to speak in front of Ricardo, she lets it drop, for now, and injects a droll tone into her voice as she says, 'I got the impression you and Rina were discussing me before we left.'

'Ah, yes,' he replies, apparently ready to admit it. 'She wants to know if I am going to make you my wife.'

Startled, as much by the question as her own reaction to it, she says, 'And what did you tell her?'

'I informed her that we are both married to other people, so the answer is no.'

She turns away feeling oddly flattened by his response, while reflecting on how right he'd been when he'd said it was better to live in the moment, because even that fleeting little dream has left her feeling as though she's lost something.

'Are you still married?' he asks carefully.

She starts to answer, but finds, for the moment, that she doesn't have the words. So she says, 'I think, after so much lasagne, that my *occhi di lupo* will have to wait for another day.'

He nods agreement, and she watches him turn to gaze out of the window, as if something else is now on his mind.

Neither of them speaks again until they reach the Porta Catania, where Ricardo drops them.

'What is it?' she asks as the car drives away. 'I can tell you're worried about something.'

He doesn't deny it, but nor does he engage with it. He simply takes her hand as they walk into the old town, and a few minutes later he says, 'I will take you to the apartment, but I'm afraid I will not be able to stay after all. There are things I must do this evening.'

Disappointed, and still worried, she says, 'That's OK.' Then, 'I've had a wonderful day, thank you.'

He smiles and raises her hand to his mouth. 'I will come to find you in the morning and bring your favourite cannoli.'

Relieved to know that he's planning to see her again so soon, she says, 'I'll make the coffee.'

'That's good.'

The next morning she wakes early and, because the weather is still like summer, she sets the table outside, before running out to the market to buy a small bunch of flowers. He hadn't said what time to expect him, but she feels sure it will be between nine and ten.

At midday, when the clocks start to chime the hour, she is still sitting alone, wishing she had his phone number, and wondering why she hasn't. It's true she's never asked for it, but is there a reason why he hasn't offered it?

Will she ever stop feeling suspicious, afraid to trust and as if she must keep doubting in order to protect herself? It doesn't seem to happen when she's with him, or not so much, but when left alone with her thoughts and misgivings and the mostly closed book of his life, is it any wonder she falls prey to the demons of her past?

CHAPTER TWENTY-EIGHT

Having Lola at her side, so capable and understanding, so ready to give everything of herself, turned out to be the miracle Catie needed to help start lifting her out of her depression. Even before Lola's two weeks were up and she had to return to work, Catie was managing to hold Matthew for short spells without fear, or self-loathing, or resentment, and Matthew, thank God, no longer screamed every time she went near him.

It was as if some awful band of tension had been snapped, allowing everyone to breathe more easily again.

Lola also dealt pretty effectively with Jude, telling her that she understood how close Jude was to Marilyn, and it was extremely kind of them both to be so concerned about Catie, but could they possibly stop caring so much and give Catie the space to begin standing on her own two feet? This would mean, Lola continued, unabashed, that they should no longer come and go from the house as if it were theirs – a truly colossal cheek on Lola's part given it actually was Marilyn's.

'You've been a tremendous support through this difficult time,' she told them on the day she left, 'but I know you've seen the improvement in Catie lately, so if you could try to start trusting her instincts a little more readily than your own, I'm sure that everything will turn out for the very best.'

Lawrence burst out laughing when he came home that night and had all this related to him, and was sorry that Lola had already left as he'd have liked to congratulate her in person. As Catie watched him, laughing too, she could feel more of the darkness that had plagued her starting to shift. Her blood felt as though it was running warm in her veins again, and her heart seemed to beat with more than just pain and grief. She loved her husband so much and now, looking at him, feeling his relief and his love, made her thank God that she hadn't lost him during this terrible time.

'Hey, that's never going to happen,' he told her tenderly when she voiced the fear. 'You mean everything to me, you know that, and so does he,' he added, smiling down at his son asleep in his mother's arms. An event they'd all started to dread might never happen.

'We've had the best day ever,' Catie whispered, gazing at Matthew's fat, flushed cheeks and tiny mouth. 'We've played and laughed.' She looked up at Lawrence. 'I swear, I made him laugh, and it just about did me in. He's so adorable. He kicked his legs like a proper footballer as I changed his nappy, I think he was actually enjoying it. I even got him into the backpack to take him for a walk down at the pools. So, it seems you're no longer the only one he's going to allow to do that.'

She didn't bother to mention how he'd punched her in the face and made her lip bleed when she'd tried to give him some tomato soup. It was obviously an accident; babies did that sort of thing to their mothers all the time.

Over the weeks that followed, to Catie's amazement, Marilyn and Jude kept their distance, only traipsing across the garden to the house when invited. (Jude was only asked because Matthew clearly adored her girls and it wouldn't be fair to stop him from seeing them.) Lola visited as often as she could, and spending time with her always seemed to give Catie an extra boost.

'I can hardly believe we are where we are,' Catie smiled one evening as she and Lola sat cosily together on a sofa with one-year-old Matthew finally asleep upstairs in his cot. He'd been screaming for most of the day, working himself into such a frenzy that he'd thrown up his food and ripped out handfuls of Catie's hair. He was teething, of course, she understood that, but the constant crying and lack of sleep were starting to get her down again.

'You mean that you're a mother and I'm still a spinster of the parish?' Lola responded dryly.

'No,' Catie protested. 'I was meaning that I'm a stay-at-home, not-very good mum, and there's you, a career-driven, highly successful and stunningly lovely young woman totally in charge of her own life.'

Lola grimaced as she laughed. 'I'd hardly call a senior air stewardess highly successful, or thirty-four young, and you're not getting away with not-very-good mum. You're fantastic with him now. OK, it's difficult while he's teething and having to be watched all the time now he's practically walking, but you're doing brilliantly.'

Catie scoffed. 'Not true, but let's stop talking about me. I want to hear more about you and your travels . . . Are you still seeing the pilot?'

Lola sipped her wine. 'You mean the *married* pilot? I'm afraid I am, but only on my terms, you understand. I know better than to build my hopes on a man who's already a cheat, so it's purely physical and . . .' Her eyes twinkled. '. . . pretty damned good.'

Catie grinned. 'Actually, Lawrence and I are finally getting it together again,' she admitted. 'And it's as amazing as ever. I can't believe how patient he's been with me.'

Lola nodded thoughtfully. 'He loves you,' she said. 'We all do.'

Catie pulled a face. 'I'm not always sure about my son . . .'

'He's just a baby.'

'And as for my mother, she still wants nothing to do with me and that really hurts, more for Matthew than it does for me. How can she not want to meet her own grandson?'

'I've no idea, and the worst part of it is how much she must be hurting herself. Have you sent her any photos of him?'

'Lawrence has, and he's tried talking to her, but the last time she ended up putting the phone down on him.'

With a sigh, Lola reached for more wine and said, 'I can't help wondering, now that Matthew's becoming more mobile, if it isn't time to start letting your mother-in-law back in.'

Though Catie balked, she said, 'It's already happening. She comes over most mornings and sits with him while I shower and dress, or if I have to go out somewhere. She's actually really good with him. In fact, he still never seems to play her up anywhere near as much as he does me. You can imagine how much she enjoys that.'

'Oh, that woman,' Lola muttered despairingly, 'how much easier her life would be if she could find it in herself to accept what a wonderful human being you are. And singer.' She slanted Catie a careful look. 'OK, clunky segue, but I promised Lawrence I'd talk to you about restarting your career.'

Surprised, Catie said, 'You and Lawrence have discussed it? When?'

'I guess it was on the phone a couple of nights ago. He keeps me up to date with how you're doing. I hope that's OK?'

Not sure whether it was or wasn't, Catie said, 'So what did the two of you decide about me restarting my career?'

Lola's smile was full of fondness. 'Actually, he told me your agent's been in touch to find out when he might start booking you out again, and apparently you're holding back.'

It was true, she hadn't yet reached a place where she could think about taking that step forward without her father being there, afraid of all the memories it would bring up. 'I know I didn't perform much with him before he died,' she said, 'but being out there, with a band . . .'

'Will probably do you the world of good. It's what you do, who you are, Catie. You've never not sung in all the years I've known you, and I can't believe you want it to go on like this.'

She shook her head. 'No, of course I don't. And actually I suppose I do want to do it, just small gigs at first, maybe with the Blue Notes . . .'

'So, you have thought about it?'

Catie smiled at being caught out. 'Yes, but what about Matthew? He's still so young and I've already let him down terribly with all my depression. I can't just up and leave him again.'

'You didn't leave him the last time, but OK, I get what you're saying. The difference now is that you'll be out mostly at night when he's sleeping and, as you say, Marilyn's already helping out during the day, when, more often than not, you'll be here too.'

Catie begins to nod, taking it in and feeling small but very definite sparks of excitement coming to life inside her. It really would be good to walk out onto a stage again, to feel herself fusing into the power of a song, being carried deeply into the soul of the music, as her father used to say.

'There is a problem actually,' she said, looking at Lola with a resigned sort of smile. 'I'm pregnant.'

Lola's eyes flew open in shock. 'You're not serious,' she cried.

'I am.'

'But . . . How?'

Catie laughed, then Lola did too.

'Sorry,' Lola said, 'it was just a bit of . . . but you're drinking wine.'

Catie shook her head. 'You obviously haven't noticed that I'm not.'

Lola checked the glass and saw that it was still full, while her own was reaching empty – again. 'Well, this is a surprise,' she declared, sitting forward to refill it. 'Does Lawrence know?'

'Not yet. He's away filming this week and I don't want to tell him on the phone. I'll do it at the weekend.'

Seeming to understand that, Lola said, cautiously, 'Are you pleased? Do you want another?'

Catie put a hand over her still flat stomach and sighed. 'I guess I don't have much of a choice now,' she replied. 'Oh, and by the way, apparently Jude's pregnant too, although she's a few months further along than me and, according to Marilyn, she's having another girl.'

Jake David MacAllister Vaughan slid almost effortlessly into the world seven and a half months later and, as soon as Catie held him, she knew that early motherhood was going to be entirely different this time around. She was able to feed him straight away, and bathe him, and laugh at his funny noises, without any of the grief that had tormented her with Matthew. And unlike his brother, Jake hardly ever cried. He simply murmured and waved his fists, or, as time went on, he'd give yells of what sounded like pure joy. No one could resist him, not even Matthew. He'd sit for minutes on end (a long time for such a hyperactive boy) just gazing at his little brother, calling him Jakey and telling him garbled stories about elephants and trains and something they eventually worked out to be Thunderbirds.

For the first time in far too long, Catie reached for her guitar, and as she began to play she wished with all her heart that she'd been able to do the same for Matthew when he was a baby. She sang to them both now, nursery rhymes and lullabies and sometimes funny little ditties that made Matthew laugh. *One fine day in the middle of the night.* Jakey always seemed transfixed by the music, staring with his big blue eyes right into his mother's, until he eventually fell asleep with a little snore. Matthew, either wanting to join in or easily bored, often stomped about the place blowing a toy trumpet, or banged loudly on a drum.

It didn't really matter, at least they were spending time together, and even Marilyn seemed to enjoy their musical hours.

Jake was close to eight months old, Matthew two and a half, when Lawrence came home from work one evening with some awful news.

'They've announced a whole slew of redundancies across the BBC,' he told Catie after she'd finished nursing Jake and laid him on the floor in his Moses basket, 'and my name's on the list.'

She looked up at him in disbelief. 'But I thought your programme was doing really well,' she protested. 'You get good viewing figures . . .'

'We did, but they've been dropping off lately and management are looking at a whole new structure, new faces, new ideas . . . Whatever, I'll get a pay-off, not sure how much yet, but by this time next month it looks like I'll be out of a job.'

'Oh God, Lawrence,' she cried, going to wrap her arms around him. 'I'm so sorry. I know how much you love working there and how good you are at what you do. Isn't there anything else, maybe on another programme? What about HTV on the Bath Road? They have a local current affairs programme, maybe they're looking for someone.'

'I'll explore all options, obviously,' he assured her, 'but it'll be a competitive field with so many of us being laid off at the same time.' Drawing her down onto his lap, he smoothed back her hair as he said, 'Actually, it's not all gloom and doom. But tell me first, where's Matthew?'

'Upstairs, fast asleep, the last time I saw him.'

'OK, I'll go check on him in a minute. Now, I know I haven't told you anything about this before, I just wanted to see where it might go first, but I've been working on an outline for a new book, and it turns out my old agent thinks he might be able to raise an advance for it.'

Stunned and thrilled she cried, 'But that's fantastic! When have you been doing it? I haven't heard the typewriter.'

'I'm using a word processor now,' he reminded her, 'and I try to grab some time when I'm at the office. At home, I just want to be with you and the boys.' He started to frown as he spotted a fat, rubbery doll in a spotted dress sitting on one of Matthew's toy trains. 'Whose is that?' he asked.

Laughing, she said, 'Jude brought Olivia over today, she must have left it behind.'

He nodded, still staring distractedly at the toy.

Dismissing it, Catie said, 'Actually, it's starting to seem serendipitous, you losing your job just when you're going to need the time to write a new book.' She pressed her mouth to his and held him so tightly that he started to choke and laugh.

'I guess you realize,' he said softly, 'that this could be a good time for you to start up again. I'll be home with the boys, Mum as backup, of course, and you, my darling, could become our breadwinner for a while.'

She laughed. 'Presuming I can earn the way I used to, and I'm not so sure of that. I've been out of the loop for a while . . .'

'But your agent still calls from time to time, so he obviously still wants you.' He reached up to stroke her face, and said, 'No pressure, it's just a thought. You know whatever you decide will be fine with me.'

She wanted to, she really did, but would it seem as though she was abandoning Matthew and Jake, especially Jake, when he was still so young? It was distressing almost beyond bearing to think of him missing her while she was away. Matthew, she felt sure, would be nothing short of delighted to have his beloved daddy around all the time, and would probably even allow himself to be put into play group if Lawrence took him and was there to pick him up.

'Let's keep talking,' she said, getting up, and going to check on Jake. 'We'll need to discuss it with your mum, obviously, although I can't see her having a problem with any of it – anything to get me out of here and you in full time. Of course, you'll have to put up with Jude popping in and out with her three . . . You know what a big crush Matthew has on her eldest, Vikki, although it seems to be turning the other way around lately – she's keener on him. Anyway, they love playing together, and I'm sure your mum and Jude will respect the fact that you're working so they won't let the children interrupt you.'

Seeming to be on board with the idea, he said, 'OK, but don't let's make it all about me and the children. It's about you too, I just don't want you forgetting us when you're rich and famous.'

Not engaging with the tease, she said, seriously, 'You three are the centre of my world, and you always will be, no matter how rich, or poor, or famous, or anything else we are, so don't ever forget that, OK? I love you all more than I'll ever be able to put into words, but don't worry, I'm going to have a damned good try at singing them.'

CHAPTER TWENTY-NINE

'So, you resumed your career and went on to become rich and famous?' Giancarlo prompts playfully as he and Catie stroll a deserted beach a few kilometres from Taormina. Ricardo and Tony had dropped them off there half an hour ago, before driving on to carry out some sort of errand for '*il capo*'. Catie hadn't understood the instructions Giancarlo gave them, only knew that they would be collected from this same beach in a couple of hours.

Matching his humorous tone, she says, 'Neither – although maybe a little bit of both, depending on how you measure it. I was never a household name, but I was known, mostly on the blues and jazz circuit, and I sang with plenty of big bands. I also did a lot of recording, sometimes for albums of my own, but more often as a duettist, or as a backing singer for leading musicians right at the top of their game – and not necessarily just jazz. I got paid extremely well for that – I still do, in royalties – and I was happy to do it because we needed the money.'

He turns to glance at her and she smiles, feeling faintly disoriented as she vacillates between those music studios of long ago, the tours, the pressure and rivalry, and this tranquil, sun-filled bay of today. How different the people who populate the scenarios – loud, demanding, even ruthless producers, and this intriguing enigma of a man.

She has no way of knowing if he really had failed to wake up until the middle of the afternoon yesterday, when he was supposed to be bringing breakfast to her apartment. Considering how tired he'd seemed the day before, she guessed it was highly possible, especially as he'd seemed to be in some sort of pain, or at least discomfort. Whatever the cause, he doesn't appear bothered by it now, and nor is she still delving into fantastical imaginings of knife wounds or beatings.

'Are you OK?' he asks.

She nods and after a moment picks up her story. 'Our problems started when I began to get bookings for festivals and concerts overseas. Copenhagen, Juan-les-Pins, Montreux, Paris, there were so many. I even went to Asia and South America, various places in the States, except Chicago. I didn't want to run into Carlin Monroe, which was crazy, of course, because he travelled even more than I did and I could have been in the same line-up as him at any time, and anywhere.'

'But you weren't?'

'Actually, I was, eventually. I think we both always knew it would happen . . .'

When she doesn't continue, he says, 'And when you saw him again, was the chemistry still there?'

Not willing to answer that yet, she uses her sunglasses to push back her hair and turns her face into the warming breeze as she says, impishly, 'How did I know you were going to ask that?'

He shrugs, 'Probably because I am predictable and transparent?'

She has to laugh, given that he's absolutely neither and he surely knows it.

When she still doesn't answer his question, he stoops to pick up a pebble and sends it skimming across the waves.

She watches him, the ease with which he shifts his weight, and the subdued strength of his movements. She's recalling the depth of her disappointment when he hadn't shown yesterday, and the relief when he'd turned up today. It was as though something heavy and anchoring had released her, allowing her to feel light-hearted again. She can't deny he's having as profound an effect on her as Carlin Monroe once had, although it's very different now. She's not that mixed-up and lonely mother any more, travelling from hotel room to hotel room, up and down motorways, across oceans; never seeing enough of her sons. Her life isn't the same at all, and nor is Giancarlo anything like Carlin Monroe.

As they start to walk on, their feet crunching the shingle, and the gentle, percussive sough of the waves mixing with the cry of gulls and distant traffic, she says, 'Carlin wasn't the issue – until he was, of course. But before that everything was about the boys, and how much of their lives I was missing.'

Giancarlo nods, almost as if expecting this, and why wouldn't he when anyone would see her long and erratic absences as a problem? And it wasn't as if she and Lawrence hadn't, they just hadn't known how to get around it.

'I'd have reduced my commitments in a heartbeat,' she says, 'worked things out so I could be at home more, but when Lawrence's second book didn't take off . . . It was published, but the sales weren't great – and then we discovered that Marilyn had lost a big chunk of her pension thanks to some really bad investments . . . Well, it meant I had to carry on.'

'Didn't Lawrence's brother step in to help his mother?'

'Oh yes. Graham was as generous as he could be, but

he and Fiona were having a difficult time as well – they'd made the same investments. In the end, things got so bad that it was decided I should buy Breemoor – the Abbotts Leigh house – with a mortgage, of course, and that way there would be enough funds for everyone to breathe a little more easily.'

Giancarlo's surprise and scepticism are audible as he says, 'So you carried the whole family?'

She couldn't deny it, nor did she want to. In some ways she was proud of it, or might have been if things had turned out differently.

'Did Lawrence continue to write?' he asks.

Sighing she says, 'Not really. Jude – yes, the dreaded Jude again – introduced him to a local MP, so he began working for him as a parliamentary assistant. It wasn't great money, although it helped, obviously, but it meant having to go up and down to London at least a couple of times a week. We did our best to work it so that I was at home when he wasn't, but of course it meant we hardly saw one another, and we were heavily dependent on Marilyn. She coped so well with the children that sometimes I felt she had a closer relationship with them than I did.' She pauses, then pushes herself to admit that, 'Looking back, she probably did, or certainly with Matthew.'

Matthew! Even thinking his name makes her heart cry tears that never really stop.

'He was often difficult with me,' she continues, 'and the older he got, the worse he seemed to become. There were times when he spoke to me as if he had nothing but contempt for me. It was so offensive that even Marilyn would reprimand him about it. Lawrence, if he witnessed it, would ground him and not let him out again until he apologized, but when he did it was clear he didn't mean it.' Realizing what a bad light she's painting her son in, she quickly adds, 'That isn't to say he couldn't be as loving and sweet as Jake when the mood took him, because he could. They were similar in so many ways, and yet entirely different in others.' Not for the first time she reflects on the truth of that, and feels her heart lift as she recalls how thrilled they both used to be when she turned up unexpectedly to watch one of their school football or rugby matches. Lawrence used to say that they never failed to score when she was there and maybe it was true.

'Matthew had this belief,' she continues, 'that I loved Jake more than I loved him. He never said it, not then, but later . . .' She stops herself and starts again. 'It wasn't true, of course, I loved them equally, but I will admit Jake was easier, and more demonstrative in ways that Matthew struggled with. For instance, Jake, right through school, even in his teens, would have a surprise waiting for me when I got home from a spell away. It could be anything from a tune he'd learned to play on the guitar; to a painting he'd done of birds, or squirrels, or some sort of wildlife; to baking a cake that was always a terrible mess. He had such a wonderful sense of humour that he never minded about his brother's fake retching, or his father's idiotic dad-dancing to tunes that were truly awful. He just thought they were hilarious. He was impossible not to love, while Matthew . . .'

A lump was closing her throat now; she needed to swallow and tilt her face to the sky to sink the tears.

Hoarsely, she says, 'I'm not sure if Matthew really believed I didn't care when it was discovered he had osteomyelitis. He was eleven, maybe twelve by then. I was in Berlin when it was discovered, but I rushed back as soon as Lawrence called me. By the time I got there, Matthew was out of surgery and, thank God, out of danger. It was lucky Lawrence had rushed him to A&E when he had, or it might have been a different story.' It still turns her cold to think of how differently it might have ended, and no harder to deal with is the way Matthew had seemed to blame her for it all. There had been no logic to his reasoning; it just seemed to be another stick to beat her with.

She pictures his young, handsome face, so like Lawrence, and yet like her too, but she doesn't see the anger and hurt, no resentment or contempt at all. Instead, she sees him laughing and leaping in triumph after scoring a goal; rocketing around the garden with Jake and Jude's girls, showing her with great pride that his height marker on the doorframe was now level with hers.

'I used to be afraid of how much he could hurt me,' she says, joining Giancarlo on the sea wall. 'Of course I knew it wasn't intentional; we all know that children have the capacity to cause immense pain without knowing it, but sometimes . . . Well, I'd almost dread going home in case he said or did something to make me wonder if he really meant it. I guess that was my own paranoia, or guilt over being away. Then I'd walk in and there they would be, the three of them, as happy as could be, reeling off dialogue from various movies. I swear they knew the entire script of *The Godfather Part II* . . . It was so funny that I'd laugh and laugh, unable to imagine why I'd felt so nervous of my own son. Then suddenly he'd turn on me again, usually over something trivial, and the arguing would start, with Jake defending me and Lawrence trying to referee . . .' She takes a breath, 'Jake was, he was . . .' Her lips are trembling so hard that she realizes she can't go on.

Giancarlo slips an arm around her shoulders and draws her gently to him. She allows herself to lean into his compassion and for a long time they simply sit quietly, watching the surf foaming over nearby rocks.

In the end he says, 'Were you still having no contact with your mother during these difficult years?'

Her eyes lose focus, as if it might allow her to see all the way to Patty's small house in Fishponds. 'No, we weren't in touch,' she replies. 'Lola spoke to her occasionally, just to make sure she was OK and to find out if she needed anything, but she didn't want to hear from me.'

'So Lola was still in your life?'

She nods absently and says, 'Less and less as time went on. Our schedules were so different . . . She gave up being an air hostess around the time the boys were eight and ten – funny how we mark the passing of time by our children's ages – and she set up as a photographer . . . It had always been her passion. She became successful quite quickly, and deservedly so. She had an inventive eye when it came to portraiture. Lawrence commissioned her to take some of the boys, most years, right up to their mid-teens, and the photographs were exceptional. So different to the standard headshots . . . They're still hanging on the walls at home. I've never been able to bring myself to take them down.'

Waiting for the roar of a helicopter passing overhead to die down, he says, 'Why would you want to do that?'

She smiles grimly and pushes herself off the wall. 'Can that be enough for today?' she asks, turning round to look at him.

'Of course,' he agrees.

'I think,' she adds, 'that I might have to write what comes next. To try and say it out loud, to put into words the way Lawrence and I . . . To tell you, anyone, what happened . . .'

'Let it go,' he says gently.

She nods and feels grateful to him for stopping her. Sometimes the past feels like a vacuum, sucking her in, holding her under until she can no longer breathe. Summoning a smile, she says, 'To put a slightly different spin on what you said at *la fattoria* the other day: there's dreaming, there's remembering and there's the here-and-now. This, right here, is where I want to be.'

He watches his own movements as he lifts a hand to sweep her hair behind one ear. 'Can we spend this evening together?' he asks.

Seeing no reason to hold back, she says, 'I was hoping we would.'

His eyes come to hers. 'Perhaps you will prepare the *occhi di lupo*?'

'Yes, I will.'

'At my apartment?'

Her breath catches on the motion in her heart. 'I'd like that,' she says, and wonders if he might have kissed her then had Ricardo and Tony not chosen that moment to return.

CHAPTER THIRTY

She hadn't seen Carlin yet. She almost didn't have to. Simply knowing that he was nearby, that at any minute they were going to come face to face, to feel the flow of memory and what-might-have-been moving between them, dissolving all the years that had passed since they'd last seen one another, was enough to unsteady her heartbeat in a way that wasn't welcome.

They'd both been booked for an event at a neo-Gothic mansion in Gloucestershire. With all its wings and towers and rolling acres of Cotswold grounds, the entire place had been taken over by Troy Ashcroft, an American hedge fund manager, for what promised to be one of the most lavish weddings she'd ever performed at.

She hadn't been around for the ceremony earlier in the day, nor the banquet for five hundred guests – other musicians had covered that. She was here for the 'jazz event', due to begin at ten this evening.

A special marquee had already been transformed into a nightclub to resemble Ronnie Scott's in London, or maybe they were aiming for a Thirties Berlin scene. Whatever, it felt authentic and atmospheric. There were fifty or more tables set around the stage, each with candles, crystal flutes and bottles of champagne. There was a frosted-glass bar and the stage itself seemed both intimate and large.

Behind this marquee was another, smaller one, 'for the artistes', it said on the sign outside. Catie had to admit, as soon as she entered the door with her name on it, that she was impressed. Everything, from the vast make-up mirror to the ornate garment rail, to the Oriental modesty screen and velvet chaise longue, evoked such a louchely exotic New Orleans scene that she could be in no doubt of the bridegroom's wealth. Or of his aristocratic bride's exquisite attention to detail.

She'd already been told, by her agent, that Carlin was an old friend of the Ashcroft family. It hadn't surprised her, for he'd always been well-connected. And apparently, she was greatly admired by Helena Grayson, the bride. It had crossed Catie's mind that Carlin might have asked for her to perform with him tonight, although why he'd do so now, when there had been so many opportunities over the years, she couldn't explain. He'd made no contact with her since the booking had been confirmed, and she hadn't been in touch with him either, or with the bride and groom. She'd simply accepted the set-list, along with the terms of the contract, not only because her agent might have fired her if she hadn't, but because she was in no position to turn down such a generous fee.

Once there had been a time when Lawrence, if he'd known Carlin was the headline act at an event where she was performing, would have done everything in his power to stop her from going. These days she wasn't sure he'd care so much. They were arguing far more often than they seemed able to speak civilly to one another, and there never seemed to be any time to make up before one of them had to leave. She'd genuinely forgotten when they'd last made love. Maybe it was the night the boys had gone for a sleepover at Jude's, back in October? But no, they'd fallen asleep before anything happened, and the next morning, a Sunday, he'd had to rush off to London for an urgent meeting with his MP.

The truth was, she missed him, and wanted their closeness back, and yet she couldn't help being irritated, even resentful of the decisions he kept making without consulting her first. The boys hadn't needed to go to Clifton College just because it was Lawrence's alma mater and a family tradition. It was too expensive, and there were plenty of other great schools in Bristol that would cost half as much. The trouble was that Matthew had set his heart on it, so he'd had to go, and by the time Jake was ready to start Upper School with him, it simply wouldn't have been fair to deprive him of the same opportunities as his brother.

So she now not only had a huge mortgage to meet, but extortionate school fees and all the extras that came with having two children at such a prestigious establishment. Of course, Lawrence paid what he could, and he was always generous, but his earnings were nowhere near as high as hers. It meant she had no choice but to take just about every gig, concert, festival or recording that came her way. As a result, she was seeing even less of them all, and over the past couple of years she'd actually started to feel like an outsider. Apart from with Jake. He was always thrilled to see her, no reticence about hugging or sharing his news. He even looked sorry when they all had to rush off to some sporting fixture or birthday event almost as soon as she was in the door.

Jake was her darling, her angel, her rock even. It was often thinking about him that got her through some of the worst parts of being away. At least she knew she'd have a warm and wonderful welcome home from her youngest son.

Hearing voices outside her door, she guessed it might be a couple of band members so went out to introduce herself. It was the caterers, delivering trays of refreshments to the dressing rooms.

Apparently, nothing had been overlooked; there was even a 'light supper menu' for anyone who might want to eat after the performance.

Knowing she probably wouldn't, she filled a glass with chilled mineral water and went to unzip the heavy bag she'd dropped on the chaise longue. She'd packed four costume changes, in spite of only needing two – it was vital to have something in reserve in case of a wardrobe malfunction.

Although she had more than an hour now to apply her make-up, fix her hair and dress, she was feeling so nervous that she knew she was going to need every minute of it. It was the thought of Carlin that kept causing her heart and stomach to flutter, and the set-list wasn't making things any easier. The music had been chosen by the bride and groom, with certain requests from friends, and it was clear that Carlin – it almost certainly would have been him – had arranged many of the pop songs to a jazz rhythm. He'd also set them in the keys he knew she'd be the most comfortable with.

Suddenly, out of nowhere, she felt the need to see him and tell him how glad she was that they were doing this together. She wanted him to know how often she'd thought about him over the years, and how hard she'd tried not to. She had no regrets, but at the same time she realized now that she'd never wanted to go the rest of her life without seeing him again.

She didn't act on the impulse; it would have been crazy even to try when she had no idea how he might feel now. He could be married, and his wife might be in the audience tonight. Certainly, he'd have moved on – how could he not have after all this time? – and yet she knew in her heart that when he'd accepted and arranged the set-list he'd been thinking of her. They'd performed many of the trad duets together before, albeit a long time ago, and some of them were amongst the greatest love songs of all time . . .

Right now, she couldn't decide whether she was more caught up in anticipation or fear.

Hearing a knock on the door she looked up, and knew instinctively it was him. It was one thing to go on stage with no rehearsal, it happened all the time, but they couldn't do it without a sound check, or without seeing one another first.

'Come in,' she called.

He pushed the door open and seeing her, sitting at the mirror in all her make-up and sparkling dress, he slipped his hands into his pockets and propped himself against the doorframe. His smile was every bit as heart-stopping as she remembered, maybe even more so. Funny how memory could fade or brighten, distort or take on its own tune. 'Catie Mac,' he drawled, and his familiar voice, so rich and yet clear, seemed to carry her back towards a past that they'd both left long ago. 'It's good to see you.'

She smiled and even laughed because she was so pleased to see him. It felt bizarrely as if almost no time had passed, although he was greyer and the lines around his eyes had noticeably deepened. He didn't seem quite as tall, she thought; however, his physique remained every bit as powerful as his charisma.

'So how are you doing?' he asked, making no attempt to come any further into the room. 'You're looking good.'

Thankful she was already made up, she said, 'So are you. It's been too long.'

He nodded and she could almost hear him thinking, *Your choice, Catie, your choice.* 'How's Lawrence?' he asked, and without waiting for a reply. 'I hear you got yourself a couple of kids now. Two boys? Is that right?'

Wondering how he knew, she said, 'Matthew and Jake. Almost fourteen and twelve.'

'Wow,' he murmured. 'That's great.'

'And you? Do you have any children?'

'Just the one. A girl. Jessica. She's gonna be twenty soon.'

So, he hadn't waited long after she'd left to find someone else, except they'd never been together so why would he? 'Are you married?' she asked.

'Not any more. Footloose and all that.' He checked the time. 'Maybe we can catch up after the show? Has anyone shown you the bungalows yet?'

'The bungalows?'

'They're where we're staying, somewhere out there on this Gatsby estate. The guys and I were there last night. They're as comfortable as everything else around here. I think you'll like yours, although I haven't personally seen it yet.'

Feeling her heart catch on the 'yet', she said, 'How many in the band?'

'Eight. I'll be doing keyboard and vocals, as usual. I'll introduce you to the others when we do the check. You've seen the set-list? Mostly traditional stuff, a lot of Porter and Berlin—'

'And Nat King Cole,' she interrupted teasingly; his voice was often likened to the great jazz maestro's, and with good reason.

His tone was dry as he said, 'As I recall you were always a fan.'

'Always,' she agreed, not sure whether he was alluding to Cole or himself, or even if she'd intended to flirt, but it was so easy . . .

Clearly amused, he said, 'Did I get the keys right?'

She nodded. 'I think I'll manage. Who's on trumpet?'

'A guy called Jim Hall. He's been with me for the past five years and he's good. Damned good.' He paused a moment before saying, 'I heard about your dad. I know that'll have been hard for you. He was a really cool guy. Playing with him at the House of Blues is still right up there in my top ten best memories.'

Swallowing, she said, 'It was a number one memory for him. Thanks for making it happen.'

He shrugged. 'It wasn't just me, but I was glad to be a part of it.' He turned as someone called out to him, and said, 'Sure, right there.'

Catie stood up. 'I guess it's time for sound checks?'

'Audience in twenty.' He held onto her gaze for a moment and said, 'It really is good to see you, Catie Mac. I'm glad you agreed to do this.'

'Did you ask for me?'

'I didn't have to, Helena's mind was already made up, but I would have if it had been left to me.'

It was the early hours of the morning by the time the show began coming to an end, and there was little doubt that every one of the three main sets had been a great success. Everyone had danced, whether to smooch, swing, slow-jive, or even Charleston to 'Anything Goes' and 'Think'. Covering Roberta Flack and Aretha Franklin numbers always took Catie to places she could never go any other way. She could feel the rhythm, the lyrics, the passion, right through to her soul. And duetting with Carlin was, as before, anything from exhilarating to hilarious to so utterly erotic that she was sure everyone else in the room must feel it.

The last number, at the request of bride and groom who, amazingly, were still there, was perfectly predictable given this was a wedding. She'd sung it so many times over the years that it had almost lost its meaning. However, she knew, even before she took up position at the side of the grand piano, and Carlin played the opening bars, that with the way the chemistry had been sparking between them throughout the show, the next few minutes were going to feel like nothing less than foreplay.

'Tonight I Celebrate My Love For You'.

As they sang, her voice as husky and mellow as his, and falling easily into the jazz rhythm he'd arranged, she allowed herself to look fully into his eyes and felt the lyrics as if they were already real. Soon they would leave this place behind, and they would be as close as it was possible for two people to be . . . She wanted it so much that she was hardly even thinking about the words any more.

When it was over, the audience rose to their feet, applauding rapturously, not for them, for the bride and groom who'd been dancing the whole time. But then it was for them, as the newlyweds turned to applaud them. She and Carlin linked hands and stepped forward to take their bows.

'Thank you,' they both said, over and over, 'thank you.'

His hand on hers was claiming her, and she was ready to go.

She looked around the room, barely taking in the small sea of happy, tired faces. She only knew the feel of him as he moved closer to her, putting a hand on her back and sending currents of desire surging all the way through her.

She started to turn away, smiling and breathless, then came to a sudden stop.

Lawrence was standing at the back of the room, staring right at her.

They had to drive home separately given they both had their cars, and Catie could only feel thankful she'd had no alcohol, or she would have had to travel with him. More than anything she needed time to collect herself; and he needed to calm down.

She had no idea yet how he'd managed to get into such a high-security private event, although she supposed if he'd explained he was the singer's husband, they'd have let him through.

Oh God, oh God, oh God.

Why on earth had he come? He *never* turned up at her gigs unannounced like that any more; he hardly came to them, full stop, even if they were close to home.

What the hell had he seen? Had he been there the whole time, watching as she virtually promised herself to another man on stage? And not just any man . . .

God only knew what Carlin was thinking now . . .

That was the least of her problems.

Lawrence arrived home first and his mother was barely out of the back door before Catie came in and he rounded on her in such a rage that she found herself taking a step back. 'You might as well have been fucking him right there on the stage,' he seethed. 'You were behaving like a whore—'

'Don't you dare—'

'No, don't you! I've got no idea how long you've been planning this, how many times it's already happened . . .'

'It hasn't.'

'But I'm telling you right now, the boys will stay with me . . .'

Stunned, she cried, 'Lawrence! For God's sake. You're taking this too far. I know how it must have looked . . .'

'If you're about to try and tell me it was all a part of the act . . . Jesus Christ, Catie! We've been through this before, with *him*, the very same man. So how fucking long has it been going on? How many years have you been out there meeting up with your lover, cheating on me, while you've got two boys at home who need you . . .'

'You have to stop,' she implored. 'I understand why you're angry, why you're thinking the way you are, but I swear tonight is the first time I've seen him since Los Angeles . . .'

'Really? And that's how long it took for you to become his bitch again . . .' He reeled back as she slapped his face.

'Don't ever call me that,' she hissed, 'and don't ever make racist comments in my hearing again.'

'What the hell are you talking about?'

'That was racist, and if you don't recognize it you need to start reassessing your values. Yes, I'm attracted to him, I always was, and I probably always will be. I'll make no excuses for it. That sort of thing happens, and tonight, yes, I'd have slept with him if you hadn't turned up. Not because I'd been planning it, but because of what's happening – or *not* happening – between us. And why the hell *did* you turn up? How did you even know where I was?'

'People that rich don't get married without it being noticed,' he growled. 'It was on the news; there was even footage of lover boy flying in. And you never mentioned a word to me.' His face suddenly twisted with contempt. 'You were disgusting the way you behaved on that stage tonight. You might just as well have stripped off and let him fuck you right there and then. Everyone was watching, they could see exactly what was going on, but you didn't care. You'd forgotten they were there. All you wanted was his cock and he was playing you along, keeping you hot . . .' His voice broke on a sob and, turning away, he slammed a hand hard into the wall.

Covering her face with her hands she tried to think what to do, to say, but there was so much awfulness between them. Their relationship was so fractured, so difficult, and they seemed so far apart that she had no idea how to get them through this to try to bring them together again.

'I want you to know,' she said, finally, 'that even if it had happened with Carlin tonight, it wouldn't have changed how much I love you.'

He spun round, riven with fury again, but she put up a hand to stop him.

'I'm doing my best, Lawrence,' she cried. 'I get that it might not be good enough, but it's all I have, and the pressure of keeping everything going, of sacrificing my relationship with our sons to make sure everyone is taken care of . . . OK, I can see you're not listening to me, that I'm saying things you don't want to hear—'

'You're saying what you've convinced yourself of,' he cut in savagely, 'what *you* want to believe in order to make this all my fault so you can cut and run on us . . .'

'For God's sake, how can you say that? If I'd wanted out, I could have gone a long time ago, and sometimes I think you wouldn't even have noticed if I had. You all manage so well without me, there's hardly room for me any more, but I'm here, I stay, because I love you. I want us – you and me - to be as close as we always were, and I accept that I'm partly to blame for how we've drifted . . .'

He was shaking his head. 'Your mea culpas aren't doing

anything for me right now. You've got no idea what it's like to be a stay-at-home parent . . .'

'Nor have you,' she shouted. 'Your mother is the one who runs things around here, and you'd better believe that if I could be that person, I would. You've just never given me the chance. Don't you think I want to be like normal mothers, doing normal things with their kids, like watching them grow up, being there when they need me, not trying to slot into their crazy schedules wherever I can? If I weren't responsible for the mortgage, the school fees . . .'

'Oh, I wondered when that was going to come up. So, let's shut it all down, shall we? Sell the house, make my mother homeless, stick the boys in some half-baked academy and you and I can go our separate ways. Just know that my sons will come with me.'

'They're mine too,' she yelled, 'and I don't understand why you're saying these things. Yes, I came close to making a terrible mistake tonight, but it didn't happen, and the last thing I'd ever want is to break up our family. You've got to know how much you all mean to me . . .' She stopped, suddenly aware that he was staring past her and, turning, she saw both boys standing at the kitchen doorway watching them, their faces white with shock and terror.

'Oh my God,' she gasped, starting towards them.

Jake ran into her arms, sobbing and clinging to her. 'Don't go, Mum, please, please,' he begged.

'I'm not going anywhere,' she assured him. 'No one is . . .'

'Matt,' Lawrence said darkly.

She looked up and her heart went into freefall as Matthew stared at her with hate in his eyes and said, 'If you take us out of school and sell our house, I'll never speak to you again.'

As he walked away, Lawrence went after him, trying to pull him back, but he broke free and raced up the stairs, Lawrence close on his heels.

Still holding Jake, Catie smoothed his fair tumble of curls while whispering softly, fervently, that she wasn't going anywhere, that she'd never ever leave him. 'You can stay at school, I promise. I wouldn't really pull you out. Oh God, I'm sorry, Jakey. I'm so sorry for frightening you like that. Daddy and I are such fools, we shouldn't say things we don't mean. No one should.'

Turning his not-quite-teenage, tear-stained face up to hers, he said, 'It's not true that we manage without you, because everything's so much nicer when you're here.' He thought about that for a moment and added, 'Except tonight, but we'll make it all better in the morning, won't we? The way we always do when something goes wrong.'

CHAPTER THIRTY-ONE

Catie is lying quietly on a lounger staring up at the moonlit sky, her eyes travelling slowly between the stars as if joining them with an invisible line. Beside her Giancarlo sits up to refill their coffee cups, then lies back down again, one hand resting behind his head. They're on the roof terrace of his palatial apartment, relaxing together in the darkness, listening to French jazz and the occasional chime of church clocks.

She can feel the warmth of his hand close to hers, and hear the steady rhythm of his breathing. She wonders what he's thinking now; if, like her, he's allowed the awful scene with Lawrence that he'd read earlier to fade back into the past, and is simply enjoying these quiet moments of being together.

They'd prepared the *occhi di lupo*, as planned, in a quaintly old-fashioned kitchen with curtained cupboards and marble worktops, and they'd eaten at the table up here. The dining room was too formal, much like the rest of the apartment, spread out over the top floor of a former palazzo. When he'd shown her around, she'd felt almost as if she were visiting a gallery. There are so many hand-painted frescoes covering the walls, and elaborate cornices carved around ceilings and doorways. Each room has a chandelier and classic antique furniture, styled more for elegance than comfort.

This roof terrace, with its vibrant Moorish ceramics, lushly planted beds and cosy seating areas could belong to another place altogether. It overlooks stepping-stones of other rooftops with satellite dishes, washing lines and flowering trees, everything descending gently towards the sea. The fragrance of a nearby shrub is scenting the night air, and soft lights from candle lamps burn and flicker strange patterns over the terrazzo floor. It's hard to imagine a more romantic setting, or anywhere else she'd rather be.

Breaking the easy silence between them, she says, 'We still haven't been to the opera.'

'Mm,' he responds, in a way that confirms his mind is returning from elsewhere.

'Or the Ancient Theatre,' she adds.

For some reason this sharpens his attention. 'You haven't visited the Ancient Theatre?' he says, surprised.

'I've tried a couple of times, but the queues are always so long.'

'Then we must talk to Tony. He will be able to take you right in.'

She wants to say she'd rather go with him, but he speaks first. 'I am going away for a day or two tomorrow,' he tells her. 'Ricardo will drive me, but we have arranged for someone to chauffeur you and Tony. Unless you go to the Ancient Theatre. You won't need a car for that.'

Not quite sure what to think of this, she simply says, 'Thank you.'

'I had thought,' he continues, 'that he could take you to Savoca, a village twenty kilometres from here, where scenes from *The Godfather* were filmed. But now I'm concerned that reminders of the film will upset you if, as you say, your husband and sons could recite from the script.'

Knowing that the reminder would be harder than he can begin to imagine, she says, 'Perhaps it's better I don't go there.'

He nods. 'As you wish, but Tony and a driver will be available to take you wherever you'd like to go.'

She turns her head to look at him. His face is lost in shadow, making it impossible to try to read him. 'Can I ask where you're going?' she prompts.

There's a moment before he says, 'I'm afraid it's necessary for me to be in Palermo again.'

When he offers no further explanation, she wants to remind him that he told her she could ask him anything, but she doesn't. She's feeling suddenly confused by him and annoyed with herself. She looks around and wonders why she's here. How has it come about that she's in the most beautiful surroundings on this distant, exotic island, so far from home, with a man she thought she was coming to know, but maybe she isn't? The connection between them no longer feels real. It's a trick of her imagination, and an old one, considering how often she's been wrong about people before.

'It's late,' she says, starting to get up, 'time for me to go back to my apartment.'

He puts out a hand to stop her. 'Wait,' he says softly. 'There's something I need to tell you.'

Experiencing an instinctive shield of self-protection, she resists the urge to leave, deciding it would just seem ill-mannered, even childish. Sitting up, she turns so she can see him in the candlelight.

Meeting her eyes, he takes one of her hands and brings it to his lips. 'This isn't going to be easy,' he tells her, 'mainly because I did not expect to develop such strong feelings for you, and certainly not this soon.' He kisses her hand again, and she wants him to stop speaking now, to allow her to tell him that she has strong feelings too, and that whatever he has to tell her won't change them. And there's so much else . . .

'I thought we could become friends,' he continues, 'that we would spend time together, helping one another through a lonely and difficult period of our lives.'

'I think we've been doing that,' she says, smoothing the backs of her fingers over his lightly bearded cheek and feeling the comfort of their connection closing around them again.

He nods. 'Yes, we have.'

'Except you never tell me why you feel lonely, or what's making things difficult for you.'

He turns his face into her palm and kisses it gently. 'It is not something I find myself willing to talk about,' he admits, 'but I know I must, or I am afraid there is a chance you will continue to think I am a *mafioso*.'

Surprise makes her laugh, and even blush slightly to know he'd read her so easily. 'Then what is it?' she asks, running her fingers to his neck and back again.

He takes a breath and brings her hand to his chest as he says, 'I go to Palermo to see a doctor who is treating me for cancer.'

She is suddenly very still, disbelieving, as if she hasn't quite understood his words. Surely to God they can't be true, and yet surely he'd never lie about something like that.

'It is melanoma,' he continues. 'I have had it before, on my leg, and it was successfully treated. Last week I had another mole removed from my shoulder, also from here.' He puts a hand to his abdomen. 'They have also taken – how do you say? – lymph nodes?'

223

She nods, not wanting to connect with the awful portent of this.

'Tomorrow, I will return to the hospital for the doctor to check my progress since the surgery. I am hoping he will give me the results of the analysis while I am there, but it is probably too soon.'

'So,' her voice is hoarse, she has to clear her throat, 'you don't know yet whether or not it's spread?'

He shakes his head. 'The doctor tells me he is optimistic. In case you're wondering, I am here in Taormina and receiving treatment in Palermo, so my mother will know nothing unless she has to.'

Still barely moving she says, 'And there's a chance she never will? Have to?'

'Correct.'

Somehow, she inhales, shakily, and turns aside for a moment as she tries to take it in. It seems incredible, unspeakably cruel even, that she should rediscover feelings she'd believed long dead simply for them to be crushed all over again. And yet how much worse it is for him . . .

Getting him through it, being there for him, is all that matters, but is she in a position to do that?

'I am telling you now,' he says, 'to give you the chance to walk away before we become any more attached to one another.'

She stares down at him, already shaking her head. 'I'm not going anywhere,' she tells him, meaning it. 'I will be here for you the way you have for me . . .'

'Oh Caterina,' he sighs, 'it's not the same . . .'

'No, it's more serious, and I won't let you do this alone. I will come with you tomorrow . . .'

'No, I don't want that, but knowing you'll be here when

I get back . . .' He smiles and reaches up to cup a hand around her face. 'You must know,' he says gruffly, 'how much I want to make love to you. Sometimes I feel it is all I think about, holding you in my arms and being as close to you as I can be.'

'I want it too,' she whispers, feeling it so deeply she almost can't bear it.

For long moments he continues to look at her then, bringing her mouth down to his, he kisses her tenderly, deeply, with a gently growing hunger.

As she pulls back to look at him, he says, 'I should not ask this of you, *cara* . . .'

'Sssh,' she murmurs, and begins to unfasten his shirt.

He tries to stop her, but she pushes his hand away and continues freeing the buttons until she can open it wide, and then she sees the angry, stapled scar across his chest. She stoops to kiss it gently and feels his hands moving into her hair.

'Let's go inside,' she says, and winces herself as he eases himself to his feet.

Minutes later they are standing beside his bed in the silvery moonlight, naked and absorbing the overwhelming pleasure of being this way with one another. Neither of them is perfect, or young, and yet his body is as strong and male and beautiful as she'd imagined, and his arousal is powerful.

Slipping a hand into his, she says, 'I know it might not be possible for you to make love to me tonight, but I can make love to you.'

As his breath catches on her words, he turns her to the bed and lies down with her, wrapping her in his arms and murmuring softly, as carefully and lovingly she begins to fulfil her promise.

A long time later, as he sleeps soundlessly beside her, she lies gazing at his long, dark lashes, the lines around his eyes, the grey flecks in his close beard and feels, very deeply, that they are a gift to one another at a time when they've needed it most.

CHAPTER THIRTY-TWO

After the terrible scene with Lawrence when he'd actually talked about them breaking up and even trying to separate her from the boys, Catie was ready to do everything she could to right things between them. It had never occurred to her that divorce had even entered his mind, or that he was feeling so let down by their marriage that he might not even consider it worth fighting for any more.

To her relief, it soon became clear that he did want to fight for it, and that he was as shocked and upset by his threats as she had been.

'You must know I didn't mean it,' he said during one of their many long talks, his voice as roughened by guilt and confusion as his appearance was strained and dishevelled. They were walking around Abbots Pool that day, the boys racing on ahead, eager to get to the fallen branch to attempt their 'tightrope walk' over one of the ponds. It was amazing how quickly they'd seemed to recover from the trauma of that night, how ready they were to accept that because Dad had made Mum laugh since and Mum had put her arms around him, all that was behind them now. No more insecurity about school, or their parents' marriage, or where they might be living, and that was exactly how it should be. Catie just hoped that the damage hadn't been buried deep inside, ready to show up in all the wrong ways later.

'I wish I could take it back,' Lawrence went on, reaching for her hand. 'I was just so . . . Seeing you . . . It's no excuse, I know . . .'

'I'm the one to blame,' she reminded him. 'I'm just thankful you turned up when you did, because if you hadn't . . . I know I wouldn't be able to live with myself now.'

His head went down as he shook it, his tousled, greying hair making him seem so vulnerable that she wanted to fold him into her arms. 'Thinking of you with another man,' he murmured, 'with anyone at all, not just him . . .'

'It isn't going to happen,' she assured him gently. 'I've never cheated on you, Lawrence. *Never*. I won't deny there have been opportunities, you must know that, and I'm sure it's been the same for you . . .'

'Why? What makes you say that?'

Confused, she said, 'Because you're an attractive man, and you're often on your own in London. I'm sure the women are flocking around you.'

Not responding to the tease, he said, 'I don't think so. Not really.'

Dropping it, she said, 'The important thing is, what we have together, who we are . . . This, us, as a family . . . It will always matter more than anything else.'

'Yes, it will,' he agreed, staring off through the trees. 'We should never have allowed things to get to where they did between us. It's my fault, of course, I should be providing for us all . . .'

'It's both our faults, and you do provide, in so many ways. You hold us all together, Lawrence. You make sense of everything, and I don't even always understand how. I just know you do. And I could never do what I do without you.'

He smiled wryly. 'Yours is a God-given talent that has nothing to do with me, and as for the boys, I think they are driven to achieve in order to show off to you.'

Touched by that, and hoping that it was at least partly true, she said, 'Even Matthew?'

'Yes, even Matthew, although I grant you, he's better at hiding it than Jake.'

She sighed and watched them both at the bottom of the wooded hill, wobbling and yelling their way over the tree-trunk bridge, calling one another horrible names that made her wince and laugh. 'I hate being away so much,' she said, quietly, 'and I know you do too.'

He didn't deny it, simply slipped an arm around her shoulders and rested his head against hers.

'We have become so dependent on your mother,' she said, 'and Jude in a way. But I worry most about your mum. It isn't fair. She isn't getting any younger . . .'

'Probably best not to let her hear you say that,' he commented dryly.

She smiled, and waved as Jake leapt off the end of the log without falling in and, beating his chest, looked up to make sure they were watching. Behind him Matthew was putting on a great show of going over at any second, tilting this way, that way, bending forwards and back, until he suddenly sprinted to dry land and wrestled his brother to the ground.

'I've been thinking,' she said, still not sure whether the idea she'd been considering for a while was a good one, but she needed to share it to find out what he thought. 'There are all kinds of gigs I could take on over and above what I do now . . . No, hear me out,' she said as he made to protest. 'I know it's going against what we're saying, but some of the cruise ships pay small fortunes for a resident singer, and we know how lucrative it can be to do backing vocals for big-name artistes. I could do more private parties, support acts at concert venues . . . Anything my agent can get me, even commercials, and maybe we could be done with the mortgage within a couple of years. Or at least we could substantially reduce it . . . I know I should have done this before. Oh God, am I delusional? I probably am. I'm just desperate to find a way for us, for me, to be a proper part of our family again before it's too late.'

Seeming perturbed, he said, 'Why too late?'

'They're growing up fast,' she pointed out.

Understanding, he smiled and turned her to him. 'You are a proper part of us,' he murmured, 'and you always will be. Nothing will ever change that, no matter what you do, and the last thing I want is you to be away more . . .'

'But it could work, you can see that, can't you?'

'Maybe, but I'm the one who should be tackling that mortgage . . .'

'And you would if you had the same opportunities. I know you're not writing any more, but everything's going well for you at Westminster, and you're loving it, it's just that we both know . . .'

'That I don't have the same earning potential as you,' he came in flatly. 'You're right, I don't, and that's why I think we should consider selling the house to get somewhere smaller.'

'No, Lawrence!'

'Your turn to hear me out,' he insisted. 'Mum can always go to live with Graham and Fiona, or we can try to get her somewhere near us. I know she won't like leaving the boys, and they probably won't be thrilled about her going—'

'No, we can't do it that way,' she interrupted. 'We owe her so much more than making her move out of the cottage,

230

and not seeing her grandsons as much. And the boys will hate changing schools, maybe even being a lot further from their friends. It's coming up to a crucial time for them . . . No, please let me do it my way – sorry, that's a bit Frank Sinatra, but you know what I mean. If I really throw myself into it all, then by the time Matthew's doing his GCSEs, I could be here a whole lot more than I am now.'

Though they continued to argue it back and forth over the next few weeks – one minute he was all for it, the next not at all – in the end, they discussed it with the boys and both, even Matthew who they'd expected to be scathing in some way, were in favour of her being home more, even if it wasn't going to happen immediately.

So, she called her agent, let it be known that she was willing to broaden her horizons, and it wasn't long before more offers started coming her way; some every bit as lucrative as she'd hoped for.

Within eighteen months they were celebrating the fact that the mortgage had been reduced to a far more manageable level, so no more three weeks – or even whole months – away. She could start easing back now, and the timing couldn't have been more perfect: Lawrence's MP, who'd become a minister a few years ago, had decided to stand down at the next election. This meant that Lawrence could, possibly, if the votes went his way, fulfil an ambition to stand for parliament himself.

The boys were so excited by the prospect of their dad being in government, shadow or otherwise, that their joy started erupting in wildly hilarious scene-enactments from *The Godfather,* their go-to play-act when they wanted to make their parents laugh. They were so proud, and kept telling anyone who'd listen that their dad was going to be the next PM. Though Lawrence did his best to calm them down, Catie could see how thrilled he was to have their support, although his nerves began to show, the closer they came to the big announcement. At one point he even talked about backing out, saying it was a mistake to think he was the right person for the job, and how were they going to cope with all the intrusion into their lives?

'All our secrets will come out,' he warned Catie. 'Is that really what you want?'

She laughed. 'What secrets? We don't have any, unless there's something you want to tell me.'

He shook his head and turned away, and because she understood how a crisis in confidence could hit during the final build-up to a huge event, she did her best to bolster him. 'We'll be here for you,' she told him gently. 'And you're going to be brilliant, I have no doubts about that, and nor will you once it's all decided and under way.'

He didn't argue, nor did he seem particularly uplifted; he simply kissed her and retreated to the room he used as an office, to make some calls, he said.

It was two nights before the big announcement. Lawrence was in London and Catie was at home with the boys, making campaign banners and feeling almost as ludicrously excited as they were about the big change that was possibly about to happen in their lives. Even Matthew, who was still edgier with her than Jake had ever been, enough to make her heart ache during the times he wouldn't allow her to hug him, was ready to fist-bump and cheer and tell her that she was going to be the best MP's wife ever. They were sixteen and fourteen by now, and developing skills and ambitions neither she nor Lawrence had seen coming, and – OK as parents they were biased – they were turning into fine young men. No drugs, no alcohol, no serious rebellion; they were all about sport and good grades, video games with their mates, and, more recently for Jake, music. His instrument of choice this month was the violin, and while Matthew took great delight in caterwauling along to an unrecognizable tune, Catie felt she could sit listening to him scraping away for ever.

When the phone rang, Matthew tilted back his chair to reach for it and said, 'Hello whoever you are, this is the MacAllister-Vaughan residence.'

Jake laughed and Catie rolled her eyes.

'Hey Jude,' Matthew replied, jarringly out of tune. 'Sure, she's here . . .' Seeing Catie shaking her head, he threw out a hand, what was he supposed to do? He'd just said she was there. 'I'll pass you over.'

Reluctantly taking the phone, Catie tried to sound more curious than unfriendly as she said, 'Hello, Jude. What can I do for you?'

Though Jude was still a frequent visitor to Marilyn's cottage, usually turning up with one or more of her girls in tow, she didn't come to the house much, at least not while Catie was there. In fact, they had surprisingly little to do with one another, considering how close the boys were to Jude's three. 'How are you?' she asked, still failing to imagine a time when she'd ever warm to her old nemesis.

'I'm fine, thanks,' Jude replied. 'I . . . I wasn't sure about making this call . . . I mean, I've talked to Marilyn, and Henry, my husband . . .'

'I know who Henry is.'

'Of course, yes – well, they both agree . . .' She was sounding so awkward that Catie glanced at the phone as if something might be wrong with the line. 'Well, I was wondering if I could come to see you,' Jude asked. 'When it's convenient, of course, but before the . . . big announcement.'

'You mean Lawrence's?'

'Yes, yes. It's important we speak before it happens.'

Not much liking the sound of this, Catie carried the phone into the sitting room and closed the door. 'Why do you want to see me?' she asked. 'Can't you just tell me now, whatever's on you mind?'

'Of course,' Jude replied, 'I just thought . . . Actually, it doesn't matter what I thought. I need to . . . I'm sorry, Catie, I really am, but Lawrence can't stand as an MP. You must know that. Surely.'

Baffled, Catie shook her head. 'What are you talking about?'

Sounding more wretched than ever, Jude said, 'Oh my God, you don't know, do you? Honestly, I don't want to be the one to tell you, but someone must . . . Catie, Lawrence has . . . He has another family.'

Catie blinked, put a hand to her head and tried to make sense of what she'd just heard. 'Are you crazy?' she demanded. 'How can he have . . .?'

'He has other children,' Jude told her quietly.

Catie felt suddenly nauseous as the most horrifying possibility swam into her head. 'Oh my God. Are you saying the girls are *his*?' she cried.

'No, no, no! That's not what I'm saying at all. It's not me, Catie. I'm not the one he has another family with. It's your friend, Lola.'

Catie was sitting at the kitchen table on her own, hands spread out in front of her, eyes staring at nothing. She'd tried calling Lawrence, but he wasn't answering his phone. She'd sent a text saying: *You need to come home. NOW!* Still no response to that either.

The boys had disappeared to their rooms half an hour ago, angry with her that she'd spoiled the mood, telling her she was just mean and never as much fun as Dad. That was Matthew, of course; Jake hadn't said much, but she'd seen that he was worried. She'd tried to convince them both that everything was fine, it was just time to pack up for the evening and start getting ready for school in the morning. Something in her manner had clearly told them not to push too far.

Hearing Matthew's heavy metal starting to thud upstairs, she clasped her hands to her ears and closed her eyes. He always did this to get his own back for something she'd said or done, but tonight she couldn't feel upset with him; couldn't even properly register his frustration. She was too stunned, too completely horrified by Jude's call to make herself think beyond it. It was as if she'd become stuck inside it, sealed up, cut off from everything else.

She was in shock, she realized that, and maybe it was where she wanted to stay because moving forward, even attempting to process this earth-shattering news, would mean she'd have to accept it, and deal with it.

She looked up at the sound of a knock on the door, and her heart thudded with dread that it might be Lawrence. She wasn't ready to face him yet, wasn't sure if she would ever be able to again. But he wouldn't knock, nor would he come in through the back.

As Marilyn let herself in, Catie saw straight away that she'd been crying and felt a spark of anger. She didn't want to deal with her mother-in-law now, she had no idea what to say to her, and she sure as hell didn't want to hear her defending her son.

'I'm sorry,' Marilyn said wretchedly. 'I should have told you myself, I know I should . . .'

'How long have you known?' Catie demanded.

Marilyn shook her head. 'I'm not sure. Maybe when the first child was—'

Cutting her off again, Catie cried, 'How many fucking children are there? And how old are they?'

Flinching, Marilyn said, 'There are two. A boy and a girl. I've never met them. They don't come here . . .'

'Well, shall we be thankful for that?' Catie seethed sarcastically.

Swallowing, Marilyn said, 'They're probably nine and seven by now.'

Catie reeled as the words hit like a blow. He'd been living a double life for that long? Splitting his time between her and the boys and whatever the fuck he had going on in London? She'd believed him when he'd said he was using the MP's flat in Pimlico. It had never even occurred to her to check up on it, and yet, apparently, all the time she'd been working her bloody ass off trying to keep their lives together, he'd been . . . She started to get up, sat down again and gave a sudden, wrenching sob of fury.

'Oh, my dear, my dear,' Marilyn said shakily. She came forward as if to offer comfort, but stopped, seeming afraid Catie might not want to be touched. She turned to the fridge and poured two large glasses of wine and brought them to the table. 'I know we haven't always got along so well,' she said, sounding completely unlike her normal, assertive self, 'and I know it's mostly my fault, but I swear I would never have wanted to see you hurt like this. It's not what you deserve. You've worked so hard . . .'

'Why didn't you ever tell me?'

'It wasn't my place . . .'

'Of course it fucking was, you're the boys' grandmother, for God's sake. Are you telling me that you just sat back while their father went off and played happy families with some . . . *slut* in London who called herself *my best friend*? Jesus Christ. What's wrong with you, Marilyn?' Before Marilyn could answer, she said, 'Do they know? The boys? Do they have any idea what their father has done?' She felt sick at the mere thought of it.

'No! No, of course not,' Marilyn assured her. 'I wasn't entirely sure about it myself for a long time. It was only when his – the – little girl fractured her skull in the playground at school that he told me. He was here when it happened and he had to leave right away . . .' She trailed off, seeming to realize Catie wasn't ready to feel sympathy for a child that meant nothing to her, and why would it?

They sat quietly for a while. Catie couldn't speak, she was too stupefied, traumatized, by the madness of it all to do more than fail to make sense of something that had no place in her life. The deception, the duplicity was on a scale so way beyond her understanding she hardly knew how to try. The shattered trust could never be repaired.

'She was all right,' Marilyn went on quietly. 'The little girl. They were worried out of their minds for a while, but she was fine, and I suppose that's a good thing. After all, she's not to blame for anything.' A moment later she added, unprompted, 'She's the eldest.'

Catie felt such a sudden and powerful need for her father that she could hardly breathe. He'd know what to do now, wouldn't he? He'd be able to sort this out . . .

'I want you to know,' Marilyn continued, 'that whatever you decide to do I will always be here for you and the boys. I know this is your house now, and you might decide you want me to leave . . .'

'I can't think that far ahead,' Catie said irritably. 'I need to speak to Lawrence. I have to find out what the hell . . .'

As her voice faltered, she put a hand to her head and tried to take in air.

'He's on his way back,' Marilyn told her. 'After Jude spoke to you, I rang him—'

'Why did you let *her* tell me?' Catie cried angrily. 'You know how I feel about her . . .'

'She said it would be better, for the boys' sake, if you hated her rather than me. I know you're not fond of me anyway . . .'

'This isn't about *you*,' Catie raged then, seeing how her words had cut, she made herself apologize. It wasn't Marilyn's fault, after all, even if she hadn't done the right thing, whatever that might be in these unbelievable circumstances.

In the end, after a horrible abyss of silence, and because there was no one else to ask, she said, hoarsely, 'What would you do now, if you were me?'

Marilyn looked helpless as she shook her head in despair. 'I've no idea,' she replied. 'I mean, I'd probably want to kill him – not literally, of course – but we have to think of Matthew and Jake. They're all that really matter. You too, of course.'

'And what about his other children? Do you know their names?'

'Martine and Nicholas.'

Catie had no idea why that seemed to hurt so much, until she realized that children with identities made the whole thing so much more real. 'Do you ever have any contact with them?' she asked.

'No, like I said . . .'

'What about their mother?' She was unable to utter Lola's name, didn't even want to picture her vile, treacherous face. No wonder she was no longer in touch, always had an excuse for them not to meet . . .

'No, not since she used to come to see you,' Marilyn said, and it took Catie a moment to remember what her question had been.

When Lola used to come to see her.

How long ago that seemed now, part of another world, when she'd been tormented with grief and post-partum depression. Was that when she and Lawrence had first . . . 'So, all the time she was helping me to get back on my feet,' she said, 'when I thought she was an angel that might have been sent by my dad, she was *fucking my husband*?'

Marilyn's face crumpled as tears fell onto her cheeks. 'I don't think it started that long ago,' she said, 'but whenever it did, they are both to blame – and I want you to know that I am ashamed of my own son.'

Catie was thinking that Lola must have come to the house while it was going on, because the photographs of the boys had been taken here and in the garden, usually while she, Catie, was away. Had she brought her own children? No, she couldn't have, or the boys would have seen them . . .

She looked up at the sound of a car coming to a stop outside.

'It'll be him,' Marilyn said.

Catie's heart thudded with a terrible, sick mix of dread and fear. Her first instinct was to rush to the door and lock him out and never let him in again. It was as if a stranger, some kind of monster, was coming to wreck her and her children's lives, and she supposed that was who he was now. Not their father, or her husband, or even Marilyn's son, but a crazy man, a delusional narcissist, who'd been living a double life maybe for as long as his eldest boy had been alive.

'What would you like me to do?' Marilyn asked anxiously. 'I'll stay if you think . . .'

'I need to speak to him alone,' Catie replied, 'but thanks for coming over. It would have been very hard sitting here on my own, waiting.'

Lawrence's face was so haggard as he came into the kitchen that Catie didn't have to ask if any of it was true. She hadn't intended to. None of this would be happening if it weren't. She loathed and despised him so much that she could hardly bear to look at him, much less hear what he had to say.

In one rapid movement she stood, snatched up her glass and hurled it right at him. He ducked, but it hit his head. 'You *hypocrite*,' she hissed, mindful of the boys upstairs, although Matthew's music was still cranked up. 'You lying, cheating, low-down fucking *hypocrite*. You threatened to break up our marriage when you saw me with Carlin, and all the time you – *you* – had *another fucking family*.'

'Catie, listen . . .'

'No, you fucking listen. You're the one who's going to lose the boys, this house, me, any ounce of respect you ever had from anyone, and as for your deluded notion of running for parliament . . . What the hell is wrong with you? You had to know it would come out . . .'

'I did, of course,' he agreed, 'and I tried to tell you, but you believed in me, and it was gaining its own momentum . . .'

'Jesus Christ!' she spat in disgust. 'When exactly did you start being such a spineless, worthless human being? How did I not see it before? I can hardly believe how blind, how *goddamned stupid* I've been. You've used me in a way I will never forgive, *ever*. You allowed me to throw away years of my life when I could have been at home with my children, being a proper mother, just so *you* could have it all. This house, their school, me, *her*, my boys and her *bastards*.' She grabbed a fruit bowl, and flung it at him so hard that it smashed on impact.

'Catie, please try to calm down . . .'

'Don't you dare,' she seethed and, snatching up a plant, she hurled that too.

'The boys will hear,' he growled, wiping blood from his head.

'Well maybe we should get them down here so you can explain what sort of father you are. Yes, let's tell them that they have a half-sister and -brother that you've been keeping secret for at least ten years, apparently. Perhaps we can tell them then that you're a bigamist. *Are you?* Is that something else you've done, Lawrence? Have you married her . . .?'

'No, I have not. Catie, please let me speak . . .'

'And what could you possibly have to say that will excuse what a despicable person you are? There is nothing, Lawrence, *nothing*, because this level of deception and betrayal, this level of total *fucking hypocrisy* can never be excused. Even your own mother is ashamed of you . . .'

'Have you seen her?'

'Yes, she was here, and frankly I blame her too, because she *knew*. She could have told me at any time, but she chose not to . . .'

'Because she didn't want to hurt you . . .'

'Whereas you couldn't care less. All that mattered to you was having it all. I'm not going to ask how it started, because I don't want to know . . .'

'We didn't mean for it to happen . . .'

'For God's sake! You have two fucking children with

241

her, so how can you say you didn't mean it to happen? What world are you living in?'

'I meant at the beginning,' he protested. 'It wasn't something we set out to do . . .'

'And yet you did it anyway, and somehow, along the way, when she was pretending to be my best friend, she managed to talk you into having babies? Or did she trick you? Don't bother to answer that, I'm sure you didn't agree to it. You were just a dupe, a sperm bank for her because she *couldn't get anyone else*.'

She spun round as if to get away from him, turned back, hardly knowing what to do with herself. He went to open a cupboard and poured himself a Scotch. Before he could get it to his lips she ran at him, snatched it away and threw the drink in his face. 'Get out of here,' she raged. 'Get out, right now. I can't bear you near me a moment longer.'

Regarding her helplessly, he said, 'I'll leave now, if that's what you want, but you know we have to talk about this, to decide what's best for the boys.'

Unable to believe he'd actually said that, she yelled, 'You should have thought about that a long time ago, back when they were the only children you had. Now, they're *mine* – do you hear me, *mine* – and I will be getting a court order to make sure you never go near them again. Now, there's the door. Get the hell out of *my* house and don't even think about coming back.'

CHAPTER THIRTY-THREE

***188: *So you've reached the point of Lawrence's other family?*

CM: *Yes, it was hard going through it again. I felt drained and breathless after writing it. Actually, a lot more than that.*

***188: *Of course. It was a terrible shock. An unforgivable deception. Have you discussed it with your friend?*

CM: *Not yet, but he's read it.*

***188: *OK. You know I'm here if you need me.*

'It's quite possible,' Giancarlo says musingly, 'that we are currently sitting in the most beautiful place on earth.'

Catie smiles as he puts an arm around her. Their seat is made of cold, hard stone, is backless and extremely uncomfortable, nevertheless she says, 'I think you're right. If only we could make all these people go away.'

He chuckles and whispers, 'Pretend it's only us. I think you can do that.'

'I think I can,' she decides, and closes her eyes for a moment to reset.

They are sitting at the very top of the Ancient Theatre's vast *cavea*, with tiers of centuries-old stone steps descending in a sweeping arc in front of them all the way down to the orchestra and stage. Crumbling Roman columns and fallen boulders provide a frame for the most stunning of all backdrops – the crystal-blue waters of the Ionian Sea, and magnificent dark slopes of Mount Etna beyond.

How can anything be this beautiful? It's quite simply breath-taking, and made even more so by the pure, cloud-less sky and translucent sunshine that's lighting it.

'I don't think I could ever get tired of this place,' he reflects, resting his head on hers.

Deciding the same, she inhales the brackish, earthen scent of their surroundings, and says, 'Have you been to many concerts here?'

'*Sì, sì,*' and she smiles because she loves it when he responds in Italian, even if it is only to say yes. 'Opera, ballet, rock, jazz . . .' He presses a kiss to her hair. 'I would love to see you on this stage, to hear you singing . . .'

'Ssh,' she chides, 'this is far too grand a venue for me . . .'

'Says someone who's performed at the Hollywood Bowl and Monte Carlo Sporting Club . . .'

'You've been looking me up again.'

'I had to do something while I was waiting at the hospital and it made me feel close to you.'

She smiles again. 'Then I'm glad you did it, because that's exactly where I want to be, close to you.'

'I know that song,' he declares, and she laughs, because there probably aren't many people of any age or nationality who don't know the Carpenters' classic.

His trip to Palermo, three days ago, had turned out to

be no more than a post-op check. So soon after the surgery they should have expected as much, although they'd hoped for some positive lab results. It was too early, of course; there would probably be another week to wait, while the staples, he'd been told, could be removed after ten days. This will happen at the Taormina hospital, so he doesn't have to return to Palermo yet.

The fact that they still have no idea if the cancer has spread to other parts of his body is a constant dark cloud in the backs of their minds, but they have agreed not to allow it to dominate their time.

'I will deal with it when I have to,' he'd told her when he'd got back.

'You mean *we* will,' she'd corrected, meaning it, and hoping with all her heart that she wouldn't have to go home before that.

Now, waiting for a tour guide behind them to finish explaining to her group the difference between a theatre and amphitheatre, Catie turns to him and smiles simply because she loves looking at him.

He says, 'I have finished reading what you wrote about the other family.' He swears under his breath, '*Porca miseria . . .*'

She isn't sure what that means, but puts a finger over his lips anyway. 'Not here,' she says. 'This is too special a place to talk about unhappy times. I just want to be with you, soaking everything up from a way more distant past, imagining the Greeks staging their plays . . .'

'And the Romans throwing Christians to the lions?'

She frowns. 'Maybe not that.'

He laughs and pulls her in closer. 'We should find out when the season starts next year. I hear that Jimmy Sax is playing, or there is *The Marriage of Figaro, Madame Butterfly . . .*'

'Any of the above,' she says, glad that he's looking forward and seeming to presume she'll still be here. Will she? It's so hard to answer that question that she doesn't even try.

Changing the subject, she asks, 'When do you think you'll go back to Turin?'

He sighs and waits for another guide, Dutch this time, to finish her spiel before moving her party on. 'It will probably have to be soon, or my mother will start to become suspicious,' he replies.

'Of what exactly?'

'Mm, maybe that I am falling for a very beautiful English *signora*.'

Her heart swells as she says, 'How would she know?'

'Word gets around.'

'And how do you think she'd feel about it?'

'I think,' he replies ponderously, 'that like most mothers, she wants her children to be happy, even if they are sixty-five.'

She laughs and nudges him playfully, while thinking, fleetingly, of her own mother and what she might have to say if she could see her now.

Later, as they stroll back to her apartment – how quickly it's become hers rather than Isabella's – they pick up a roast chicken and some salad from the deli, and several bottles of wine to share between the rack and the fridge.

The place is stuffy and dark as they walk in, but he goes to open the shutters and throws wide the doors to the terrace. 'You know, I like it here,' he decides as a waft of cooling air rises from the sea. 'It's . . . *molto accogliente* . . . very comfortable, and you seem quite at home.'

'I am,' she confirms, turning from watching him stretching

out his long limbs in the late afternoon sun to begin piling ripe red plum tomatoes into a bowl. 'In fact, I shall be very sad to leave when the time comes. Shall we have wine now, or wait until we eat?'

Not reacting to her change of subject, he says, 'I'll open a bottle,' and he comes into the kitchen to do the honours. 'Did you pick up any olives?' he asks, searching for a cooler.

'They're in the bag,' she replies, reflecting on how much she's enjoying their easy domesticity. Only two nights of sleeping together, added to a small wealth of stories about who they were before she came here, and it feels as though they've known one another forever.

After laying out the aperitifs, and popping the chicken into the oven to keep warm, he waits until she joins him outside and says, 'I must tell you I was very shocked by the "other family". I know years have passed since you found out, but I still find it very hard to think of how terrible it was for you.'

Wryly, she says, 'You mean after my temper died down, and Lawrence's injuries healed? Yes, it was pretty horrible; one of the worst times of my life, in fact. I can't remember how long I kept wondering why it wasn't possible to stop loving him when I hated him so much, but I know it ran into years. I couldn't stand to be with him, and yet I wanted him there all the time rather than think of him with her.'

'Did you speak to her at all?'

'Not once. It was best we stayed away from one another. I don't think she had the courage to face me, and I was afraid of what I might do if I saw her.'

'But surely he gave her up in order to keep you together?'

She gives an incredulous laugh. 'No, he didn't, and he wouldn't let me go either. He said he loved us both, that it had been impossible for him to choose all these years,

247

and it still was. So, if we were able to carry on the way we were, then none of the children would suffer.'

His eyes widen in shock.

'I know, crazy, beyond insane,' she agrees, 'but it's what we did. Obviously, his plans to become an MP were dead in the water after that night. Why he ever thought they could happen, only he knows, although I found out later that Lola had played a part in convincing him he could carry on having two families without the press finding out. I think she did it because she was afraid he'd leave her if he had to make a choice. So, I guess that made her as delusional as him. She certainly had a lot of influence over him, and he was so much weaker than I'd ever realized.

'Anyway, after he pulled out of the race that hadn't even started, he ended up with a job in the Foreign Office and continued to split his time between London and Bristol, when he wasn't travelling. I only agreed to it because I couldn't bear to think of *her* children having a full-time father while mine didn't. Matthew and Jake were so close to him, loved him so much and, in spite of all his faults, no one could ever accuse him of not being a great dad. Although obviously great dads don't do what he did.'

She takes a sip of wine, sets the glass down and starts to feel something close to shame as she says, 'I allowed that awful double life to go on for three entire years. It seems inconceivable now, as if it happened to someone else, or in another world. My only excuse is that I wasn't in my right mind after the shock of his betrayal. You understand we were no longer sleeping together, although there were nights when I felt so heartbroken and lonely I might have weakened if he'd been there. When he was, I simply couldn't take the pretence that far. God knows it was difficult enough being in the same room as him at times . . .' She stops, feeling strained and scattered by how crazy it had all been.

'Christmas was the worst,' she continues after a while. 'It only worked because we lied and he did lots of driving. Of course the boys knew something wasn't right, how could they not? But it was as if they were afraid to ask in case everything fell apart around them, and somehow that made it even worse.'

'So how many days a week was he with you, outside of holidays?'

'His job meant that he was away quite a lot, but when he was around he was quite scrupulous about sharing his time. Whenever he came to Bristol, I tried to make sure I was away. At least then he could have the boys to himself, and I wouldn't have to pretend everything was normal and that I could stand things the way they were.

'Marilyn continued to make it all possible, of course. We'd never have been able to do it without her, but it took a toll on her. Anyone could see that, she was aging before our eyes, although Lawrence refused to accept it. I'd never realized just how self-centred and oblivious he was until then. All his worst traits were so plain to see once I was no longer in love with him that I came to wonder how I'd married him in the first place.'

Topping up her glass, he says, 'You mentioned it went on for three years, so what happened to change it?'

She shudders as she remembers and wonders how anyone else who'd been a part of that terrible time thinks of it now. Those who are still living, of course. 'I'd already made up my mind I would file for divorce as soon as both boys left home,' she says, 'but everything came to a head much sooner than that, when Matthew started talking about going to university . . . He had his heart set on UCL, and even before we went to look around, he was getting excited about seeing his dad in London.'

She stops, looks at Giancarlo and reaches for his hand, though whether to reassure him she's still with him, or to anchor herself back in the present for a moment, she isn't sure.

'Enough?' he asks.

She shakes her head, and pushes herself on. 'I wasn't there when Lawrence told him about his "other family", I only know how devastated he was after, and then how incredibly quickly he seemed to get over it. Lawrence took him to meet his half-brother and -sister – obviously he already knew Lola, although he hadn't seen her in years – and when he got his place at UCL he was a regular visitor to their Battersea home. By then Lola was quite a legend in her world; everyone who was anyone wanted her to stage their portrait photos, even royalty. I'm not sure if Matthew was impressed by the celebrity, it's hard to imagine he wasn't, at his age. I never discussed it with him, we didn't mention her at all when we got together, and I did my best to make sure he never knew that I felt almost as betrayed by him as I did by his father.'

'And what about Jake? Did he start a relationship with the other family too?'

She nods. 'Eventually, because Jake always wanted to please everyone, but I could see how torn he was, and concerned about me. Not that Matthew was entirely detached; he was just better at compartmentalizing things, like his father, I suppose.'

She smiles wryly as she considers what she's going to say next. 'You might be surprised to hear that Marilyn and Jude were my greatest friends and supporters during that time. Especially Jude. I didn't want to lean on Marilyn any more than I already had to with the boys, but Jude was different. She seemed to want to be there for me, to chat things through about our past, of course, and how crazy she'd been as a youngster, and how embarrassed and sorry she was for it now. But all that was a long way behind us. I realized she was a different person now, and I was so grateful for her friendship, for her willingness to talk about my marriage, and drink wine with me late into the night.

'We took long, bracing walks together, and she was always ready with advice when it was needed, and not if it wasn't. She turned out to be the best friend I didn't know I had. Actually, I'm not sure I could have found the heart to carry on singing during that time if it weren't for her. But it wasn't only during those awful years when I was struggling so hard; it was later, when it *really* mattered. She was there at the very, very worst time of my life, and I'll never forget all that she did for me.'

She knows he's waiting for her to continue, to explain what happened for Jude to prove herself so loyal and indispensable, but she can't do it now. So she says, 'It's time we ate, and after, if you're very lucky, I'll spare you what comes next in my story and do something I think you'll like a lot better instead.'

His eyes narrow at the suggestiveness in her tone. 'You're going to make a tiramisu?' he guesses.

She laughs and gets up from the table. 'If that's what you want . . .'

He catches her hand and pulls her onto his lap. 'I know what comes next,' he says, stroking her hair, 'so you don't have to tell me.'

She isn't surprised. 'You looked that up too?' she asks.

'I didn't have to. It was there without a search, but if

you want to put it into your words, or if you want me to read it—'

She stops him with a kiss, knowing that for the moment she can't even think about it, much less sink herself into the depths of writing it.

CHAPTER THIRTY-FOUR

'Mum! Where are you?' Jake yelled, crashing in through the front door as if he'd forgotten to open it and dropping his school bags with a thud on the floor. 'I know you're here so stop hiding.'

Laughing, she shouted, 'Take a guess.'

A moment later he appeared at the music-room door, all five foot ten of him practically filling the space. 'Of course, you're here,' he grinned. He looked so dishevelled and muddy and utterly gorgeous that she wanted to hug him to within an inch of his life. He was going to be seventeen soon, was finally shaving, and had grown so fast in the last year that he might just end up being taller than his brother. Not that there was a competition going on between them, except of course there was.

'Great news!' he announced, his navy eyes sparkling with infectious delight. 'I only passed the audition.'

She gave a gasp of surprise. 'No! I mean, yes, of course you did,' and leaping up from the piano, she laughed and cheered as he swung her around while delivering one of Shakespeare's most famous lines, '"Some are born great, some achieve greatness, and some have greatness thrust upon 'em".'

'I knew you'd get it,' she told him, gazing up at his adorably flushed cheeks and tousled dark hair. He was such a crazy mix of her and Lawrence, and even Mac was there in his jawline and thickening eyebrows.

'Born actor, me,' he declared, thumping his chest and still grinning all over his face, while somehow managing to remind her of the time, aged six or seven, when he'd refused to take off his Spiderman costume. He'd even slept in it, for five full nights in a row, and what a tantrum he'd thrown when Lawrence had held him down so she could peel it off him. 'We start rehearsals next week, straight after school,' he told her, 'so I won't be home until late on Tuesdays, Wednesdays and Thursdays. I've already told Gran.'

'Where is she? Didn't she bring you home?'

'She dropped me off and went back into Clifton to pick up the dry cleaning she forgot. Oh, guess who's playing Olivia?'

'Tell me.'

'Olivia,' and he laughed as if it were the most hilarious joke.

'That's fantastic. Does Jude know?'

'I guess so, by now. We have to celebrate.'

'We certainly do. I'll call Jude . . .'

She broke off as her mobile rang and, seeing who it was Jake said, 'Spooky or what? I'm going to get something to eat. No! I have to ring Dad and Matt first. They've got to be there for opening night.'

'Which is when?' she asked, clicking on the line.

'December the something. I can't remember off the top. Hey Jude,' he replied, hitting the wrong notes as usual.

'He's so funny,' Jude commented dryly. 'But he'll be a great Malvolio. Olivia's beside herself. I thought she was going to combust when she told me. We have to do something with them.'

'I was about to ring you to say the same. I'm guessing the favourite will be the Clifton Sausage?'

'I'll call and see if we can get in. It's a Tuesday, so we should be OK. Will Marilyn join us?'

'I'm sure she will. Text to let me know what time, and we'll see you there.' As she rang off, Catie couldn't help feeling sorry that Lawrence wasn't at home to share the moment, not because she wanted it for him, or herself, but she did for Jake, because she knew how much it would mean to him. Getting such a key part in *Twelfth Night* was a dream come true – or one of the many, given that Jake was on three sports teams, football, cricket and hockey, and often talked about lifting the cup at Wembley, or Lord's, or Lee Valley. He was, in fact, a pretty damned good actor, and Catie knew she wasn't the only one who wondered if it was because he'd had to do so much of it at home. Marilyn had commented on it once to Lawrence who'd reacted in his usual tin-eared way saying, 'It's good for him to put his experiences to good use.'

'Oh wow! That is totally awesome,' she heard Jake shouting down the phone, presumably to his father or brother. 'Definitely count me in. Who else is going? No way! It's going to be so cool. Tell me the dates again.' His tone was suddenly downbeat as he said, 'I don't think I'll have broken up from school by then, Matt, and it might clash with the reason I'm ringing you. I only got the part of Malvolio . . . I know, amazing isn't it? Olivia's playing Olivia, which is totally cool . . . Listen, I'll try and sort things out because I definitely want to come with you guys. Have you told Dad about it? Yeah, he would be. Sure, she's right here, want to say hello?'

'Hi, Mum,' Matthew shouted.

'Hi, you,' she shouted back. 'What are you talking your brother into this time?'

'He'll tell you. Great news about the play, Jakey. Let's hope it doesn't clash, because no way do I want to miss it.'

As Jake put the phone down, Catie went to make a sandwich to keep her permanently hungry boy going until they ate at the Sausage. 'So, what was all that about?' she asked, opening up the bread bin.

'Matt and some of his mates are going skiing in December and there's an extra place, so Matt's asked me if I want to take it. Isn't that cool? I really wanted to go last year when they all . . .' He trailed off, belatedly remembering that last year's ski trip had been with Lawrence and the other family. Matt had gone, but Jake had turned it down saying he had too much on, but she knew the real reason was so she wouldn't have to think of them all enjoying themselves without her. 'Sorry,' he said awkwardly.

'Don't be,' she said. 'I knew you wanted to go and I should have let you . . .'

'You didn't stop me,' he reminded her.

It was true, she hadn't, but she almost certainly would have tried if he hadn't taken the decision himself. She'd have stopped Matt too, given half a chance, but he'd been in his first year at uni by then, and no longer had to listen to her, about anything. It wasn't that she didn't want them spending any more time with the other family than they already did, although of course she didn't. No, it had much more to do with how reckless both boys could be when throwing themselves body and soul into a sport, and skiing was infamously dangerous.

'So, you think this trip of Matt's might clash with the play?' she asked chattily as she tried to slice the cheese with crossed fingers.

Practically inhaling an apple, he said, 'Even if it doesn't, exactly, I'll probably be in rehearsals. Shit! Why did they both have to come up at the same time?'

Smiling at his frustration, she said, 'You still need to call Dad to tell him you're going to be the next Kenneth Branagh.'

'Who?'

She looked up in surprise and, seeing he was teasing her, threw a teacloth at him.

As it turned out there wasn't a clash. The three-night run of *Twelfth Night* would be over by the time Matt and his friends were booked to fly out. And the last day of term before the Christmas break was two days before the big trip.

So, the only excuse she had for not wanting him to go was the real one. 'I'm scared,' she told Lawrence, when he sat down to talk to her about it. She knew Jake had probably asked him to, no doubt Matt had weighed in as well, wanting to put on the pressure, but she was no more likely to be persuaded by their father than she was by them. Probably less likely, in fact.

'They can be crazy, the pair of them,' she reminded him, 'and if you're not there . . .'

'They'll be fine,' he insisted. 'They're not stupid. They're young men now, and being a bit daredevil at times is the kind of thing healthy young males do.'

'And it's how they end up getting horribly injured. No, Lawrence, I want you to talk him out of it. I know Matt won't listen, but if you can talk sense into him too . . .'

'I'm not going to do it, Catie. Matt was a great skier by the time we left the slopes last year, and Jake will be too . . .'

'Can't you go with them? At least then they might not be so wild.'

Lawrence smiled. 'They don't want an old bloke like me hanging around, cramping their style while they're trying to show off to the girls. Christ, I don't even want to think about what Matt would say if I as much as suggested it. No, Catie. You're just going to have to accept that they're growing up and you can't mollycoddle them for ever.'

'I don't do that,' she snapped. 'I just care about what happens to them . . .'

'And I don't?'

'I'm not saying that, I just wish you weren't encouraging Jake to go.'

'Has he asked you to pay for it yet?'

She frowned in confusion. 'Is he expecting me to?'

'I think so. He knows I can't, not right now, so I told him to talk to you.'

Feeling terrible for the position her lovely boy was in, she said, 'He knows I won't give him the money. It'll be why he's been off with me lately; he's been trying to pluck up the courage to ask when he knows what the answer will be.'

'Well, it would be one way of stopping him, to withhold the funds, but it's not the way I'd advise.'

She turned away, at a loss for how else to make her case when she knew that telling him she had a bad feeling about it would just make him roll his eyes.

'Listen,' he said, his tone warm and conciliatory, 'if this is about Christmas then you don't need to worry. They'll be back on the twenty-fourth, I'll pick them up at the airport and bring them straight here—'

'You're not really listening to me, are you?' she snapped.

'I am, but I don't think you're listening to yourself. He deserves this, Catie, and you know it. He works hard, gets really good grades and he'll do a fantastic job with that

258

play, we both know it. I think the real problem is you're struggling with the fact that he's starting to become less dependent on you. But you're never going to lose him, any more than you've ever lost Matt. They just grow wings, like every other kid, and fly the nest. You don't want to be the one to keep him tied to your apron strings.'

Though she didn't continue the discussion then, more were had during the weeks that followed, some descending into full-scale rows. Jake didn't argue with her himself; it wasn't his way. Instead he waited until the play's opening night to try to make a deal with her.

'If we get more than three curtain calls, I can go? Yes?'

It was clear he took her failure to answer as a win; however, even after four curtain calls she still wouldn't budge. It tore her apart to see how frustrated and unhappy he was because of her decision, but she'd come this far and wasn't going to back down now.

In the end, it was while she was performing a Christmas party gig at a famous actor's Devonshire pile that Matthew drove to Bristol, helped his brother to pack and took him back to London with him. They flew out early the next morning, even before she'd realized Jake wasn't at home.

'How did he pay for it?' she shouted at Lawrence as soon as she got him on the phone. 'I thought you said—'

'What does it matter who paid? They're there now.'

'*She* gave him the money, didn't she?' Her voice was shaking with fury. 'Tell me the truth, Lawrence. Did you allow her to pay for his trip, knowing how I felt about it?'

'As I said, they're there now. They'll have a fantastic time and when we see them on Christmas Eve . . .'

She slammed the phone down and gave an agonized seethe of rage. 'How dare she?' she cried to Marilyn. 'How fucking dare she?'

'It was wrong of her, and of Lawrence,' Marilyn agreed. 'They should never have gone behind your back like that.'

'Here,' Jude said, putting a cup of tea in front of her. 'Or maybe we need something stronger?'

'I'm working tonight,' Catie reminded her.

'Do you want me to drive you?' Jude offered. 'Actually, before you answer that, where is it?'

'Newcastle.'

Jude's eyes rounded.

Catie smiled. 'Celtic Manor,' she admitted, 'just over the bridge, but you don't have to take me. I'll be fine.'

Jude was already opening up her phone. 'I'll call Henry now to make sure he's OK with it. He might even want to come. Will we be able to get in?'

'I'm sure it won't be a problem if you're with me.'

'Room for one more?' Marilyn asked, holding up a hand. 'It's been too long since I last saw you sing, and if you're doing Christmassy songs . . .'

'I am,' Catie assured her, 'although it's the last thing I'm feeling right now.'

'But you'll be fine once you get into the rhythm,' Jude reminded her, 'you always are. So, off you go and get yourself ready, while I persuade Henry to let us take his car. He'll probably offer to come just to stop me getting behind the wheel of his precious BMW.'

Six days later, Catie was in her music room arranging a set-list for a New Year's Eve gig, when she heard someone letting themselves in through the front door. Presuming, hoping, the boys were back early, she abandoned her task and went out to the hall, already feeling thrilled to see them, though still cross about the way they'd tricked her.

It was Lawrence, and the instant she saw him she knew.

It wasn't only the way he seemed somehow smaller, older, less of himself, it was the way her heart stopped beating.

'Which one?' she said croakily.

He started to speak but had to try three times before he could heave enough air into his voice to say, 'Jake.'

Her head was swimming. 'How bad is it?'

He looked away.

'I said *how bad is it*?' she shouted, unable to curb the panic.

His eyes flicked to hers, haunted and bloodshot, before he shook his head and started to break down. 'He didn't make it,' he sobbed. 'Oh God, Catie, he didn't make it.'

CHAPTER THIRTY-FIVE

Catie is lying quietly on the bed in Giancarlo's arms, listening to the gentle beat of his heart and comforting rhythm of his breath. She is no longer crying for her precious boy; the tears have dried on her cheeks, but they will come again, she knows that as surely as she knows the sun will rise again tomorrow. She has cried so much and so savagely over the years, has torn herself to pieces with grief, because there is no cure for the loss of a child. It is something no parent can get over, no matter how long they live.

She feels tired now, and grateful to Giancarlo for being here, for the way he seems to care so much, and how tenderly he's holding her. She's starting to realize that she could never have done this alone. The reliving, the telling, the writing of her story, wouldn't have got this far if she'd had no one to help her bear it. She'd have shied from it and tucked it all away again, allowing it to stop her from moving forward. She still isn't sure how much this form of therapy is helping, but she does know that she's just pushed herself up against an immovable barrier, and maybe even a small way past.

Today is the first time she's spoken Jake's name for a very long time. She's hardly spoken it since the accident that claimed his life. Not even when she and Lawrence flew to Austria to bring back his broken and beautiful young body did she utter it, unless she had to for an official. She had no words for Lawrence or Matthew. She had nothing to offer them, no desire to reach out to them and no forgiveness to ease their suffering.

There had been nothing anyone could do to help her through the pain and grief. She didn't want anyone's solace, or advice, or support. She only wanted to be left alone with her boy living on in her heart, forever seventeen, forever her crazy, talented superhero who had more fun, sensitivity and kindness in his soul than anyone she'd ever known.

Maybe Giancarlo is proving an exception.

She remembers the therapist telling her once, 'Sometimes people come into our lives for a short time, when they are needed, and when their purpose is fulfilled, they leave again.'

Is that how it will be with Giancarlo?

When she's sure he's sleeping, she gets quietly up from the bed and goes to her phone.

She isn't surprised to find a message,

***188: *Have you reached the part about Jake yet?*

CM: *Yes.*

***188: *How are you?*

CM: *OK, I think. Actually, that's not true.*

***188: *No, I'm sure it isn't, but not too much further to go now. Be strong.*

CM: *No turning back?*

***188: *No turning back.*

CHAPTER THIRTY-SIX

It was the day before Jake's funeral.

Catie was at home alone, unusually, for there seemed to be some kind of pact between Jude and Marilyn that someone should always be with her. She was grateful for their kindness and knew she probably wouldn't be coping without it, but during the moments she could wrench herself from the depths of her heavily tranquillized state, she was worried about the strain it was putting on Marilyn. The shock of losing her beloved grandson, and in such a needless and tragic way, had aged her terribly. It had aged them all, but Marilyn's devastation seemed to be consuming her. Not that Catie's wasn't; at times she felt she no longer existed outside of it, but Marilyn was becoming forgetful and confused to such a degree that Graham and Fiona had come to stay at the cottage to keep an eye on her. Matthew and Lawrence visited her too, but Catie had made it known that she wasn't ready to see either of them yet, so they didn't come to the house.

She knew she'd have to make her peace with Matthew soon, that she couldn't go on letting him suffer this terrible, insupportable loss without her, but she just didn't seem able to make herself reach out. She wasn't even sure he wanted to see her; it was quite probable he didn't. What excuse could he give for stealing Jake away in the night like that? How could he possibly explain why he'd done it when he'd never been in any doubt about how she'd felt about Jake going skiing? Rational or not, she'd *known* it was the wrong thing to do, and now, God help them, she'd been proved right.

Now, alone in the sitting room where they'd shared so much as a family, birthdays, Christmases, big matches on TV, movies, tears, rows, laughter, it was a few moments before she realized that someone was knocking on the front door. She turned her head to look out into the hall, but could see nothing from where she was, on the sofa, in the space that had always been considered Jake's. It still smelled of him.

She guessed it was the head of school come early to talk through the service tomorrow; or the priest; or someone else with food she was never going to eat. Everyone had been so kind, and she was grateful to them all while wishing they would stay away; their generosity was a brutal reminder of what she'd lost.

Just thank God for the drugs. They might not stop her from thinking, or feeling, and did nothing to fill the terrible, bottomless hole in her world, but they did seem to dull some of the worst moments of wrenching grief.

The knock came again, not hard or insistent, quite gentle really, but whoever it was clearly wasn't going to go away. Deep down inside, somewhere past the stultifying and ragingly conflicting emotions, she knew she wanted it to be Lawrence. But not the Lawrence of today. The Lawrence she'd known before his other family, when they'd have turned automatically to one another at this terrible time.

If they'd still been properly together, if he hadn't betrayed her with Lola Higgins, there would be no need for comfort because the accident would never have happened.

Getting up from the sofa, she went to find out who it was.

At first, she didn't recognize the elderly woman standing there, smartly dressed, neat grey hair, large handbag over one shoulder . . . Then she realized who it was and her heart seemed to stop beating.

The woman gave a small, hesitant smile, her watery eyes were bright, wary, determined. 'Hello,' she said.

Catie could only stare, couldn't speak, until suddenly she was sobbing.

'Come here, my girl,' her mother said, raising her arms, and Catie stumbled forward right into them. *Her mother was here. Was it a dream? Nothing seemed real any more.*

'Sssh, there now, I've got you,' Patty soothed, holding her tight, and it was strangely as if only days had passed since they'd last seen one another, rather than almost twenty years.

'Oh Mum, Mum,' Catie choked. 'My boy . . . I didn't . . . How . . . How did you know?'

'It was on the news,' Patty told her, and Catie heard the catch in her voice. 'I wasn't sure if you'd want to see me . . .'

'Oh God, I do. More than anything.' It was true, so true, and she hadn't even known it until now. 'Come in. Please,' she urged. 'There's no one else here. Will you come in?'

'Of course.'

She took Patty's hand and led her through to the kitchen, where the table and countertops were overflowing with casseroles and cakes, flowers, cards, unopened letters, soothing bath salts, aromatherapy candles . . .

'People are obviously being very thoughtful,' Patty commented, taking it all in, the size of the kitchen too, the hand-painted cupboards, beechwood surfaces, bay window overlooking the garden. It couldn't be more different to the kitchen in her own Fishponds home.

Catie couldn't stop staring at her. It was as if the only way to keep her here, to stop her from becoming an apparition, was not to blink, just hold onto her with her eyes.

Patty turned to her and Catie cried, 'Oh God, Mum . . .' She had to catch her breath. 'I didn't realize how badly I needed to see you, how much it would mean, until suddenly . . . here you are . . .'

Patty's habitual reserve softened as she smiled and Catie's heart folded around it.

'We – I – should never have let it get this far,' Patty said, putting a hand to Catie's cheek with a tenderness that never used to come naturally to her. 'I blame myself. I know it was my fault—'

'Mine too,' Catie insisted. 'I should have got in touch a long time ago.'

'Maybe,' Patty acknowledged, 'but I'm not sure it would have done any good if you had. I was so ashamed of what I did to you, the way I created that bonfire of everything that was precious to you both. In my head, maybe even my heart . . . But you don't want to hear about all that now . . .'

'No, I do. Tell me, please. Talk to me.'

Allowing herself to be pulled down into a chair, Patty unbuttoned her coat and let her bag drop to the floor.

'I should make us some tea,' Catie said, getting up again. 'Or would you prefer something stronger?'

'Tea's fine. Why don't I make it?'

'I know where everything is.' She was shaking, trembling so hard with relief and shock and confusion that her movements felt wrong and heavy.

'Let me,' Patty insisted, and Catie did, because Patty was

so much more capable than anyone else she knew, and it felt right for her to be in charge, even in this house that she'd never been to before, and of a daughter she hadn't seen in almost two decades.

When the tea was made, Patty cleared some space on the table and set the mugs down. Catie came to sit next to her, eager to be close to her, to hear everything she had to say. She still couldn't be sure she wasn't dreaming; perhaps she'd wake up in a minute and find herself alone again, but for as long as she believed her mother was here she could cope with her life.

Patty took a sip of tea and put her mug down. 'We've got a lot of things to say to one another,' she began, 'but all that matters now is you and what you're going through.'

Feeling herself hit a wall, as she always did when Jake came back into focus, Catie struggled to swallow her tears.

'It's all right to cry,' Patty told her.

Catie nodded. 'It's just that . . .'

'It's OK, I get that me turning up like this is hard to deal with on top of everything else. It's been a shock for you . . . I should have called first, and I thought about it, I even picked up the phone a few times, but I have to be honest, I was afraid of what you might say when you knew it was me. I still was when I knocked on the door, but I thought if a daughter ever needed her mother . . . And if you were going to give me my marching orders, then we probably ought to see one another one last time.'

Welling up again, Catie said, 'I'm glad you did it this way. I think, if you'd rung . . . I'd have been so nervous waiting, knowing you were on your way, that we were about to meet after so long . . . Given how things are with me, I'd have made life even more impossible for everyone than I'm already managing.'

Ever the pragmatist, Patty said, 'So who's taking care of you? I hope someone is.'

'Yes, they are. I don't know if you remember Jude Penrose?'

Patty frowned, but it didn't take her long to say, 'Wasn't she the girl you socked outside the Town's Talk all those years ago?'

Catie choked on a laugh. 'That's her, but a lot's changed. She's . . . Well, I guess you could say she's my best friend now . . . Who saw that coming, eh? Believe it or not, I even get along with Lawrence's mother these days . . . Actually, it took Lawrence starting another . . .' Realizing she was about to go too far, she looked at her mother in painful dismay.

'I know about Lola Higgins,' Patty told her darkly. 'I heard it from her mother. We haven't had much to do with one another since.'

Realizing that Patty had taken her side without her knowing about it, Catie struggled for the right thing to say. There was so much clamouring for attention in her head, questions that needed answers, confusions that required clarity, an urge to explain herself, to make her mother understand why she'd allowed the double life . . .

'I've got to admit,' Patty said, circling a hand around her mug, 'I never imagined in my wildest dreams that Lawrence would do anything like that. Your dad and I, we loved him like he was the son we never had. It was difficult at first, you know, when you got together with him, you were so young, the two of you, but over time, we saw – *I* saw, your father always knew it – how right you were for one another.

'*Her*, on the other hand, that Lola, she's a different story. She was always jealous of you, wanted everything you had . . .'

'I don't remember that,' Catie said. 'I thought we were close.'

'Oh, you were, but that doesn't mean she didn't hanker after being as pretty and talented and popular as you. Everyone knew that except you. She wouldn't have had any friends if it wasn't for you, even her own mother admits to it. I know she's changed now, got herself all glammed up – the publicity she gets with her celebrity photos and the like, I've seen her, but we know from what she's done to you that she's only different on the outside. On the inside she's proved she's the same old Lola wanting what's our Catie's . . .' She shook her head in distaste and dislike. 'Still, speaking ill of her now isn't going to change anything, is it? I'm just glad your father didn't have to see it. It would have broken his heart as sure as it must have broken yours.'

Catie didn't answer, she had no need to, because her mother clearly already understood how devastating and humiliating it had been. But nothing, nothing at all, would ever compare to what she was going through now.

Patty continued to look at her and at last Catie saw the shadows of pain and loneliness in her silvery-grey eyes, the longing to be accepted and understood in spite of what she'd done. Softly she said, 'Do you still miss him?'

'Every day,' Patty answered, with no hesitation, 'and I know you do too. Oh, he's not in the forefront of our minds any more, but he's always *there*. He meant everything to us both, and in so many ways, we could probably never name them all.' She seemed bothered, lost for an instant, then gave a fleeting smile. 'You're still like him,' she declared, seeming happy to land on that. 'I knew it was what I'd find hard when I came here, seeing him in you. I suppose it's part of what kept me away. I was afraid to face him, and you, with who I was, what I'd done.' She took a breath.

'All that resentment I'd bottled up over the years towards my own daughter, and that bloody bonfire . . .' She paused again and her sad eyes lost focus as she returned to that dreadful, long-ago time. 'I did it to punish him for dying,' she stated, 'and to hurt you, because he'd loved you so much more than he loved me.'

'Oh, but he didn't, Mum,' Catie protested. 'It was just different, that's all.'

'Of course, it was. I know that now, but . . .' Patty lifted a knotted hand, as if to put it somewhere, but let it drop back into her lap. 'I had a lot of very bad things going round in my head for a very long time,' she confessed. 'I was stubborn and full of bitterness towards the whole world, towards God I suppose, for taking him away . . . And before that, for not making me a part of what you two had. I kept seeing myself as the sensible, boring one who just got in the way. He always took your side in everything and that used to drive me wild. What a stupid, selfish, pathetic woman I was. I reckon I'd still have all that nonsense going on in my head, doing all its wickedness if it weren't for . . . Well, let's just say I've seen the error of my ways, and would you believe I'm trying to mend them? Of course, I've still got a long way to go, big old sinner that I am, but there's a minister at the old people's home where I work sometimes, and she's been helping me.'

Catie regarded her in surprise.

'Don't worry, I haven't got God, or anything like that,' Patty assured her. 'Well, maybe I have a bit, but it doesn't mean I'm here to try and preach to you. I'm here because Sarah – the minister – convinced me that I didn't have to be afraid to face you any more. She said, there would never be a time in your life when you needed me more, and if I didn't understand that, then I wasn't the person she thought

I was. We won't get into what she actually thinks of me, but I can tell you it's a bit savoury at times. She plays the trumpet, you know? She's probably got hairs on her chest too, but I've never asked. Anyway, she doesn't play as well as Dad, obviously, but she's quite good. I think you'd like her, if you met her. I'm not saying you have to, but if you do, it'll be for another time . . . You've got a lot going on right now and I don't want to be burdening you with all my stuff. I just want to help in any way I can.'

Realizing her mother's emotions were getting the better of her, Catie enveloped her in a hug – and how wonderful it felt to be holding onto one of her family, her own flesh and blood. The last time had been with Jake, and how small he'd started to make her feel all wrapped up in his muscly arms. Growing so fast . . . 'I'm so glad you're here,' she said softly. 'I know this might sound silly, but I feel as though Dad brought you. He realized we needed one another and well, here you are.'

Patty's eyes were teary and wry as she patted Catie's hand. 'Could be you're right,' she said. 'It's a nice thought anyway, and I mean it, I'm here to help in any way I can.'

Catie didn't stop to consider it. 'Will you come tomorrow?' she asked. 'To the funeral, I mean. Having you there will make a big difference for me.'

Clearly moved, Patty said, 'Of course, I'll be there, you don't need to worry about that. I just wish I'd . . .' They both looked up as the back door opened and Jude came in.

'Gosh, I'm sorry,' Jude exclaimed. 'I didn't realize you had company.'

'Jude,' Catie said, keeping hold of Patty's hand as she stood up, 'I don't know if you remember my mother, Patty MacAllister. Mum, this is Jude.'

'Oh my goodness!' Jude gasped, clasping a hand to her chest. 'This is . . . Wonderful?' she said, glancing at Catie.

Catie nodded.

'I am so pleased you're here,' Jude gushed, coming to seize Patty in an extravagant embrace. 'But you mustn't let me interrupt. I didn't see a car outside or I'd never have crashed in.'

'How did you get here?' Catie asked her mother.

'How do you think? I got the bus. Well, two actually, and then I walked from the main road. It's quite nice around here, I can see why you like it. All the big houses and lovely trees.'

'Mum's coming to the funeral tomorrow,' Catie told Jude, her heart immediately trying to reject the horror of what lay in store. 'You'll sit with me, won't you?' she asked.

'If that's what you want,' Patty answered. 'Just tell me what time to be here.'

'It's at two o'clock, but why don't you stay, now, tonight?' Catie urged, suddenly unable to bear the thought of her leaving.

'I don't have anything with me,' Patty objected.

'No problem, I can run you home to get what you need,' Jude told her.

'Oh no, I can't be putting you to all that trouble. It's all right, I can go back the way I came, and—'

'No, I've made up my mind,' Jude cut in. 'Are you still living in Fishponds?'

'Of course, where else would I be? It's your father's house,' she reminded Catie. 'There's only one way I'll be leaving there and it's in a box.' Her eyes rounded in horror as she realized what she'd said. 'Oh, my word,' she murmured as Catie and Jude started to laugh. 'I didn't mean . . .'

'I know,' Catie said, her heart making a small space for

the only moment of black humour she'd known since the day before Christmas Eve. And wasn't it amazing, unbelievable even, that it had come from her mother?

Hundreds of mourners turned out the next day, most of them young – school friends, team-mates, fellow actors, the devastated skiing party, teenagers Catie had never even seen before. Each one of them looked as shell-shocked and grief-stricken as the next. Teachers, coaches, neighbours, old friends and new acquaintances came to pay their respects. The school choir sang the coffin in, and four of his closest friends read tributes they'd written themselves. Two girls sang a song composed in his honour and his head of house told short, wry stories of Jake's misdemeanours and boisterousness, citing incidents the man probably shouldn't have known about, and the fact that he did made the students laugh and cry.

Though Lawrence tried to deliver the eulogy, he wasn't able to get through it, so his brother stepped quietly up to the podium to take over.

With her mother one side of her and Marilyn the other, Catie kept her eyes lowered throughout. She'd taken more tranquillizers that morning; it was as if by not really engaging with anything she could render it unreal, put herself at a distance she didn't have to bridge. She hadn't looked at Matthew, who was seated with his father, uncle and aunt; the only words they'd exchanged today had been out of necessity, nothing to do with tenderness or comfort.

There was no sign of Lola, and Catie wondered if it was because she hadn't been able to find the courage to face her, or maybe Lawrence had asked her not to come. She didn't care which, could only feel thankful that she wasn't there.

She didn't join in with any of the hymns, merely listened to the words and somehow managed to admire the choir's excellence. She knew, almost with no feeling, that she would never sing again. Her heart was with Jake now and that was where it would stay. No one could sing without a heart.

The school orchestra accompanied the choir for Leonard Cohen's 'Hallelujah' as the coffin was carried out, and the magnificence of the voices soaring to the rafters, the sheer beauty of it, and soulful depth, was overwhelming. Catie felt Marilyn start to slump and moved quickly to catch her. Jude was there too, and then Graham. Patty took Catie's hand and they slipped in between Lawrence and Matthew to walk back down the aisle. Catie wanted to reach out to her eldest son, to put a hand on his back and let him know she forgave him, but she still wasn't sure that she did.

Later, much later, after the sun had gone down and the youngsters began turning the reception into a party to celebrate Jake's life, Catie and her mother returned to the house. Marilyn had already gone home with Graham and Fiona, while Jude, along with others, remained at the hall to make sure things didn't get out of hand.

Catie felt so exhausted – so utterly drained and raw – that she could only sink into a chair, still in her coat, as Patty poured large shots of whisky into their tea and brought it to the table. It was her first taste of alcohol today and it was so much more of a comfort than all the expressions of sorrow she'd heard over and over for the past five hours. Certainly, more than the young girls who'd clung to her in tears wanting her to know how much they'd loved Jake, and seeming to expect her to offer them solace.

For a long time neither she nor her mother attempted to speak. There were no words, only platitudes, and what was the point of them? This was a day Catie had somehow managed to get through, only because of the Alprazolam, but there were going to be so many more . . .

She looked up at the unexpected sound of someone coming down the stairs. Her heart turned inside out. It had to be Jake. He was the only one who lived here now, apart from her, so today, the last three weeks, all of it, must have been a nightmare. He'd been in his room all along and she was finally waking up.

Except her mother was here and that was real.

She stared through the open kitchen door into the hall, certain she was going to see him at any second; too afraid of it not being him to move.

It was Matthew who appeared at the bottom of the stairs and dropped a heavy bag on the floor.

He turned to start along the hall, and came to a dead stop as he saw her. His face was pinched and white, his whole body seeming rigid to the point of breaking. A long, terrible moment passed, before he said, 'I didn't hear you come in.'

She closed her eyes, having no idea what to say.

'It's OK, I'm going,' he told her gruffly. 'I just came to pick up some stuff.'

She shook her head, trying to make herself connect with his words.

'I said, *I'm going*,' he shouted. 'I'm getting out of here so you'll never have to see me again.'

She attempted to speak, but he was still shouting.

'I know you blame me, and you're right, it was my fault, but it's not the only reason you hate me, is it? Ever since I was born you've hated me, and you've always tried to push me away. Jake was the one you loved. He could never do anything wrong in your eyes and I could never do anything right.' His voice snagged on a sob of anger and grief. 'Have you got any idea how it felt growing up knowing my own mother didn't really care about me? You were all about yourself, going off to your gigs and concerts, and when you came back it was only Jake you couldn't wait to see, never me. You went to his matches, his plays, his parents' evenings, but no way did you want anything to do with mine. I was never good enough for you. And look at you now, you can't even be bothered to speak to me, and he was *my brother*! I didn't mean for it to happen. If I'd known it would, I'd never have taken him, and it's killing me that I'll never see him again. But you don't need to worry, you'll never have to see me. I'm out of here . . .'

Stepping around the table so he could see her, Patty said, 'Don't go like this, Matthew.'

He stared at her uncomprehendingly. 'Who are you?' he demanded.

'I'm your grandmother and if—'

'Oh, the grandmother who's been here for us all our lives?' he cut in scathingly. 'Well, old lady, don't think you can tell me what to do now. You've got no idea about anything around here. It's no wonder Dad wanted another family—'

'Take that back,' Patty instructed.

'Forget it! I'm only speaking the truth and if you, or she, can't take it, then I'm sorry, too bad . . .'

'Matthew,' Catie croaked.

'Don't even speak my name. I'm done with you. You didn't lose one son today, you lost them both,' and grabbing his bag he threw it out into the porch and slammed the door behind him.

'I'll get him back,' Patty said, starting down the hall, but by the time she stepped outside he was already piling into a friend's car and they were driving away.

CHAPTER THIRTY-SEVEN

Catie's eyes are bleary and sore after a near sleepless night. When she'd left Giancarlo in bed during the early hours to go and check her phone, she hadn't intended to write about the devastating heartbreak of Jake's death. Or the harrowing scene with Matthew that had followed, but for whatever reason it had happened. Maybe because she'd felt compelled to try proving to herself that finally, after all this time, she was starting to move forward.

After all, it's the reason she's here.

Giancarlo has been up for a while now, showered and shaved, and as she looks across the table he exhales a long, low breath while lowering the lid of her laptop. She can see how disturbed he is by what he's just read, as a parent, as a human being, how could he not be?

'How long ago was this?' he asks, reaching for the coffee she's just poured him. They are sitting inside the apartment this morning with the terrace doors open to allow in a refreshing breeze. After a downpour during the night everything seems shiny and slick, more alive somehow, ready to blossom and burst with new shoots and new beginnings.

'Ten years,' she replies, and even as she says the words, she feels the truth of them churning the pain in her heart. Has Jake really been gone that long? It's still almost impossible to believe, or accept, in spite of how hard she's tried. He'd be twenty-seven by now, could be running his own business, coaching a sports team, seizing everything life had to offer with all his indefatigable passion and exuberance. He might have a girlfriend, or a wife even, if he'd turned out to be as romantic and impulsive as his father.

'Have you spoken to Matthew again in that time?' Giancarlo asks, his voice coming distantly into her thoughts.

She shakes her head and feels the lightness of Jake's possibilities yield to the darkness of Matthew realities. 'More happened after he left that day,' she replies, hoarsely, 'quite a lot more . . .' She takes a moment to brace herself, to try to fight down the build-up of resistance. 'He fell apart,' she says, and her voice caught on the words, as though she might do the same. 'He couldn't handle what had happened to his brother – what boy could? And how much harder it was for him to know that his mother couldn't find it in her heart to forgive him.' Her hands tighten on the table, but she forces them open again, as though unlocking the next words. 'He refused to talk about it, with anyone, and he kept his word to have no more to do with me. I sent him letters, emails, texts . . . I don't think he even read them, and he never replied to the voice messages I left begging him to be in touch with his father even if he wasn't with me.

'Eventually he contacted Lawrence, not to let us know where he was – he'd dropped out of uni by then – but because he needed money. We both feared he'd got into drugs, although we had no evidence of it then, and anyway, how could we refuse him when we didn't know anything for certain. Maybe he'd fallen behind with his rent, or needed something to tide him over until he was paid.

We gave ourselves all the excuses we could think of . . . He was our son, so why wouldn't we, but then Lawrence got a call late one Friday night – this was a year or more after we'd lost Jake – to tell him that Matthew had over- dosed and was in A&E.

'I happened to be in London at the time, so I went straight to the hospital and stayed with him, day and night, until he finally came round. He wasn't interested in talking to me, and he didn't relate much to Lawrence either, but at least he was out of danger. I went to my hotel to catch a nap and change clothes. By the time I got back, he'd managed to discharge himself and had disappeared again.'

She inhales shakily and takes a sip of coffee. Funny how words and thoughts had the power to make things seem real and immediate again, could even rerun the fear and pain, the guilt and terrible heartache. 'We tried to find him,' she continues, 'but we hardly even knew where to begin. His life was a totally mystery to us by then; we knew none of his friends, had no idea where he lived or worked, if he had a job at all. If he was even still in London. Weeks, months, went by and the only contact we had with him was when he needed money. It was always Lawrence he asked, never me, and we struggled terribly over whether or not to give it to him, knowing he was almost certainly going to use it to buy drugs. In the end we usually did, because denying him just never felt like the right option.'

She watches Giancarlo refill her cup and feels the surreal- ness of being between these two worlds, one darkened by the past, the other so beautifully here. 'I was afraid Lola might be giving him money,' she says. 'Lawrence always denied it, but I wasn't so sure.'

'Did she ever contact you after Jake's death?'

She shakes her head. 'She didn't show up at the hospital when Matthew OD'd either. I can't imagine what I'd have done if she had, but thankfully it never happened.' She sighs heavily and pushes herself on, never willing to dwell on Lola for long. 'None of his old friends could tell us anything about him; they hadn't heard from him since he'd dropped out and not even a private investigator was much help. By the time we got to wherever he'd been spotted, he'd already gone . . . I spent months, over a year, walking the streets, visiting homeless shelters, constantly checking hospitals in an effort to find him. Sometimes my mother or Jude came with me, but mostly I was alone. Jude had her own family to care for, and it was too much for Patty in spite of what she might try to tell you. I followed leads to Manchester, Glasgow, even to Dublin. Whether or not they were real, I had no idea, but I had to try. Sometimes I felt as though I was only a couple of steps behind him; other times I was close to despair of ever finding him.

'Then he overdosed again and was rushed to St Thomas's. Whether he'd been in London all along we had no idea, but at least we knew where he was now. Thankfully he got through it again. The big difference this time, after the crisis had passed, was that he agreed to go into rehab.

'I arranged it all and paid for it. We weren't allowed to visit, but a caseworker gave us regular updates and they were usually good. He stayed for three months and then one day, out of the blue, Lawrence received a call from him saying he was in Australia. We had no idea if it was the truth, but he'd certainly left the clinic, and several weeks after the call he got in touch again to ask for five thousand pounds to be sent to a bank in Sydney. He sent an email afterwards, saying he was making a go of things there and he'd pay everything back as soon as he was able.'

She takes a breath and then another, before she realizes that maybe she isn't feeling quite as panicked or anxious as she usually does when trying to talk about this part of her life. She looks at Giancarlo.

'Go on,' he says.

She collects her thoughts and looks out at the bay, as she says, 'While we waited for more news of him, I came to suspect, with my mother's and Jude's help, that Lola had paid for his ticket out there. We had no proof, but it felt like the kind of thing she'd do behind all our backs. We'd already worked out that his view of his childhood, and his relationship with me, had very probably been influenced by Lola for years. She knew all about my postnatal depression, of course, and she could well have used it to deepen his insecurities and drive a wedge between us. I guess she hoped it would bring him closer to her. I could imagine her telling him she was the one who'd come to save him as a baby, who hadn't allowed his self-absorbed mother to give him up when things got really bad. And then she was making his father happy, and who didn't want Lawrence to be happy after all he'd been through with me? Because all I really wanted was to be out there singing, performing, jetting from one exotic venue to the next . . . While what Lola wanted was Matthew and Jake to be a part of *her* family.'

'So, it wasn't enough for her that she had his children too?' Giancarlo says, making it more of a statement.

Catie's mind whirls. There are so many ways to answer that question, and probably most of them aren't known to her, so she gets up to go and fetch his mobile phone from the kitchen. It's buzzed several times in the last few minutes but, so far, he's ignored it. 'I think,' she says, giving the easiest answer right now, 'that when you've betrayed someone the way she betrayed me, then it's almost impossible to feel secure in the world you've constructed based on their pain. She wanted to reel my boys in, keep them close, and that way she'd keep Lawrence close too. Are you going to answer?' she asks, handing him the phone as it rings again. 'It's Ricardo.'

He nods as he takes it. 'He's expecting to drive me to *la fattoria* this morning. One of the local wine-growers is interested in making an offer for our land.'

'Just the land? What about the house?'

'They go together, he knows that, but I fear he's intending to demolish *la fattoria* if he is successful in his bid. My brother and I will not agree to this, so it's not likely he will be successful.'

'But you'll meet him anyway?'

'It's only polite, but it doesn't need to be today. Or,' he added, regarding her closely, 'maybe I should go and allow you to sleep?'

Although she feels drained, wretched even, she's also wired, so she says, 'Why don't I come with you?'

He smiles. 'That was my plan, but no, *cara*, you need to rest and it won't be interesting for you if all the talk is of business.' A mischievous look comes into his eyes. 'Anyway, I have a surprise for you later, so I would like it if you are fully awake.'

Her eyebrows show her interest. 'What sort of surprise?'

He seems momentarily puzzled. 'Actually, I can't tell you yet, but I'm sure I will think of one.'

She laughs and goes to kiss him on the forehead, but he tilts his head back and, as she sinks into his lap, many more minutes pass before he's ready to ring Ricardo with instructions on how the day is to unfold.

* * *

Although it's her intention to sleep after he's gone, she realizes, as she watches him from the terrace, walking through the narrow street full of cafés and delis, always waving and greeting someone, that she feels ready now to try to exorcize the very worst of her shame. The pain has already been laid bare, but she can't have come this far only to back away from her crimes now. It isn't something she wants him to read, but she won't allow it to remain unspoken or unwritten. If she does, it will continue to have power over her, to be like a sore festering inside her, and that would be the same as allowing Lola to control her.

Before sitting down with her laptop she makes more coffee and opens up her phone.

CM: *Are you there?*

***188: *I am now. How are you?*

CM: *OK, I think.*

***188: *I've had a phone call.*

CM: *Do I need to be worried?*

***188: *I'll answer that when I know more.*

CM: *No police involved?*

***188: *Please don't worry.*

CM: *Can I call you?*

***188: *You don't have to ask. It was you who made the decision you wouldn't.*

CM: *OK.*

***188: *I get the impression you're almost there now.*

CM: *I am.*

***188: *And then you'll be ready to come back?*

She doesn't know how to answer the final question, so rather than try she shuts the phone down and carries a fresh pot of coffee to her laptop.

CHAPTER THIRTY-EIGHT

'The answer is no, Lawrence, absolutely *no*!'

'But Catie, it's not your decision to make,' he reminded her coolly. 'She's my mother . . .'

'And she would not want Lola bloody *Higgins* at her funeral. You have to know that, and so does *she*. So why the hell does she want to be there?'

'She wants to support me . . .'

'Are you serious? Are you really that stupid? What she wants is to rub my face in the fact that she's Mrs Vaughan now, mother of *all* Lawrence's children – oh, except, that's right, one has gone to the other side of the world to get away from us all, and the other is dead.' She was getting far too worked up over this, surging towards hysteria, and right after this call she had to go back into the recording studio, not to sing, she never did that now, but to oversee some mixing of old tracks. So she needed to calm down, to get herself back to a place of faked equilibrium, at least for the next few hours.

'Catie, let me come and see you so we can talk this through. I have to be in Bristol tomorrow . . .'

'I'm not in Bristol. I don't want to see you, and there's nothing to talk about. Just tell me how Matthew is. Have you spoken to him recently? Does he know about his grand-mother?'

'I told him last night. He's upset, obviously, but he's not coming back for the funeral.'

That stung, badly, for herself as well as for Marilyn, though she couldn't say it was a surprise. It had been almost four years since she'd last seen or spoken to him, and, in truth, it didn't always help to hear that he was doing well in Sydney. Not that she wanted him to do badly, for God's sake she'd never want that; it was just that she longed desperately to be a part of his life.

Still, at least he'd been in touch with his grandmother during these last few months of her illness. It had meant the world to Marilyn to hear his voice, had probably even kept her going longer than she might have if she hadn't had his calls to look forward to.

'Are you still there?' Lawrence asked.

'So Matthew's not coming,' she snapped, 'and you thought you'd bring Lola instead. Well, forget it . . .'

'Catie, try to be reasonable. You won't have to speak to her if you don't want to . . .'

'Of course, I don't fucking want to, and she's not coming, Lawrence. Tell her that now! Right now! She is not welcome at the church and she sure as hell will not be setting foot inside my home.'

She was about to hang up when he said, 'Let me remind you again, she's *my* mother . . .'

'I know who she is,' she tried not to scream, 'and now tell me this: who's been there for all this time, taking her to doctors' appointments; showering and dressing her, some-times feeding her? Not you, Lawrence. And who saw her through the worst of losing Jake? Who broke her heart even before that with his *second family*? You are a disgrace,

Lawrence Vaughan, as a husband, a father and a son.' And before he could whip her into an even greater fury, she ended the call and turned her face to the wall.

'Hey, Catie? You OK?' Jason the sound recordist asked, coming out of the studio. 'That seemed like a pretty heavy call. If you want to take a break . . .'

'I do,' she told him shakily. 'Thanks. I need to go. I'm not sure when I'll be back . . . Sorry.'

After snatching up her bag and coat she ran out of the building to the car park. She didn't usually drive to London, but today she had and now she was glad of it, because she didn't want the ordeal of trying to find a taxi.

She had no clear idea yet of what she intended to do when she got to Lola's studio. She only knew, as she navigated the heavy traffic around Hammersmith into Fulham, that something inside her had finally snapped. Why it had happened over Marilyn's funeral and not over Jake or Matthew, she couldn't say, but all the anger, pain and hatred that had been building for years was suddenly no longer under control.

'She'll get her comeuppance,' Jude had once promised, 'karma will take care of it. You just need to focus on you.'

Well, to hell with karma. It was time for Lola Higgins to pay for what she'd done, and she, Catie, didn't give a damn about what it might end up costing her.

When she got to the right street in Clapham, the photography studio was easy to find. One huge, expensive-looking shop front, with white wooden blinds protecting the windows and preventing anyone from peering in, and a single black-and-white photograph of a well-known actor seeming to float mid-air.

Leaving her car on a yellow line, she crossed over the quiet road and was surprised when she pushed at the door to find it opened.

'Hello? How can I help you?' a young lad with punky black hair and piercings enquired cheerily.

'Where is she?' Catie demanded, barely looking at him.

He was instantly worried. 'I'm sorry, do you have the correct . . .?'

Ignoring him, she marched behind his reception desk straight through a door marked Private. It too opened.

The room beyond turned out to be bigger than she'd expected, and was set up like a gallery, exhibiting dozens of photographs against stark white fabric-covered walls, most of them suspended from ceiling wires. There was a gantry at the top of an iron staircase, full of lights and other paraphernalia; the floor was whitewashed and pristine and, at the centre of the room, encased in a tall glass display case, was an antique-looking box-camera and tripod.

No doubt a prized possession – or maybe just a prop. What did she know or care?

'Please, you shouldn't be in here,' the boy objected, seeming to want to wrestle her out, but not daring to touch her.

'Where is she?' Catie asked again.

'If you mean Lola . . .'

'Yes, I mean Lola . . .'

'She's not here right now. Is there something I can help with?'

'When will she be back?' Catie was taking in the candle lamps now, strategically placed about the studio on small white plinths, their small flickering flames softening the sterile ambience, and suggesting a client might be due at any minute.

'It's OK, Joe, I'll handle this.'

Catie looked up and there she was, her nemesis, the woman she loathed above all others, watching them from the gantry.

'Can I . . . get some . . . coffee?' the lad asked anxiously.

'Just go,' Catie told him, keeping her eyes on Lola. 'Or stay if you want to, it makes no odds to me.'

Lola was halfway down the steps now, and nodded for her assistant to leave. Catie had to hand it to her, she looked the part in her lumberjack shirt and black leggings, hair skewed into a high ponytail and face as smooth as a cosmetic surgeon could make it. Top photographer at work, looking good, but not good enough to compete with the more glamorous clients.

'Why are you here?' Lola asked, almost imperiously, as she reached the bottom of the steps. There wasn't enough light to tell if she was nervous, but she surely had to be, and guilty and embarrassed and full of shame. Any normal person would feel all that and more . . .

Unfazed by the show of calm, Catie said, 'To begin with, I've come to tell you what Lawrence doesn't have the guts to: that you are not welcome at Marilyn's funeral.'

Lola's expression tightened. 'I don't see that as your decision . . .'

'Take it from me, it is. No one wants you there.'

'Lawrence does, and as Matthew can't make it . . .'

At the mention of her son's name, Catie felt the little control she had left slip anchor. 'What the hell is wrong with you?' she snarled. 'What did I ever do to you to make you want to ruin my life?'

Lola shrugged, as if irritated by the question, but Catie could see it had hit a mark. 'You've ruined your own life, Catie,' she replied. 'No one had to help, least of all me.'

'*What?*'

'Maybe if you hadn't always put yourself first, hadn't neglected your husband and . . .'

'Is that what he told you? That I neglected him?' Her tone

was incredulous, scornful. 'Or is that what you tell yourself to try and justify the way you wheedled yourself into his bed? To make it possible to live with yourself after I *trusted* you . . .'

'To take care of your son? Yes, I did that, and we all know what would have happened to him if I hadn't.'

Catie's eyes rounded with shock. 'Tell me,' she challenged with icy calm. 'What would have happened to him?'

Lola glanced away, clearly not as willing to answer this as Catie had been to ask it. 'Let's just say everyone thought he was in harm's way . . .'

'No! No one thought that! It's a story you've spun for yourself to try to excuse how you took advantage of a depressed *friend* and her husband who you'd always had the hots for. I admit I didn't see it at the time, I had no idea, and I don't think he did either until you managed to get to him. He's a weak man, we all know that now, and you are a scheming, vindictive, soulless bitch who deserves to be exposed for who you really are.'

'You're being hysterical . . .'

'Yes! I'm hysterical. I'm also the mother of a wonderful young man who'd be alive today if it weren't for you.'

'That's not true.'

'My son! Lola! My youngest boy, who you know damned well should never have been on that ski trip – and he wouldn't have been if *you* hadn't given him the money . . .'

'He asked me because *you—*'

'And you could have said no, but instead you colluded with Matthew to fly him out before I knew anything about it. And we all know what happened after. Then you did the same with Matthew. You gave him money to go to Australia to be as far from me as he could get. You did that, didn't you? I don't know why you wanted to hurt me so much, why you still seem hell-bent on pushing your way into my life, and I sure as hell don't know how you sleep at night, knowing what you've done to my family? How can you even face yourself in the mirror, knowing who you really are? And how the fuck does Lawrence look at you, knowing what you did?'

Lola's face had paled, suggesting she probably didn't sleep, and maybe she didn't know how Lawrence could tolerate her either. Nevertheless she said, 'What happened to Jake was an accident, Catie. No one pushed him . . .'

'But he wouldn't have been there if *you hadn't paid for him to go*. His blood is all over your hands and you know it. He was smashed apart on those rocks, just like this!' And giving the display case an almighty shove, she sent it crashing to the ground in a shower of shattered glass and metal.

'For God's sake!' Lola cried, running forward as if to rescue it. 'Do you have any idea—?'

'Don't you dare tell me how much it's worth,' Catie seethed, 'because *nothing* is worth more than my son. And the way you've turned Matthew against me . . . You've dripped your poison into his ears, made him believe I never cared about him, and *you know that's not true*. You are evil, Lola Higgins. Rotten to your rancid core, and all I ever did was believe in you as a friend. You need to count yourself lucky that I've never gone in search of *your* children to make them pay for your crimes, but I know this place means just as much to you, and now here's what I think of it . . .'

Lola gasped and shrieked as Catie began pushing over the candle lamps, smashing them to smithereens and barely even noticing as a stray flame snagged hold of a fabric wall. 'Stop! For God's sake!' Lola cried, trying to get to her, but

Catie was moving too fast – with too much fury and hatred – to hear, much less to pause.

Not until every last lamp was destroyed did she allow herself to draw breath, but even then, she was too blinded by rage and grief to realize there was a fire.

'Joe!' Lola was shouting, struggling to stay upright on the broken glass as she tried to get to the drapes. 'Joe! Bring . . .'. She grunted as she went down, hitting the floor hard, cracking her face against a corner of the old camera.

Catie walked past her, crunching the glass, but staying upright as Joe raced past her with a fire extinguisher, yelling that she was a psycho and he'd rung 999.

She didn't stop, simply continued out to her car, unaware of the cuts on her hands dripping blood over her clothes, not even seeing the crowd that was starting to gather outside the shop.

Less than twenty-four hours later, the police came to arrest her at Breemoor.

So, in the end, neither she, nor Lola, attended Marilyn's funeral – she was in custody, and Lola was in hospital fighting for her life.

CHAPTER THIRTY-NINE

Catie walks quietly through from the bedroom, wearing only a short, semi-transparent chemise, to find Giancarlo in the kitchen dropping dried fennel, rosemary, lemon juice and salt into a small bowl of olive oil.

She smiles and moves in close to him, using a crouton to taste the mix. 'Mmm, delicious,' she murmurs. 'How long have you been here?'

'Almost an hour,' he replies, brushing a kiss to her forehead and using a paper towel to wipe his fingers. 'Good sleep?'

She nods and says, 'Am I allowed to double-dip?'

'As it's you. Tony is going to bring us some fresh tuna for dinner.' He checks the time. 'He should be here soon.'

She turns into the circle of his arms and tilts her face up to his, aware that she isn't looking her best, but it's not as if he hasn't seen her with bed-hair and no make-up before this, and he hasn't run away yet. 'How did it go today?' she asks. 'Was there a deal to be done?'

He smooths her face with the back of one hand and gazes thoughtfully into her eyes. 'I'm not sure,' he replies. 'Giorgio Rizzo is an . . . *interesting* man, with some equally interesting connections, but he is prepared to make a very good offer for the land.'

'What about the house?'

'He says he will renovate and turn it into a holiday rental, but I'm afraid Giorgio is not always a man of his word.'

'But if it's in a legal contract?'

'You are in Sicily,' he reminds her, with no small irony, 'there are many ways of doing things here, but maybe we are a step further in our negotiations. Would you like some wine?'

She shakes her head. 'I need to take a shower.' She narrows her eyes playfully. 'Care to join me?'

He throws out his hands. 'If not for these staples, you know I would. Plus, we are expecting Tony.'

Noticing that the strain of tiredness around his eyes has deepened, she says, 'Are you OK? Have you had any news from Palermo?'

He's about to reply when the door-buzzer alerts them to Tony's arrival. 'I'll go to let him in,' he says, touching a brief kiss to her lips.

'Is he eating with us?'

'No, he has other arrangements this evening.'

She starts to move away but he keeps hold of her hand. 'I see you were writing while I was out,' he says. 'Can I read it?'

Aware of what a terrible light she is soon to be painted in, she makes herself say, 'It isn't finished yet, but yes, you can read what's there.'

When she returns from the bathroom half an hour later, she finds Tony lounging on the terrace checking messages on his phone.

'Ah, Catie,' he smiles, getting up from his chair with a jaunty raise of his hat. 'It is good to see you. Giancarlo has to go out for a moment, but he will be back soon.'

Puzzled, she says, 'Where did he go?'

'Oh, not far, nearby, to take a phone call. All is good. How are you enjoying the flat?'

Bothered by Giancarlo's disappearance, considering what he'd presumably read while she was in the bathroom, it takes her a moment to connect with Tony's enquiry. 'Oh, yes, very much, thanks,' she replies. 'Please tell Isabella I'm taking good care of it.'

He beams. 'She is happy to know this. May I ask how long you are staying? No rush for you to leave, of course. This is just, how you say, idle chat?'

As she goes to open some wine, she's still trying to shake a growing sense of disquiet as she offers him a drink.

'Ah, no, thank you. I must go home soon; I have a friend waiting for me.'

She pours herself a glass and takes it onto the terrace. Though she can't believe Giancarlo would walk out without a word after reading about what she'd done to Lola, she can't recall him ever needing to go outside to take a call. Something unusual is happening, she just can't think what it might be.

'The sun is back,' Tony announces cheerily as she sits down. 'Nice weather again for next few days.'

'Did Giancarlo ask you to stay and . . .?'

'Ah, *sì, sì,* he not want you to come back and find no one here. He will not be long time. Ah, good news, here he is.'

She hears the security gate clang outside and looks round as Giancarlo comes in. His eyes come straight to hers, serious, unreadable, and her heart twists with a further sense of unease. 'Is everything all right?' she asks.

Going to pour himself some wine, he says, 'The reception is not always good in this flat. Tony, *grazie per avermi aspettato. Tutto è preparato. Ti vedrò domani mattina.*'

After Tony has embraced them both farewell, Giancarlo comes to join her on the terrace. He's grave, detached, seeming to be elsewhere in his mind.

'What did you say to Tony before he left?' she asks, wondering if she really wants to know.

He sighs and pushes a hand through his hair. 'I thanked him for waiting,' he replies.

'Is that all?'

He looks at her, but instead of answering the question he says, 'I have read what you wrote today.'

Her tension increases. He knows now that she's quite possibly a convicted criminal who's either been to prison, or is here escaping justice. Has that changed anything for him? Of course it has, even without him knowing the details.

'I am very keen to know what happened next,' he says.

His failure to mention the attack, along with his unusual abruptness, unsettles her badly. However, she can't back away from this now, and nor will she. She takes a sip of her drink to bolster her courage and says, 'Lola lost an eye when she fell onto the camera.'

He sits quietly with that for a moment, presumably taking in the horror of what such an injury would mean for anyone, especially a photographer. 'And you?' he prompts.

Steeling herself, she says, 'I was charged with lesser culpability arson and S20 GBH, for which I was sentenced to five years in prison.'

Seeming neither shocked nor surprised, he simply says, 'S20 GBH?'

'Grievous Bodily Harm without intent,' she explains. 'Lola and her lawyers tried to push for S18, which covers intent, and I suppose they had a point. After all, it could be said I went there intending to cause harm. Not that sort of harm, obviously, but I wasn't in my right mind that day – I don't suppose I had been since losing Jake. Maybe even since my marriage had broken up. But losing Jake, I'm sure it's what . . .' She's breathless for a moment. 'Everything had been building up inside me for so long, to a point where, according to my lawyers and a psychiatrist, I lost control of my actions. I think it was the reason the prosecution ended up settling for S20.'

Seeming to understand that, he says, 'And Lawrence? Where was he during this time of your arrest and her . . . treatment?'

Realizing she doesn't exactly know, she says, 'Supporting her, I suppose. Well, obviously he would have been. I didn't see him. He made no contact with me at all until after the sentencing. I pleaded guilty, by the way. Obviously I had to.'

Brushing past that, he says, 'Did he visit you in prison?'

'No, he wrote to tell me how heartbroken he was over the way things had turned out. He said he didn't blame me for anything, and that a part of him would always love me, but he was sure I understood that it was time to separate our assets now we were no longer married.'

His eyes darken as he says, 'So you had to sell the house?'

She shakes her head. 'Jude and my mother found a lawyer for me to make sure he didn't try to overstate his claims, but in the end he didn't really ask for much. And, I have to admit, he was good about keeping me up to date about Matthew. Always by letter, he never came to see me and I didn't try to ring.'

'Didn't Matthew get in touch himself?'

How much it still hurts to answer no to that question, so badly that she feels herself tensing against the pain. Her eldest son, who exists now only in the photographs and messages Lawrence sends, who's soon going to be thirty years old, and there is still no contact between them. It's unthinkable, completely unbearable. 'Lawrence has tried to persuade him to see me,' she says, 'but he's still refusing.' She takes an unsteady breath and, in order to get away from that devastating truth, she pushes herself on. 'I ended up serving fourteen months of my sentence before the pandemic hit and I was released to serve the rest of my term on licence.'

He nods slowly, thoughtfully, showing no signs of how her story is affecting him. 'So, you swapped one sort of lockdown for another?' he comments.

Her smile has no humour. 'I guess you could say that.'

'Were you alone for that time?'

'No, my mother came to stay, and we saw Jude and her family when we were allowed to bubble.' She wants to ask how he and his family coped, but since it's not the point of the conversation, she lets it go.

'Is your son still in Australia?'

'Yes, and apparently he's still doing very well in his job. He's the communications manager for a PR and marketing firm, based in Melbourne, so he's no longer in Sydney. He has a girlfriend who he's living with, and there's some talk of marriage . . .' Speaking the words out loud makes their truth feel so harsh, so isolating . . . It's still too hard to accept.

'And you?' Giancarlo asks. 'Do you remain on . . . licence? This is probation?'

She nods and, stealing herself for the next terrible admission, she says, 'It's due to end in February, so in three months' time.' She waits for a reaction to the fact that, legally, she shouldn't be here, but it's not clear yet whether he's connected with the seriousness of what she's just told him. 'The system is in chaos,' she explains. 'I almost never see my probation officer, and even when I do, months pass before the next time. So far no one has contacted my mother to find out where I am, but I'm sure it'll happen at some point.' Maybe it already has, but she's not going to think about that now.

'And if it's discovered you've left the country?' he asks. 'What then?'

'I'm not sure. It could be they'll send me back to prison, but I think it's more likely they'll extend the licence and take away my passport.'

He says nothing and, as she continues to look at him, so silent and still, she suddenly realizes that she needs to explain herself much better than this. 'I know I should have told you everything at the start,' she says, 'and I'm sorry. I truly am. I must seem so . . . deceitful now . . . My only excuse is that I had no idea we'd become so close, and when we did . . .' She takes a breath. 'I've loved, cherished, every minute of the time we've spent together, but I swear I'd give it all up so I'd never have to see you looking at me the way you are now.'

He appears puzzled, bewildered even, as if not quite understanding what she's saying, until clearly he does and he reaches for her hand. '*Oh cara mia, mi dispiace,*' he says, looking directly into her eyes. 'There are things . . .' He shakes his head and starts again, 'What happened was terrible, for both you and Lola, but you are my only concern. It's hard to think of your suffering, of how much you've lost, the ordeals you have faced . . . And now I . . .' He lets her hand go and gets up from the table.

'What?' she says, not understanding as he goes into the apartment then turns back again. 'What is it?'

'The phone call just now,' he says, 'it was to tell me that the results of my tests are . . .' He raises a hand as she gasps. 'The doctor requires a second opinion,' he explains, 'but he insists I must not read too much into it. This means, however, that I will not have an answer until there is news from a laboratory in Roma . . .'

Before he can go on, she's on her feet embracing him, and overflowing with relief and fear as she says, 'Whatever the outcome, you know I'll be with you, at least for as long as I can . . .'

To her surprise, he takes her arms from around his neck and holds her hands between his. '*Cara*, I cannot let you do this, and not only because it is too much for you after all you have been through. You do not need to attach yourself to a man who has my problems, you must not . . .'

'It's my decision . . .'

'But I'm afraid I need to return to Turin, *cara mia*. I thought maybe I'd have some more time here, to spend with you, to be as we are together, but my brother . . . There is a crisis in the company and he needs me there. I want to ask you to come with me, but my wife is still in the house . . .'

'Ssh,' she says, somehow managing to sound calm in spite of already falling apart inside. 'I understand. It's OK. We always knew this would probably have to end, and we've made no promises . . .'

'It's true, we have not, but I wish I could make them now. I want to tell you everything that's in my heart, to do whatever I can to make you happy . . .'

'You have made me happy. Everything about you makes me feel glad to be alive, and I truly never thought that would be possible again. I'm not even sure I deserve it . . .'

'You deserve it, *cara*,' he murmurs, cupping his hands around her face. 'I just want to be the one to give it to you, and if I could you know I would.'

301

'Of course, but what's important is this time we've shared. It has meant more to me than I'll ever be able to put into words. Just tell me when you have to leave.'

His face seems to blanch as he says, 'I will take a flight tomorrow evening.'

His reply is a terrible blow to her heart. 'So soon? So little time left . . .'

'What will you do when I go?' he asks.

Without having to think, she says, 'I'll go home too. My mother keeps insisting she isn't waiting, but I know she is.'

'You're in touch with her?'

'We text most days, and yesterday she told me that someone has called her.'

'Do you know who it was?'

'I'm guessing it was my probation officer, but that's for tomorrow. Please, let's make tonight about us.'

Later, when she eventually falls asleep with Giancarlo's arms around her, she has a strange and terrible dream about the accident that killed his wife. Except it isn't Vittoria who dies, it's him. He is crushed by an oncoming lorry, killed outright, and Vittoria is screaming that it was all his fault.

She comes awake suddenly, the horror of it still beating in her heart as she tries to recognize her surroundings.

She's in Isabella's flat, of course, and he's right here with her, as real as the love in her heart. She turns to slip her arms around him, but the bed where he should be is empty. The sheets are turned back, the pillow scrunched against the headboard. He was there, but now he's not . . .

Still shaken by the nightmare, and praying he hasn't already left in the early hours to make parting less painful, she hurries out to the sitting room and almost collapses with relief to see him in the kitchen, making coffee. Early morning sunlight is streaming through the open windows, and the sea beyond is silver and bright.

'I thought . . .' she gasps. 'I was afraid . . .' Not bothering to finish, she wraps her arms around him, resting her cheek against his bare chest, feeling the coolness of the staples holding his incisions together and the warmth of his skin. He is wearing only a towel around his waist and she is wearing only his shirt.

'Did you think I'd gone?' he asks curiously, tilting her face up to his.

She shakes her head, then nods. 'I had a dream . . . It felt so real I couldn't . . .' She shakes her head again. 'It doesn't matter . . . It made no sense anyway. Are you OK? Couldn't you sleep?'

His smile is teasingly intimate. 'I don't remember last night being much about sleep.'

She laughs. It had been a truly memorable few hours of making love, talking for a while, listening to music and gazing into one another's eyes as they made love again. All the time she'd felt the pain of losing him, had been aware of it as if it were a spectre in the corner of the room that she'd refused to allow to trespass on the joy of being with him.

She isn't going to let it spoil today either.

Removing his towel, she circles a hand around him and closes her eyes as he lowers his mouth to hers. He is more able to take control now, to make love to her in a way she knows she will never get enough of. They don't have to be quite so gentle, or tentative, or afraid of the fervency of their passion. It's true there can be no wild abandon, but the way they can make one another feel is everything.

The sun is much higher in the sky by the time they are dressed and ready to wander up to Piazza Belvedere for breakfast. They sip coffee and watch tourists stroll past, saying little to one another, and trying not to notice the time ticking by. It feels surreal to think of all the years, decades, that have passed without them knowing anything about one another. They've lived their lives, loved, laughed, suffered and lost with no idea of each other's existence, much less that fate would bring them together like this. It's almost impossible to imagine being in this world without him now, but by this time tomorrow it will all be over. She doesn't want to let him go, is desperate to hold onto him, but she won't do or say anything to make this any harder. Later, after he's gone, she'll book her own flight home. Staying here without him will deepen her loneliness and make her feel sadder than she can bear.

Eventually he puts a ten-euro note on the table and reaches for her hand. 'I want to hold you again,' he murmurs. 'Let's go back to the apartment.'

As they leave the café, the owner comes to speak to him, and a few minutes later, on the Corso Umberto, someone else claims his attention. In the sunken garden of Naumachie, he's waylaid again. He's always friendly, engaged, never allows anyone to feel his impatience, but she knows it in the way he squeezes her hand.

Once inside the apartment, with the windows open and a sea breeze sailing softly in, they stand with their arms around one another, as if imprinting, memorizing the feel of one another.

After a while, she says what she's certain is in both their minds, 'I think it will be for the best if we don't try to stay in touch. Our lives are too different, too separate.'

He tightens his hold on her, and she understands it's a silent agreement.

'But I will want to know the results of your tests,' she tells him.

'Of course.'

She tilts her head back to look up at him and wonders, would he actually admit it if the news was bad? Maybe he already knows and is keeping it from her.

'I don't want to let you go,' he murmurs, his voice deepened by feeling. 'I want to keep you safe from any more harm, to show you how much you mean to me.'

'I want the same,' she whispers. 'You have brought so much that is good and wonderful into my life.' She smiles self-consciously. 'I know I shouldn't really be here, but the world feels like a far better place than it did before I came.'

'It is like this for me,' he tells her. 'It is as if we were meant to be, even if only for this time.'

'Thank you for all you've given me.' She wants to add, *for the hope, the laughter, the love, the dreams*, but her throat is too tight, her heart too full. 'I'll always treasure the memories we've made together . . .'

He stops her words with a kiss that is so full of feeling, and so deeply intimate that she wants it never to stop.

'Maybe it's true,' she says unsteadily, 'that people come into our lives at the time we need them, and when that time, or the need, has passed, they go again.' She swallows and almost adds, *I don't want you to go*.

'There is a saying in Italy,' he tells her, '*Il primo amore non si scorda mai*. It means the first love is never forgotten. For me it will be this one, the last.'

As her heart swells with emotion, she fights back tears and loses herself in the searing tenderness of another kiss.

There is no need to check the time, the clocks are starting to strike, and somewhere out there, on the outskirts of town, Ricardo is heading for Giancarlo's apartment. She wants to walk there with him, to stay until he finally gets into the car and drives away, but finding her way back alone will be too hard.

'Tony will be here if you need anything,' he tells her, touching his fingers to her cheek. 'And when you're ready to leave, Ricardo will take you to the airport.'

'Don't worry about me,' she says, not able to believe yet that this is the last time she'll look into his eyes.

His smile is ironic and tender. 'Are you sure we should not stay in touch?' he asks, seeming doubtful.

No, she isn't, but she says, 'You can't live in England and I can't even speak Italian . . .'

'You could learn.'

She puts her fingers to his lips. 'Please don't let's make it any harder by creating dreams that can't come true. What we've had has been just about perfect. To draw it out, to put it under the strain of everyday life – I don't want to spoil it.'

He takes her hand and kisses her palm. 'Then I wish you happiness and love and everything else your heart desires.'

Knowing that he is everything she desires, she says, 'Please, don't forget to let me know if you're all right. I won't be able to breathe easily until you do.'

'I will,' he promises. Then, in a whisper, '*Arrivederci, cara mia.*'

As the door closes behind him, she listens to the sound of his footsteps receding and is aware of her breath shuddering as she tries not to cry out. Her father, her sons, her liberty and now Giancarlo . . . She feels she can't bear it, and yet knows she has to.

She must see him one more time.

She goes to the side terrace and there he is, climbing the steps back into town, nodding to those who greet him, seeming – as he always does – friendly, interested, ready with a kind word, and yet she can tell he's as torn apart by their parting as she is.

She watches until he disappears from view, and it's strangely as though time stops for a moment, while the world continues. She feels disoriented, unsure of what to do next. She wants to call out for him to come back, to stop him from going forward, from being swallowed into the past . . .

'Oh God, oh God,' she murmurs, turning her face to the sky. She still feels their connection, their affinity, in spite of the distance increasing between them. She imagines him reaching Corso Umberto, and climbing more steps towards his apartment. She thinks of the wonderful times they've shared here on this island, and in this apartment. The laughter, the tears, the discoveries and, most of all, the love . . . Then she's listening for his footsteps, for a knock on the door that doesn't come.

She sinks into the chair behind her, and tries to remind herself that she's survived grief before. But she was younger then, stronger, and somehow still able to believe that some good might come from it all.

She doesn't believe that now. She's not sure she believes anything at all.

CHAPTER FORTY

Though Catie's heart is still dark with despair, the instant she sees Jude in the Arrivals hall it's as if a small shred of sunlight is trying to push its way through. She hadn't known Jude would be there, couldn't have imagined how pleased she'd be to see her.

'How did you know which flight I'd be on?' she asks as they hug tightly and tearfully. 'Mum must have told you.'

'She did,' Jude confirms, her round, fleshy face as lively and lovely as ever. 'You look amazing. I mean, you always do, but obviously the weather was good, wherever you were.'

Knowing she looks dreadful, Catie accepts the compliment and smiles at the mischief in Jude's eyes. 'Mum told you that as well,' she states. 'I should have known.'

'I was worried, so of course she did, but I hope you appreciate the iron will I showed in not being in touch to fuss you. You know you could have told me though, even though it was the wrong thing to do. I'd have understood.'

'I know, but I didn't want you to have to lie if anyone came looking for me. It was bad enough that Mum knew, but obviously I couldn't have left without telling her.'

'No, I get that, and thanks for leaving the note. It didn't tell me anything, but I was glad not to be completely forgotten.

And, amazingly, it seems you've got away with it, because as far as I'm aware, no one from officialdom has been trying to find out where you are. Now, come on, let's get you home where you belong.'

Though the words *home* and *belong* are difficult for Catie to hear after finding it such a wrench to leave Isabella's apartment, she somehow holds onto her smile as they wheel her luggage out to the car. The skies over west London are grey and low, drizzle is clogging the wintry air, and a sharp wind is whistling between the terminal buildings. It could hardly be a more depressing contrast to the glorious weather she left little more than three hours ago.

For a moment she reflects on how her homecoming from LA, over twenty-five years ago, had been very much the same, leaving warmth and sunshine, palm trees and glorious skies, to return to England at its dreariest. Her father had been there to meet her that time, and now it was Jude. How strange, how utterly unpredictable and perverse, and also kind and healing life could be.

Where is Giancarlo now? How is he? Is he thinking of me?

'So, Sicily,' Jude declares as they motor off towards the M4. 'Taormina, to be more specific. Henry and I visited once, back in the day. We were on a Mediterranean cruise that stopped off in Naxos. Gorgeous hillside town as I recall, with an ancient theatre?'

Catie's heart contracts as she gazes out of the window, recalling the mesmerizing scene down over a crystal blue bay, all the way across to the blackened swell of a volcano. Why hadn't she taken any photographs while she was there? It seems crazy now to realize she hadn't even thought of it.

Does he regret it too? Has it even occurred to him that the only memories we have of one another live in our minds?

Except he can always go online to be reminded of me, if he wants to. Maybe he'll find it easier not to.

'I know I'm probably not supposed to ask,' Jude is saying, indicating to overtake a coach, 'but I'm going to anyway. Did it help, escaping for a while? It has to have done. I know you were going nuts needing to get out of the house, to try and find something beyond those four walls.'

After mulling the question, Catie decides it has so many different and complex answers that for now all she says is, 'Yes, it helped, mostly in ways I didn't expect, while in others . . .' She sighs quietly and tries not to think of him in Turin. Whatever she can conjure will be false, when she's never visited the city and has no idea of his home or his life there.

It'll be the same for him, having never visited Bristol, although she's told him so much about her past that it might be easier for him to picture her in Abbots Leigh than it is for her to imagine him in his home town.

What is she going to do now? How will she fill her days, her weeks and years going forward? She'll find something, she's certain of that, she just needs a little time to reset and start making plans. How hard it is to try to imagine the future when her heart is so entrenched in the past.

'I hope you don't mind,' Jude says, 'but Patty mentioned you'd made a friend?'

Her eagerness to know more is so apparent that Catie can't help but smile. 'His name is Giancarlo,' she says, 'and he's probably the most wonderful man I've ever met, but would you mind if we talk about him later?'

'No, of course not. Whenever you're ready.'

She smiles again and says, 'Tell me about you. What have you been up to all this time? And how are Henry and the girls?'

Jude shoots her a quick glance. 'I'll answer that,' she says, 'because I can tell you need the distraction, but if it gets too much just tune me out or shut me up.'

Catie's eyes close; she's so glad of their friendship, of how easy Jude always seems to make things, that she might have hugged her if it had been possible.

Soon, maybe even later today, she'll tell Jude about the spin of the globe that had made her decision on where to go for her escape, and the map that Patty had bought the next day for her to narrow the destination down to a single village or town. It always had been a crazy idea, an enormous risk, but, as Jude had said, thank God she'd got away with it, and – even if she hadn't – she knew she could never regret the time she'd spent with Giancarlo.

'Your mother's already at the house,' Jude says as they finally leave the motorway to start towards Abbots Leigh. 'Obviously, she's mad keen to see you, and the last I heard she was planning to cook something Sicilian for supper.'

Catie's impressed. 'That sounds exotic for my mother.'

'Maybe, but she's been looking up recipes online so that you won't – to quote her – have too much of a culture shock when you get back.'

Catie laughs.

'She's also got some news for you, but I'll let her tell it.'

A pang of nerves hits Catie's heart. 'Is it good or bad?' she prompts.

'Mm, I guess that depends on how it shapes up.'

Catie scowls at her.

'I'm sorry,' Jude cries defensively, 'it's for Patty to tell you, not me. I probably shouldn't even have mentioned it, but I will say this, whatever the gods are playing at, or Mac – Patty thinks it's Mac – in my opinion it's a good thing you came home now.'

* * *

311

Ten minutes later, they turn into the driveway of Breemoor, where the trees have already shed their autumn colours, and the old swing is still dangling from a low-hanging branch. As they pull up alongside a dark blue Audi A6, Catie is too distracted by it to consider how she feels about seeing her home again.

'Whose is that?' she asks, thinking of her probation officer who usually drives a Vauxhall Opel. Maybe it's someone more senior; a police officer, even.

Jude frowns. 'I don't know. I haven't seen it before.'

Absurdly, Catie suddenly wonders if it's a car Giancarlo rented from Bristol Airport. If there was a flight it would have got him here sooner than she could have made it from Heathrow. So, it could be his – and actually it was the kind of thing he'd do to surprise her.

In spite of knowing this is nonsense, she is so ready, so able to believe it that even when her mother comes to the door looking worried she still holds on to the hope.

'Catie!' Patty declares, almost as if she'd had no idea Catie was about to turn up. 'Are you all right? Was the flight on time? I see Jude found you.'

'Wasn't difficult,' Jude pipes up. 'She still looks the same, apart from the tan.'

'Lovely tan,' Patty agrees, nodding approval.

'Can I have a hug?' Catie asks, holding out her arms.

'Oh, all that palaver,' Patty chides, walking straight into the embrace. 'Yes, yes,' she mutters, patting Catie's back. 'Are you all right?' she asks again. 'If you're tired . . .'

'It's not that long a flight, Mum,' Catie points out, 'and it's bloody freezing out here. Can we go in?'

Patty stands aside. 'I just want you to know that this wasn't my doing,' she says. 'Well, not exactly,' she adds as Catie enters the house.

Having no idea what her mother is talking about, Catie inhales the familiar scent of the place and finds it more welcoming and comforting than she'd expected. It's always good being with old and dear friends at a time of sadness and loss, and heaven knows this house has seen her through so much of it. She looks around, taking in the old photographs of the boys that still climb the stairs, the new light-fitting she'd bought just before leaving, the worn hall carpet she's always meant to replace but never has.

What would Giancarlo think of it?

He'll never see it.

She knows that as surely as she knows that Patty is chatting away to Jude behind her, saying she hopes Jude will stay for a while, and Jude is agreeing. Catie is hardly listening as she takes off her coat and hangs it on the rack that used to be full of anoraks and waxed jackets, long woollen scarves and bobble hats. There are no wellies cluttering up the porch now, or football boots or school bags, and she can't think why she's missing them when they'd disappeared such a long time ago.

She turns towards the kitchen, but comes to a halting stop as a tall, broad-shouldered man steps out of the sitting room into the hall.

She blinks.

Lawrence?

Her heart turns over and her hands fly to her mouth, too late to stifle a sob.

'Hello, Mum,' he says, and to her confusion, he adds, 'I hope you don't mind me just turning up like this.'

'Matthew?' she whispers. 'Oh my God, *Matthew*.'

His smile is awkward, nervous. 'Yes, it's me. The prodigal and all that. I . . . hope this is OK.'

How many years have passed since they last laid eyes on one another? She can't count them now, can only register that he is a grown, healthy man – and he's here!

She wants to reach for him but isn't sure if it's the right thing to do. She tries to speak but can only sob again as she wonders what this visit might mean, and whether she should feel afraid or relieved or even hopeful that he might stay awhile.

'Patty said I should wait until tomorrow,' he tells her, 'to give you a chance to settle in, but I—'

'But he can't do as he's told,' Patty interrupts chippily, 'so here he is, great big handsome thing that he is. Just turned up on me half an hour ago and insisted on waiting . . .'

'I wanted to see you,' Matthew says to Catie, 'but if you'd rather I left and—'

'No! No,' she cries quickly. 'I want you to stay. I just . . . It's such a surprise . . . I had no idea . . .'

'None of us did until he showed up at my front door the day before yesterday,' Patty declares tartly.

'Actually,' Jude puts in, 'he came to mine first, and I told him where to find his granny. I thought,' she explains to Catie, 'that if anyone was going to tell him where you were, it had to be your mother.'

'Of course it had to be me,' Patty agrees, 'but then I get a message from you saying you're on your way back, and now, well . . .' She throws out her hands. 'Here we are.'

Catie is unable to take her eyes off Matthew, drinking in just how like Lawrence he is with his dark, curly hair and intense brown eyes, the shape of his nose and even his mouth. His jawline is firmer, and he has a more determined, even self-assured air about him. He seems anxious too, a stranger amongst three women he barely knows any more, and realizing this can't be easy for him she says, 'Shall we go and sit down? You and me? I'd love to hear all your news.'

'I'll make some tea,' Patty immediately informs them.

'And I'll pour wine,' Jude adds. 'Do you drink?' she asks Matthew worriedly.

He laughs and the sound of it makes Catie's heart melt. 'Sure, I drink,' he tells her, 'but it's kind of early so maybe some tea first?'

'Of course. Your grandmother is the best tea-maker I've ever known . . .'

'Do you think I didn't make him a cup when he came to see me?' Patty asks archly. 'Black, no sugar,' she states, letting him know she remembers.

'Same for me,' Jude says, going after her into the kitchen.

'I thought you were having wine?'

'I would if I could be sure you wouldn't call AA on me.'

'You're past help, my girl,' Patty snips as the door falls closed behind them.

Matthew's eyes are simmering with laughter as he turns to Catie. 'Girl?' he repeats incredulously.

Loving the unexpected moment of humour, Catie says, 'Patty's almost eighty-four, so to her I guess that's what Jude is.'

'Patty!' he states, shaking his head almost disbelievingly as they go into the sitting room. 'She's something else, isn't she? I don't think I've ever met anyone quite like her before.'

Certain her mother would take this as a compliment, Catie says, 'She's different, I'll allow you that.'

The fire is already lit so she goes to drop another log into the flames, hopefully giving him a moment to decide where he might want to sit. When she turns round, he's still standing, and seems anxious again.

Before she can speak, to remind him that this is his home, that all he needs to do is make himself comfortable, he says, 'I keep trying to work out how to start, but nothing feels right. Or I get it all mixed up in my head and I'm afraid it'll come out wrong, so maybe it's best not to say anything.'

Slipping, without thinking, into the role of parent, she says, 'Why don't you just tell me about your life Down Under?'

He nods, then shakes his head in a way that really does seem to mean no. 'I will,' he assures her, 'but first . . .' He takes a breath, as if he's about to dive into deep water, and the next words come tumbling out so fast it takes her a moment to catch up. 'First I need to say I'm sorry, like *really* sorry, but that's not nearly enough. I just don't know any other words to make it bigger and better and more . . . Oh God, you'd think someone who does what I do for a living wouldn't have a problem, but look at me. I'm all over the place and I thought, before I came here, that it would be easy, or easier than this.'

Going to take his hand, she says, 'All that matters, Matthew, is that you're here. I've been so afraid I'd never see you again and—'

'That's just it,' he interrupts forcefully, 'I shouldn't have done that to you. You didn't deserve it . . . Any of it. Taking off to Australia, the drugs, the way I spoke to you after Jake died . . .'

'You were grieving. We all were.'

'Sure, but after, once I started getting my act together, I could have contacted you. It was all just so . . . I couldn't make myself do it. I felt so guilty on top of all the other guilt over Jake. I was a coward. I didn't know how to face you, and I was always haunted by the terrible things I said the day of the funeral . . .'

'Why don't we sit down?' Catie says, gently, and still holding his hand, she pulls him onto the sofa beside her. 'Before you go any further,' she begins, turning to him, 'try to remember that we all do and say things we don't mean at times, every one of us, and what you were going through after we lost Jake, what I put you through because I couldn't bring myself to forgive . . .'

'But you did forgive me. Dad kept telling me that, and I know you did too . . . I guess it's just that I couldn't forgive myself and for a long time it was easier to blame you . . .'

'That happens,' she smiles, tenderly. 'It's almost second nature to blame your mother for things. But, like I said, what really matters is that you're here now, and from what I've heard you've turned your life around . . .'

'Sure, I have, and I'll tell you about it, I swear, but I need to do this, Mum. I need to tell you that I can't stop thinking about what I put you through, all the things I did and said . . . The way I made out like you never cared for me, that you always preferred Jake and you wished you hadn't had me, and none of it was true. OK, we used to yell at each other and even chuck things around, well I did. I was horrible and obnoxious and downright mean to you . . .'

'No, Matthew, you were just trying to express how frustrated you felt about me being away so much. I wasn't here for you the way I should have been . . .'

'But you *were here*, way more than I realized until I really started getting to grips with it all. When I go back over everything . . .' He takes a breath, as if needing to slow himself down again. 'Jake was always easier; we know that. It's just the way he was. It's why we all loved him so much. He was like you, kind, ready to have fun, into

317

everything and everyone, and if I'm like anyone, it has to be my gorgon of a granny out there.'

Catie's eyebrows go up.

'That's what she called herself when we had a chat the other day,' he explains with a teary laugh. 'She told me about what she did to you all those years ago, and what a "stupid, ridiculous woman" she was to have let the rift between you go on for so long. And now I've done the same. I allowed myself to believe things about you that I should never even have been told, much less listened to.'

Tensing slightly, Catie says, 'And who told you?'

'Who do you think? I mean, Dad admitted you'd had a bad time after I was born . . .'

'But he never said I didn't want you?'

'No, no, he never said that. He told me about your dad and how close you were to him, and how hard you found his death. And then how helpful *Lola* was when it came to getting you back on your feet. I guess that's when she and Dad first . . .' His jaw tightens as he fights against his father's betrayal. 'Actually, I don't know when they first got together,' he says, 'and I don't want to know. It's taken me a long time, too long, but I can see now how weak he was, and so fucking duplicitous, pardon my French. Don't get me wrong, I still love him, he's my dad, but I hate him too for what he did to our family. And as for what Lola did to you . . . Christ Almighty, that woman! I can see now how she was doing everything she could to poison me against you, even before Jake went, and then after . . .' He swallows down a fierce rise of emotion. 'She is such a bitch,' he growls, 'even her own children say that about her, or they do now. They never used to when they were younger, obviously, but Martine, she's the eldest, reckons she got really scared after Jake died that Dad would go back to you.' His voice falters and his mouth trembles as he says, 'Everyone felt so guilty about what happened. Me most of all, with good reason, because if it weren't for me, he'd never have been there.'

'Ssh,' Catie soothes, understanding that his journey, the struggle to deal with his grief and loss, has been even more difficult and complex than her own. 'You couldn't have known it would happen . . .'

'But *you* did. It's why you didn't want him to go, and then I—'

'I didn't *know* anything. I just had a bad feeling about it . . .'

'Which I ignored. Or I thought it was stupid, and because I was so bloody arrogant, so totally up myself and convinced I was always right, I wanted to show you that everything would be fine and you were just paranoid about your favourite son . . .'

Seeing he's about to break down, Catie pulls him into her arms and holds him close, tears falling from her own eyes as the enormity of this moment, and of what they mean to one another, along with the overwhelming might of their grief, binds them even more tightly together.

'I think about him all the time,' he sobs into her shoulder, 'the way he used to laugh when things went wrong, how nothing ever got him down . . . I even talk to him in my head . . . Oh God, Mum, I still miss him so much. I keep thinking about what he'd be doing now, where he could be, like he's really still out there somewhere. Does that sound crazy?'

'No,' she whispers, stroking his hair. 'I do it too.'

He draws back to look at her, clearly appreciating that he isn't on his own with his imaginings. 'I reckon he'd have gone to Cambridge, don't you?' he says. 'He was that clever.

Or sometimes I think he'd have thrown himself into drama school and he'd be a movie star or West End actor by now. Or maybe he'd be playing professional football . . .'

With a broken smile, she says, 'He wasn't that good.'

Matthew laughs and sniffs. 'No, he wasn't, but no one ever threw themselves into the game more. I wish . . . I wish . . .' He tries to catch his breath. 'I wish it had been me who hit that rock . . .'

'Oh God no, Matthew, don't ever say that,' she cries, tightening her hold on him, horrified by the mere thought of it. 'Please, if we've learned anything from losing him, it's that we don't have control over what happens . . .'

'But we do!' he splutters. 'We always did. If I hadn't taken him . . .'

'Matthew, you mustn't do this. You can't go on blaming yourself. I understand it's hard, that you can only see your own part in it, but try to remember that he was seventeen, old enough to make his own decisions. No one forced him to go.'

He shakes his head. 'No, I didn't force him, but I took Lola's money and I listened to her when she said, "If he wants to go with you, find a way to make it happen."'

Catie's eyes close as she rests her head on her son's. She's aware that it would be the easiest thing in the world now to give in to a renewed surge of hatred towards Lola, to wish her straight to hell and eternal damnation, but she isn't going to do it to herself. It will only make her Lola's victim again, caught up in a blinding fury and the burning need for vengeance, and she already knows where that can lead. More importantly, it will do nothing to bring Jake back or heal things between her and Matthew.

After a while he sits up and, as he looks at her, his eyes wet, his cheeks flushed and mouth still trembling, the love she feels is so visceral, so powerful that she can only wonder how she's continued all this time without him.

'Did you get counselling?' she asks softly.

He nods. 'I don't think I'd ever have found the courage to come back if I hadn't.'

She smiles and brings his hand to her lips. 'I'm glad. We all needed it after Jake went.'

'Did you have some too?'

She nods. 'Mostly while I was in prison, but don't let's talk about that particular darkness now. How long are you staying?'

He seems confused. 'You mean now?'

'No, in the country. When are you going back to Australia?'

'Oh, right. Actually, I'm not. I . . . Sandy and I moved to London last month. She's my girlfriend, fiancée, actually. She's English too, but grew up in Adelaide. We've both got jobs, starting mid-Jan, and . . . Oh God,' he laughs, and wipes his eyes again, 'talk about landing everything on you at once, but here goes . . . We're expecting a baby next June.'

Catie's eyes fly open in amazement as her heart erupts with joy. 'You're going to be a father?' she cries, wanting to hold the child right now this minute.

'It'll make you a granny,' he warns. 'Is that OK?'

Laughing, she says, 'Of course, of course, as long as he or she calls me Catie.'

'She. It's a girl.'

More thrilled by that than she could ever have known she'd be, she says, 'We have a great deal of catching up to do, you and I. We've only touched the surface today, but I'm so proud of you for making it happen, for finding that courage, not only to come here, but to get yourself the help you needed.'

'Yeah, it was a bit of a journey,' he admits. 'Kind of ongoing, I guess.'

She nods. 'For me too, but tell me more about Sandy.'

His eyes show right away how in love he is. 'She's amazing,' he says. 'Really beautiful and clever . . . Actually, she's the one who made me get help, and she went through a lot of it with me. Kind of beyond the cause, eh?'

Catie smiles. 'She sounds very special. When can I meet her?'

'Like today! She's already here, in Bristol. We're staying at the Clifton Hotel du Vin. You'll love her, Mum. You really will.'

Feeling certain of it, she smiles to herself as the words echo down the years to when she'd told her parents the same about Lawrence. 'Two things before you call her,' she says as he takes out his phone. 'First, I'd love it if you came to stay here – only if you want to, of course . . .'

'Are you kidding? We'd love to. It'll give us two, you and me, a great chance to talk, and for you and Sands to get to know one another. Did I already say you'll love her?'

She laughs. 'You did. And now second. Does Dad know you're here?'

He pulls an awkward face. 'I haven't even told him we're back yet,' he admits. 'I will, obvs, but Sands and I agreed it was more important to get things sorted with you first. And, if I'm being totally honest, we've decided we don't want to see Lola.'

Wondering how she's supposed to feel anything but pleased about that, Catie says, 'And you're not sure how Dad will react if you tell him that?'

'Frankly, I don't really care what he thinks, but knowing Lola she'll try to push her way in and the next thing she'll be telling Sands how you ruined her business and deliberately tried to blind her. I know this, because she does her best to bring it up every time I speak to her, which is not very often, or it hasn't been in the last couple of years. I get Dad to send me a list of times when he's on his own so we don't have to deal with her.'

'So, when exactly are you intending to tell him you're back?'

He shrugs. 'I guess it'll have to be soon, because Martine and Nick know and it's not fair to ask them to keep it a secret for much longer.'

'You mean you're in regular touch with your half-brother and -sister?'

He grimaces awkwardly. 'Do you mind? I mean, none of it's their fault, and they're good guys.'

'Of course I don't mind.' And actually, she doesn't. 'Now, if you want to make that call to Sandy – Sands – I'll go and find out what's happening with that cup of tea, because it seems to have gone very quiet out there. Probably because they're right outside the door with their ear trumpets.'

As she gets to her feet, he stands too, and she isn't sure who reaches for who first; it happens so naturally, so fluidly, and feeling his arms around her is beyond wonderful. Tears well in her eyes, of happiness and relief, and with the deepest and most lasting love of all, that of a mother.

How dearly she'd love to tell Giancarlo all about it.

CHAPTER FORTY-ONE

'But why aren't you able to tell Giancarlo?' Jude demands as she and Catie stroll through the trees, heading for the pools. They're both wrapped up warm against the cold, and wearing heavy boots to prevent too many slides in the mud. 'What is wrong with staying in touch when you clearly bonded so well?'

Sighing, Catie pulls up her scarf to huff warm air onto her face. 'It's just an impossible situation,' she replies, loving being able to talk about him in spite of how it increases the longing. It'll diminish over time, she keeps reminding herself, it's just these next few weeks, maybe months that she has to get through. 'He can't live here,' she points out, 'his whole life is in Turin – his company, family, friends – and I can't live there. I don't even speak Italian, so what would I do?'

'Well, it can't be that hard to learn the language and, who knows, maybe you'll get back into singing.'

Catie slants her a look.

Jude stops and turns Catie to face her. 'Brutal truth,' she declares, 'you're not getting any younger, so to be given another chance at love, and with someone who sounds as though he might actually deserve you . . . You can't just dismiss it over something as banal as not speaking his language.'

'It's not just that though, is it?' Catie cries, and she turns to walk on, keen to catch up with Matthew and Sands, who'd left the house a few minutes ahead of them. 'There are huge cultural differences that I won't have any idea how to surmount. Plus, let's not forget he's married . . .'

'Pfft!' Jude scoffs. 'If everything he's told you is true, she's already on her way out.'

Realizing she'd never doubted him, Catie almost snaps back, but swallows the irritation and says, 'There's also Mum. Leaving her for six weeks is one thing, going for good . . .'

'Patty will want whatever makes you happy, and she can always visit.'

Catie smiles. 'Can you see her in Italy?'

'Yes! As a matter of fact, I can see Patty wherever she wants to be. Not much fazes that woman, and she's back to her sparky old self since you returned. Although that probably also has a lot to do with getting to know Matthew and Sands.'

Catie sighs and stoops to pick up half a dozen pine cones, thinking of the brightly coloured ceramic versions all over Taormina – symbols of prosperity and enlightenment. These small brown ones will either be used as kindling, or decorated for Christmas. 'What do you think of Sands?' she asks, needing to steer the conversation, even her thoughts, away from Giancarlo. She spends so much time thinking about him, reliving the precious moments they were together, dreaming of how things might have been, she can't let it dominate her time with friends and family as well.

'I absolutely love her,' Jude replies without hesitation. 'OK, we've only known her a week, but she's swept into that house like a breath of fresh air. Don't you agree?'

Catie smiles. 'I do,' and adds, 'if I'd been lucky enough to have a daughter, I'd want one just like her. Or one of your three, who I completely adore. Are they coming home for Christmas?'

'Olivia and Harriet will, complete with partners, one child and one dog. Vikki has to go to the in-laws in Wales this year. Why don't you and yours join us? We'd love to have you over. The more the merrier.'

'I'd say yes right away,' Catie replies, meaning it, 'but I know that Mum and Sands have already ordered the turkey and Matthew is digging out old games for us to play before we collapse in front of a movie. Maybe we can do Boxing Day together, all of us?'

Jude claps her gloved hands. 'Brilliant idea. Let's book a table at the George, then no one will have to cook, or wash up.'

'Hey, Mum! Over here!' Matthew shouts, waving from a stone footbridge dividing two pools. Sands is beside him, wearing a pink bobble hat and navy padded coat, her gorgeous mane of honey-coloured hair streaming down her back, and her beautiful freckly face flushed with happiness and cold. 'She looks like Alice in Wonderland,' Patty had commented when they'd first met her, not as *sotto voce* as she'd thought.

'You're not the only one to say that,' Sands had laughed. 'But don't worry, I'm careful to avoid rabbit holes.'

Patty had found that so witty that the others had laughed at her laughing. It had probably, Catie reflected after, been the bonding moment between Patty and Sands, because ever since they'd been almost inseparable. Patty wasn't even going home to Fishponds any more, apart from when Matthew and Sands took her to pick up something else she might need.

So, they are all now fully ensconced in Breemoor, Matt and Sands in Matt's old room, complete with new bed, an extra wardrobe and a bathroom to themselves. Patty has her suite overlooking the front garden, which they'd made hers during the lockdowns: 'No way are you putting me in that spooky old cottage out there like I'm some nasty little troll,' she'd protested when Catie had offered it to her. And Catie is in her room, different now to when she and Lawrence had shared it, for she, Marilyn and Patty had decorated and refurnished it about a year after they'd lost Jake. It had been clear by then that Lawrence wouldn't be coming back, and Catie had wanted as few reminders of him as possible.

'Hey!' Sands smiles happily as Catie and Jude join her to watch Matthew, arms outstretched, wobbling across a fallen log below.

'Not so easy now,' he shouts up to his mother while circling his arms frantically to try to stay upright. 'Come on, you were always good at . . . Oh shit!' and suddenly he's knee-deep in the sludge.

As they all laugh and cheer as if he's performed some amazing feat of balance, he wades heavily to the bank, laughing too, and reminding Catie so much of Jake, who'd always found his own pratfalls hilarious, that she can't stop the loss tightening her throat.

'Your turn!' Matthew insists, trying to take her hand.

'No way am I going to end up like you,' she protests, pulling away.

'So, show us how it's done and finish it.'

'Do you know how old I am? I haven't crossed that log in at least twenty years.'

'Core strength and a bit of speed,' Jude advises. 'You'll be across in no time.'

'Don't encourage him. Tell you what, you do it.'

'You've got to be joking. Look at the size of me. I'll break the damn thing if I get on it.'

Catie looks at Sands.

'Pregnancy pass here,' Sands grins. 'Go on, Catie, do it for the team!'

Laughing, while knowing she's going to end up in the same state as Matthew, she steps up to the end of the log and presses one foot into it. It doesn't move, not that she'd expected it to when it's been there for decades. Next, she stands on it, wobbles, and leaps back to the bank.

'Boooo!' Matthew shouts.

She shoots him a menacing look, then takes a deep breath before placing one foot carefully in front of the other, arms out wide to grab thin air for balance.

If I can make it to the other side without falling, I'll see Giancarlo again.

Foolish, of course, and childish, but it keeps her going, slowly, steadily, inch by inch, until suddenly she slips and lands on her hands and knees in the muck. 'Oh no!' she cries, laughing and groaning, and reminding herself that her failure has nothing to do with the fate of her and Giancarlo.

'Sorry,' Matthew cries, coming to haul her to the bank. 'Are you OK?'

'You mean apart from soaked right through and bloody freezing?' she replies, using the back of a wet, gloved hand to push the hair from her face and smearing herself with green mire.

'I honestly thought you'd do it,' he tells her.

'I will next time,' she promises.

'I can't wait to hear what Patty has to say when she sees you both,' Sands laughs.

'Don't worry, the pine cones are OK,' Jude cries, holding up Catie's bag.

Catie has to laugh.

'Prosperity's safe then,' Matthew grins.

Surprised, Catie looks at him.

He shrugs. 'Isn't that what they're about?' he asks. 'Something like that, anyway. Hey, did you hurt yourself?'

'No, I'm fine,' Catie assures him, blinking back the silly rush of tears. 'I just need to get out of these revolting clothes is all, and into a hot bath.'

Much later, after the sun has gone down and the latest storm has passed, Catie is snuggled up in front of the fire listening to Etta James on an old CD player while checking her phone. Just in case. She can't help it; she does it all the time and wishes she could find a way to make herself stop.

She glances up as Patty comes in carrying a tray of mini sausage rolls fresh from the oven, and two large glasses of Prosecco.

'The others are still upstairs,' she says, referring to Matthew and Sands, 'so I thought we could take the opportunity to have a little chat, just the two of us.'

Experiencing a stirring of unease, Catie says, 'Of course. You're OK, are you?'

'Better than new,' Patty replies, setting the tray down. Or had she said, *better than you*?

Handing her a glass, Patty clinks her own against it and sinks into the other fireside chair. In typical Patty fashion, she doesn't beat about the bush. 'Has he let you know his test results yet?' she asks.

Catie's heart catches as she shakes her head. 'I don't know whether no news is good news,' she sighs. 'Or if he just doesn't want to burden me . . .'

'You need to call him and find out,' Patty tells her.

'And if it's bad news? Actually, I don't think he'd tell me even if it is. He won't want me to worry.'

'But you're worried anyway, and if it turns out it has spread, you'll want to be there for him.'

Catie's eyes flicker to her mother and away again. 'Of course I will,' she says, 'but if it's not what he wants . . .'

'Men never know what they want,' Patty scoffs, 'much less what's good for them.'

Catie smiles. 'Did you used to think that about Dad?'

'All the time, daft bugger that he was over all sorts of things. Good job he had me, I kept telling him, except I let him down in the end. I didn't know he had a weak heart.'

'You couldn't have known . . .'

'Maybe not, but you do know this man of yours has cancer. OK, we're not sure how serious it is yet, but that's what you need to find out. Don't just sit here waiting for him to be in touch. Do what anyone else would do, who's not all mixed up with emotion – get on the phone and speak to him. Or at the very least send him a text to ask how he is.'

Catie looks down at her mobile. 'I've already done that,' she admits, 'and he hasn't replied.'

'When did you send it?'

'Yesterday.' She'd also told him she was missing him and thinking about him all the time, which meant he hadn't responded to that either.

'OK, well, maybe he's waiting until he has something concrete to say,' Patty ventures. 'But if you haven't heard by next week . . . Actually, is there someone else you can contact to ask how he is? His brother, or someone he works with?'

She shakes her head. 'There's Tony, but he's in Taormina, and I'm not sure how much he knows.'

'Why not give him a call and find out?'

'But what if he doesn't know? I can't be the one to tell him.'

Reaching for a sausage roll, Patty eats it slowly and is

about to speak again when Catie says, 'Why don't we talk about Christmas trees and when we're going to get ours?'

Patty nods slowly, seeming reluctant to let the subject change, but in the end she says, 'Matthew and Sands are hoping the four of us will go tomorrow. He wants to dig one up, the way you used to when he was young. I missed out on all that, stupid woman that I am.'

Knowing there's an admonishment in there for her too, Catie sips her Prosecco and says, 'What's important is that you're here now and he loves you every bit as much as I do.'

'Oh, stop all that soppy nonsense. He hardly even knows me.'

'But to know you, Patty McAllister, is to love you,' and though it's a wonderful thing to say, and she really means it, it makes them both cry because she's just quoted her dad.

CHAPTER FORTY-TWO

Cara mia, I am thinking of you all the time, and missing you too. It is hard to let go, we both know this, but I believe you were right to say we must try. Many things are happening here with my family, some good, some not so good. I very much want to receive news of you, but I am afraid that it will make the letting go even harder. Already it has been a month since I last held you, but I must stop counting the days. Christmas is almost here. My daughter is coming with her family – this is my good news. The not so good mostly concerns the company, but we shall get through it.

I am glad to say the staples are gone and the scars are almost healed. The test results are now much clearer and nothing for you to worry about.

You have my heart, Caterina.

As Patty finishes reading the text, she looks at Catie and passes the phone to Jude.

Before anyone else can say it, Catie announces the first omission. 'He hasn't mentioned his wife,' she says, 'so presumably she hasn't left.'

Patty frowns, as if she hadn't thought of that, while Jude says, 'I'm not sure I'd rush to that conclusion. Maybe he just didn't feel it was important enough to mention.'

'She's his *wife*,' Catie says, letting the emphasis make the point. 'If she'd left, I think he'd have said so. Or maybe he just doesn't want me to read anything into it when we've already agreed that we can't have a future together.'

Seeming not to know how to argue with that, Jude looks at Patty who, after a while, says, 'He's quite vague about the test results.'

It's what is bothering Catie most about the message. 'Saying they're much clearer isn't the same as saying they're clear,' she states, almost angrily.

'A classic sort of obfuscation,' Jude comments.

'Whatever that is,' Patty retorts. 'If you ask me, I reckon he's honouring his promise to tell you the results, while not actually telling you what they are.'

Jude arches an eyebrow and Catie hides a smile, although it's soon gone. 'He's detaching,' she says, knowing it and trying to make herself accept it. 'This is exactly the way he'd do it, as gently as he can . . .'

'Which can only mean,' Jude runs on as if Catie hasn't spoken, 'that if there is a spread, he doesn't want you to use up your life being there for him.'

Catie's face is pale as she stares at her. 'It could be that his wife is going to be at his side,' she says. '*If* there is a spread.'

'Well, I don't see how we're going to know if you don't ask him?' Patty sighs, reaching for the phone to read the text again.

'You're missing the point, Mum,' Catie tells her. 'That message is him fulfilling his promise to tell me what I need to know, and we can put as much spin on it as we like, but what he's actually doing is closing things down between us. Now I have to do the same.' She gets to her feet and goes to check on the Christmas puddings steaming on the stove.

After adding more water to both, she turns back to find Jude and her mother staring helplessly at one another.

'It's OK,' she tells them, annoyed by the shake in her voice. 'I've already prepared myself for this, you know that, so now we just have to get on with things here and start looking forward to Christmas.' When they don't react, she throws out her hands, as if to try to cheer them, 'Matthew's going to be with us,' she reminds her mother. 'We never imagined this time last year that we'd be saying that today, and you're going to be a great-granny in June. Think how special that will be.'

Jude checks the time and gets to her feet.

'Are you leaving?' Patty asks, surprised. 'I thought you were staying for supper.'

'I am, but it's six o'clock, time for a glass?'

'I'm surprised you waited this long,' Patty mutters. 'Make mine a large one. Catie's too. What time are we expecting your husband?'

'In about an hour,' Jude replies, opening the fridge.

'Matt and Sands should be back by then,' Patty says, going to fetch a jar of olives she'd marinated under Catie's instructions. 'I wonder how they got on with Lawrence and the One-Eyed-Witch.'

Catie turns to her, genuinely appalled. 'Mum! You can't call her that,' she protests.

'Just telling it like it is,' Patty grunts. 'I just hope if she started on with her drip, drip, drip of nastiness about you again that Matt stood his ground and put her in her place.'

'Actually, Lola wasn't there,' Matthew tells them later, after he and Sands have kicked off their shoes and settled into the warmth of the kitchen. 'Apparently, she had an important client meeting. She's into events coordination or something, these days, or so the story goes. Personally, I reckon she was avoiding us, or maybe Dad told her to make herself scarce. Either way worked for us.'

'Drastic,' Jude mutters. And in the next breath, 'Is their relationship on the rocks yet?'

Catie scowls at her, but is interested to hear the answer.

It's Sands who says, 'Apparently Lola wants to move out of London, but Lawrence isn't keen, so they might end up with two places. I guess we read into that what we will.'

'She'll bully him into doing what she wants,' Patty states with a curl of her lip.

Suspecting that might be true, and finding she has no more interest in their affairs, Catie says, 'I expect he was thrilled to hear about the baby?'

To her surprise, Matt and Sands exchange glances before Matt says, 'I think he was, yes, but actually it was pretty obvious he's not in a good place. He mostly wanted to talk about himself, so that's what happened.'

'He's about to retire,' Sands continues, 'and he's not sure what to do next with his life.'

'Nick and Martine don't visit very often,' Matt tells them, 'and, I don't know if you want to hear this, Mum, but he actually admitted that he really misses you.'

Catie can't help her insides reacting to that as Patty snorts, 'It's a bit late for him to be thinking about that now.'

It is, of course, but Catie is still quite stunned to hear it.

Moving things on in the way only she can, Jude says, 'Is he ageing well?'

Catie shoots her a look, but again she's keen to know the answer.

Matthew shrugs. 'He seems OK for a man in his sixties.'

'He's not like you,' Sands tells Catie. 'You know, just by

looking at him, that he's the age he is, whereas you don't look a day over fifty.'

'She has my genes,' Patty reminds them.

As everyone laughs, Catie says, 'I'm sorry to hear that he's not happy.'

'Not that you're going to do anything about it,' Jude warns, eyeing her suspiciously.

'How can I?' Catie cries. 'I never see him and I have no desire to, but I don't wish him ill.' To Matthew she says, 'Did he say what they're doing for Christmas?'

'You are *not* to invite him here,' Patty cuts in before Matthew can draw breath.

'Apparently Lola's father is going to stay with them,' Sands replies.

'Oh, that's right,' Patty remarks, 'her mother died back during the pandemic. I'm not sure I'd have gone to the funeral anyway, but thankfully I didn't have to make a decision. Sands, have you asked your mother yet if she'd like to join us for Christmas?'

'Oh, yes I did,' Sands replies brightly, 'and she said she'd love to if she wasn't already coming in May for the baby.'

'She also said,' Matthew continues, 'that she hopes we'll all go over there next year and have Christmas on the beach.'

Patty blinks. 'That doesn't seem right, does it? Christmas on the beach. Although, I have to say, I wouldn't mind giving it a go. I'll look out my rubber ring.'

As the others laugh, Catie says, 'You think you're up to doing that flight?'

Patty shrugs. 'I won't know unless I try, but Dad and I used to make it to LA and back without too much trouble. Of course, we were a lot younger then, but as I keep telling myself, you're a long time dead, Patty McAllister, so best get on with everything while you still can.' Her eyes are fixed meaningfully on Catie's, as Jude says, 'I'll drink to that.'

In the end Christmas turns out to be both relaxing and enjoyable, mainly thanks to Matthew and Sands being around. There isn't so much time to think about Giancarlo when present opening turns into a noisy and hilarious affair. Champagne is served – soda for Sands – and Patty carries in a delicious batch of homemade cheese straws to munch in front of the fire as they listen to carols on the TV and inspect all the gifts for the baby. Before long Matthew is regaling them with stories of Christmases past, and seems to remember them so clearly that Catie finds herself transported back to the happy times she hadn't thought about in too long. There are so many more than she'd allowed herself to recall over recent times, and watching him, laughing along with him, she feels silently and deeply grateful to him for reminding her.

'My gift to you,' she tells him, pulling the last one out from under the tree, 'is all that I wrote while I was in Taormina. I'm not sure what you'll think of it, or of me after you've read it, but it might tell you a lot of things that have been going through my mind, and that I'd find difficult to put into words as we carry on talking through our past.'

'Oh wow, Mum!' he exclaims, clearly locking in immediately with how special this is. And, tearing off the paper, he finds a glossy A4 box containing a printed manuscript titled *For My Beloved Son, Matthew*. Before going any further, he gets up from the floor and comes to sweep her into an embrace. 'I just want to know,' he says, deadpan, 'is it going to make me blush?'

As Catie laughs, Patty says tartly, 'I expect it will if she's written anything about Giancarlo.'

Matt's eyes grow round with surprise and intrigue. 'Giancarlo?' he asks, drawing out the name as he looks from Patty to Catie and back again.

'There's nothing about him in there,' Catie says, glowering at her mother.

'Giancarlo,' Patty explains, unabashed, 'is someone your mother fell in love with while she was writing all that. So, in my book, I'd say he's a big part of it. Pardon the pun, by the way.'

Matthew is regarding Catie with as much interest as concern now. 'So, what happened to him?' he asks. 'Where is he now?'

'Good question,' Patty responds, approvingly.

'It's over,' Catie says. 'It was only . . . I suppose you'd call it a holiday romance.' Even as she utters the words, she can feel the demeaning effect on what they'd shared. It had been so much more than that, at least to her it had, she believed to him too, but now maybe that's the only way to see it.

'There's more to this,' Sands observes quietly. 'You might be telling us it's over, but I'm not feeling it.'

'You're very astute,' Patty informs her. 'I don't think it's over either, but—'

'Can we just leave it there?' Catie cuts in, knowing that today, of all days, will be too hard to think of him without becoming emotional. 'We need to start getting the veg under way, and later, when we're all full up and too fat to move, I'll tell you my news.'

Matthew is instantly alert. 'Is it about him?' he asks, warily, hopefully.

'No, it's not about him. It's about us, as a family, and whether or not a decision I've come to will work for us all.'

* * *

'You're kidding,' Matthew cries, seeming both stunned and bewildered, and even, Catie is daring to hope, a little bit excited?

'That's a big step,' Patty says darkly, then adds, 'but for the most part I think it could be a good one.'

Sands says nothing, and Catie realizes she probably doesn't feel she should have a voice in this, given that it's not her home they're discussing.

'Are you sure?' Matthew asks. 'We've lived here for so long, and it was Dad's home before . . . I mean, it has to be your decision, Mum. I don't want you to stay here because you think it's what I want, but . . . Well, to start with, where will you go?'

Catie glances at her mother. 'Patty and I can discuss that,' she replies, 'but this place is far too big for the two of us, and like I said just now, you guys are going to need some help getting started in London. Everything's so expensive there, and this house is worth over two million – more if we decide to fix it up first, but I don't think we want to do that. Do we?' she asks Patty.

Looking faintly dazed, Patty shakes her head. 'Are you thinking about coming back to Fishponds with me?' she asks, clearly trying to imagine how that would work.

Catie laughs. 'I'm thinking it's time you gave that house up so a family that needs it can move in, and then you and I will get a nice three-bed place, four even, so that when Matthew and Sands come to stay we'll have room for them and the baby.'

'But you can't live with me,' Patty protests. 'You're still young.'

'Not very,' Catie corrects, 'and I'm living with you now. However, if you prefer, I'll get you somewhere in a retirement village . . .'

Patty's eyes pop.

'Or,' Catie continues, turning back to Matt and Sands, 'we can move to London, and be nearby if you need a babysitter.'

Matthew is clearly still having some difficulty taking it all in. 'You can't do all this for us, Mum,' he says finally. 'You're going to need the money to see you through your retirement – OK, I know the royalties are still good, but nevertheless . . . We'll be fine, we'll both be earning well.'

'But you don't want to spend it all on a massive rent,' Catie points out. 'Anyway, we can keep talking, and throw in anything that comes to mind, but unless you want me to hold on to this house, I think the time has come to let it go.'

CHAPTER FORTY-THREE

It's the second week of January, the day before Matthew and Sands are due to drive back to London to settle into their rented flat and start their new jobs. Catie is at her desk in the music room listening to Stevie Nicks while going through a pile of paperwork, and is so engrossed that it's a moment before she realizes Matt is in the doorway.

'Hey, Mum,' he says, and comes to perch on the piano stool next to her. He's looking a little pale, Catie notices, and . . . worried?

'Is everything OK?' she asks, turning to give him her full attention.

He nods. 'Sure, cool. We're more or less packed.' He glances at her and down at his hands. A grown man, and yet she can still see her boy. 'I've really loved being here with you all this time,' he says. 'We both have. It's been really special . . .' He comes to a stop and she says, gently, 'But?'

He shakes his head. 'No buts. It's meant the world to me, reconnecting with you. I just want you to know that.'

'Oh, Matt,' she smiles, reaching for his hand. 'It's meant the world to me too.'

He watches their fingers entwine and pushes himself on. 'I've read what you wrote about the past,' he says, 'you know, when I was born, and your depression after; when Jake and I were growing up, then what happened . . .' He swallows, clears his throat and says, 'I was wondering if you'd mind me adding some of my own memories to it.'

Thrilled and surprised, she says, 'Of course. That would be wonderful. And it's yours now, you can do as you please with it . . .'

'I just want to set the record straight, that's all,' he tells her.

His tone makes her wonder if he's picked up on something that's upset him and, given what's there, it's certainly possible. 'Obviously there are many sides to a story,' she says, 'and the one I gave you isn't really complete. It's just me venting, I guess, trying to sort through things—'

'That's just it,' he interrupts, 'you don't seem to realize what a great mum you were. It's like you've thrown a blanket over most of the good bits so that no one can see all the great things you did for us. How you always seemed to know what we needed even before we did, all the fun you made it to be a kid, even if you were a brat like me.'

'You weren't a brat . . .'

'I was, and you know it – and I'm sorry.'

'You were a child.'

'OK, make excuses for me if you must, but it's like you've forgotten, or won't allow yourself to remember all the craziness that made us so happy . . . All our mates wanted to be here, in this house, to be in your sphere, because you were magic. They loved you, and you haven't written anything about that . . . You have to remember how this place was always full of small boys – and girls, with Jude's three. You weren't houseproud or full of rules . . . There was always music, any kind of music, and we'd all sing – shout, more like – and you'd record us and we'd laugh so much when you played it back. You drove us to beaches and surfed with us; took us to Center Parcs and did all the rides with us. We'd have mad games in the garden, play hide-and-seek in the woods. You helped with our homework, even made tidying our rooms a weird kind of fun, the way you'd get us to do it before a song stopped playing. OK, I'm not saying there weren't bad times, we know there were, but every family has them, and ours definitely weren't your fault. They just happened; we were all to blame in our different ways for all sorts of screw-ups, but especially Dad in the end. But before that, the fact that you felt like an outsider at times just about kills me, because I can see now that sometimes we treated you that way. We got so busy with our *stuff*, me, Jake and Dad, all the sports and movies and God knows what else we had going on that had us rushing out the door as you came in. I mean, you always tried to join in, but you were tired, needed to sleep, and we just went off and forgot all about you . . .'

'Oh, Matt . . .'

'And then Dad got his job in London, and Grandma M kind of took over while you were away. I didn't mind, because I loved her, but I really wanted you to be there all the time, and I used to get angry and resentful when you weren't . . .' He looks down at their joined hands and turns hers over in his. 'And then, what Dad put you through,' he murmurs brokenly, 'the way he betrayed you . . .'

'Darling, it's all in the past now, please don't—'

'I know it's in the past, but I want to set the record straight, I mean about those early years, so that my daughter, and any other children I might have, will know just how special you are.'

As tears fill her eyes again, she puts her arms around him. He's crying too, and holds her tightly. 'So,' he says, after a while, 'it's all right with you if I add my and Jake's two pennies' worth to the story?'

And Jake's? Who else could speak better for her beloved lost child than his brother? 'Yes,' she says hoarsely, 'I'd like that very much indeed.'

He pulls back and clears his throat, dashes a hand across his cheeks and says, deadpan, 'I think I'll start with this:
'*One fine day in the middle of the night,*
Two dead men got up to fight.
Back to back they faced each other,
Drew their swords and shot each other.'

By the time he's finished, they're both laughing and crying. 'I used to love it when you recited that,' he tells her. 'You always did it when we were miserable, or in a state about something, and can you remember how it used to drive Jake nuts trying to work it out?'

How could she ever forget it, and why hadn't she put it in to her story for them, as well as for herself with Mac?

'I know we've still got a lot of talking to do,' he says, 'but I feel like this project, or book, whatever we want to call it, is going to be really special for our family. We can add to it as memories come back to us, or as new things happen . . .' He breaks into a smile. 'It'll be the MacAllister family bible according to Catie and Matthew.'

'Oh, Matt,' she laughs, 'I'm starting to feel lost for words . . .'

'And maybe,' he continues, clearly warming to his theme, 'while we've still got her, we could ask Patty to share something with us?'

A surge of love pushes another laugh from Catie's throat. 'Yes, we should definitely do that,' she agrees, thinking of how wonderful it would be if she'd done something like this with her father all those years ago.

He hasn't finished. 'I think Dad's forfeited the right to add anything,' he says, 'but maybe we'll want to revisit that further down the line. We'll see.'

Feeling certain they would, she says, 'I'll let you decide when the time is right.'

He smiles, says, 'Cool,' and glances towards the door. 'Someone's going to come looking for us any minute, but I'm really glad we had this chat before Sands and I take off.'

'I am too,' she whispers, stroking his cheek. 'I'm going to miss you. Patty and I have loved having you here, but I'm excited for your new life in London—'

'Which you will be a *huge* part of,' he tells her. 'Promise?'

'Cross my heart.'

He regards her sceptically, but she can tell he believes her, and so he should, because she couldn't want it more if she tried. 'You know,' he says, 'I feel like Sands and I should be taking you and Patty out tonight to say thank you.'

'But the evening's already planned,' she reminds him, 'and you won't want to be the one to tell Patty that all her preparations have been in vain.'

He laughs and rolls his eyes. 'God forbid.' Then after a moment, 'She's the best, isn't she?'

Catie nods. 'She is, and so are you. Now, I'd say it's time to go and start giving her a hand?'

As they leave the room, she rubs a hand over his broad back and knows that she'll never love another human being as much as she loves him, apart from his child, perhaps. And of course, there's Patty. What they share as a family – as inextricably linked members of three different generations – runs in their veins, it's a part of their DNA, of who they are as individuals, and it will always, no matter what, keep them together, even during the times they're apart.

She isn't looking forward to him and Sands leaving, she's going to miss them terribly, but at least they won't be too far away and she'll be able to see them regularly.

'So how many are we going to be in total?' Patty asks, moving aside a tray of champagne glasses to make room for the baked camembert she's about to take from the oven.

'About sixteen,' Matthew tells her, and goes to check there's enough wine and beer in the fridge while running through the list of old school and neighbourhood friends he's invited. Catie is only half-listening. She's focusing more on her plans to sell the house while going through the mechanics of folding napkins and tucking them between side plates. It really is going to be a big upheaval, a complete change of life probably, but as daunting as it feels, she knows it's the right thing to do. What she isn't anywhere near as sure of is where she and Patty should go next.

Finding her attention drawn to something on the radio news she pauses, certain they've just mentioned Sicily. A moment later, she is turning cold as the report continues:

'. . . one of the world's most-wanted criminals, the Mafia boss, Matteo Messina Denaro, has been arrested at a private clinic in Palermo, where he has been receiving treatment for a tumour . . .'

'What is it?' Patty asks as Catie drops the plate she's holding.

'Sssh,' Catie whispers.

'. . . he's been using the false name of Andrea Bonafede. Denaro has been on the run for thirty years . . .'

Catie rushes into the sitting room and turns on the TV. She flicks from one news channel to another to another, before remembering how to access the headlines. Eventually she has the story on the screen in front of her, and as she watches, tense with dread, ready to be devastated and deceived all over again, she realizes she isn't seeing footage of Giancarlo being escorted into custody. The man they have is a stranger. He looks nothing like Giancarlo. He is small, hunched and *old*.

Relief makes her head spin, and as she sinks onto the sofa, Matthew comes into the room and regards her with concern. 'What's going on?' he asks, looking from her to the TV and back again. 'And what's so funny?'

Only realizing now that she's laughing, she says, 'It's nothing. Sorry, I just . . .' She flicks off the news, gets up and links his arm. Giancarlo would find her moment of panic hilarious were she ever able to tell him, but she won't think about that now. 'So, what music shall we play tonight?' she asks. 'Have you sorted out a playlist yet?'

'I thought you could do that,' he replies. 'Some of your old favourites, maybe, and Grandpa Mac's, if you and Patty can bear it.'

Catie melts as she smiles. '*The Great American Songbook*,' she murmurs, feeling the words almost as if they are musical notes playing inside her. 'Yes, I think we can manage that.'

'Maybe you'll sing?' he suggests, hopefully, tentatively.

She tilts her head, wondering if it might be possible at last, until she remembers how out of practice she is. 'Maybe next time,' she says, and sweeping on ahead she goes to sort through her and her father's vinyl collection. It's all downloaded now, of course, can even be played on Alexa if they want to go that route, but making choices always comes more easily to her if she consults the albums.

She's almost done when she remembers the song Mac always used to play for Patty, whether on his trumpet, the piano, or maybe he'd sing it. Though certain her mother would love to hear it, she decides she ought to check first, so getting up she goes through to the kitchen.

'I'm her mother,' Patty is saying into the phone, 'can I help you? Oh, I see, yes, yes of course. She's right here,' and, holding out the mobile to Catie, her eyes twinkle madly as she says, 'It's for you, *Caterina*.'

As shock rushes into her heart, Catie comes to a stop, and for one strangely hypnotic moment she's afraid to take the phone from her mother.

Patty thrusts it at her, turns her into the laundry room and closes the door.

'Catie? Is it you?' he asks as she puts the mobile to her ear.

His voice is so much better than music, so everything she needs to hear that she only wants to carry on listening, but manages to say, 'Yes, it's me. I . . . How are you?'

'I am thinking,' he replies in the wonderfully ironic tone she remembers so well, 'that your idea of us not being in contact with one another is not working very well for me.'

Her heart swells almost beyond endurance as she says, 'No, it isn't for me either.'

'I can come there,' he tells her.

She takes only a moment to think before she says, 'No, I will come there.'

'To Taormina?'

'Yes, to Taormina.'

'When?'

Loving that she's about to surprise him, she says, '*Presto amore mio, molto presto.* Soon my love, very soon.'

He chuckles softly. 'I am impressed. And now, I have a suggestion.'

'I'm listening,' she replies, and when she hears what it is, she knows right away what she must do.

CHAPTER FORTY-FOUR

Three weeks later

It's cooler, quieter, but still so exhilaratingly the same that Catie simply can't get enough of being here. She is sitting at the very top of the Ancient Theatre, her eyes moving slowly, appreciatively down to the stage, out past the broken Roman pillars and fallen masonry to nature's incomparable backdrop of azure bay and monstrous, snow-capped Etna.

She inhales deeply, gladly, as she tracks a cluster of white clouds, spreading and shifting as they float through the greyish-blue sky to merge with the volcano's sulphurous vapour.

In spite of the sunny day, there are almost no tourists around, it isn't the time of year for them, although a few intrepid souls are climbing from the orchestra, up through the wide, crescented *cavea*, to take photographs from the top, while marvelling at the sublime amalgam of history and nature.

She'd come early, simply for the pleasure of soaking it all up, and is almost lost in imagining Greek audiences from over two thousand years ago, rapt by performances enacted in the original amphitheatre, when her eyes are drawn to an archway at the side of the stage.

Her heart turns over, and is filled with so much joy that she almost can't bear it. He is leaning one shoulder against the stonework, arms folded, legs crossed at the ankles as he waits for her to see him. She could be imagining him, but knows she isn't.

'Meet me at the world's most special place,' he'd said when they'd spoken on the phone yesterday, and so, here she is, and now here he is too.

She stands as he starts climbing the ancient steps to join her, keeping her eyes on his and feeling as though the power of her joy might make her fly.

'Caterina,' he murmurs, reaching her and cupping a hand around her face. The tone of his voice, as it always does, turns her name into a caress.

'*Amore mio*,' she whispers, and as his mouth covers hers, powerfully, tenderly, intimately, she holds him as closely as he holds her, moulding their bodies together as if there can be no parting.

She has no idea how much time passes, how many have stopped to stare, or try not to notice, before finally, reluctantly, he raises his head to gaze into her eyes. His own are dark, deep with love and irony, and she finds herself laughing softly at the expression, and how right, how perfect it feels to be with him again.

'Shall we sit?' he says and, keeping an arm around her, he draws her down to the step behind them, reaching for her hands and pulling them to his heart to warm them.

'So tell me you're here legally this time,' he mutters drolly.

Nudging a reproof, she says, 'You know I am.'

He allows himself a grin. 'Your visa is for six months? That is correct? This is all Brexit will allow?'

'I'm afraid so.'

'But if you have residency? That would make a difference?'

350

'Of course, but . . .'

He puts a finger to her lips. 'We will ensure your residency, then you can come and go as you please.'

She arches an eyebrow, 'And how will you do that, Signor Santori?' she wants to know.

He shrugs. 'There are many ways, but maybe the most favourable would be to make you *Signora* Santori?'

Her heart stutters and somersaults as she turns to look at him, eyes wide with disbelief. 'Did you just . . .? Was that . . .?'

He nods, and laughs as she suddenly throws her arms around him. 'Will you say yes?' he asks.

Still in a state of blissful shock she murmurs, 'Yes, yes, yes, yes.'

When finally they are simply gazing at one another again, he says, 'Maybe we will save this news for a little while, keep it as our secret until today is over?'

She regards him suspiciously, 'Do you mean until you're officially a free man?'

'Mm, that too,' he concedes wryly.

She laughs and hugs him again, more than ready to wait when she knows even better than he does how much is planned for the coming hours. And maybe she needs some time to take it in. *Signora* Santori. It has such a wonderful ring to it, and how proud she already feels to think that the name will be hers.

'Is everyone here?' she asks, unable to stop looking at him.

He smiles as he nods. 'They arrived this morning.'

'On the same flight as you?'

'*Sì. Lo stesso volo.*'

'Tell me who came.'

Narrowing his eyes, he says, 'My mother, Fiorella; my brother Eduardo and his wife, Allegra. My daughter,

Angelina, and her husband Giovanni. My son, Luca, is hoping to join us by this evening, but his flight from Beijing is delayed. Now tell me who has come with you, *cara mia*.'

Winding her fingers more comfortably around his, she says, 'My mother flew in with me yesterday and she is still trying to work out how a volcano can have snow on it.'

He laughs and hugs her more tightly. 'I can't wait to meet her,' he says.

'The feeling's mutual,' and because she knows he'll want to hear it, she tells him about the conversation she had with her mother on the balcony of Patty's room last night.

'You know I don't go in for all the soppy nonsense,' Patty had begun, gripping a glass of Prosecco as if it might be trying to escape, 'but I want to say this.' Her frown deepened. 'Yes, I'm going to say it. Right now, I'm going to say it.'

'I'm listening,' Catie laughed quietly.

'OK, right. Here goes. I will never, I mean *never*, forgive myself for what I did to you all those years ago, or for the way I let you go . . .'

'Oh, Mum!'

'Listen please. I know we've been back together a long time now, ever since Jake, so it's well overdue for me to say this . . . Your father would be proud of you, my girl, and I am too.'

Catie made to speak, but Patty said, 'I've nearly finished, so please wait,' and after taking a breath, she looked into Catie's eyes and said, 'Thank you . . . thank you, for taking me back. I didn't deserve it . . .'

'Come here,' Catie urged and, putting her glass down, she forced Patty into an awkward and quite hilarious embrace. Even Patty laughed as she said, 'Well, I'm glad no one saw that.' Then stroking Catie's face she said, tenderly, 'You deserve to be happy, my love, and from all you've told me about him . . . Well, do what's right for you now, and don't think about me. OK?'

'We've already discussed this,' Catie reminded her.

'I know, and I'm not arguing. I just want you to put yourself and Giancarlo first.'

As she finishes her story, Catie is watching Giancarlo shaking his head in quiet amazement and can almost feel how moved he is by her mother's words. 'I will talk to her myself,' he says. 'I want her to know she is welcome, whatever she decides.'

Catie smiles and presses a kiss to his cheek. 'Thank you,' she whispers. 'I think she might be persuaded to spend winters with us, having just left England in February to come to this.' She indicates the sunny perfection of where they are. 'Plus, she's spent the last three weeks learning Italian online, and I hate to admit, I think she's better than me.'

He laughs, clearly enjoying the suggestion of one-upmanship. 'And Matthew?' he prompts. 'Is he here yet?'

She takes out her phone to show him the latest text. 'They've just landed at Catania Airport. Jude and Henry were on . . . *lo stesso volo*?'

Delighting in her use of Italian, he kisses her lips and takes some time to search her face with his eyes, as if trying to make himself believe she really is here. 'And you are all staying at the Metropole?' he asks.

'*Sì.* All of us. Isabella has returned to her flat for this weekend. Apparently she's claimed some patronage of our story and so she wants to meet me. You, she already knows, of course.'

He seems surprised, and pleased. 'It will be good to see her,' he says. 'Is she joining us this evening?'

Catie nods and feels such an upsurge of excitement and nerves that she starts to laugh.

'Are you going to tell me what is happening?' he prompts, laughing too.

She shakes her head, then concedes and says, 'You already know that everyone will meet at the Mocambo for drinks, and to be introduced to one another. Would you believe my mother has been practising how to curtsey?'

He gives a laugh of astonishment.

'It's to wind me up,' she assures him. 'I'm sure she won't do it really.'

Still laughing, he says, 'My mother has watched you on YouTube and insists you are probably too good for me.'

Catie ponders this, and says, 'Mm, she could be right.'

Loving her humour, he squeezes her hard and turns to gaze out at the almost dreamlike perfection of the view. 'There is so much I want to tell you,' he says, 'things I need to share with you. I hardly know where to begin.'

'We have time,' she reminds him.

'But maybe not as much as we would like.'

'Because we're old?'

He smiles. 'Because they have only given me five years . . .'

'Which could be six, or ten, or fifteen. We just don't know yet. What matters is that we spend the time together. Besides, I think you'll make it to a hundred.'

'But only if you are with me?'

'Of course I'll be with you, that goes without saying, but I still think you should let me buy *la fattoria*. When the sale of my house goes through—'

'Ssh,' he says, putting a finger to her lips. 'We have already discussed this on the phone, and *la fattoria* will be a gift from me to you . . .'

'But I'll take care of the renovation. No, please don't argue.

I have already made up my mind. I want it to be *ours*, something we create together, and it'll keep me busy when you have to be in Turin.'

'Which will be less often now that Eduardo has taken over the helm and Luca is returning to become a director.'

'But you'll still have to go from time to time?'

He nods. 'For treatment, probably. And you will come with me?'

Now that his soon-to-be-ex-wife has left, she doesn't hesitate to assure him that she will.

'Meantime,' he continues, 'while we are fixing *la fattoria* we can live in the apartment, and maybe you can make it feel a little more like home.'

Though they've already discussed this too, the prospect of continuing their lives together, for however long it might be, fills her with so much happiness and anticipation that she feels she can go on making plans for ever.

Resting his head against hers, he says, '*Parlami in italiano.*'

She doesn't have to think for long. '*Io ti amo, mio caro.*'

He takes a breath and, bringing her to him, he murmurs, 'Is there somewhere we can be alone together? It's not enough to tell you I love you too, I want to show you.'

'I have a hotel room,' she reminds him.

He stands and, bringing her to him, he walks her back down through the *cavea* towards the exit, only pausing when someone calls their names.

'Hey! Giancarlo! Catie!'

Tony is waving from the stage. 'It is very nice to see you,' he tells them.

'*Che cosa fa qui?*' Giancarlo asks.

'I have some visitors,' Tony explains. 'They will join me soon. I am very much looking forward to meeting your family this evening, Catie.'

'Same goes for them,' she assures him. 'Five p.m. at the Mocambo.'

As Tony gives them a thumbs-up, they walk on, still arm-in-arm and fixed on where they're going, until Catie throws a quick glance back. It's all she can do not to laugh as Tony breaks into a mad dance of a thousand thumbs-up. It's his way of letting her know that everything is going to plan.

'Catie! There you are! And here we are!' Jude cries as Catie and Giancarlo enter the hotel's reception area. 'And you must be – yes, of course you are. It's such a pleasure to meet you, Giancarlo. I'm Jude, this is Henry, my husband, and I can't tell you how much I've been looking forward to this.'

'It is a great pleasure to meet you too,' he tells her, and everything about him is so friendly, so uniquely him, that Catie almost bursts with pride. 'Welcome to Taormina,' he says, including Henry. 'I have heard much about you.'

'Only believe the good bits,' Jude advises. 'I promise I'm not as weird now as I was when I was young.'

'Says you,' Henry mutters.

Laughing, Giancarlo turns to Matthew and Sands, who are still embracing Catie.

'Giancarlo,' Matthew declares, grasping Giancarlo's hand in both of his. 'This is truly amazing. When Mum told us about you . . . Wow! You've made such a difference to her life. After you rang, it was like she came back to life . . .'

'You might have to stop there,' Sands cautions under her breath and, going up on tiptoe, she plants a kiss on each of Giancarlo's cheeks.

'Congratulations on the baby,' he says, smiling down at her. 'This is very good news.'

'She'll make a gorgeous granny, won't she?' Jude ventures.

'Thank you,' Catie says, smiling through her teeth.

Slipping an arm around her, Giancarlo says, 'I am already a grandfather, and now, together, we will be many things besides.'

As Catie looks up at him, she knows how adoring her eyes are, but she doesn't care.

'Tell me, Giancarlo,' Henry says, 'have you met *la suocera* yet?'

'Who?' Jude asks, confused.

'The mother-in-law,' Patty translates, appearing from the marble staircase behind them in a manner that makes her seem as though she might have been born to this old palazzo.

Giancarlo's face lights up, and so does Patty's. 'Well, my boy,' she declares as he comes to greet her, 'you're definitely as good looking as she told me. And, I might say, if I were twenty years younger I'd be giving her a run for her money.'

As everyone laughs, Catie groans and mutters, 'You can take the girl out of Fishponds . . .'

'I heard that,' Patty tells her, 'and, by the way, I'm not *una suocera* yet, Henry, but if you do want to marry her, Giancarlo, you have my blessing.'

'Mum!' Catie cries as the others applaud.

'This is very good to know, Patty,' Giancarlo informs her and, slipping an arm around her, he steers her out to the terrace. 'But there are certain things I would like to learn first . . .'

'Don't encourage her,' Catie calls after them.

'*Non preoccuparti,*' Patty calls back over her shoulder, '*i tuoi segreti sono al sicuro con me.*'

'What?' Jude and Sands demand in unison.

'I think she just told me my secrets are safe with her,' Catie replies. 'As if! God, she's a dreadful woman.'

'I heard that too,' Patty shouts from the terrace.

Laughing, Matthew says, 'She's got better hearing than a bat.'

And she's just hijacked my siesta, Catie reflects moodily. However, she perks up no end when she remembers that she still has a few things to sort out for later, and maybe having Giancarlo out of the way for a while will work just fine.

CHAPTER FORTY-FIVE

It was the day after Giancarlo had rung to say that being apart wasn't working for him, that Catie had first called Tony to seek his help with an idea she'd had. He'd become so excited, had overflowed with so many crazy and wonderful ideas to make her dream come true that she'd ended up having to talk him down from some seriously dizzying heights. She began to wonder if he really could keep a secret, but she needn't have worried, after daily, sometimes hourly phone calls, he'd somehow managed to achieve the impossible.

So now she's nervous, excited, even slightly overwhelmed by what she's hoping to pull off, and yet she knows in her heart she can do it. She's rehearsed over and over, written and rewritten, changed the melody many times and returned to the original. For the past week she's been connecting on Zoom with a band from Messina, all seasoned and talented musicians, every one of them known to Tony. As soon as she sent the lyrics, the guitarist came back with a sensational riff that took her song to a whole other level. Last night they got to rehearse together in the jazz bar at the Metropole, and it had gone so well she feared they might already have hit their peak.

Everyone but Giancarlo knows what's going to happen tonight, even his family, who she's received messages from in recent days wishing her *buona fortuna*, and telling her, in Italian, that they are looking forward to meeting her, or they are honoured to be included. And from his mother, in English: *This is a beautiful thing you are doing, my dear. I am very happy for my son that he has met you. I now look forward to the pleasure myself. Your friend, Fiorella Santori.*

CHAPTER FORTY-SIX

At a few minutes before five, Catie and her small party leave the hotel to walk the short distance to the Café Mocambo. The late afternoon sun still has warmth, but the temperature is dropping so they're all carrying coats and hats for later. Catie's dress is black, knee-length and fitted to her slender figure, with gold detailing at the cuffs, and around the mandarin collar. Her hair is a messy bundle of curls tumbling from the slides Jude clipped in earlier, and her eyes, blazing with happiness, belong to the thirty-year old she feels inside.

'Are you all right?' Patty asks as they go through the Byzantine arch onto the piazza.

'I'm fine,' Catie assures her, knowing that she is, in spite of all the apprehension and soaring emotions. 'Are you?'

'Bit nervous,' Patty admits.

'You'll be great,' Matthew assures her from behind. 'At least you speak the language.'

'C'est vrai.'

'That was French,' he whispers.

Patty gives a laugh and presses her fingers to her lips. She's wearing a pale blue skirt suit with a white silk shirt and sturdy shoes to keep herself upright on the cobbles.

'There they are,' Catie murmurs, her heart swelling with

love and happiness as Giancarlo turns from the small knot of his family to watch them approach. He looks so incredibly handsome and stylish in a black linen suit and white silk polo neck, nothing like a man in his sixties, more a man in his prime. As he comes towards her, he says, 'My beautiful love. I don't know what surprise you are planning this evening, but I think I might have guessed.'

'I knew you would,' she tells him, not minding at all, 'at least, a part of it anyway.' She looks past him as an older woman with soft grey curls and opaque blue eyes comes to greet her. 'My dear, I am Fiorella,' she tells her, holding one of Catie's hands in both of hers. She is wearing a navy bouclé suit with a tie-neck blouse and a large gold brooch. So elegant, so very Italian. 'Thank you for bringing us all to Taormina,' she says. 'It is too long since we were here.'

'I'm glad you could come,' Catie smiles, and turns to introduce her mother.

'Ah, Patty, I have looked forward to this meeting,' Fiorella smiles warmly. 'Welcome to Sicily and to our beautiful town.'

'*Grazie,*' Patty responds with a barely noticeable little bob that Catie knows is for her benefit. '*È un onore conoscerla.*'

Fiorella says, '*Vedo che parla l'Italiano – complimenti! Mi farebbe piacere se conoscesse mia famiglia.*'

As Patty's eyes dilate with alarm, Fiorella pats her hand reassuringly, 'Don't worry, everyone speaks English, and they are all very keen to meet you.' She tucks Patty's arm under hers and leads her onto the café terrace as a waiter comes forward with a tray of Prosecco and hands them each a glass.

'My brother, Eduardo,' Giancarlo tells Catie as a slightly balding man with deep frown lines between his eyes and a broad smile comes to meet her. He barely resembles his brother, shorter and stockier, however the way in which he exudes warmth seems to be a family trait. 'And my daughter, Angelina,' Giancarlo adds, taking the hand of an exceptionally striking young woman to bring her forward. She has a mane of thick black hair, and a slender face with high cheekbones – and her father's stunning blue eyes.

Catie can tell right away that she's nervous, unsure of the right thing to say, and trying to cover it with a poise that could almost be hostile.

Having been prepared for this by Giancarlo, she says, 'It's such a pleasure to meet you in person, Angelina. I have been looking forward to it since I saw the fashion show you staged at Casa Cuseni last year. I watched on YouTube and I was blown away by your amazing use of colour and light and music. It's no surprise that it was such a great success.'

Angelina looks astonished, perplexed, then finally a smile starts to break through. 'Have you visited Casa Cuseni?' she asks, glancing at Giancarlo, clearly guessing he'd set this up, but not seeming to mind too much.

Catie says, 'Yes, I have. I've also read Daphne Phelps's book, *A House in Sicily* . . .'

'Oh, I'm so glad. I mean, you would, of course, because you're English, but it's a wonderful portrait of Taormina, don't you think?'

'I do,' Catie agrees, warmly. 'I almost felt as though she was holding my hand during my first stay here. I learned so much from her . . .'

Giancarlo leaves them then to go and introduce Matthew, Sands, Jude and Henry to everyone else, ushering them onto the terrace and making sure they all have a drink. Meanwhile, Angelina presents Catie to the rest of her family, seeming genuinely pleased to be doing it, showing no signs at all of the recently healed rift between her and Giancarlo.

Tony joins the gathering with Isabella, who's as round as she is jolly; shortly afterwards, everyone is being urged to finish their drinks and start following Tony to their mystery venue. Of course, everyone but Giancarlo knows where they're going, and so they're aware that there isn't too much time to spare, as the sun is already starting to go down.

Catie walks along the Corso Umberto between Jude and Angelina, telling them about the bus that has been arranged to take them to *la fattoria* the next day.

'I am so happy that you are going to live in my great-grandmother's house,' Angelina tells her. 'It is a special place and Papa says your mother might join you?'

'At least for part of the year,' Catie replies, watching Patty ahead of them, arm in arm with Fiorella, and what a pair of schoolgirls, the way they're whispering and giggling.

'What do you think they're talking about?' Angelina whispers to Catie.

'Just what I was about to ask,' Jude says.

Barely looking back, Patty calls out, 'I'm explaining about Fishponds and how there aren't many fish or ponds, but we had a lido once.'

Jude laughs as Catie covers her face and Angelina says, 'I believe there is not only one match made in heaven here tonight.'

Ten minutes later, coats and hats are going on as they approach the Ancient Theatre and, coming to take Catie by the hand, Giancarlo pulls her to one side. She can see the emotion in his eyes, the love and disbelief and concern.

'You will do this for me?' he asks.

'Everything is for you,' she tells him, and tilts her mouth for a kiss.

The band is already on stage, smart and proud in their navy-blue suits and pink shirts; chairs are set out in the orchestra for the twenty-strong VIP audience, and lights are ready to take over after the sun has disappeared behind Etna.

Catie is about to make her way to the wings when her mother catches her hand and says, 'Your father's here tonight. I can feel him.'

Tears well in Catie's eyes as she pulls Patty into a fulsome embrace. 'I can feel him too,' she whispers, and turns her face to the sky, certain he's watching them. 'Thank you for letting me share your song with Giancarlo,' she says to both her parents.

'It's yours now,' Patty tells her. 'All yours, my love, but even more special is . . .'

Catie puts a finger to her mother's lips, kisses her and walks on.

As everyone takes their seats, the band is playing from *The Great American Songbook*, jaunty numbers such as, 'It Don't Mean a Thing (If You Ain't Got that Swing)', 'Sweet Georgia Brown', 'Lullaby of Birdland'.

Catie enters the *versura*, the West Hall, or the wings. She's thinking of the thousands of artists, over more than two millennia, who have waited here, in this very space, for the cue to begin. She is just one small person in the vast, indefinable arena of time who has felt nervous, on the brink of elation, yet strangely but utterly calm. She can't remember when she last wanted to sing so much, when the need for it felt like a life force running through her.

At last the pianist glances her way. She nods, and as he plays the opening bars of her parents' favourite tune, 'Too Young', she walks onto the stage, feeling the night air sweeping around her and the breathlessness of those who are waiting.

It takes her only a moment to find Giancarlo and, as he recognizes the music, she sees him start to laugh. She wants to laugh too, but instead she reaches for the mic and, as she starts to sing, she hears more laughter and applause.

Of all the songs she could have chosen to open this small, exclusive show, this is the most inappropriate, and yet it feels so poignant, for her, for them, and for her mother. And the sound of her own voice, free at last, flying with spirit and purity into the night air, is like nothing she's ever felt before.

The others are feeling it too, she can tell. They're smiling and listening, taking in the lyrics and music and, like her, they are watching Giancarlo, pressing hands to hearts and suppressing wider smiles as she sings her own version of the last line, '*and who cares that we're not so young at all.*'

As everyone cheers and applauds, Giancarlo rises to his feet and claps the loudest and the longest, his pride, his joy seeming to fill the night as potently as her music and all the stories that have gone before. She laughs and bows, blows him a kiss and then, as subtly as she can, she gestures for him to sit down again.

Behind her the sun is sinking into Etna's open mouth, and the darkening sky is filling with stars. A single spotlight finds her and, as everything falls silent, she brings the mic back to her lips. 'This next song,' she says to Giancarlo, 'is something I wrote specially for you. It's kind of jazz, a bit folk maybe . . . I guess it's a lot of things, I just hope you're going to like it and, and you don't mind sharing it with everyone else, but just for tonight.'

Someone cheers, others clap and Giancarlo, clearly holding onto his emotions, simply looks at her and nods.

With a full heart she waits for the standard AABA rhythm to play her in, and on the fourth bar she begins to sing.

A Sicilian Affair

The first time I saw you our eyes met,
Did we know then, caro mio, did we know then?
There were no words,
I didn't know your name, and you didn't know mine,
Do you recall that time? Do you recall that time?

I don't know what brought me here,
But I'm glad I came, so glad I came.
I'm going to love you for ever, together, for ever and ever.

You told me to meet you at nine,
I think, this is too late to dine,
And who is he anyway? I won't go.
I was there at nine, and so were you.

I don't know what brought me here,
But I'm glad I came, so glad I came.
I'm going to love you for ever, together, for ever and ever.

We walked on the beach,
We swam in the sea,
We drank wine, and I knew
It was real this time.

I don't know what brought me here,
But I'm glad I came, so glad I came.
I'm going to love you for ever, together, for ever and ever.

We have lived our lives, now the best is to come
Our stories are old, but our hearts are young
I don't know how you do this to me,
But I'm glad you do. I'm glad you do.
The look in your eyes,

The way you say my name,
I'll be here for it again and again,
I'm going to love you for ever, together, for ever and ever.

As Giancarlo steps up onto the stage, she replaces the mic on its stand and lets the band take over as she moves into his arms. He holds her tenderly, lovingly, and as they dance in the moonlight, their shadows seeming to stretch away and across the centuries, they wait for the final notes to play and she sings as he whispers, 'I'm going to love you for ever, together, for ever and ever.'

ACKNOWLEDGEMENTS

One of the most exciting and pleasurable parts of being a writer is the time spent in beautiful locations absorbing, plotting and losing myself in the surroundings. Sicily, most specifically, Taormina, is the setting for much of this book and I can't thank Gerry Reiner enough for making my stays there so special and fruitful. There is almost nothing he doesn't know about his hometown and his generosity in sharing opened my eyes and my heart to it all. From Casa Cuseni, to the Mount Etna vineyards, to Isola Bella, Piazza Belvedere, the village of Savoca (location for *The Godfather*), Palazzo San Domenica (location for *The White Lotus*) and, best of all for me, the Ancient Theatre where I regularly 'saw' Catie Mac and Giancarlo together, Gerry left me with nothing not to love.

The day I knew I had the main character for the story was the day I watched Natalie Williams perform at one of our most iconic jazz clubs, Ronnie Scott's. I had no idea then how Catie Mac was going to do justice to a world I knew nothing about, but after a fabulously inspirational meeting at The Ivy in Covent Garden with Natalie, where much wine was consumed and jazz stories shared, I was on my way. So thank you, thank you, Natalie, for helping me to bring Catie Mac to life, and take her into the wonderful world of soul and jazz. If anyone wants to treat themselves to one of Natalie's Soul Sundays at Ronnie Scott's you won't regret it. You'd also love her Christmas specials when she lavishes all her amazing talent on the season's favourite songs.

Closer to home, for me, there is another fantastic singer, Hannah Wedlock who regularly fronts the Blue Notes Jazz Band (thanks so much for letting me use your brilliant name) at the Undercroft in Bristol. Another very productive lunch at The Ivy, this time in Bath, helped me move the story along and I can't thank Hannah enough for so much valuable input and inspiration. Again, if anyone around my hometown of Bristol should want to indulge in a very enjoyable evening of jazz and good food, maybe a little dancing too, don't hold back. The Blue Notes play alternate Wednesdays; the Undercroft is a part of St Mary Redcliffe, a landmark every Bristolian will know.

The biggest and most lavish of thanks to my wonderful agent, Luigi Bonomi, who provided the Italian translations for the book, giving it an authenticity and sense of romance I'd never have achieved otherwise. We had so much fun doing it that I'm considering setting another book in Italy just so we can collaborate again.

Even closer to home is my husband, James, who I have to thank with all my heart for so much patience and memory-searching when it came to the scenes set in Bristol during the Eighties. Although I was born and grew up in the city, it made all the difference to be able to check and combine my history with his given how different our experiences and worlds were back then.

I'm not sure my publishing team ever read the acknowledgements, but I'm not going to let that stop me. Kimberley Young and Belinda Toor, I can't thank you enough for the amazing reception you gave this book. It seems you love it as much as I do and for the first time ever, I had virtually no editing notes. Does this mean, after fifty books, I'm finally getting it right? A huge thank you and great big glasses of champagne to Katelyn Wood in editorial, Olivia French in marketing, Liz Dawson and Maud Davies in publicity and to everyone in every department who works so cleverly and tirelessly to bring my books to you, the reader.

Don't miss Susan's gripping new thriller,
Nothing to See Here

COMING AUTUMN 2024

Read on for a sneak peek . . .

PROLOGUE

Sixteen Years Earlier

It was a glorious sunny June day, just after four in the afternoon, when Flora Gibson turned her truck and trailer off a leafy lane in the Berkeley Vale into the driveway of Kellon Manse. The wooden gates were usually open, so nothing unusual there, and the gravelled patch just off to the right, under a giant horse chestnut, was empty so plenty of room for her to park and unload. She was only here to do the lawns today, front and back, maybe a bit of weeding, so it shouldn't be more than an hour before she was off to her last call of the day.

What a joy it was being a gardener in this sort of weather, warm, a little breezy and full of sublime countryside sounds and smells. And so peaceful, not unusual for around here. She was already picking up a tan, and the escaped strands of her knotted fair hair were lightening by the day. She might not be a beauty; actually, with her large nose, close set eyes and slightly jutting jaw, she was a long way short, but the goodness in her soul radiated through her gentle nature, making her a favourite with most. She was going to be twenty-five next week and Jack, her live-in partner whose dad owned the landscaping company they both worked for, had some sort of barbecue-party planned. She was looking forward to it. Jack was good at parties.

It took only a few minutes to unhitch the ride-on mower, to turn it around, clamp on her earphones and get started on the Manse's left side front lawn. It was identical to the right side, with a gravelled drive surging through the centre, sloping up to the main house where Flora could see Lexie Gaudion's white Volvo in the wisteria-covered carport. A blue Audi was also there, suggesting Lexie had a visitor. No doubt they were around the back enjoying a cold drink on the terrace while taking in the spectacular view. This meant Flora and her roaring engine and flying grass probably wouldn't be welcome beyond the long row of beech hedges that separated the front and back gardens. However, she hadn't received a text asking her not to come today, so she ploughed on for the time being – Lexie would pop out and let her know if she'd rather the lawns waited for another day.

Half an hour later, she'd completed both lawns and emptied the grass catcher a couple of times, and as no one had appeared to stop her, she chugged the mower through a gap in the beech hedge to go on round to the back.

No sign of anyone on the terrace, although the kitchen and sunroom doors were open so if the noise was going to be a bother she'd soon find out.

She could only dream of one day living in a house as lovely as this with its redbrick walls, black slate roof and white framed windows. It was Edwardian in style, she thought, but wasn't sure, and like many of the properties around these parts, it belonged to the Kellon Estate. Now that was an amazing house if ever there was one, Kellon Hall. Jack and his father took care of the grounds there; there was such a lot of acreage that it was a full-time job for four of their gardeners. Flora helped out from time to time, mostly with weeding and mowing and strimming. The house itself, in spite of being seriously grand and massive, was, in her humble opinion, the kind of place that appeared out of the mist in horror films. All those medieval turrets and pointy-topped window frames, not to mention the clinging ivy and poky-looking attics. Inside wasn't much better from the occasional glimpses she'd managed to sneak. All dark wood panels, towering fireplaces and scary portraits. From where she was now, behind the Manse, she could see a couple of the Hall's tallest chimneys soaring up through the treetops – unsurprising when the properties adjoined one another, although the Hall had to be at least a quarter of a mile away.

The weird, maybe sad, part of the Hall today was that Lexie's mother, Mean Margaret, lived there all on her own. She didn't even have a Mrs Danvers to take care of her, just a few cleaners from an agency who did their stuff once a week, and the locals who came each day to muck out the stables and exercise the horses.

Finally, Flora was ready to pack up and leave.

She glanced over at the open doors, surprised and, weirdly, a little bit bothered that no one had come out. She probably ought just to mind her own business and be on her way, but for some reason she found herself going across the terrace, not sure if she thought something wasn't right, maybe just wanting to be sure nothing was wrong.

'Hello!' she called, stepping into the empty kitchen. It was seriously grand, all black granite and white wood cupboards, a huge centre island with a bowl of china fruit and loads of stuff like letters, colouring books, some weigh scales and table mats with the family's names on. David, Lexie, Rosaria, Amelia. 'Anyone at home?' she shouted.

No reply.

She listened, peering down the hall towards the half-open front door. No sound of anyone chatting.

Venturing a few more steps in, she called out again. 'Lexie! Are you in here?'

Still nothing.

It occurred to her that the BMW might belong to a bloke who could be, right this minute, upstairs giving Lexie one.

Best not get involved in that, she reflected, although it would be funny to hear them at it, wouldn't it?

She moved into the hall quietly, gingerly, and looked up the stairs. No sign of anyone and no rhythmic thumping or grunting or orgasmic shrieking.

She turned back and glanced into the sitting room. That was when her heart stopped beating.

'Oh fuck! Oh God!' she choked, clapping a hand to her mouth.

For a moment she wasn't sure she was actually seeing right. It was like some sort of massacre had happened.

She began to shake, uncontrollably, almost sank to her knees, but somehow she forced herself to run before anyone realized she was there. She had to get out of here, *now*. She needed to summon help. Just please God, don't let anyone catch her first.